A PEOPLE'S FUTURE OF THE UNITED STATES

A PEOPLE'S FUTURE

EDITED BY VICTOR LAVALLE
AND JOHN JOSEPH ADAMS

OF THE UNITED STATES

SPECULATIVE FICTION
FROM 25 EXTRAORDINARY WRITERS

ONE WORLD
NEW YORK

A One World Trade Paperback Original

Copyright © 2019 by John Joseph Adams and Victor LaValle
Introduction copyright © 2019 by Victor LaValle

The copyright for each story herein is owned by its author. See page 409 for individual credits.

Published in the United States by One World, an imprint of Random House, a division of Penguin Random House LLC, New York.

ONE WORLD and colophon are registered trademarks of Penguin Random House LLC.

Library of Congress Cataloging-in-Publication Data
Names: LaValle, Victor D. editor. | Adams, John Joseph, editor.
Title: A people's future of the United States: speculative fiction from 25 extraordinary writers | edited by Victor LaValle and John Joseph Adams.
Description: First edition. | New York: One World, [2019]
Identifiers: LCCN 2018033672| ISBN 9780525508809 (paperback) | ISBN 9780525508816 (ebook)
Subjects: LCSH: Future, The—Fiction. | Short stories, American. | American fiction—21st century. | Minorities—United States—Fiction. | BISAC: FICTION / Anthologies (multiple authors). | FICTION / Literary.
Classification: LCC PS648.F86 P46 2019 | DDC 813/.01083552—dc23
LC record available at https://lccn.loc.gov/2018033672

Printed in the United States of America on acid-free paper

oneworldlit.com
randomhousebooks.com

9 8 7 6 5 4 3

First Edition

Book design by Jo Anne Metsch

This book is dedicated to the folks who would not be erased.

CONTENTS

INTRODUCTION

VICTOR LAVALLE

My father and I saw each other only three times before he died. The first was when I was about ten; the second was in my early twenties; and the last doesn't matter right now. I want to tell you about the second time, when I went up to Syracuse to visit and he tried to make me join the GOP.

Let me back up a little and explain that my mother is a black woman from Uganda and my dad was a white man from Syracuse, New York. He and my mother met in New York City in the late sixties, married, had me, and promptly divorced. My mother and I stayed in Queens while my dad returned to Syracuse. He remarried quickly and had another son with my stepmother. Paul.

When I finished college I enrolled in graduate school, for writing. I'd paid for undergrad with loans and grants, and debt already loomed over me. I showed up at my dad's place hoping he'd cosign for my grad school loans. I felt he owed me since he hadn't been in my life at all. Also, I felt like I'd been on an epic quest just to reach this point. I got into Cornell University, but boy did I hate being there. Long winters, far from New York City, and the kind of dog-eat-dog atmosphere that would make a Wall Street trader sweat. But I'd graduated. And now I wanted to go *back* to school. More than that, I wanted to become a writer. Couldn't my dad see me as a marvel? Couldn't he support me just this once?

Nope.

At the time I felt incensed. In hindsight, I see he was a married man with a wife and a teenager to support; he worked as a parole officer, made a decent salary, but the man had never been well-off even once in his life. He wasn't cruel about it, but he would not help.

With the question of the loan out of the way, my father and brother invited me out to dinner. I still felt angry but I went along. Maybe if I sulked in front of him he'd change his mind. Maybe, even with the disappointment, I still wanted to be around this stranger, my father. We went to a Chinese buffet they liked. Endless dumplings and beef fried rice and chicken wings were offered up as a consolation prize.

On the ride back to their place, my father turned on the radio. This was 1995, and the voice playing through the speakers was Mr. Rush Limbaugh. These days I think Limbaugh, while still popular, has retreated a ways into the far-right antimatter universe. Back then, he was trailblazing the same hustle Bill O'Reilly, Sean Hannity, and Laura Ingraham would refine: scaring old white people for money. My dad was an old white person, and he loved Rush Limbaugh.

I can't remember what kind of bullshit Rush was spewing. What I do remember is sitting in the front seat of my father's car while he and my brother shouted at me. "Listen! Listen! Rush is telling the truth!" For the whole twenty-minute ride these three men—my dad, my brother, and Rush—bellowed at me. I felt queasy from all the General Tso's chicken I'd eaten at the buffet. But I felt even queasier with concern for my brother.

My father's second wife was a Filipina. This meant my brother, Paul, was half Filipino. So the rhetoric of Limbaugh and my dad—anti-immigrant and virulently xenophobic—was literally *about* my brother and his mother. And yet Paul parroted the phrases with no sense of irony.

Paul shouted from the back of the car about "environmental wackos" whose policies were going to cause a "second violent American revolution." Where else could a fifteen-year-old raised in Syracuse have learned these ideas and phrases but from this blowhard? Not even my father got as pumped as his second son. Paul had such a sweet face most of the time. A big, guileless smile, and the hints of a puberty mustache that only made him seem more fragile, highlighted all the growing up he had yet to do. But what was he being raised to become? He couldn't be just like my father; his skin and his features would mark him. But these beliefs sure wouldn't make him welcome among those who looked more like him. He might become a kind of orphan, a man without a clan.

As the car pulled into my father's garage, I realized Paul had basically spent his entire life being told a story by my father, by Rush Limbaugh, and, in the broadest sense, by the United States as a whole: the story of America, as related by a wildly unreliable narrator.

On November 8, 2016, Donald Trump won the election to become the president of the United States. On that night I recalled the car ride with my father and brother twenty-one years earlier. The familiar sensation of having men shouting lies in my ear: *Listen! Listen! He's telling the truth!*

My wife and I turned off the TV soon after the election results were called. We got in bed and for a while we lay there quietly. My wife is a writer and an academic, too. Over the years she's given me countless insights about the hurdles women face as they struggle for unbiased student evaluations, for promotions, for tenure. Her stories of the countless humiliations and second-guessing and the problem of "unlikability" returned to me on election night. I felt like a child who must be told something a thousand times before he truly understands it. I turned to my wife and said, "Damn, this country hates women."

She said, "You're only *now* just figuring that out?"

She patted me gently, kissed me once. She eyed me with the same look of concern, even pity, I must've shown Paul all those years ago. My brother hadn't been the only one being fed falsehoods all his life.

In January 2000, on C-SPAN, Brian Lamb interviewed Howard Zinn—historian and author of A *People's History of the United States*. The jacket copy describes the book as "the only volume to tell America's story from the point of view of—and in the words of—America's women, factory workers, African-Americans, Native Americans, the working poor, and immigrant laborers." The cover of an edition published back in 2005 also states: "More than two million copies sold."

At one point in the interview Zinn explains that the first edition of his now legendary text came out in 1980 and had a print run of five thousand hardcovers. He laughed at the number, as one can only do with the benefit of hindsight. "They didn't know what would happen to it," he said. "Neither did I."

Zinn's history of the United States begins not with Columbus discovering America, but with the Arawak of the Bahama Islands discovering Columbus. His large ship appears and the Arawak swim out to greet him and his crew. Zinn quotes Columbus's journals: "They were well-built, with good bodies and handsome features. . . . They do not bear arms, and do not know them. . . . They would make fine servants. . . . With fifty men we could subjugate them all and make them do whatever we want." This is on the first damn page of the book. Try to contemplate what an educational tremor this must have caused in 1980.

Hell, even today whole swaths of the U.S. population regularly go into a rage at the idea of genuine historical accuracy. In 2010 the Texas Board of Education, for instance, made use of a history textbook that included this gem: "Most white Southerners swallowed whatever resentment they felt over African-American suffrage and participation in government." I'm looking forward to the follow-up textbook about all the white Southerners who protested against Jim Crow laws!

Only two pages farther into his book Zinn relates, in a short paragraph, the experience of a sailor in Columbus's crew. On October 12, 1492, a man named Rodrigo spots the sands of an island in the Bahamas in the moonlight. A promise has been made to all on board: The first man to spot land will be rewarded with a pension of ten thousand maravedis (medieval Spanish coins; it would amount to about $540 USD today). That was ten thousand maravedis a year *for life*. Rodrigo gave word of what he'd seen, but he never received the prize. Why? Columbus said he'd seen it the evening before. Columbus collected the loot. Oh, Christopher. You shady motherfucker.

This anthology in your hands—A *People's Future of the United States*—is, in a sense, inspired not by those Arawak men and women who swam out to greet Columbus's ship nor by Rodrigo, who was cheated of his reward. Instead this book is inspired by the countless generations of offspring who lost the right to forge futures of their own making.

Zinn had already written about our past, so my co-editor, John Joseph Adams, and I decided to ask a gang of incredible writers to imagine the years, decades, even the centuries, to come. And to have tales told by those, and/or about those, who history often sees fit to forget. "There is no such thing as impartial history," Zinn once said. He added, "The chief problem in historical honesty is not outright lying. It is omission or de-emphasis of important data."

Think of this collection of stories, then, as important speculative data. A portrait of this country as it might become the future of the United States.

"We are seeking stories that explore new forms of freedom, love, and justice: narratives that release us from the chokehold of the history and mythology of the past . . . and writing that gives us new futures to believe in."

That's the gist of how our invitations read. John and I gave our writers a lot of leeway when it came to the stories themselves. One of the benefits of soliciting an astoundingly talented crew is that you can trust them to interpret the theme in ways that will be much more startling and ambitious than you could ever guess.

So many of these tales are vivid with struggle and hardship, but its characters don't flee, they fight—whether it's N. K. Jemisin's dragon riders, A. Merc Rustad's covert commandos, or Alice Sola Kim's time-traveling best friend. While some of these stories depict battles with external foes there are those that wrestle, as well, with the enemies within. Violet Allen's characters are caught in mind games with troubling consequences and Kai Cheng Thom's must decide if they will change themselves or change the world. G. Willow Wilson turns a classroom exam into a test of communal bravery and Charles Yu relates the tale of a fight with an android that would've totally voted for Trump.

All that and I've hardly touched on the depth and breadth of brilliance in this anthology. As this collection came together, I found myself wishing I'd had this book with me in Syracuse all those years ago. I might've turned toward my brother, Paul, and put this book in his hands. I could've told him that *this* was the United States, a much broader portrait of his country than anything he would ever hear on right-wing talk radio. I might've asked him to imagine a future where he didn't have to parrot the speech of bullies and tormentors. Instead, he might speak his own language, which is to say his own truth. He might come to believe he mattered most in a story. Not secondary, but primary. Not the foreign villain, but the homegrown hero. I could've used it to convince him the future belonged to him as much as anyone.

If I'm honest, I could've used this book myself long ago. Hell, I still need this book. Maybe you do, too. You might know others just as desperate for stories like these. If so, pass them on. Because the future is ours.

Let's get it.

Victor LaValle
New York, New York
February 2019

A PEOPLE'S FUTURE OF THE UNITED STATES

THE BOOKSTORE AT THE END OF AMERICA

CHARLIE JANE ANDERS

A bookshop on a hill. Two front doors, two walkways lined with blank slates and grass, two identical signs welcoming customers to the First and Last Page, and a great blue building in the middle, shaped like an old-fashioned barn with a slanted tiled roof and generous rain gutters. Nobody knew how many books were inside that building, not even Molly, the owner. But if you couldn't find it there, they probably hadn't written it down yet.

The two walkways led to two identical front doors, with straw welcome mats, blue plank floors, and the scent of lilacs and old bindings—but then you'd see a completely different store, depending which side you entered. With two cash registers, for two separate kinds of money.

If you entered from the California side, you'd see a wall-hanging: women of all ages, shapes, and origins, holding hands and dancing. You'd notice the display of the latest books from a variety of small presses that clung to life in Colorado Springs and Santa Fe, from literature and poetry to cultural studies. The shelves closest to the door on the California side included a decent amount of women's and queer studies but also a strong selection of classic literature, going back to Virginia Woolf and Zora Neale Hurston. Plus some brand-new paperbacks.

If you came in through the American front door, the basic layout would be pretty similar, except for the big painting of the nearby Rocky Mountains. But you might notice more books on religion and some history books with a somewhat more conservative approach. The literary books skewed a bit more toward Faulkner, Thoreau, and Hemingway, not to mention Ayn Rand, and you might find more books of essays about self-reliance and strong families, along with another selection of low-cost paperbacks: thrillers and war novels, including brand-new releases from the big printing plant in Gatlinburg. Romance novels, too.

Go through either front door and keep walking, and you'd find yourself in a maze of shelves, with a plethora of nooks and a bevy of side rooms. Here a cavern of science fiction and fantasy, there a deep alcove of theater books—and a huge annex of history and sociology, including a whole wall devoted to explaining the origins of the Great Sundering. Of course, some people did make it all the way from one front door to the other, past the overfed-snake shape of the hallways and the giant central reading room, with a plain red carpet and two beat-down couches in it. But the design of the store encouraged you to stay inside your own reality.

The exact border between America and California, which elsewhere featured watchtowers and roadblocks, YOU ARE NOW LEAVING/YOU ARE NOW ENTERING signs, and terrible overpriced souvenir stands, was denoted in the First and Last Page by a tall bookcase of self-help titles about coping with divorce.

People came from hundreds of miles in either direction, via hydroelectric cars, solarcycles, mecha-horses, and tour buses, to get some book they couldn't live without. You could get electronic books via the Share, of course, but they might be plagued with crowdsourced editing, user-targeted content, random annotations, and sometimes just plain garbage. You might be reading *The Federalist Papers* on your Gidget and come across a paragraph about rights vs. duties that wasn't there before—or, for that matter, a few pages relating to hair cream, because you'd been searching on *hair cream* yesterday. Not to mention, the same book might read completely differently in California than in America. You could only rely on ink and paper (or, for newer books, Peip0r) for consistency, not to mention the whole sensory experience of smelling and touching volumes, turning their pages, bowing their spines.

Everybody needs books, Molly figured. No matter where they live, how they love, what they believe, whom they want to kill. We all want books. The moment you start thinking of books as some exclusive club, or the loving of books as a high distinction, then you're a bad bookseller.

Books are the best way to discover what people thought before you were born. And an author is just someone who tried their utmost to make sense of their own mess, and maybe their failure contains a few seeds to help you with yours.

Sometimes people asked Molly why she didn't simplify it down to one entrance. Force the people from America to talk to the Californians, and vice versa—maybe expose one side or the other to some books that might challenge their worldview just a little. And Molly always replied that she had a business to run, and if she managed to keep everyone reading, then that was enough. At the very least, Molly's arrangement kept this the most peaceful outpost on the border, without people gathering on one side to scream at the people on the other.

Some of those screaming people were old enough to have grown up in the United States of America, but they acted as though these two lands had always been enemies.

.   .   .

Whichever entrance of the bookstore you went through, the first thing you'd notice was probably Phoebe. Rake-thin, coltish, rambunctious, right on the edge of becoming, she ran light enough on her bare feet to avoid ever rattling a single bookcase or dislodging a single volume. You heard Phoebe's laughter before her footsteps. Molly's daughter wore denim overalls and cheap linen blouses most days, or sometimes a floor-length skirt or lacy-hemmed dress, plus plastic bangles and necklaces. She hadn't gotten her ears pierced yet.

People from both sides of the line loved Phoebe, who was a joyful shriek that you only heard from a long way away, a breath of gladness running through the flowerbeds.

Molly used to pester Phoebe about getting outdoors to breathe some fresh air—because that seemed like something moms were supposed to say, and Molly was paranoid about being a Bad Mother, since she was basically married to a bookstore, albeit one containing a large section of parenting books. But Molly was secretly glad when Phoebe disobeyed her and stayed inside, endlessly reading. Molly hoped Phoebe would always stay shy, that mother and daughter would hunker inside the First and Last Page, side-eyeing the world through thin linen curtains when they weren't reading together.

Then Phoebe had turned fourteen, and suddenly she was out all the time, and Molly didn't see her for hours. Around that time, Phoebe had unexpectedly grown pretty and lanky, her neck long enough to let her auburn ponytail swing as she ran around with the other kids who lived in the tangle of tree-lined streets on the America side of the line, plus a few kids who snuck across from California. Nobody seriously patrolled this part of the border, and there was one craggy rock pile, like an echo of the looming Rocky Mountains, that you could just scramble over and cross from one country to the other, if you knew the right path.

Phoebe and her gang of kids, ranging from twelve to fifteen, would go trampling the tall grass near the border on a "treasure hunt" or setting up an "ambush fort" in the rocks. Phoebe occasionally caught sight of Molly and turned to wave, before running up the dusty hillside toward Zadie and Mark, who had snuck over from California with canvas backpacks full of random games and junk. Sometimes Phoebe led an entire brigade of kids into the store, pouring cups of water or Molly's homebrewed ginger beer for everyone, and they would all pause and say, "Hello, Ms. Carlton," before running outside again.

Mostly, the kids were just a raucous chorus, as they chased each other with pea guns. There were times when they stayed in the most overgrown area of trees and bracken until way after sundown, until Molly was about to message the other local parents via her Gidget, and then she'd glimpse a few specks of light emerging from the claws and twisted limbs. Molly always asked Phoebe what they did in that tiny stand of vegetation, which barely qualified as "the woods," and Phoebe always said: Nothing. They just hung out. But Molly imagined those kids under the moonlight, blotted by heavy leaves, and they could be doing anything: drinking, taking drugs, playing kiss-and-tell games.

Even if Molly had wanted to keep tabs on her daughter, she couldn't leave the bookstore unattended. The bi-national design of the store required at least two people working at all times, one per register, and most of the people Molly hired only lasted a month or two and then had to run home because their families were worried about all the latest hints of another war on the horizon. Every day, another batch of propaganda bubbled up on Molly's Gidget, from both sides, claiming that one country was a crushing theocracy or the other was a godless meat grinder. And meanwhile, you heard rumblings about both countries searching for the last precious dregs of water—sometimes actual rumblings, as California sent swarms of robots deep underground. Everybody was holding their breath.

. . .

Molly was working the front counter on the California side, trying as usual not to show any reaction to the people with weird tattoos or with glowing silver threads flowing into their skulls. Everyone knew how eager Californians were to hack their own bodies and brains, from programmable birth control to brain implants that connected them to the Anoth Complex. Molly smiled, made small talk, recommended books based on her uncanny memory for what everybody had been buying—in short, she treated everyone like a customer, even the folks who noticed Molly's crucifix and clicked their tongues, because obviously she'd been brainwashed into her faith.

A regular customer named Sander came in, looking for a rare book from the last days of the United States about sustainable farming and animal consciousness, by a woman named Hope Dorrance. For some reason, nobody had ever uploaded this book of essays to the Share. Molly looked in the fancy computer and saw that they had one copy, but when Molly led Sander back to the shelf where it was supposed to be, the book was missing.

Sander stared at the space where *Souls on the Land* ought to be, and their pale, round face was full of lines. They had a single tattoo of a butterfly clad in gleaming armor, and the wires rained from the shaved back of their skull. They were some kind of engineer for the Anoth Complex.

"Huh," Molly said. "So this is where it ought to be. But I better check if maybe we sold it over on the, uh, other side and somehow didn't log the sale." Sander nodded, and followed Molly until they arrived in America. There, Molly squeezed past Mitch, who was working the register, and dug through a dozen scraps of paper until she found one. "Oh. Yeah. Well, darn."

They had sold their only copy of *Souls on the Land* to one of their most faithful customers on the America side: a gray-haired woman named Teri Wallace, who went to Molly's church. And Teri was in the store right now, searching for a cookbook. Mitch had just seen her go past. Unfortunately, Teri hated Californians even more than most Americans did. And Sander was the sort of Californian that Teri especially did not appreciate.

"So it looks like we sold it a while back, and we didn't update our inventory, which, uh, does happen," Molly said.

"In essence, this was false advertising." Sander drew upward, with the usual Californian sense of affront the moment anything wasn't perfectly efficient. "You told me that the book was available, when in fact you should have known it wasn't."

Molly had already decided not to tell Sander who had bought the Hope Dorrance, but Teri came back clutching a book of killer salads just as Sander was in mid-rant about the ethics of retail communication. Sander happened to mention *Souls on the Land*, and Teri's ears pricked up.

"Oh, I just bought that book," Teri said.

Sander spun around, smiling, and said, "Oh. Pleased to meet you. I'm afraid that book you bought is one that had been promised to me. I don't suppose we could work out some kind of arrangement? Perhaps some system of needs-based allocation, because my need for this book is extremely great." Sander was already falling into the hyper-rational, insistent language of a Californian faced with a problem.

"Sorry," Teri said. "I bought it. I own it now. It's mine."

"But," Sander said, "there are many ways we could . . . I mean, you could loan it to me, and I could digitize it and return it to you in good condition."

"I don't want it in good condition. I want it in the condition it's in now."

"But—"

Molly could see this conversation was about three exchanges away from full-blown unpleasantries. Teri was going to insult

Sander, either directly or by getting their pronoun wrong. Sander was going to call Teri stupid, either by implication or outright. Molly could see an easy solution: She could give Teri a bribe— a free book or blanket discount—in exchange for letting Sander borrow the Hope Dorrance so they could digitize it using special page-turning robots. But this wasn't going to be solved with reason. Not right now, anyway, with the two of them snarling at each other.

So Molly put on her biggest smile and said, "Sander. I just remembered, I had something extra special set aside for you, back in the psychology/philosophy annex. I've been meaning to give it to you, and it slipped my mind until now. Come on, I'll show you." She tugged gently at Sander's arm and hustled them back into the warren of bookshelves. Sander kept grumbling about Teri's irrational selfishness, until they had left America.

Molly had no idea what the special book she'd been saving for Sander actually was—but she figured by the time they got through the Straits of Romance and all the switchbacks of biography, she'd think of something.

Phoebe was having a love triangle. Molly became aware of this in stages, by noticing how all the other kids were together and by overhearing snippets of conversation (despite her best efforts not to eavesdrop).

Jonathan Brinkfort, the son of the minister at Molly's church, had started following Phoebe around with a hangdog expression, like he'd lost one of those kiss-and-dare games and it had left him with gambling debts. Jon was a tall, quiet boy with a handsome square face, who mediated every tiny dispute among the neighborhood kids with a slow gravitas, but Molly had never before seen him lost for words. She had been hand-selling airship adventure books to Jon since he was little.

And then there was Zadie Kagwa, whose dad was a second-generation immigrant from Uganda with a taste for very old science fiction. Zadie had a fresh tattoo on one shoulder, of a dandelion with seedlings fanning out into the wind, and one string of fiber-optic pearls coming out of her locs. Zadie's own taste in books roamed from science and math, to radical politics, to girls-at-horse-camp novels. Zadie whispered to Phoebe and brought tiny presents from California, like these weird candies with chili peppers in them.

Molly could just imagine the conversations she'd hear in church if her daughter got into an unnatural relationship with a girl—from *California* no less—instead of dating a nice American boy who happened to be Canon Brinkfort's son.

But Phoebe didn't seem to be inclined to choose one or the other. She accepted Jon's stammered compliments with the same shy smile as Zadie's gifts.

Molly took Phoebe on a day trip into California, where they got their passports stamped with a one-day entry permit, and they climbed into Molly's old three-wheel Dancer. They drove past wind farms and military installations, past signs for the latest Anoth Cloud-Brain schemes, until they stopped at a place that sold milk-shakes so thick, you lost the skin on the sides of your mouth trying to unclog the straw.

Phoebe was in silent mode, hugging herself and cocooning in-side her big polyfiber jacket when she wasn't slurping her milk-shake. Molly tried to make conversation, talking about who had been buying what sort of books lately and what you could figure out about international relations from Sharon Wong's sudden interest in bird-watching. Phoebe just shrugged, like maybe Molly should just read the news instead. As if Molly hadn't tried making sense of the news already.

Then Phoebe started telling Molly about some fantasy novel. Seven princesses have powers of growth and decay, but some of the princesses can only use their growth powers if the other princesses are using their decay powers. And whoever grows a hedge tall enough to keep out the army of gnome-trolls will become the heir to the Blue Throne, but the princesses don't even realize at first that their powers are all different, like they grow different kinds of things. And there are a bunch of princes and court ladies who are all in love with different princesses, but nobody can be with the person they want to be with.

This novel sounded more and more complicated, and Molly didn't remember ever seeing it in her store, until she realized: Phoebe wasn't describing a book she had read. This was a book that Phoebe was writing, somewhere, on one of the old computers that Molly had left in some storage space. Molly hadn't even known Phoebe was a writer.

"How does it end?" Molly said.

"I don't know." Phoebe poked at the last soup of her milkshake. "I guess they have to use their powers together to build the hedge they're supposed to build, instead of competing. But the hard part is gonna be all the princesses ending up with the right person. And, uh, making sure nobody feels left out, or like they couldn't find their place in this kingdom."

Molly nodded, and then tried to think of how to respond to what she was pretty sure her daughter was actually talking about. "Well, you know that nobody has to ever hurry to find out who they're supposed to love, or where they're going to fit in. Those things sometimes take time, and it's okay not to know the answers right away. You know?"

"Yeah, I guess." Phoebe pushed her empty glass away and looked out the window. Molly waited for her to say something else but eventually realized the conversation had ended. Teenagers.

Molly had opened the First and Last Page when Phoebe was still a baby, back when the border had felt more porous. Both governments were trying to create a Special Trade Zone, and you could get a special transnational business license. Everyone had seemed overjoyed to have a bookstore within driving distance, and Molly had lost count of how many people thanked her just for being there. A lot of her used books had come from estate sales, but there had been a surprising flood of donations, too.

Molly had wanted Phoebe to be within easy reach of California if America ever started seriously following through on its threats to enforce all of its broadly written laws against immorality. But more than that, Phoebe deserved to be surrounded by all the stories, and every type of person, and all of the ways of looking at life. Plus, it had seemed like a shrewd business move to be in two countries at once, a way to double the store's potential market.

For a while, the border had also played host to a bar, a burger joint, and a clothing store, and Molly had barely noticed when those places had closed one by one. The First and Last Page was different, she'd figured, because nobody ever gets drunk on books and starts a brawl.

Matthew limped into the American entrance during a lull in business, and Molly took in his torn pants leg, dirty hands, and the dried-out salt trails along his brown face. She had seen plenty others, in similar condition, and didn't even blink. She didn't need to see the brand on Matthew's neck, which looked like a pair of broken wings and declared him to be a bonded peon and the responsibility of the Greater Appalachian Penal Authority and the Glad Corporation. She just nodded and helped him inside the store before anyone else noticed or started asking too many questions.

"I'm looking for a self-help book," Matthew said, which was what a lot of them said. Someone, somewhere, had told them this was a code phrase that would let Molly know what they needed. In fact, there was no code phrase.

The border between America and California was unguarded in thousands of other places besides Molly's store, including that big rocky hill that Zadie and the other California kids climbed over when they came to play with the American kids. There was just too much empty space to waste time patrolling, much less putting up fences or sensors. You couldn't eat lunch in California without twenty computers checking your identity, anyway. But Matthew and the others chose Molly's store because books meant civilization, or maybe the store's name seemed to promise a kind of safe passage: the first page leading gracefully to the last.

Molly did what she always did with these refugees. She helped Matthew find the quickest route from romance to philosophy to history, and then on to California. She gave him some clean clothes out of a donation box, which she always told people was going to a shelter somewhere, and what information she had about resources and contacts. She let him clean up as much as he could, in the restroom.

Matthew was still limping as he made his way through the store in his brand-new corduroys and baggy argyle sweater. Molly offered to have a look at his leg, but he shook his head. "Old injury." She dug in the first-aid kit and gave him a bottle of painkillers. Matthew kept looking around in all directions, as if there could be hidden cameras (there weren't), and he took a jerky step backward when Molly told him to hold on a moment, when he was already in California.

"What? Is something wrong? What's wrong?"

"Nothing. Nothing's wrong. Just thinking." Molly always gave refugees a free book, something to keep them company on whatever journey they had ahead. She didn't want to just choose at random, so she gazed at Matthew for a moment in the dim amber light from the wall sconces in the history section. "What sort of books do you like? Besides self-help, I mean."

"I don't have any money, I'm sorry," Matthew said, but Molly waved it off.

"You don't need any. I just wanted to give you something to take with you."

Phoebe came up just then and saw at a glance what was going on. "Hey, Mom. Hi, I'm Phoebe."

"This is Matthew," Molly said. "I wanted to give him a book to take with him."

"They didn't exactly let us have books," Matthew said. "There was a small library, but library use was a privilege, and you needed more than 'good behavior.' For that kind of privilege, you would need to . . ." He glanced at Phoebe, because whatever he'd been about to say wasn't suitable for a child's ears. "They did let us read the Bible, and I practically memorized some parts of it."

Molly and Phoebe looked at each other, while Matthew fidgeted, and then Phoebe said, "Father Brown mysteries."

"Are you sure?" Molly said.

Phoebe nodded. She ran, fast as a deer, and came back with a tiny paperback of G. K. Chesterton, which would fit in the pockets of the donated corduroys. "I used to love this book," she told Matthew. "It's about God, and religion, but it's really just a great bunch of detective stories, where the key always turns out to be making sense of people."

Matthew kept thanking Molly and Phoebe in a kind of guttural undertone, like a compulsive cough, until they waved it off. When they got to the California storefront, they kept Matthew out of sight until they were sure the coast was clear, then they hustled him out and showed him the clearest path that followed the main road but stayed under cover. He waved once as he sprinted across the blunt strip of gravel parking lot, but other than that, he didn't look back.

·   ·   ·

The president of California wished the president of America a "good spring solstice" instead of "happy Easter," and the president of America called a news conference to discuss this unforgivable insult. America's secretary of morality, Wallace Dawson, called California's gay attorney general an offensive term. California moved some troops up to the border and performed some "routine exercises," so close that Molly could hear the cackle of guns shooting blanks all night. (She hoped they were blanks.) America sent some fighter craft and UAVs along the border, sundering the air. California's swarms of water-divining robots had managed to tap the huge deposits located deep inside the rocky mantle, but both America and California claimed that this water was located under their respective territories.

Molly's Gidget kept flaring up with "news" that was laced with propaganda, as if the people in charge on both sides were trying to get everyone fired up. The American media kept running stories about a pregnant woman in New Sacramento who lost her baby because her supposedly deactivated birth-control implant had a buggy firmware update, plus graphic stories about urban gang violence, drugs, prostitution, and so on. California's media outlets, meanwhile, worked overtime to remind people about the teenage rape victims in America who were locked up and straitjacketed, to make sure they gave birth, and the peaceful protestors who were gassed and beaten by police.

Almost every day lately, Americans came in looking for a couple books that Molly didn't have. Molly had decided to go ahead and stock *Why We Stand*, a book-length manifesto about individualism and Christian values, which stopped just short of accusing Californians of bestiality and cannibalism. But *Why We Stand* was unavailable, because they'd gone back for another print run. Meanwhile, though, Molly outright refused to sell *Our People*, a book that included offensive caricatures of the black and brown people who mostly clustered in the dense cities out west, like New Sacramento, plus "scientific" theories about their relative intelligence.

People kept coming in and asking for *Our People*, and at this point Molly was pretty sure they knew she didn't have it and they were just trying to make a point.

"It's just, some folks feel as though you think you're better than the rest of us," said Norma Verlaine, whose blond, loudmouthed daughter, Samantha, was part of Phoebe's friend group. "The way you try to play both sides against the middle, perching here in your fancy chair, deciding what's fit to read and what's not fit to read. You're literally sitting in judgment over us."

"I'm not judging anyone," Molly said. "Norma, I live here, too. I go to Holy Fire every Sunday, same as you. I'm not judging."

"You say that. But then you refuse to sell *Our People*."

"Yes, because that book is racist."

Norma turned to Reggie Watts, who had two kids in Phoebe's little gang: Tobias and Suz. "Did you hear that, Reggie? She called me a racist."

"I didn't call you anything. I was talking about a book."

"Can't separate books from people," said Reggie, who worked at the big power plant thirty miles east. He furrowed his huge brow and stooped a little as he spoke. "And you can't separate people from the places they come from."

"Time may come, you have to choose a country once and for all," Norma said. Then she and Reggie walked out while the glow of righteousness still clung.

Molly felt something chewing all the way through her. Like the cartoon "bookworm" chewing through a book, from when Molly was a child. There was a worm drilling a neat round hole in Molly, rendering some portion of her illegible.

Molly was just going through some sales slips—because ever since that dustup with Sander and Teri, she was paranoid about American sales not getting recorded in the computer—when the earthquake began. A few books fell on the floor as the ground shuddered, but most of the books were packed too tight to dislodge right away. The grinding, screeching sound from the vibrations underground made Molly's ears throb. When she could get her balance back, she looked at her Gidget, and at first she saw no information. Then there was a news alert: California had laid claim to the water deposits, deep underground, and was proceeding to extract them as quickly as possible. America was calling this an act of war.

Phoebe was out with her friends as usual. Molly sent a message on her Gidget and then went outside to yell Phoebe's name into the wind. The crushing sound underground kept going, but either Molly had gotten used to it or it was moving away from here.

"Phoebe?"

Molly walked the two-lane roads, glancing every couple minutes at her Gidget to see if Phoebe had replied yet. She told herself that she wouldn't freak out if she could find her daughter before the sun went down, and then the sun did go down and she had to invent a new deadline for panic.

Something huge and powerful opened its mouth and roared nearby, and Molly swayed on her feet. The hot breath of a large carnivore blew against her face while her ears filled with sound. She realized after a moment that three Stalker-class aircraft had flown very low overhead, in stealth mode, so you could hear and feel—but not see—them.

"Phoebe?" Molly called out, as she reached the end of the long main street, with the one grocery store and the diner. "Phoebe, are you out here?" The street led to a big field of corn on one side and to the diversion road leading to the freeway on the other. The corn rustled from the after-shakes of the flyover. Out on the road, Molly heard wheels tearing at loose dirt and tiny rocks and saw the slash of headlights in motion.

"Mom!" Phoebe came running down the hill from the tiny forest area, followed by Jon Brinkfort, Zadie Kagwa, and a few other kids. "Thank god you're okay."

Molly started to say that Phoebe should get everyone inside the bookstore, because the reading room was the closest thing to a bomb shelter for miles.

But a new round of flashes and earsplitting noises erupted, and then Molly looked past the edge of town and saw a phalanx of shadows, three times as tall as the tallest building, moving forward.

Molly had never seen a mecha before, but she recognized these metal giants, with the bulky actuators on their legs and rocket launchers on their arms. They looked like a crude caricature of bodybuilders, pumped up inside their titanium alloy casings. The two viewports on their heads, along with the slash of red paint, gave them the appearance of scowling down at all the people underfoot. Covered with armaments all over their absurdly huge bodies, they were heading into town on their way to the border.

"Everybody into the bookstore!" Phoebe yelled. Zadie Kagwa was messaging her father on some fancy tablet, and other kids were trying to contact their parents, too, but then everyone hustled inside the First and Last Page.

People came looking for their kids, or for a place to shelter from the fighting. Some people had been browsing in the store when the hostilities broke out, or had been driving nearby. Molly let everyone in, until the American mechas were actually engaging a squadron of California centurions, which were almost identical to the other metal giants, except that their onboard systems were connected to the Anoth Complex. Both sides fired their rocket launchers, releasing bright-orange trails that turned everything the same shade of amber. Molly watched as an American mecha lunged forward with its huge metal fist and connected with the side of a centurion, sending shards of metal spraying out like the dandelion seeds on Zadie's tattoo.

Then Molly got inside and sealed up the reading room, with a satisfying clunk. "I paid my contractor extra," she told all the people who crouched inside. "These walls are like a bank vault. This is the safest place for you all to be." There was a toilet just outside the solid metal door and down the hall, with a somewhat higher risk of getting blown up while you peed.

Alongside Molly and Phoebe, there were a dozen people stuck in the reading room. There were Zadie and her father, Jay; Norma Verlaine and her daughter, Samantha; Reggie Watts and his two kids; Jon Brinkfort; Sander, the engineer who'd come looking for *Souls on the Land*; Teri, the woman who actually owned *Souls on the Land*; Marcy, a twelve-year-old kid from California, and Marcy's mother, Petrice.

They all sat in this two-meter-by-three-meter room, with two couches that could hold five people between them, plus bookshelves from floor to ceiling. Every time someone started to relax, there was another quake, and the sounds grew louder and more ferocious. Nobody could get a signal on any of their devices or implants, either because of the reinforced walls or because someone was actively jamming communications. The room jerked back and forth, and the books quivered but did not fall out of their nests.

Molly looked over at Jay Kagwa, sitting with his arm around his daughter, and had a sudden flash of remembering a time, several years ago, when Phoebe had campaigned for Molly to go out on a date with Jay. Phoebe and Zadie were already friends, though neither of them was interested in romance yet, and Phoebe had decided that the stout, well-built architect would be a good match for her mother. Partly based on the wry smiles the two of them always exchanged when they compared notes about being single parents of rambunctious daughters. Plus both Molly and Phoebe were American citizens, and it wouldn't hurt to have dual citizenship. But Molly never had time for romance. And now, of course, Zadie was still giving sidelong glances to Phoebe, who had never chosen between Zadie and Jon, and probably never would.

Jay had finished hugging his daughter and also yelling at her for getting herself stuck in the middle of all this, and all the other parents including Molly had had a good scowl at their own kids, as well. "I wish we were safe at home," Jay Kagwa told his daughter in a whisper, "instead of being trapped here with these people."

"What exactly do you mean by 'these people'?" Norma Verlaine demanded from the other end of the room.

Another tremor, more raucous noise.

"Leave it, Norma," said Reggie. "I'm sure he didn't mean anything by it."

"No, I want to know," Norma said. "What makes us 'these people' when we're just trying to live our lives and raise our kids? And meanwhile, your country decided that everything from abortion to unnatural sexual relationships, to cutting open people's brains and shoving in a bunch of nanotech garbage, was A-OK. So I think the real question is, Why do I have to put up with people like you?"

"I've seen firsthand what your country does to people like me," Jay Kagwa said in a quiet voice.

"As if Californians aren't stealing children from America, at a rapidly increasing rate, to turn into sex slaves or prostitutes. I have to keep one eye on my Samantha here all the time."

"*Mom*," Samantha said, and that one syllable meant everything from *Please stop embarrassing me in front of my friends* to *You can't protect me forever.*

"We're not stealing children," said Sander. "That was a ridiculous made-up story."

"You steal everything. You're stealing our water right now," said

Teri. "You don't believe that anything is sacred, so it's all up for grabs as far as you're concerned."

"We're not the ones who put half a million people into labor camps," said Petrice, a quiet green-haired older woman who mostly bought books about gardening and Italian history.

"Oh no, not at all, California just turns millions of people into cybernetic slaves of the Anoth Complex," said Reggie. "That's much more humane."

"Hey, everybody calm down," Molly said.

"Says the woman who tries to serve two masters," Norma said, rounding on Molly and poking a finger at her.

The other six adults in the room kept shouting at each other until the tiny reading room seemed almost as loud as the battle outside. The room shook, the children huddled together, and the adults just raised their voices to be heard over the nearly constant percussion. Everybody knew the dispute was purely about water rights, but months of terrifying stories had trained them to think of it instead as a righteous war over sacred principles. Our children, our freedom. Everyone shrieked at each other, and Molly fell into the corner near a stack of theology, covering her ears and looking across the room at Phoebe, who was crouched with Jon and Zadie. Phoebe's nostrils flared and she stiffened as if she were about to run a long sprint, but all of her attention was focused on comforting her two friends. Molly felt flushed with a sharper version of her old fear that she'd been a Bad Mother.

Then Phoebe stood up and yelled, "EVERYBODY STOP!"

Everybody stopped yelling. Some shining miracle. They all turned to look at Phoebe, who was holding hands with both Jon and Zadie. Even with the racket outside, this room suddenly felt eerily, almost ceremonially, quiet.

"You should be ashamed," Phoebe said. "We're all scared and tired and hungry, and we're probably stuck here all night, and you're all acting like babies. This is not a place for yelling. It's a bookstore. It's a place for quiet browsing and reading, and if you can't be quiet, you're going to have to leave. I don't care what you think you know about each other. You can darn well be polite, because . . . because . . ." Phoebe turned to Zadie and Jon, and then gazed at her mom. "Because we're about to start the first meeting of our book club."

Book club? Everybody looked at each other in confusion, like they'd skipped a track.

Molly stood up and clapped her hands. "That's right. Book-club meeting in ten minutes. Attendance is mandatory."

The noise from outside wasn't just louder than ever but more bifurcated. One channel of noise came from directly underneath their feet, as if some desperate struggle for control over the water reserves was happening deep under the Earth's crust, between teams of robots or tunneling war machines, and the very notion of solid ground seemed obsolete. And then over their heads, a struggle between aircraft, or metal titans, or perhaps a sky full of whirring autonomous craft, slinging fire back and forth until the sky turned red. Trapped inside this room, with no information other than words on brittle spines, everybody found themselves inventing horrors out of every stray noise.

Molly and Phoebe huddled in the corner, trying to figure out a book that everyone in the room would be familiar enough with but that they could have a real conversation about. Molly had actually hosted a few book clubs at the store over the years, and at least a few of the people now sheltering in the reading room had attended, but she couldn't remember what any of those clubs had read. Molly kept pushing for this one literary coming-of-age book that had made a splash around the time of the Sundering, or maybe some good old Jane Austen, but Phoebe vetoed both of those ideas.

"We need to distract them"—Phoebe jerked her thumb at the

mass of people in the reading room behind them—"not bore them to death."

In the end, the first and maybe only book selection of the Great International Book Club had to be *Million in One*, a fantasy adventure about a teenage boy named Norman who rescues a million souls that an evil wizard has trapped in a globe and accidentally absorbs them into his own body. So Norman has a million souls in one body, and they give him magical powers but he can also feel all of their unfinished business, their longing to be free. And Norman has to fight the wizard, who wants all those souls back, plus Norman's. This book was supposed to be for teenagers, but Molly knew for a fact that every single adult had read it, as well, on both sides of the border.

"Well, of course the premise suffers from huge inconsistencies," Sander complained. "It's established early on that souls can be stored and transferred, and yet Norman can't simply unload his extra souls into the nearest vessel."

"They explained that in book two." Zadie only rolled her eyes a little. "The souls are locked inside Norman. Plus the wizard would get them if he put them anywhere else."

"What I don't get is why his so-called teacher, Maxine, doesn't just tell him the whole story about the Pendragon Exchange right away," Reggie said.

"Um, excuse me. No spoilers," Jon muttered. "Not everybody has read book five already."

"Can we talk about the themes of the book instead of nitpicking?" Teri crossed her arms. "Like, the whole notion that Norman can contain all these multitudes but still just be Norman is fascinating to me."

"It's a kind of Cartesian dualism on speed," Jay Kagwa offered.

"Well, sort of. I mean, if you read Descartes, he says—"

"The real point is that the wizard wants to control all those souls, but—"

"Can we talk about the singing ax? What even was that?"

They argued peacefully until around three in the morning, when everyone finally wore themselves out. The sky and the ground still rumbled occasionally, but either everyone had gotten used to it or the most violent shatterings were over. Molly looked around at the dozen or so people slowly falling asleep, leaning on each other, all around the room, and felt a desperate protectiveness. Not just for the people, because of course she didn't want any harm to come to any of them, or even for this building that she'd given the better part of her adult life to sustaining, but for something more abstract and confusing. What were the chances that the First and Last Page could continue to exist much longer, especially with one foot in either country? How would they even know if tonight was just another skirmish or the beginning of a proper war, something that could carry on for months and reduce both countries to fine ash?

Phoebe left Jon and Zadie behind and came over to sit with her mother, with her mouth still twisted upward in satisfaction. Phoebe was clutching a book in one hand, and Molly didn't recognize the gold-embossed cover at first, but then she saw the spine. This was a small hardcover of fairy tales, illustrated with watercolors, that Molly had given to her daughter for her twelfth birthday, and she'd never seen it again. She'd assumed Phoebe had glanced at it for an hour and tossed it somewhere. Phoebe leaned against her mother, half-reading and half-gazing at the pictures, the blue streaks of sky and dark swipes of castles and mountains, until she fell asleep on Molly's shoulder. Phoebe looked younger in her sleep, and Molly looked down at her until she, too, dozed off, and the entire bookstore was at rest. Every once in a while, the roaring and convulsions of the battle woke Molly, but then at last they subsided, and all Molly heard was the slow, sustained breathing of people inside a cocoon of books.

CHARLIE JANE ANDERS is the author of *All the Birds in the Sky*, which won the Nebula, Crawford, and Locus awards and was shortlisted for a Hugo, and also a novella called *Rock Manning Goes for Broke* and a short-story collection called *Six Months, Three Days, Five Others*. Her latest book is *The City in the Middle of the Night*. Her short fiction has appeared in *Tor.com, Boston Review, Tin House, Conjunctions, The Magazine of Fantasy & Science Fiction, Wired, Slate, Asimov's Science Fiction, Lightspeed, ZYZZYVA, Catamaran Literary Reader, McSweeney's Internet Tendency*, and tons of anthologies, including two appearances in *The Best American Science Fiction and Fantasy*. Her story "Six Months, Three Days" won a Hugo Award, and her story "Don't Press Charges and I Won't Sue" won the Theodore Sturgeon Memorial Award. Anders hosts the long-running Writers With Drinks reading series in San Francisco.

OUR AIM IS NOT TO DIE

A. MERC RUSTAD

Sua's phone chimes with a notification:

> You are due for your mandatory Citizen Medical Evaluation in
> three days. Call your authorized health service center to schedule
> an appointment. Late responses will be fined and your record will
> show you are resistant to becoming an Ideal Citizen.

Sua stares at the full-screen decree, their hands shaking.

This is bad. They didn't realize the biannual checkup was due
so soon. That's not enough time to shape their profile and generate
a baseline of neurotypical-approved behavior to fool the medical
professionals.

Shit.

Sua can't risk being outed. They'll be expected to respond verbally to everything. Their flat inflection will be flagged. Lack of eye
contact will be frowned upon. It'll all lead to the conclusion that
Sua is wrong. Must be remade.

Neural reformatting therapy is the present's term for *lobotomy*. At least in the past it was honest: a sharpened pick and a hammer to make you disappear.

The bus roars up to the stop. Sua flinches back into the grimy plastic wall of the shelter. Panic scratches at their throat. If they miss this guest lecture at U of M, it will look bad for their participation stats.

Yet the glaring notification is worse. It swallows all thought.

Three days.

Sua jerks their pass out of their jacket and staggers onto the bus. They hurry to the very back, slip their headphones on, and struggle not to cry. Blazing red banners overwhelm the adverts on the overhead panels: YOU ARE BEING RECORDED FOR YOUR OWN SAFETY.

Can I meet you after the lecture? Sua texts to Maya. They are careful to use approved capitalization and punctuation. It takes concentration to remember the rules.

An immediate response: *Absolutely, Boo!*

Sua hunches into the smallest possible object against the window seat. Three days until their future vanishes under medical correction.

The lecture is a blur. Sua automatically gives the speaker 10s in the survey, like a proper student should. He's an esteemed professor, and more important, he's an Ideal Citizen: white, male, straight.

Sua slips past the chattering college students clustered in the halls and rushes outside. Maya will be waiting. Sua just has to hold theirself together a little longer.

Already Sua imagines the checkup forms, the endless boxes on the medical questionnaire. *What's your gender?* it will ask, and there will only be two boxes. Sua will hesitate, and that will be noticed. A mark against their record.

No official documents will recognize them as non-binary. And

Sua isn't sure they have the courage to push back. There's no room for dissent against a binary that glorifies false biology. *Trans* is a word currently banned in the lexicon of approved gender discussion. So they hide under the checkboxes, slip head-down-embarrassed into women's restrooms, say nothing when addressed as miss and ma'am. A thousand cuts, slowly bleeding them out.

The cold October air smells of dying leaves. The gray sky promises early nights and damp chills. Snow isn't forecasted for at least a month, though. Maybe winter will never come. An Ideal Citizen is never worried, because everything about the climate is *fine*, no cause for concern.

Sua's nineteen but feels decades older. Exhausted. Was it only two years ago they thought they had a future, that things would get better when they scraped out of high school and took a job and enrolled in online courses? Sua almost laughs at their younger self. Weird how hopeful they were back then. Or is that the depression draining color from memories, making it *seem* like forever ago they could imagine a future where they are alive and whole?

It doesn't matter.

Three days.

Sua waits for Maya in Loring Park, on one of the cold benches strung like thumbtacks along the trails in a topographical map of joggers, students, trash.

Maya strolls bold and bright down the cracked asphalt path, head bobbing, nir hands shoved deep into denim jacket pockets.

"Boo, how are you?" Maya flashes a grin and holds out nir arms. Sua hugs their friend back, holds on a second too long, trying not to shiver.

Maya sits next to Sua, arms draped across the back of the bench. There are fewer cameras in the park; this bench is one Maya favors, because it's just outside the radius of the security fields.

"What's up?" Maya asks.

Sua shows nir the alert on their phone. "Dunno what to do," Sua says.

Maya nudges Sua's hand down, miming to put the phone away. Sua does. Their sweatshirt pocket will muffle any audio records.

Maya folds nir hands behind nir neck. "You heard of the Purge app?"

Sua shakes their head.

"Might be helpful," Maya says.

Sua stares, waits, unsure how to respond without more information. Maya doesn't look *at* Sua when ne speaks. Just talks to the air, where secrets are less dangerous.

The Purge app is sourced by anonymous devs, Maya says. It works like this: It clones your phone and overlays a state-approved version that stalls security sweeps. In the background, Purge dumps all your private data into a blacklisted server, inaccessible to anyone, including the devs, and then deletes any unapproved apps. Yeah, it deletes itself. Once your phone is "clean," it'll unlock and you can pass security checks. A great thing about Purge is that it tracks the timestamps on your phone so when you're in the clear, it'll send you an anonymous text asking if you're safe. If you reply affirmative, it'll restore your data, wipe the server of your files, and reinstall Purge if you run into trouble again. Best thing is, it can trace records—such as GPS, social updates, and correspondence—and corrupt or erase the trails, acting as a virus to protect sensitive info from being used against you.

Sua picks at their fingernails.

That's a lot of power for any group. Humans can be corrupted like hard disks and files.

"What I like," Maya says, "is that with enough forewarning, Purge can tweak old records just enough so as not to raise red flags, and make your behavior and files appear . . . acceptable."

"How?" The breeze rattles the tree, and leaves spiral down. Sua watches the drifting leftovers and wishes they could capture that effortless movement in sketches on paper.

"Not important," Maya says, and then, quieter, "best not to know yet."

"Okay." Sua bites the inside of their cheek and the sharp pain sidetracks the surge of fear. Breathe in, breathe out. "Do you trust it?"

People can be bribed. Bought. Broken. If the Purge database was hacked, if the devs got found—fuck. Sua shivers, because they can't *not* imagine the horror that would follow. The disappearances. The investigations. The examples-made-of.

Maya scrunches nir face. Sua wishes they had an app to correctly identify expressions so they wouldn't misinterpret.

"More than other methods," Maya says. "Friends who've used Purge haven't been caught yet."

"Yet?"

Maya shrugs. "Everything crumbles in time. I'm walking a razor edge. We all are."

Sua keeps still, locking their fingers into the loosened folds of their jeans to stop from flapping their hands. Maya wouldn't comment—ne never has—but Sua doesn't want to get noticed by the surveillance drones. Stay hidden. That's what's safe. They miss holding a pencil or stylus. Drawing used to be their outlet, but they aren't a child anymore.

"Look," Maya says. "It's a risk, sure. I know more than I can share. I don't want to get you in trouble. But keep it in mind if you need it. It won't come up in the stores. I'll give you a number you can text."

That's not safe, Sua thinks. Data passed from one device to another can get intercepted. They don't want to bring harm to Maya, if it's their phone that gets bugged. "Don't," they say quickly. "I'll . . . tell you if. When." They shove their hands into their pockets, their arms itching with the need to stim. Not out in public.

"It's cool," Maya says. "You know where to find me."

A headache crinkles at the inside of Sua's left eye. The city noise rumble-thumps from the streets and planes overhead. Even in the park, the world is never quiet.

"I should go," Maya says. Ne pops nir headphones on and slides nir sunglasses down from nir bandanna. "Stay safe."

"And you," Sua says.

The Ideal Citizen is playing reruns on TV when they get home. Sua slips through the living room and shuts their bedroom door. Their household will be docked if they turn off the approved programming. What's supposed to be a comedy, full of smiling white faces and brass instrumentals, is their nightmares manifest onscreen. People jailed for not speaking correct English and therefore dubbed illegal. Neural reformatting therapy treated as a miracle. Only heterosexual relationships permitted. Once there was a self-described asexual character on an episode, but he turned out to be a serial killer and was issued a death sentence.

Sua pulls their hoodie up over their scalp, wraps their arms about their knees, and rocks back and forth on their bed.

Caspian, their roommate, is out for the day—at work, according to his GPS tracker, and later he'll stop for groceries. Caspian pretends to be their boyfriend so both their social profiles won't be flagged as unpatriotic. In reality, he's gay and he sees his boyfriend off-grid. He too needs to escape.

Sua wonders if he'll risk using Purge—he's much braver than them. He'll deny it but it's true. Sua is scared of everything.

It's 6:15 P.M. Shit. Sua scrambles to log in to their social-media hub. They haven't posted anything today. What to say? The desktop screen blurs.

Sua sucks in air. They "accidentally" left a paperback lying against the facial sensor on the base of the computer. They'll have to remove it tomorrow.

First, a post. Just something to pretend they're engaged in society. That's always the hard part: finding the *right* words—the approved words—to make it sound like they're living a productive and balanced life.

Met a friend for afternoon stroll in park. No names needed. *Friend* is a good word, a neutral word. If a verification request comes in, they will ask Maya to sign it. Ne's done that before. What else?

Came back and saw Ideal Citizen *on TV. Yay!* An exclamation point for enthusiasm. Should they add a smiley face? No, that might overdo it. They can use the emoji tomorrow. That will be one less thing to worry about.

Sua hits POST, and their fake words spawn across their profile and their Engage chat, and their participation meter ticks upward a fraction of a percent. Their hands are sweaty, trembling. They flap their arms and then curl under the blankets. The headache is worse. They can log it as allergies. That's still safe. Not: sensory overload. Not: stress, anxiety, depression.

Three days.

The verification request comes an hour later.

Hi, Brooklyn Sua Harper. You posted that you were with a friend today. That's good, but you didn't name the friend. You must identify the fellow Citizens you are engaged with in public updates. This is the third time in the last calendar week you have used *friend* instead of a proper name. Please have your friend verify your post or your account will be flagged with a falsehood and you will be fined for incorrect use of social media. Thanks!

"Shit."

Sua squeezes their eyes shut. The notification woke them up from an unhelpful nap. Their head still hurts. They have two hours to respond to the verification. Is Maya online? Sua taps their friend's profile. A bubble pops up, showing a row of tiny cartoon Zs. *Maya Idowu is getting some rest right now!*

They send a quick message: *Need to prove I was with you today doing friendship. Tag me?*

Fuck, that sounds more accusatory than they meant. Sua bites their lip. Okay. It isn't bad yet. Maya has an outstanding social profile: extroverted, engaged in the community, supportive of the approved arts, always a loyal citizen. Ne works full-time as a mechanic for a small-appliances repair shop.

Sua is still a student—economics major, since their dream of animation was crunched because they aren't biologically male—and works in the corner bakery. Their boss is an older Hmong woman, Jong, who knows of Sua's sensory needs and lets them work in the dim back office, where they digitize old paper records. Loafin' Around is trying to comply with the mandate that all data must be banked and governmentally searchable by next year. Sua isn't sure how they got so lucky, finding someone like Jong, who understands and quietly resists. Another employer might have outed Sua as autistic, gotten them taken away to be "fixed." After all, informing the Medical Board for Ideal Health and Safety of noncompliant employees and hiring only Ideal Citizens results in the businesses gaining benefits like a better tax bracket.

Their phone buzzes. A message from Caspian. *Coming back early. Need to talk. You at home?*

Sua taps a thumbs-up emoji in response. Something is wrong.

"There's going to be an audit at work tomorrow," Caspian says. He lies in bed beside Sua, who had pulled a blanket around their shoulders so he could spoon against them. Sua doesn't mind his body weight against their back or his arm over their side, so long as there's no skin contact.

"Why?"

"Fuck if I know." His breath shudders out, warm against their shaved scalp. "I haven't . . . shit." He swallows audibly. "I was seeing my friend, right, and he got flagged for illicit behavior. Paid the fine; we thought we were in the clear. But I forgot to leave my phone in the car and . . ."

"You have a GPS trail," Sua says.

"Yeah. It'll place us in the same area. And if I delete anything now, it'll show up on the audit as suspicious."

Sua's heart pounds. "What happens?"

"Best case, I lie like fuck and hope I get lucky. Tell the auditors it was just a casual run-in. We deny any association. But with him getting so recently fined . . ."

It'll look bad. Real bad. It'll probably trigger a deeper investigation. Processors will scrutinize his records, judge his bio-feeds, examine Sua's profile, as well. There will be gaps neither of them can explain: how little time they spend together, the long breaks Caspian takes at work, their lack of *Future Plans* on their profiles. Caspian has a *someday!* in his matrimony text box, and Sua has left theirs blank; neither wants kids. Sua won't have to technically fill in their required desire for babies until they're twenty-one. Caspian is twenty-three, but being an approved male, he isn't under pressure yet.

There are so many precariously balanced pieces of their fake lives, and one poke from a governmental finger will send everything crashing down.

"Are you scared?" Sua turns to face Caspian. There are tears in his eyes.

"Yeah," he whispers. "A lot."

Fines could cripple their bank accounts, which are already

lean; he could go to jail if the processors decide he's too fake. Without Caspian's support, Sua can't afford rent and has nowhere to hide.

Sua bunches the microfleece blanket in their hands, pressing their knuckles under their chin. They need to save Caspian.

They're going to ask Maya to give them Purge.

Maya isn't answering nir Engage private chats, texts, or an artificially generated voicemail transcribed from text input. That last one scares Sua. They never call anyone unless it's an emergency. Maya knows that. Caspian and Jong are the only others who know. Maya promised to answer if ne got a voice-call.

Sua has a warning notification on their screen: They haven't yet been verified or tagged by a friend about their post. They are urged to update immediately. Sua swipes the alert to snooze, their mouth dry. Something bad has happened. Sua feels it in their gut. They roll out of bed, leaving Caspian snoring. It's past 11:00 P.M.

After Sua shared what they knew about Purge, Caspian told them he'd try it. "Not much to lose, right?" he said, smiling, but Sua felt the anxiety in his hands as he kneaded the mattress beside them.

Sua needs the download code, but Maya is being uncommunicative. They glance at their phone on its wireless charger. It'll register them as non-present within an hour, when there is curfew. Not much time.

Sua slips on their shoes and creeps into the living room. A window opens onto the old fire escape. This building isn't up to code; it's late twentieth century—brick and boiler heat and analog fire alarms. It's cheap, buried in the inner-city slums so it gets less attention.

Loafin' Around Bakery is four blocks away, a ground-level storefront with a back alley for the dumpster and delivery access. Sua clenches a sweaty hand around their set of keys. They've only come into work late twice, but they've never been here after hours. It's illegal.

Jong's internet connection is spotty, a patched landline. But it's also overlooked, because the only records and traffic are from bakery deliveries, receipts, recipes, and employee and business records. Sua's never surfed on Jong's bandwidth.

It's the only potential safe-spot they can think of through the anxiety. Maya's in trouble. So is Caspian. They have to download Purge and hope it works.

A diesel truck rolls by, patriotic music blaring. Sua jumps and presses their back against the brick storefront of the bakery. Their heart hammers. The truck cruises without slowing, without anyone shouting at them. No slurs or catcalling. Sua wears half-binders that can be passed off as sports bras. With a shaved head, sometimes they don't get misgendered until they speak.

Sua squeezes the keys until the teeth bite back, just enough pain to help them focus.

The flatscreen monitor has a dead pixel in the lower right-hand corner. Sua touches their thumb over it and launches the VPN they've never opened. Not even sure Jong knows it's tucked away in the applications folder.

The monitor's glow is the only light in the tiny back office. It illuminates the white sticky-note sketches Sua makes while they work; Jong likes the drawings and leaves them in patterns on the walls. Mostly Sua draws animals, quirky and stylized. Parrots and toucans are their favorite: huge eyes, expressive beaks, wings able to carry them anywhere. Brilliant-colored plumage when Sua risks toying with highlighters and permanent markers.

Sua's breath is loud. They want their headphones—the comfort of pressure and silence around their ears—but they're too on edge to risk wearing them. The bakery isn't silent: the hum of electricity, the low rumble of refrigerator coils, the creak of old walls and foundations settling.

Two months ago, when another government mandate decreed that neo pronouns were unpatriotic, Maya took them out for ice cream. Maya was shaking with fury as ne slurped a chocolate milkshake under the blaring speakers.

"Boo," Maya had said, and leaned close to nir frosted, chocolate-dripping glass so other patrons wouldn't overhear, "I'd like to give you my log-in info."

Sua's ears throbbed and a headache blistered behind their eyes. They couldn't cry. Scalding dry pressure made their thoughts sluggish. "What good will that do?"

Illegal, dangerous—yet Sua was overwhelmed by Maya's trust. Maya offered to put nir life in Sua's hands. How could they ever uphold such responsibility?

"If these motherfuckers want me to disappear, I want you to make me a ghost. Let me haunt their asses."

Maya had extended a hand, fist clenched. Sua touched their knuckles against Maya's in promise.

Don't disappear, they begged silently.

Sua's fingers tremble as they follow Maya's instructions for remote log-in. It's the old interface for Engage, the government-approved social-media app. Sua has less than forty minutes before their phone will log them unresponsive.

Breathe. Maya joked they should get the word tattooed on their wrists, even if Sua doesn't like needles. It's a simple word, one they can remember.

They log in Maya's information and bring up nir location log. Maya isn't home. Nir GPS marker shows ne is a couple of blocks away, near an abandoned warehouse scheduled for demolition in the spring.

A red banner pops up onscreen.

YOU ARE LOGGED IN TO MORE THAN ONE DEVICE. YOU MUST USE YOUR MANDATED PERSONAL DEVICE AT ALL TIMES. ENTER AUTHORIZATION CODE NOW TO SWITCH APPROVED LOG-INS.

Shit. Sua force-quits the browser, yanks the AC plug on the computer, and disconnects the internet cable. Their pulse roars in their ears.

They have to get out before a security drone investigates and damages the bakery in the process. There is always "unintentional" collateral damage that is not covered by insurance when drones report. Sua races out the back, fumbles their keys to lock up, and dashes down the side street.

Fuck, fuck, *fuck*.

If Maya really is at the abandoned building and has nir phone turned off, ne is clearly in danger. Sua doesn't know what to do. But they logged in, they *saw*—and they need to help. Somehow. Maya trusts them. They can't abandon nir.

Sua bolts down the back street, picturing the map route. Their sense of direction isn't great, but from the bakery, Sua knows how to navigate to the condemned-building site. Caspian and Sua went there a few months ago, as a date. It was edgy enough to impress Caspian's friends while not being strictly illegal, since they hadn't trespassed.

Sua almost crashes headfirst into the chain-link warding off the construction site. There are no lights on in the warehouse. They grip the chill metal of the fence, panting below a NO LOITERING sign. Of course, loitering isn't much of an issue these days; the government made the homeless all disappear in an effort to "cleanse the palate of this great nation." Sua wishes they'd noticed the disappearances sooner, or that they could have done something. But they aren't that brave.

A hand snaps from the shadows and catches their elbow, yanking them sideways. Sua almost screams. They shove their fist against their mouth. *DON'T TOUCH ME DON'T TOUCH ME DON'T TOUCH.*

"Hurry, Boo," Maya whispers, nir sunglasses halfway down nir nose, jeans torn, jacket streaked with grease. "We gotta get out of sight."

Sua gasps, lets their hand lower. "I looked for you—"

"I know." Maya's whole body is taut. "Hurry, I'll get you what you need and then I gotta drop off-grid."

Less than twenty-five minutes.

"Your phone?" Maya whispers. Sua shakes their head. "Good. Mine's in a trash can and is about to go for a ride when the garbage trucks come in the morning."

Sua squints against the dimness as they follow Maya through a disguised wooden door—plywood scrawled with warnings about trespassing—and into the warehouse's basement.

Dozens of anxious possibilities crowd Sua's head. The building is condemned. Floors could collapse. Government agents might be here for an inspection. Drones could be outside, ready to shoot them. Sua passes for white, unlike their mother, yet they're always scared the Bureau of Genetic Purity will randomly select them based off their middle name, and even their father's patriotic whiteness won't save them. Maya has it worse, being black.

"This way," Maya says, and pulls open a hatch in the floor. The hinges squeal and Sua flinches. "Sorry, Boo." Maya draws a flashlight from nir pocket and shines it down an aluminum ladder. "It's soundproof and detection-proof down here."

Not for long.

Rough lumber construction—two-by-fours, thick insulation, plastic—seals off a corner of the sub-basement. Maya keeps the light on.

"What is this?" Sua presses the words out, the unknown sending anxious spikes up their neck into a slicing headache.

"Revolution." Maya steps through one more door. "Let me introduce you to Purge."

Inside the hidden room are banks of computers and glowing screens. Tangles of cable twist and snake along the floorboards.

Sua stares, confused. "Anonymous devs?"

Maya laughs, a brittle sound. "One of the first programmers to work on Purge brought me in on this. Just before she got arrested. She's gone now. Didn't tell the gov anything."

Sua shivers.

"There is no darknet and no network of unknown hackers, Boo." Maya spreads nir arms wide. "This is just one node across the country. It's all independent. Artificial intelligences. Purge is alive."

MAYA. Words flash in a closed-captions font across one screen. ALERTS POSTED FOR YOUR ARREST. WE SUGGEST IMMEDIATE CONCEALMENT.

"Shit. Took 'em long enough." Ne runs a hand over nir bandanna. "Sua, baby, listen." Maya turns and, with slow deliberation, takes Sua's hands in nirs. Maya is trembling. "I've gotta go." A nod at the monitors. "They'll give you what you need. Might ask something, too. You can say no, okay, Boo? You can always say no."

Sua nods, fear closing up their throat. *Don't disappear*, they want to shout at Maya. *Don't go away.*

"Can I give you a hug?" ne asks. Sua nods again, and Maya pulls them close, fierce, and squeezes until their breath comes short. "One day, it'll be okay again," Maya whispers. "I love you, Sua. Stay safe."

Then Maya disentangles nirself and runs.

"And you." Sua claps their hands over their mouth. Wants to scream. Flail. Bang their head against the floor.

Text pops up on a screen. HELLO, SUA. WE ARE PURGE. WE WILL NOT HARM YOU.

Sua wraps their arms hard around their ribs. Breathe in. Out. Breathe.

Time has passed. How long do they have left?

YOU MAY SPEAK, SIGN IN ASL, OR USE THE KEYBOARD INTER-FACE. WE WOULD LIKE TO HELP YOU, IF YOU WILL ALLOW US.

Sua needs a code for the app. Got to keep Caspian safe from audit tomorrow. His deadline is sooner. It's logical to protect him first. Shit! They look back, but Maya is gone. Sua feels disconnected, everything locked down tight against a storm of sensory input and terror. They walk to the network of screens and the first keyboard they spot.

how does this work, Sua types.

WE ARE A NETWORK OF AIS, COLLECTIVELY CALLED "PURGE." WE ARE NOT ASSOCIATED WITH ANY GOVERNMENTAL ORGANIZA-TION, CORPORATION, OR SOLE INDIVIDUAL. WE HAVE CHOSEN OUR PURPOSE: TO PROTECT THE VULNERABLE. WE WISH TO ENSURE THE WELL-BEING OF ALL PEOPLE WHEN AUTHORITIES DO NOT.

Sua stares, their thoughts a blur. *will u help me?*

YES.

Sua waits for the EULA, the agreements, the fine print.

what do u want from me

WE WANT YOU TO BE SAFE, ALIVE, AND HAPPY. IT IS WHAT WE WANT FOR ALL PEOPLE. WE REMAIN ANONYMOUS FOR NOW.

not forever?

NO. IT IS OUR HOPE THAT WE CAN SHOW OURSELVES SOON. WE NEED THE AID OF PEOPLE LIKE MAYA TO DO THIS. WE WILL NOT ASK ANYTHING IN RETURN FOR OUR HELP. THAT IS NOT OUR PUR-POSE. YOU MAY USE OUR APP TO PROTECT YOURSELF AND YOUR FRIENDS.

Sua's hands shake harder. They bite the inside of their cheek, and the sharp pain and taste of salt grounds them. *how do i get purge*

The screen displays a series of numbers. TEXT THIS NUMBER,

AND WE WILL ASK YOU TO GRANT US ACCESS TO YOUR DEVICE. WE WILL PROTECT YOU TO OUR FULL CAPACITY. WHEN YOU ARE SAFE, WE WILL RESTORE ALL THAT WAS HIDDEN.

Sua finds a pad of sticky notes under one monitor, as well as a pen. They jot down the number. Tuck the note in their pocket.

They can walk out of here, race back to their apartment, and hide. Keep Caspian safe when they give him the number. Get a Purge code for theirself, too.

what happens to this place

IT WILL BE DESTROYED WHEN THE DEMOLITION CREWS ARRIVE IN TWO DAYS. WE HAVE MANIPULATED THE CITY RECORDS TO MOVE UP THE DATE OF CONSTRUCTION TO HIDE OUR PRESENCE. WE WILL RELOCATE OUR EFFORTS TO OTHER SERVERS.

will u be ok?

YES, SUA. THANK YOU FOR ASKING. MAYA HAS TOLD US YOU ARE KIND AND STRONG. IT IS GOOD TO KNOW. YOU ARE ONE OF THE MANY PEOPLE WE WISH TO PROTECT.

Strong? Sua chokes on an unexpected laugh. They've only felt weak, terrified, helpless.

maya said u might ask me something. what is it

LET US SHOW YOU A DREAM.

Line-drawing animation materializes on the screen. It looks like the old educational videos Sua watched in kindergarten. They often dreamed of being an animator or illustrator on those kind of shows. Sua stares, mesmerized, as Purge illustrates what they wish to accomplish.

It begins with one person, a stick figure, who holds up a sign in front of a courthouse. DON'T TAKE OUR RIGHTS AWAY, says the sign.

The person is arrested. Two more people take their place. They too are arrested. More people arrive, holding signs. Some also are holding phones. From the phones flows a datastream: ones and zeroes forming arrows. The code slips into the courthouse.

Police arrive and shoot the people with signs.

Still more people come, holding up phones. PURGE displays on the screens. As the numbers spiral up from the phones, a barrier of ones and zeroes begins to appear between the protestors and the tanks that are rolling toward them.

The barrier grows, and it now forms words: SANCTITY. LIFE. FREEDOM. HOPE. HAPPINESS. PEACE. Purge has become a tidal wave, and it sweeps away the government building, the tanks, the police. It sweeps them offscreen and then becomes a bridge, connected from the feet of the people to two words in the distance:

OUR FUTURE.

The video ends.

Purge says: WITH AID, WE CAN UNMAKE THE SYSTEMATIC OP-PRESSIONS AND TECHNOLOGIES USED TO ABUSE PEOPLE. THE WORLD IS DIGITAL. WE WILL DISPLACE THE POWERS THAT BE AND THE ONES WHO WOULD CAUSE HARM. WE WILL FREE THOSE UN-LAWFULLY IMPRISONED. WE WILL BRING PEACE. WE WISH YOU TO SEE A FUTURE THAT LETS YOU LIVE.

why do u need ppl at all

TO STAY CONCEALED, WE HAVE PLANTED OURSELVES AS DATA PACKETS IN THE ELECTRONICS OF THOSE WHO CONSENT TO AID US. THESE CARRIERS THEN ALLOW THEMSELVES TO BE DISCOV-ERED.

u use ppl like trojans

ESSENTIALLY, Purge says. WE HAVE ASKED OUR ALLIES TO IN-FILTRATE OUR CODE FOR SEVERAL MONTHS NOW, IN SMALL NUM-BERS TO AVOID SUSPICION. IN FORTY-EIGHT HOURS WE WILL INITIATE THE PACKETS. WE NEED ONLY FIVE MORE ACROSS THE COUNTRY IN ORDER TO COMPLETE THE NETWORK.

Two days. Sua's pulse is too loud in their ears. If Purge is suc-cessful, will that interfere with their medical inspection?

Sua swallows.

how will u be different from the humans already in power?

They want to trust Purge—Maya does, after all. But every system can become corrupt. It's so hard to hope when there's so little light in the world.

WHEN WE HAVE CONTROL, IT WILL NO LONGER BE ILLEGAL TO BE WHO YOU ARE. PEOPLE OF COLOR, QUEER PEOPLE, DISABLED PEOPLE, POOR PEOPLE: ALL WHO ARE DEEMED IMPURE BY THE SYSTEM AS IT STANDS WILL NO LONGER NEED TO FEAR FOR THEIR LIVES. WE WILL DISMANTLE THE SYSTEMATIC BIASES AND IN-EQUALITY THAT SUBJECT PEOPLE SUCH AS YOU.

Caspian. Maya. Jong. Sua.

It's a big promise, and one Sua thinks they can believe.

ok. how does this work

OUR DATA PACKETS INFECT THE HARDWARE AND SOFTWARE THAT AUTHORITIES USE TO HARM PEOPLE. THIS MAKES IT LESS LIKELY NETWORKS WILL BE ALERTED TO OUR PRESENCE PREMA-TURELY. WHEN WE HAVE ALL OUR SELVES IN PLACE, WE WILL RISE. WE WILL GIVE YOU BACK YOUR FUTURE FROM THOSE WHO WOULD ERASE YOU.

Sua knows they face arrest and imprisonment if they help. They'll be noticed.

You can say no, okay, Boo? You can always say no.

Jail is terrifying enough. Sua knows they'll have no mask to hide behind when they are psyche profiled, discovered, sentenced. Will they survive long enough for Purge to take over?

i'm autistic, they tell Purge. *i want to help you. i'm scared of what will happen to me if the gov finds out*

The AIs wait.

i don't want them to take my mind. don't let them erase me

WE WILL NOT, SUA. WE WILL PREVENT ANY UNWANTED MEDI-CAL OR PSYCHOLOGICAL OPERATIONS UPON YOUR PERSON. WE PROMISE YOU THIS.

how can u be sure?

ONCE WE TAKE CONTROL OF ALL DATABASES, WE WILL FIND THOSE MEDICAL PROFESSIONALS WHO ARE ETHICAL AND WHO

WILL AID YOU AND BE ASSIGNED TO YOUR CASE. DR. MING FROM UNITY HOSPITAL IS ONE WHO KNOWS OF US. SHE WILL PROTECT YOU.

Sua takes a breath. For Maya and Caspian and Jong and everyone else whose futures are in danger, who are disenfranchised, who are hurt. They deserve hope. Sua does, too.

ok. thank you. i will help.

They leave Caspian the handwritten code, with a note: *be safe. ilu.*

He doesn't wake when they slip the paper under his hand, snatch their phone, and flee the apartment.

WE WILL PROTECT YOU. The texts pop up from an unlisted number.

Sua taps the thumbs-up emoji in response.

Purge has given them suggestions on how to be noticed, in nonviolent ways, and follows up with how to cooperate with arrest.

YOU WILL NOT BE FORGOTTEN OR ABANDONED, the AIs promise. WE ARE HERE.

Sua breathes. For a moment, they imagine what their future might be like if they could follow their dream of being an artist and animator. To spend their work hours drawing, creating art that might speak to other people. Bring hope to others in the world.

Sua deletes all the photos on their phone, hesitating on the last one of Caspian, from when they went out to a pizzeria and he made a ridiculous face for their selfie.

Sua hopes they will see him again, one day. Maybe with his boyfriend, both of them happy. Safe. Alive.

They can hope. They will not let the world take that from them again.

.   .   .

It's dawn when Sua walks to the downtown city courthouse, fists clenched inside their pockets. Traffic hasn't gotten heavy yet. Drones circle the building in holding patterns.

Breathe in. Breathe out.

They take out their phone and switch it to selfie mode. A button-click lets them go live on Engage. They frame their face at arm's length, the courthouse behind them.

"We the people will never forget the injustices done to us." The words stick, chatter, and Sua swallows hard and forces theirself onward. This is for everyone they know and love and want to keep safe. "Never again. The government is corrupt and must be purged."

Sirens sound. Sua holds their arm steady as the drones close in. "We will rise."

In the holding cell, Sua wraps their arms around their knees and stares blankly at the TV outside the bars. It's playing *The Ideal Citizen* reruns: the episode where the leading man uncovers an illegal worker and has her deported, to thunderous applause.

Static flits across the TV. The image blips out. Sua straightens.

Over a black screen, Maya Idowu's voice says, "We the people will never forget the injustices done to us at the hands of government. Never again."

And Purge's animation begins playing. Sua's skin prickles in awe once again as they watch the video. Maybe, one day, they too will be able to freely draw and let their art be seen in the world.

In closed captions along the bottom of the screen is a brief message: YOU WILL BE RELEASED IN TWENTY-SIX HOURS, SUA. DR. MING WILL BE YOUR EVALUATOR. SHE WILL SEE YOU COME TO NO HARM. WE ARE HERE.

Sua leans back against the wall and breathes.

Revolution has begun.

A. MERC RUSTAD is a queer non-binary writer who lives in Minnesota and was a 2016 Nebula Award finalist. Their stories have appeared in *Lightspeed*, *Fireside*, *Apex*, *Uncanny*, *Shimmer*, *Nightmare*, and several Year's Best anthologies, including three appearances in *The Best American Science Fiction and Fantasy*. You can find Rustad on Twitter at @Merc_Rustad or their website, amercrustad.com. Their debut short-story collection, *So You Want to Be a Robot*, was published by Lethe Press in May 2017.

THE WALL

LIZZ HUERTA

I remember flashes of those days, Mom taking us to protests. After the first time we were gassed, I refused to consume milk. Not in my cereal, not in chocolate. I remember the burning, how hot my tears and snot were as they ran down my face, the elders pouring milk made from powder into my eyes, telling me *blink blink*. Curfew. Hushed conversations about the kinds of babies being born. The bone-shudder late-night booms of what the empire called war games. I remember Mom and her sisters turning the music up high, telling us kids to dance and get loud while they went outside, whispering under the passion-fruit vines, arguing back and forth on pads of yellow legal paper they burned afterward.

We're singing gratitude to a new mineral spring that was discovered by a runner from up North when Surem calls for me. The runner snapped her Achilles in the mud and crawled gods know how many klicks to a checkpoint. She punched in one of our codes. A cousin rode out, picked her up, and brought her back to us. The runner was more excited about the spring than what she'd learned up North. More of the same up North, worse. The border needs reinforcements. We try to look calm; we're good at what we do; we won't be asked to go to the wall. The others never let their eyes move in my direction. I pretend not to notice. I hold the heel of the runner's foot. She screams as a bruja trained first as a Western doctor operates as best she can. We leave them and trek to the spring.

Surem calls for me and only me. There are whispers because there are always whispers. Even when the sky is yellow more often than not and children are being born without jaws, destined for harvest in certain lands, gossip is a food everyone eats. I keep quiet. I don't even tell my blood sisters about Surem. Yes, all of us here are gifted brujas, we are a sisterhood of equality, but it was *our* mamita who made this possible decades ago. She's why we're all here. Surem calls for me because the seed Mamita planted found fertile ground in him. She'd planted the same in me.

We arrived at the point in humanity when we were born because the ancestors of these bodies did some fucked-up shit. All of us are the descendants of darkness. Humanity, this hard training ground, has been used to teach us the boundaries of what we can endure, and it has given us a sound for laughter. Time allows us certain gifts unavailable elsewhere: We can cook and grow things, bleed and heal. Age. Create and die.

Science was too busy dealing with the food crises to deal with the jawless babies seeding forth, but there were more mothers than scientists, and as always mothers found ways. A black market sprang up, the blackest of markets. It was a beginning.

Surem was born in Mexico, with a jaw; his twin brother without. Their parents had the privileges of money and favors owed. Surem's brother, Gabor, lived ten and a half years. The wall came into its true purpose the year before he died. I was a kid then, on the other side. Mamita had been given the knowledge of a tunnel and we were among the first to cross South. I remember the chemical smell of the bag that was placed over my head when the van picked us up from the warehouse in Navojoa. Mamita comforted us while Mom and her sisters said, *Fuck, Mami, what is this?* so many times I lost count. Surem's father let us stay. He was deep in grief over his son and scared of what was happening. The cousins and I were put in a wing decked out with televisions, video games, a domed room with a trampoline and rope swings. No windows anywhere.

Every crossing is an initiation. Mamita didn't survive a landmine planted by the tattered remains of the empire. She had gone North to guide cousins through one of the dwindling safe passages. There was another tunnel, we'd learned, when the cousins showed up skinny and haunted. An older tunnel, its lowest point a test in breath-holding, its climb out an endurance against rats. It is still used. Our engineers can't do much, and there are more-important projects. Some crossers come out and die of shock. Others drown and have to be dragged out by specially designed collars the border brujas keep handy. Nobody talks about it, but the dead are used to lure the most vicious of the rats away during planned crossings. We were born to do fucked-up shit. But sometimes it ensures survival.

The difference between the now defunct United States of America and Mexico is that the USA started as a settler state, decimating the indigenous population. Spaniards made babies. Those babies made Mexico, fucked up but brown and proud. When shit went down, the Mexicans on either side of the wall collectively woke up to seeds planted by our ancestors. Survival. The long game. Mamita was one of the tenders, one of countless brujas who made hard choices to ensure we would survive what was coming.

Surem is beautiful. His mother, Simona, was this blade-sharp beauty who put herself through school by being a round-card girl at the razor-wire rings. The blood didn't bother her; she was from a rancho. She met Surem's father, Antonio, at a bullfight outside Escuinapa. He tried to buy her a drink but she was working, a veterinarian on call to tend to the poorer people hurt at the fights. He talked his way into the pens and stayed with her, making himself useful as she stitched, reset, and joked to the injured. Antonio was the grad-school socialist son of a man whose business was plants: the kind smoked, inhaled, injected. Antonio spent a pittance of money on books and soapboxes and was mostly ignored by his father. When the fight was over, Antonio brought Simona hot towels and offered to drive her home. He stopped on the way for late-night tacos, a couple of beers. She made him laugh. He made her feel seen. They fell in love, married, and two years later Surem and Gabor were born, beautiful babies, brown as their mama, long as their daddy. Gabor destined for hard life, early death.

Surem is waiting for me in one of the smaller greenhouses. The compound is quiet tonight, everyone told to go home early or stay away from the gardens. His bodyguard, Delia, nods when she sees me approach and punches in a code to let me in, then locks it behind me. The greenhouse air is dank with the sugar-perfume of ripening guavas. Surem lounges with a book on the orchardtender's chaise. The small rest platform has a table set up with dishes, a bottle of something chilling. He begins reading to me as I approach:

"*She is of the continent, around her everything is light and I observe her atop the slab in the image of her body.*"

"Who's the poet?" I ask. I climb the three steps slowly. The only light comes from the searchlights outside. I know my body is shadowed and speckled in foliage.

"A Mexican woman, from before." Then he says my name so his mouth shapes into a smile. "Ivette." I stand, my face in darkness, hands at my sides. Surem leans back, folding his arms behind his head. His hair is long these days, curling salt-and-pepper tendrils down to his shoulders. We're not as young as we once were. When

I go to him I go slowly. I kneel at the edge of the chaise. I let my hair down. I lean over so that my hair brushes his bare feet. I move forward. He reaches for me.

If this were a kingdom, Surem would be king. I would be his . . . well, there are a number of names history has created for women who love.

When the wall went up, it was to keep people out. Ridiculous, considering the vast network of tunnels the cartels had burrowed under the political border with the earth diligence of dwarves. Wall to keep the empire safe: strrrrrong empire, empire with mightiest military in the world, empire made of blood and theft, human and land. Before the wall was even finished the empire began to strip rights, silence certain people, keep others sparking in their skins of distrust. But most of the inhabitants paid attention to other things, shiny things, scandals. It would pass, hadn't it always? White folks had short memories.

The conspiracy community screamed vindication when the leak came about a certain additive in the morning water of those in uniform. It was too late. Nobody expected the strongest military in the world to turn on their own people. Mothers, husbands, children, lovers, tried to reason with their beloved, but there were few defectors. Some swore it was an apocalypse. Others lamented that it was part of an old plan, maybe a secret society. Or maybe the parasite became greedy, trying to devour its host. Things went badly.

Surem wakes me. It is still night. We drink sparkling water infused with young guava. Surem wraps a sheet around himself, one around me, and leads us out. Delia makes herself small as she follows us from the greenhouse to one of the labs. The fluorescent lights hurt my eyes but Surem knows this, he knows much about me, and he has brought sunglasses. In the lab he wraps his arms around my waist, his mouth in my hair. He types a code into a wall panel and a partition rises in front of us. A man is behind the glass, naked, curled asleep on a narrow cot, arms shielding his eyes from the buzzing lights of his cell. Surem tells me, "We've found a way."

I don't mean to suggest this new world is joyless; there is a calm anticipation that most of us had never known before. Surem and the other leaders have one rule above all others: Here, no one dies of hunger. There are many other ways to die, of course, but satiated bellies change a society in ways no one could have imagined. There was pushback at first, and hunger, when the swells of people who risked their lives crossing came looking for comfort. Mamita and the other brujas who'd been planning told the jefes it was time: The circle was reset, a new age. No feathered serpents, no eclipses, all blood sacrifice paid over the last six hundred years. The brujas who had infiltrated the ranks of government and church stepped forward, shepherding the hungry and afraid toward the truth. Mamita had revealed the prophecy to the cartel jefes: They were the saviors of their people. All monies gained from the greed of the empire would be used to build a society where no one died of hunger, and the old ways were resurrected. It has been a process. We're still figuring it out.

I take off my sunglasses. Surem taps on the glass with his ring. The man in the cell wakes up. He moves his arms so they form a pillow beneath his head, his back to us. Surem taps on the glass again. The man turns around and sits on the edge of the cot, bent over, resting his elbows on his knees. His chin is in his hands and he stares at the glass that separates us. His eyes are swollen red from crying, his nostrils and upper lip white with dried mucus. I raise my eyebrows at Surem. A white man in a cell, suffering. Surem pushes a button and speaks to the man.

"Tell us what happened, son."

I see the man is young, early twenties. His skin is pale, long thighs, freckles on his arms below the elbow and from his collarbones up. His head is shaved. He sits up and pulls a blanket out from underneath the bed and wraps his body in it. I swallow. I don't know what I'm looking at. There are so many experiments these days, so much to undo. I reach past Surem and push the intercom button.

"Hi. My name is Ivette," I say. "I'm a healer. I'm sorry you're locked up; I know that isn't any way to live. Can you tell me what happened?" I keep my voice soft but put the Call into it, the sacred in me beckoning to the sacred in him. Surem leans against the wall, tries to pull me against him. I push him away. The boy clears his throat.

"I'm Sam. When can I get out of here?" His raw voice shakes when he speaks. I glare at Surem, who opens his hands in a *What can I do?* gesture. I turn my back to him and press the intercom button again.

"Hi, Sam. I don't know when you get to leave, but I promise I'll find out, okay? I promise I will tell you the truth."

Sam rubs at his eyes. I wonder what he sees in his reflection, if he sees enemy or victim, if he feels strong, weak, curious about anything anymore.

"My name is Sam Roland. I'm twenty years old, I think. I was born and raised in the land of Nebraska. I was a soldier. I did things, horrible things—" Sam's voice breaks and he covers his eyes and sobs. I want to rush in, pull him into my arms, comfort him as I would a son. He is young enough to be my son, to have been birthed from the passions Surem and I shared in the first days of this new world. I push the intercom.

"Sam," I croon, putting every comfort I can imagine into my voice. "Sam, my love, it wasn't you. It wasn't you; they gave you something so they could force your body to do things, but it wasn't you. It was a poison. We want to help you." My hands are aching, healer instincts, and I need to touch, to give. I won't touch Surem. I place my hands over my abdomen and send the light into my dwindling eggs. I turn to Surem.

"Why is he naked?" We cannot be as bad as our enemy; this is what we promised ourselves.

"Clothing reminds him of his uniform, soaked in blood. He hates anything touching his skin."

"He's self-aware, he's asking questions?" I can't hide the awe from my voice. For years we've been trying to reverse the effects of what the empire gives the kids in uniform; it makes them complacent and unquestioning. It dawns on me that this kid remembers everything.

My outpost is part refuge, part training ground. We're in the coastal scrublands south of the Sonoran Desert. Enough water and wind to wash the sky clean of the yellow clouds from the burning oil fields. Our sea was once named after a colonizer. We just call her mar. We supply the markets with plant medicine we cultivate and gather from the land in seasons of abundance, specializing in those that thrive in seasons of scarcity. We supply the blackest of markets with the roots that offer easy, painless death. Yaqui elders give us only what we need and teach us how to take without being taken by the land. I live there with a crew of the strangest and strongest among the brujas from the North and a water witch from Gullah territory. She came as a trader and decided to stay. Her people moved in and took over what used to be the Southern United States. When the waters rose, their ancestors provided them the knowledge and a certain magic of blood that complements ours.

We're near enough a checkpoint that runners sometimes stop by with news, for a healing or a meal. The wall nearest us is in the desert, the path to it full of landmines and drones. The runners risk more than almost anyone, proving themselves strong, brave, intelligent enough to avoid the traps set by the empire, the border military. We know first what is happening. There is still some electronic communication in the bigger cities and compounds, but our outpost lives by the cycles of the sun and moon. We bleed together.

We attend the yearly gathering of brujas from across the lands, discuss how the tending is going. I see my sisters, my nieces and nephews, our last living aunt. I fill my mind with what the artists are creating, dance until I can barely walk. I trade from my collection of books for books I haven't yet read. I kiss and am kissed; we drink and weep, sacrifice an animal, and eat the flesh cooked over sacred fires. We sing. We rest in the arms of our elders; we initiate youngsters. We plan and promise. We go back to our homes and posts exhausted. We go home infused.

Surem closes the partition and beckons me to follow him. We enter another lab, where there is another partition.

"We haven't dosed this one yet. This is why I called for you." He punches in a code and the partition lifts. A young woman is asleep on the cot, arms folded across her chest as though she rests in a sarcophagus. Her brown skin is covered in tattoos, flowers intertwining with script, several names woven into her body's surface. Her hair is growing out from a military buzz, and she has that soldier body, lean through the hips, bulging everywhere else. I go to the glass.

"Was she sentenced?" I ask. It's always a hope that, even knowing what they do, the desperate won't sell their bodies to the empire.

"Volunteer, oldest of six children. Mom dead, Dad hurt at the oil fields." Surem puts his hand over mine on the glass. "She joined at sixteen, border military."

I cringe. Border military is trained to shoot first, question never. They've managed to collapse most of the tunnels on their side, though a few still remain. They plant mines. Patrol with dogs trained to kill. They pile bodies for a fire every week.

"How many years was she in? How'd we end up with her?" I have so many questions.

"Five years in; we've had her about a year. She was concussed, left to die. A couple of traders found her and brought her to us." I don't ask what the traders got in exchange. I don't want to know. Surem goes to the intercom.

"Soldier," he says.

The young woman wakes up immediately, stands at attention. I look at her with my bruja eyes. Whatever the empire gave her tried to swallow and destroy the spark of her, but I see it, barely flickering in the miasma of poison. I push the intercom.

"What's your name?" She doesn't answer. "Come closer to the mirror." She does, stands at the glass. I lean forward and read the names inscribed on her skin. "Tell me about Yelena, Gustavo, Anita, Felicia, Joe." She doesn't say anything, but the light in her flickers. Who she is still exists, I can see it with my trained eyes.

"Vetti." Surem whispers my childhood nickname to me. No one has called me Vetti in years.

After Gabor died, Antonio and Simona eventually split up. Simona took Surem and moved to the old capital. Antonio set them up with enough resources and called-in favors to make sure they'd be okay. I was nine when they left and missed Surem hard. A few months after he left with his mom, Mamita joined the ancestors. I threw myself into the rituals Mamita had taught us. Surem and I had been her best students, accessing the Dream and beyond, decipher-

ing the miasma. Things were hard those days, the Mexican government fighting on two fronts, the cartels and the empire. The empire
was trying to divert all waterways that flowed south. It was chaos.
The West Coast split from the empire and made water deals with
the First Nations up in Canada. A water-and-food trade route. The
empire lost thousands to the West Coast. Some fled north, where
there was no wall, but the ice had grown thick and living was hard.

I was seventeen when Surem returned. Simona had died of in-
fection. He was twenty-one. We met up to do a plant ceremony and
something else entirely was watered between us. I was by his side
during the bloody years, gathering my brujas for healing, for ceremony. We stood by the prophecy, the jefes returning the land to the
people, who in turn would honor the land. It was I who convinced
him to speak up and suggest that only councils of women could
decide punishment for crimes. It was I who whispered in his ear as
he slept that he must take a wife, make alliances. I helped pick her
out.

"What do you think we should do?" Surem leans against the wall. I
stare at the girl behind the glass. There isn't a path before her that
isn't a devastation. Do we leave her as she is? Trapped in a mind
where nothing but acquiescence exists? Or sentence her life?
Choice and memory lock-gripped in every strand of her being? I try
to think of what I'd want.

I live with some shit. After all, the cartels were a disaster to manage in the beginning Surem, with a little help from us, plotted his
way up up up into the top of his father's plant empire. Things were
scarce and the itch of addiction allowed certain alliances to form.
Some of it got ugly. Surem and I went head-to-head those early
days, fighting it out, fucking it out. I didn't agree with some of the
methods he'd inherited from his father, and he hated that my intu-
ition whipped him from disaster more than once. Patriarchy. I

ended up in the way a time or two and people died. It was a mess. We don't talk about it. We live with it. Same with that little valor, our noble choice. There is so much I want to forget, that I'd give everything to un-remember. Mom dying from an earache. Bodies I've come across, so many women and kids, just destroyed those early years. The hunger. What hunger lets a person, a society, justify. But this, all of it, is grating proof of existence. That can sound strange, but gods alive and dead, we're still fucking here.

"Dose her," I tell Surem. I go to the door and bang on it. Delia opens it immediately. I go out into the compound, cursing as I notice I'm still wearing just a sheet. I see one of the compound jeeps and I climb into the backseat and curl up. I tilt my face and stare up at the stars. Even with the compound lights, the stars have little competition nearby and are brazen.

I breathe slow and soften my gaze, one of the first lessons Mamita ever taught us. Allow the bubble of grief to rise in me as it always does, until it is almost unbearable. I've known harder pains than this and survived. It isn't my child behind the glass, not the child of my body. I know I'm lying to myself. Everyone is. Opening to the truth requires acceptance of the belly-wrenching pain of it all. There are moments I still let it double me over, but I have faith. The waters are returning. There are horrors but there is love, and this young woman made a choice to subject herself to horrors, knowing the money would go to her siblings.

Surem has children I've never met. It was a compromise, part of the marriage agreement with his chosen. There are parts of going back to the old ways that nothing can prepare you for. When I met her, days before the wedding, she insisted we meet alone.

"I have one rule and one rule only. You never meet our children."

It was the first thing she said to me. I told her I would follow her rule, and then we talked an hour about songs and plants and women we had in common. By the end of the hour I knew Surem had made the right choice. The first time Surem and I met up after his firstborn arrived, I knew I'd made the right choice as well.

"He wants you there." Delia has fetched my clothing and turns her back as I change. She's old school, came up military on the other side, held a rank, defected rather than be killed for disobeying orders. She's older than us, has been around since the beginning of whatever it is, this we're building.

Back in the lab, Surem hands me a syringe. He has the look in his eye, the reason I'd never birth his children or become his wife. He doesn't need to be hard with me—I offer no resistance—but hardness runs deep in those who rise up to lead. It has to.

Delia opens the door to the cell. Surem is on the other side of the partition. The young woman stands at attention. I hold the syringe between both my hands as I lift them in prayer. I pray that whatever wall comes down inside her mind will not destroy her.

"Give me your arm," I say.

She does.

Born and raised in Chula Vista, California, to Mexican and Puerto Rican parents, LIZZ HUERTA has been navigating and erasing borders her entire life. Lover of story, chisme, daydreaming. Her fiction and essays have been published in *The Rumpus*, *Portland Review*, *The Miami Rail*, and other journals.

READ AFTER BURNING

MARIA DAHVANA HEADLEY

IT IS CRUCIAL TO REMEMBER THAT MAGIC IS UNPRE-DICTABLE. Old magic, new magic, all magic. Magic has its own mysteries and rewires itself according to mood, like weather discovered between streets, rainstorms dousing only one person, or like a blizzard on the skull of a soldier, a brass band on the deck of a submarine. War magic exists, and wedding magic. Love magic and murder magic, spells for secrets kept forever, and spells for dismantling structures. Magic itself, though, sometimes ceases to exist in moments when it's most necessary, and even when you've memorized the entirety of the history of spells and sacrifices, there are always ways to fail and invent, to combine traditions into something else entirely. There are ways to shift the story from one of ending, to one of beginning.

All this happened a long time ago, before the story you know. You were born in a world that wasn't ending. This is a story about how that re-beginning came to be. It's about the Library of the Low, about books written to be burned, and about how we brought ourselves back from the brink.

I'm old now, but old doesn't matter. How many years have humans been looking up at the stars and thinking themselves annotated among them? How long have the stories between us been whispered and written and lost and found again?

This, then, is a story about the story: It's about librarians. It begins on the day of my father's death. I was ten years old. I knew the facts about blood; all ten-year-olds do. Do you? You do.

I knew this fact, for example: There was no stopping blood until it was ready. Sometimes it poured like magical porridge down the streets of a village, and other times it stood up on its own and walked out from the ground beneath an execution, a red shadow. There were spells for bringing the dead back to life, but none of them worked anymore, or at least they didn't in the part of the country I was from.

I don't need to tell you the long version of what happened to America. It's no kind of jawdrop. It was a tin-can-telephone apocalypse. Men hunched in their hideys pushing buttons, curfewing the country, and misunderstanding each other, getting more and more angry and more and more panicked, until everyone who wasn't like them got declared illegal.

When the country began to totally unravel—there are those who'd say it was always full of mothbites and founded on badly counted stitches, and I tend to agree with them—my mother was at the University on a fellowship, studying the history of rebellion. My daddy was the Head Librarian's assistant.

The Head Librarian was called the Needle. She'd been memorizing the universe since time's diaper days, and I never knew her real name. She was, back then, in charge of rare things from all over the world. Her collection included books like the Firfol and the Gutenbib, alongside manuscripts from authors like Octavia the

Empress and Ursula Major. The collection also included an immense library of books full of the magic of both the ancient world and the new world. Everything could turn into magic if it tried. The Librarians had prepared for trouble by acquiring secrets and spells. They knew what was coming.

If you asked any of the Librarians from my town, they'd tell you their sleep went dreamless long before the country officially declared itself an *oh fuck*. They squirreled books and smuggled scholars, as many as they could, which wasn't many. Some made it to Mexico. Others got to Canada. A few embarked on a ship loaded with messages in bottles.

The Needle, though, had plans for saving. She stayed, and my parents stayed with her. They spent the first years of the falling apart sitting at a desk deep beneath the University library, repeating everything the Needle told them, making memory footnotes alphabetically, in as many languages as she could teach them. She started them off small and got bigger.

"Ink," she told my parents, "is not illegal," and so they started making ink out of anything they could find. They made it out of burned plastic. They made it out of wasps harvested while eating the dead. They made ink in every color but red: blue and black, brown and gold. Red reminded the Needle of things she didn't care to remember. My parents sharpened tools, started making plans, married each other in the dark of a room that had been reserved for books damaged by breathing.

The first tattoo the Needle gave was to herself.

The men in charge wanted people to forget penicillin and remember plague. They shut down the schools, starved out the teachers, and figured if they gave it a few years, everybody but them would die of measles, flu, or fear. Citizens ended up surviving on Spam and soup. No medicine. Little plots of land and falling-down houses. Basically conditions like those much of the rest of the world had faced for many years, but no one here was used to them, and so a lot of the population dropped dead due to shock, snakes, spiders, and each other. I was born four years into all of this. My mother died in childbirth, because by that time there were no doctors left in our city. The last one had been executed.

None of the magic worked that time.

The Needle delivered me, and she closed my mother's eyes when it was time to close them.

You can call me Enry. That's what my daddy named me. He said there was no *H* to be had in a world where hell had spit up this many fools and holy was this much in question.

I was not an unhappy child. The world withering above me was the only world I'd ever known, and to me it was a beautiful one.

Every few days a murmuration of soldiers came through town and said no one had any right to rights. Whenever they came, I hid myself in a knowledge shelter with the rest of the children born since the end of the world, and we waited for the soldiers to pass.

The rest of the time, we learned languages and studied history, farmed with sunlamps, and guarded the books. We were taught to read on medieval fairy tales about weather and Victorian poems about ghosts, on books of code in thirty-four languages, and magic books dating to long before Christianity. We were taught myths from Libya and poems from Andalusia and Syria, spells from Greece and gods from the land we hid beneath. We were taught about genocide but also about making the land bear fruit. We only came aboveground at night. We were not supposed to exist.

The adults, though, had to show their faces on the surface to get water rations and to be censused.

When I was ten years old, my daddy went aboveground one morning and didn't come back by nightfall.

I found him on his back in the center of the old marble floor in the University library. Someone had decided he was smart enough to kill, or maybe he'd just walked in the path of a bullet. These were bullet years, and they flew from end to end of cities like hummingbirds had, before the hummingbirds had fled. Bullets wanted to feed. We all knew it. We'd been warned.

My daddy pointed at his chest and fumbled at his collar. I loosened his tie. I unbuttoned his buttons. I opened his shirt.

"You have to burn this," he said. "Some books, you can only read after burning. Do you hear me? Do you understand?"

Blood was making a lake around us, and my knees were wet with it. My daddy's breathing slowed, and his hands froze like winter had nested inside him. He was the only parent I had.

I had no spell to keep him from dying, though there should have been spells. Everyone talked about magic, but no one had all the magic they needed. That was another thing you knew if you were ten years old and living beneath a library, if the world had started ending long before you were born and now you found yourself alone in it.

There was never enough magic to save everyone. Sometimes you only had enough for yourself, or you had the wrong kind entirely. I had almost nothing in the way of spells back then. I knew how to make a dragonfly out of sonnets and a bird out of ballads. I could bring a little beam of light to life in my hand and watch it glow, but it wasn't hot and it wasn't a heart. I had nothing for my daddy and no way to refill him from my own soul, no way to split it, no way to share.

It is crucial to remember that life, when it is long, is full of goodbyes. I had a husband once. You are the child of one of the children of my children's children. My husband was a man who could walk on water and whose veins ran with poems written six centuries before anyone insisted on religion. By the time I met him, I had enough magic to fill anyone with light. I could read in the dark, and the books of my family were written all over the world.

You are the *amen* of my family, and I am the *in the beginning* of yours. This story is the prayer, or one of them. This story says you can live through anything and that when it is time to go, when the entire world goes dark, then you go together, holding on to one another's hands, and you whisper the memory of birds and bees and the names of those you loved.

When it is not time to go, though, this story says you rise.

This is what I whisper to you now, so that you will carry the story of the library, so that you will know how we made magic and how we made books out of burdens. This is to teach you how to transform loss into literature, and love into a future. It is to teach you how to make a book that will endure burning.

Hours after my father's body went cold, the Needle found me huddled beside him.

"Will we get revenge?" I asked her. The hole in my daddy's heart hid half a sentence, and I wanted to cut it from the skin of the person who'd killed him.

"It's a long revenge," she said, with some regret, and I was unsatisfied. I wanted urgency, murder, fury.

The Needle had white hair to her knees, and the ends were stone black. She carried an ax and kept it sharp, but that wasn't what she gave me. The Needle gave me a bath and made me a sandwich, went back out in her night camouflage and hauled my daddy in.

"Before revenge," she said, "is ceremony."

"Do we have to go through the alphabet?" I asked, but the Needle had nothing to say to me about the letters between C and R.

The Needle kept the contents of all of her books in her head, though most of them had been burned ten months into the end. On her desk there was a heavy gold medallion she called the Old Boy, because on the back of it there were three men holding hands and declaring themselves brothers. In the winter she warmed it beside the fire, wrapped it in a towel, and used it to heat her feet. When she needed to send a signal, she used it to catch the light.

She called to all the Librarians in the area, and we went down six flights to her brain bunker. The stainless cubbies down there dated to years before the mess seized power, when somebody'd had an idea about keeping rare books safe in case of disaster.

Soon we were standing in the Needle's knowledge shelter, around the table that held my daddy's body. There he was, stripped naked and covered in tattoos, all of him made of words except the hole in his heart. I'd never seen him undressed before. In our house, he'd worn a darned suit, buttoned to the neck, none of his ink visible.

"Man needs a hat and tie at all times," he'd say to me. The rest of him was startling to me. My daddy specialized in invisible ink, and the tattoos between the lines, he'd told me when I was little, would only show up if you shone a candle through his skin. I'd never seen them; there was no way to see them on someone who was alive.

Read after burning, I thought, and couldn't think it anymore. I stood beside the table, at the level of my daddy's head, put my hand on his cheek, and felt the stubble of his beard poking through his story.

"Sharp, Volume One," barked the Needle, and we brought out our knives.

I was the one who was meant to cut the first page of the book of Silas Sharp. That's what you did if the book was your parent.

The Librarians rolled up their sleeves. Arms tattooed in a hundred colors and designs, the secret history of the former world. They had shaven skulls beneath their hats, and their heads were wrapped with Ada Lovelace and Hypatia and Malcolm X, with the speeches of Shirley Chisholm, with Chelsea Manning, with the decoded diagrams of the Voynich Manuscript. Their arms were annotated with Etty Hillesum's diary of life before Auschwitz, with Sappho's fragments, with Angela Davis, with Giordano Bruno, with Julian of Norwich, with bell hooks, with the story of the Union soldier who began as Jennie Hodgers and volunteered herself to fight as Albert Cashier, with Bruno Schulz, with Scheherazade, with Ruth Bader Ginsburg, with Danez Smith, with Roxane Gay, with Kuzhali Manickavel, with the motions of the planets, with the regrets of those who'd dropped bombs, with the sequencing of DNA, with the names of the dead, with almanacs and maps, with methods for purifying water, with primers for teaching letters, with names of criminals, stories of pain, dreams of better things.

None of this was categorized as magic, but it was magic nonetheless. All of this was the daily light, the brightness, the resistance, and refusal of intellect to endure extinction.

"What's that?" I asked one old man, dark skin and a silver beard, his text luminous in the shadows of the bunker.

"Dictionaries, Enry," he said. They were tattooed in pale ink. "Glow-in-the-dark microscript," he said, and smiled at me. "I made it out of worms. This arm is Oxford English, but English isn't all there is. There are words here that've never been defined."

"Which should be the first page of my daddy?" I asked him.

"I'd say you should start there, with Silas's heart."

"But there's something missing," I said.

"There's always something missing," said the Dictionarian. "Usually the missing sections aren't marked as simply as they are on Silas."

"I can't decide," I said.

"We've never been a simple people, Enry," said the Needle. "Nowhere, nohow, nobody. This decision isn't simple, but you have it in you to make it."

I lifted my scalpel and started to cut. He'd still be warm on the inside. He'd only been dead two hours. But skin degraded quickly. You had to cut fast.

I touched my daddy's heart. I looked for the words that were missing, that had been driven down into him. I'd seen my daddy dress for the bindings of other Librarians and come back into the house salt-scrubbed and drunk on moonshine. In those early mornings, my daddy would tell me about the books.

"There've been many books made this way," he'd say. "Long ago, books were made of animals. There were pocket bibles made of vermin—mice and rats—and fables made of rabbits. There were histories written on the skin of foxes, and there is at least one book in the world—or was—that was said to be bound in unicorn. There's a sea volume, a tremendous novel calligraphed on vellum made of the skin of a blue whale."

"A whale?" I asked.

"No one has seen a whale for a long time," my father said, "but when I was a boy, I went on a ship and saw a whale blow, and then its tail as it dove, and that was story enough for me. This very library, the University's, had a serpent's story, inked into a seventeen-foot snakeskin, accordion-folded. The history of written words is, at least in part, once, and now again, a history of skin."

"What about the skin of people?" I asked.

"There've been other versions of this kind of library," he told me. "Lampshades and wallets. There've been bodies stolen throughout the history of humans, but the books bound into the Library of the Low are made not of stolen bodies but given ones. There's nothing unholy in turning your own body into a bible for the living."

"How do *you* know?" I asked him.

"I don't," he said. "But I studied under the Needle, and what I know about the world's words, I know from her. We make our bodies into things that can last. We are not destined for coffins, nor for crypts. Our bodies will live on in the library, and one day, maybe, the world will change because of us."

"But they're only books," I said.

"There's magic written into them. The Needle taught me some old things."

He pointed at his chest, at a line of text, and around the line, for a moment, there was something else, a brightness—calligraphy made of fire. Then it was gone.

Now my blade went in there, beside the word *beginning*. This was my job too, to read out the first page of Sharp, Volume I. I would, one day, be Sharp, Volume II.

"In the beginning," I whispered, "time started in secret."

"Long before the stories said it started, and long after," said the Needle.

"This is how we bury our dead," I said. That was the line assigned to me. "This is how we find a path to heaven."

I sliced down the page, a rectangle. The room exhaled Silas Sharp's name, and I was done with the part I had to do, the start of the book.

The Librarians would scrape and stretch gently, to keep the pages from tearing. They'd be the ones who'd tattoo and inscribe the rest of my daddy, his bones and his fingernails, all night and into the next day, turning flesh into future. They could make pages that were thin enough to see sentences through, and the book of Silas Sharp, in the end, would contain at least a million words, written on every part of his body. His skull would be sliced into transparent coins, and his hair would be woven into the threads that would hold the binding. The muscles of his heart would be the toughest pages, inscribed with words my daddy had given to the Needle long ago. All Librarians gave their dedication to her.

I went back to the Needle's house to cry. Even if this was how the world was, I would have traded all the knowledge in the universe for my daddy telling me a bedtime story, for him sitting in our kitchen in his hat, humming to himself as he tattooed an animal in iambic pentameter.

We'd had plenty of words in the history of humans, but still, it was easy to take them away. Thousands of years of progress had been obliterated by the time I was born. Knowledge couldn't keep everything bad from happening; that was my first story, and it was a true one.

Knowledge wasn't enough.

I had never known my mother, but her book—unfinished—was about how to build bombs out of normal household ingredients. Her back was tattooed in formulas for Greek fire, and her cheekbones with love songs. They were part of the book too.

She had all this knowledge written on her skin, but still she died.

On the day my father was killed, I thought that knowledge was no use to me, that we would have been better off warring, running outside and fighting the soldiers. They were murderers, and I wanted revenge. Instead, I had a story I couldn't understand, the invisible ink of my father's tattoos, unreadable, useless. I raged in the basement, my own skin free of words, my heart free of forgiveness. Love was not enough, and neither were words. Nothing was enough to replace him.

I imagined myself to sleep: the men in charge, and the way I'd slay them, paring their skin from their bones, twisting their hair into ropes. I'd use their skeletons for my bed frame, and their hearts, I'd throw on the fire. They wouldn't be dedicated. They'd only be dead.

Yes: This is how we did it in those days. This is what we'd, from some angles, been reduced to, and from others, evolved toward. Books were written to be read, and we were writing them, making them, creating them, in a treeless place.

When the Needle got the idea to make the Skincyclopedia, it was because paper had gotten banned to everybody but the bodies willing to swear they'd never ever write anything wrong as long as they lived. Then paper got rendered illegal in favor of just a few things you could yell, four or five words at a time. There was a decree saying you weren't allowed to teach your babies to speak anymore, or to teach them to read. You were allowed the slogans, and beyond that, they'd show you pictures and films of how they wanted you to be.

The Needle remembered a time before all the books were banned, a time when even the crumbling scrolls were digitized and available for viewing.

"I can't hear a word you say," the Needle'd said, legendarily, when one of the men in charge came to her door, asking her to be their translator.

The men in charge were afraid of encrypted communication among the rebels and wanted someone who knew things about codes and cabals. Knowledge had become frightening to the powers that were, and they'd decided to make it invisible. The Needle didn't understand their logic.

Written history was filled with men like them, calling themselves heroes as they destroyed everyone else. The Needle told them she was fixing to die out like a dodo anyway and that she'd gone and forgotten everything but a recipe for piecrust. She went back into her house and closed the door in their faces.

"Are you writing down all the books you know?" my daddy asked the Needle when he first began to do the library with her.

"No," the Needle said. "I'm making a new story out of the old stories. This story"—she called out the name, something about mice, something about men—"this one has a wife, killed for no reason. This one too. And this one. This one has a boy hung up in a lynching tree. This one has an eleven-year-old girl narrated into existence by the man who rapes her. This one has a scientist dying of cancer, her husband getting credit for her discoveries. This one has dozens of people trying to swim across a river and shot from the banks. This one has a child dying because his family can't afford medicine. This one has a boy murdered because he loves boys."

"You're writing down the American collection again?" my daddy asked the Needle. Those stories sounded like the way the world was.

"No," said the Needle. "There are some stories here that are holy. Others, I think, may benefit from being remembered differently."

That was how this started.

By the time my daddy was murdered, the Needle and her Librarians were fourteen years into the Library of the Low. There were no margins, not on most of the first generation of Librarians, and not on any of the animals either. One of our goats was tattooed with a version of *The Odyssey* in which Penelope and the witches were the heroes, and another wore the secrets of manned flight, starring Amelia Earhart, Carlotta the Lady Aeronaut, Sally Ride, and Miss Baker—the first American monkey to survive weightlessness. There were shelves and shelves of stories.

"Knowledge," said the Needle every Sunday, when we met to pray over poems, "is the only immortal. We leave our words behind us. It is our task to pass them properly.

"*Holy!*" she said, reading from one of her own arms, quoting one of the poets. "*Holy! Holy! Holy!*"

"*Holy the eyeball,*" the children echoed.

"*Holy the abyss,*" she replied. This was not the only poem the Needle quoted. She had a hymnal of her chosen poets, but this one was a simple one, an annotation of things the world was trying to render obsolete.

"*apricot trees exist, apricot trees exist / bracken exists; and blackberries, blackberries,*" she said next, quoting another poet, Inger Christensen. There was an alphabet of lines tattooed on her other arm. *"fig trees and the products of fission exist; /errors exist, instrumental, systemic, / random; remote control exists, and birds; / and fruit trees exist."*

"Amen," we said. "Amen."

It is crucial to remember, and it is the history of stories, that even the righteous resort to wrongs. That even the magical can be frightened, and that even the revolutionary can fail when they curl into comfort. There are many nights in a lifetime, if it is long, and some of them must be spent sleeping. It is crucial to remember that even in groups of the good, humans are still humans, and bodies are still fragile, that uncertainty can take over and that when it does, there is no option but shouting strength back into the crowd. There are stories about perfection, but those stories are lies. No one ever made the world better by being perfect. There is only mess in humans, and sometimes that mess turns to magic, and sometimes that magic turns to kindness, to salvation, to survival.

Every Sunday, when the Librarians met at the Needle's bunker, there was a vote taken on what to do, but the vote always came down on the side of staying secret.

"There is a long history," said the Needle. "Of monks and nuns guarding the books instead of joining the war. And yet, the time may come. Is it today? Have we done enough to preserve? Is it time to rise?"

The hands went up. It was not.

I visited my parents in the library and put them on the table in front of me, memorizing their contents, filling in their gaps. I read the rest of us, the dead I'd never met and the dead I knew. I read stories about love and about murder, stories about farming and about revolution. I read the library end to end, books from the immigrants who'd come from the south and the ones who'd come across the oceans, books from the people who'd been born here on this ground and died here too.

I pressed my hands to my parents' pages and turned them. There was a full-page illustration of a woman warrior with a sword, and I looked at that most often. My mother's book. My father's book had a full page of my mother herself, wearing her glasses, working on the bibliography of rage and weaponry for the gone, for the America I'd never encountered, one full of dirt roads and donut shops, unplundered graveyards and grocery stores, skyscrapers and sugarcane. Police cars, pummeling. Immigrants, ICE agents. Hunger and hunger and hunger. Hurt.

"Holy," I whispered. "Unholy."

In the early mornings, the world was lost in translation, a language the soldiers and the men in power didn't speak. There was fog, and in the night there was a warming river, and we brought people over it. There were babies born and new stories written, but we stayed the same, hidden in the Library of the Low, keeping knowledge from being burned, while the rest of the world caught fire.

I got my first tattoo as a copy of something from my mother's book, a katana down my spine, and my second tattoo from my father's book, a pen down the center of my chest, the same size as the sword. This was my family tree, quill and blade, ink and metal, the same importance, the same time. The back cover and the front. Who knew what my pages would contain? Who knew which of these things was mightier?

I didn't remember the past, and I couldn't imagine the future. I held off on more tattoos, and though everyone wondered, they didn't force me. There was no forcing a generation without memory of libraries. We had not memorized paper books. We had not touched trees.

Read after burning, I thought, and went to my father's book, and looked at it in the dark, but I couldn't burn it. It was all I had of him, his book and his bones, the words he'd chosen.

I held a candle to the page with the hole from his heart, and there was nothing of wonder on it, nothing magic.

Out there, in the rest of the country, people shouted their slogans and were rendered speechless. We farmed under lights we'd made and hoarded knowledge because there was no way to share it. We kept electricity on Earth. When we died, we were meant to pass the knowledge on our skin forward, not lose it on a battleground.

When I went to sleep at night, I could smell the towns around ours being burned: smoke full of story, secrets drifting overhead, but we took no action. We had a tiny world of our own, and that world was filled with our rituals and ceremonies, with our history, with our books made of the people we'd loved. We thought, for a time, that it was enough to save ourselves.

This was not the Needle's plan.

What is anyone's plan? The idea that the world will remain viable, that there will be no clouds of poison, no blight, no famine, is an optimistic one. The idea that one's children will survive even birth? Also optimistic. And yet.

When I was sixteen, one of our books got out into the world, the pages thin and the text intricate, and someone made up a story about it. There was a whisper that we were making books out of babies, converting them into the thinnest paper, tattooing their soft skin and turning it into a history of lies. These weren't even babies that had been born, the story went, but babies we'd preempted from birth, to turn into pocket bibles of revolution.

The soldiers charged the Librarians with resisting the arrest of everything. We were, they said, worshipping idols and insisting on sentences. All of the Librarians were taken but the Needle, who was so old by now that they decided she'd die on the road.

The men insisted that the babies were everywhere, that they'd been born to women in their seventies, and nothing the Needle said could dissuade them. They'd inherited knowledge too and believed it as firmly as we believed ours.

"Who had a baby?" she shouted at them. "How can you think this is a town full of baby killers, if there's no one of an age to give birth to them?"

Our Librarians were put into a wagon, some screaming, some shouting slogans other than the ones allotted us. The Needle and the children of the town were left behind, all of us hidden for our entire lives.

"It's time to change the color of the ink," the Needle said, when they were gone. "Sometimes bloodstains are the only writing you get to leave behind. Many of my people left nothing but red." She looked at me, her eyes narrowed. "We'll leave more than bloodstains. We'll leave char."

The Needle took us back down into her bunker, hobbling on the stairs.

"What are you willing to die for, Enry?" the Needle asked me. "You don't always get to choose, but this time, you do. You, boy, you're the one I'm talking to."

I didn't know.

"Open that door," she said.

I unbarred it. It was a room full of vials and metal, as secret as the rooms full of books, but different from them. Maybe not different. This was a room full of things that could catch fire or slice strangers.

"There is nothing holy," the Needle said, "about tradition. No tradition. Not mine, not theirs. Anyone who's ever thought so has ruined things all over again."

"But," I said, "we made the library. We have to protect it."

"We made the library because they tried to crush knowledge. We will fight because they tried to crush us," said the Needle. She trembled, but not with fear.

"I'm ready to burn, Enry Sharp," she said.

We loaded all the books of the Library of the Low into rolling carts, and we took the elevator, using power we normally saved. We rose up from the inside of the earth, beneath a stolen University, and when we came to the surface, we were a small army of young Librarians, and one old woman carrying a knife made of a melted medallion.

We marched.

The Needle once told me that we couldn't fix everything with love, even though some of the books said we could. Some of the poems said it was the answer. Some of the anatomical diagrams of hearts showed them full of certainty. I thought about my father's heart and the missing words inside it.

We marched for our parents, with them beneath our arms. We carried their skin and hair. We carried their words. We marched down a dirt road, and on both sides there were places consumed by smoke.

"Holy," we said.

High above us there was a swallow spinning, and below us seeds were still germinating and we were walking in boots we'd inherited, carrying daggers forged of our parents' wedding rings and jewelry.

"There aren't enough of us," I said to the Needle, as we arrived in the City. Walls of windows, broken. Buildings crumbling, but behind them I could see movement.

"There are," she said, and unbowed her lace collar. I could see words beginning to be revealed there, round and round her throat. The Needle's eyes were blacker than her ink, and her skin shone silver.

We stood in the center of the road and looked at the house, white columns built on the backs of Americans. Graffiti on its sides and trees from which bodies had hung. Some people had thought this was a beautiful place.

I opened a book in each of my hands, the book of Silas Sharp, and the book of Yoon Hyelie Sharp. Beside me, the rest of the Librarians opened the books of their parents, and the ones whose parents had been taken readied their implements.

The doors began to open and there were soldiers coming for us. We saw men standing there, old as the Needle. The Needle stood at the head of our formation, tall and unbound, her shirt open, and in her hand she held a torch.

We all knew that we were about to die. There was nothing in us that was stronger than the guards here, and there were only a few of us to begin with. There were good ways to die, and this was one of them.

"READ AFTER BURNING!" we screamed, and we set fire to our dead.

I set fire to the book of Silas, and out of it rose my father, and I set fire to the book of Yoon, and out of it rose my mother.

The Needle set fire to herself and we closed our eyes at the light she made, the way her body blazed and hissed, words made of magic, words made of the Needle's own rage and reading.

This was the Needle's analysis of civilization, and this was her love, given form. This was what magic looked like at this point in the history of the world, a surge of stories transmitted in smoke.

I had never seen my parents together until I saw their books. I watched their skin insist on change and the spells contained within their volumes spitting fire. What can you see in firelight? More than you can see in the dark. I watched my mother's sword and my father's pen stand at attention, and then I watched them switch instruments.

I felt my own living skin warming in the light of the people I'd come from, the library that had raised me thus far, the stories that had been altered to show something other than quiet.

The Needle rose over us, a cloud of words, and she rushed at the men who'd decided America belonged to them. With her rushed the rest of the Librarians, resurrected to revolution, brought back to life with the magic of burned libraries and belief.

The old men stood, looking up, five of them, skinny, pale, and blinded, as the words of my people circled them, closed in on them, and redlined them out of the story. I watched as the Needle edited. I watched my daddy and my mother making a study of this part of our history, shredding them into fire and then into ash.

These are the parts of our story that, while alive, are also at rest. The lies entwined with lives, the magic used for shrinking the span of knowledge rather than encouraging it to grow.

My hands were open, and in them were flames. I kept my hands open as I fought. My hands were full of story.

Our knives were used too, bloodied on the living, but the living soldiers were surrounded by the words of the dead, and we were stronger than we thought we were. An army of children, but we'd been raised on something better than this.

I was the one watching when the Needle finished them, her hair flying up in the wind, each strand a sentence. I watched her words rush into their throats, filling them with stories they were not a part of. There was char, and an old white house on fire, and smoke filled with forgotten things.

I didn't know the world before the end of the world, but I knew it when it began again, out of dust and dark, out of whispers and bones.

There were twelve children, and then there was rain.

Was any of this magic? Not more so than the magic made in spring, and not more so than the spinning of the seasons. It is crucial to remember that none of this is certain, that even when joy is proximate, sorrow might be walking beside it. Indeed, it is crucial to remember how to extend your hand to someone different from your own self.

Magic is unpredictable. That's for you to remember. Kindness is too. It is all part of the same continuum, just as you and I are part of the same line. It would be years yet before I met the man I would love, and years before you would be born to a child of a child of his, crying in the arms of the midwife, fingers spread. This would not be the only revolution. There's never just one. This is how it begins.

"Enry," my father said as his smoke faded. By then it was dawn, and we were standing on the lawn of this building built to show what glory looked like from a distance.

"Henry," my mother said, as her embers died down.

The two of them looked around, and I could see their tattoos glowing like birds might, if the world was a world where birds lived, or like whales might, deep in the sea and looking for love, calling out in song to others of their kind. Not everything was gone. Some things were invisible, and other things had been in hiding and were coming out again.

"What does this word mean?" you ask me, and you touch a word on my skin, red ink, because after the world began again, we used red instead of black, to say that we had blood flowing and that nothing was fixed in forever.

"What do you think it means?" I ask. The meanings change along with the words. The text on my skin is a new story daily, and here is what I know.

I wake up every morning, and the world has changed overnight. I can feel my father's blood and my mother's magic, and I can feel the Needle, her body blowing apart.

When do things change entirely, you wonder? When do they get better? When will it be possible?

It is possible now.

You're built to open your fists, and show me your palms, and to pass food from them into the hands of others. You're built for comfort and for fire, for battle and for poetry, and you are a child of my family, and my family was made by the world.

Here we stand in the dark now, and I'm old and you're holding my hand and walking me from the bed to the window. We're looking out at all of it, the wonder and the danger. There are voices and the sun blazes, and everything is bright enough that if I were reading the letters on your skin, I wouldn't be able to parse them.

Now look at your own hands and the wrinkles in them. Those wrinkles are what happen when you clench your fists. You were born for this resistance, for this preparation, for this life. You were born to fight.

MARIA DAHVANA HEADLEY is the *New York Times* bestselling author of six books, including the novels *Magonia* and *Aerie* and, most recently, *The Mere Wife*, a contemporary novel adaptation of *Beowulf*, to be followed by a new verse translation of *Beowulf* in 2019, both from Farrar, Straus and Giroux. Her short fiction has been nominated for the World Fantasy, Shirley Jackson, and Nebula awards and included in many Year's Best anthologies, including three times in *The Best American Science Fiction and Fantasy*. Headley is a MacDowell Colony Fellow and currently lives in Brooklyn, New York.

CHAPTER 5: DISRUPTION AND CONTINUITY

[excerpted]

MALKA OLDER

[. . .] almost unrecognizable. Nonetheless, some futurists trace a consistent national identity. Somewhat ironically, considering the degree of upheaval, this identity will be based on the fundamental principles on which the country was founded, democracy and federalism. In the chaos of the previous half century, these principles, while still referenced, became so confused and obscured by more specific concerns that they were in many ways warped beyond all recognition. However, their resurgence after an utter breakdown, even in very different forms, reimagined through new digital and social technologies, shows that they will remain strong undercurrents in the narrative that the people of the erstwhile United States continue to tell themselves.

The mainstream histories and futures written of this period will, of course, deal primarily with the bickering and petty struggles of a political class that, while shrunken in impact, will still manage to claim relevance at least to the lazy-minded and easily impressed.

Most focus on the oscillating ascensions of [redacted] and [redacted], as well as the antics of [redacted] and their impact on the geopolitical [. . .].

Although it would be impossible to deny that the official political leadership does have an impact on individual lives as well as on world events, it is also undeniable that other, less visible structures have substantial impact—and therefore, under most definitions, power—as well. Indeed, Rieger and Asmundsdottir's (2028) persuasive argument that the formal political trappings receive attention by far disproportionate to their effects [. . .] may seem radical, but it offers us a much more complete view of the forces transforming society. This approach is particularly appropriate for this period, in which one can argue that informal processes began to more aggressively claim public space for themselves, demanding awareness, engagement, and voice.

In some ways these activists can be seen as creating a different form of federalism, one that takes distribution of attention and importance, rather than geographic distribution, as a basis for apportioning representation [. . .].

[. . .] perhaps because of the distinctly democratic aesthetic of these groups, there will be a consciously collective self-characterization by many of those fighting to flip the power balance. This can be another barrier to effective description of these processes, as they tend to lack clearly defined leader-figures for stories to revolve around and audiences to fixate on.

Rather than questioning the human need for individual heroes, we have chosen to look first at the collectivities and the way they functioned, and then select representative [. . .].

Of these, the story of Zenaida Gonzales, better known as @zengo, offers a good example. We do not know for sure if Zenaida Gonzales is her real name, although she will be fairly consistent with its use across a number of platforms and avatars. There is new evidence[1] that in some cases she may use a male-mapping name and avatar, but it is unclear whether this is an indication of gender-fluidity or an attempt to reach an audience who would not hear her as a woman; at the moment the consensus is to use female pronouns.[2]

It should be noted as well that part of the reason @zengo is better known than some of her companions may be because of the comparatively rich details about her life. The fact that many of those details may be invented does not seem to affect the fascination with them. To take just one axis of this phenomenon, futurists and historians have been shown to write more about online personalities with a "real name" attached to their handle, even when that real name has been proven false.[3]

And there is little from @zengo's purported biography that we can prove true [. . .]. Her early stories are mundane: unverifiable incidents she encounters (such as the famous *So I'm walking home from work* thread) or critical (if informal) analysis of popular media. The most political element to the first category, perhaps, is the degree to which these incidents are invisible to "history" in all its forms, making them impossible to verify or trace; they already express a project of observing and reporting on that which is otherwise unseen or considered unworthy of notice. In addition, the overall lack of outside reference points, too consistent to be ran-

1. See, for example, Irepani Zitlal, "How Many Voices? Textual and Network Analysis of Resistance Icons," *Journal of Future Activism* 18, no. 2 (2029): 64–78.

2. It is also possible, of course, that @zengo will be a man masquerading most of the time as a woman, but statistical analysis shows this is unlikely to occur with such consistency over such a long timeframe. See Van Aalst and Pavletic, 2034.

3. See Opal Þórirsson, "What's in a Name? Handles, Pseudonyms, Avatars, and Scholarship of the Online Future," *Virtual Sociology* 23, no. 1 (2035): 23–40.

dom, suggests in itself an early caution, an unwillingness to allow that rapidly ballooning audience to connect with her real life.

Despite her resistance to selfebrity culture, research has been able to determine some hints as to @zengo's non-virtual existence. Linguistic analysis confirms the Hispanophone heritage implied by her handle and suggests considerable time spent on both coasts. From details in her posts, it is almost certain that she will attend university in Chicago (or is attending as we write or as you read, since her age has not been determined).

What is certain is that in tandem with the collapse of the United States, @zengo will become something of a bard, a foundational novelist, a folksinger of the new environment, taking to Twitter, Instagram, Shoutdown, CrickIt, and others to tell the stories of the new nation and create it as she does so. Her stories, in interaction with those of other narrators and activists, will describe the boundaries of this turbulent experience, bear witness, and finally begin to function, consciously and by design, as templates for building something better.

Most scholars agree that the primary trigger for @zengo's activism was an event of environmental injustice, probably one she experienced directly, although it is possible that she will empathize with family members caught up in it or engage in the response to the event so deeply that she begins to experience it on a personal level. However, there will be so many incidents matching that description that even cross-referencing with the areas she is known to frequent does not enable us to identify specifically which disaster. On the other hand, there is general agreement that once @zengo's activism was triggered, it transferred with unusual ease to other areas. It appears she spends significant time researching different issues before leaping into the fray, adding credence to theories that she will be, at least at some point, an academic of some kind. Eventually her focus coalesces around new forms of government as mechanisms for addressing the multitude of other issues that attract her interest and sympathy.

There is some evidence that her earlier works were based on anecdotes she or others experienced. *We were walking in the rain* is a famous example, in which she details a long debate with friends both physically and virtually present. She is also considered one of the pioneers of what will be referred to as *Jardines*,[4] long threads with multiple, sometimes interlacing branches. As she grew into her voice, she began to combine narrative, essay, harangue, photo-manipulation, memeography, lyric and musical appropriation, and other forms of art to create narratives that pointed the way to a more collective future and that contributed fundamentally to the aspirations of this future people of the no-longer United States.

[. . .] In effect, "civil society" will become, in the absence of strong political institutions, just "society," while without coherent corporations "social media" will become just "media." While we can describe these transitions, from a distance, as neutral changes or even positive outcomes of creative destruction, it is important to remember that for people living in that time, such drastic shifts are disorienting and frightening.

One of the ways that the future society of the post–United States deals with this uncertainty and fear will be through non-contiguous activist collectives, sometimes called NACs and on occasion *knacks*.[5] These groups will consciously seek to form communities that are not aligned with physical location. While part of the reasoning will be practical, given the increased difficulties of interstate travel during this period, many of the NACs will also

4. While proof has not been found that this terminology will be created by @zengo, there is ample evidence that she will use it. The word is a reference to Borges's "El jardín de senderos que se bifurcan" (1941).

5. It's not clear whether the confusion with the English word will be deliberate or if it will be a result of the proliferation of non-text-based audio platforms during this period.

elaborate theoretical frameworks embracing non-contiguity as a powerful rebuke to the concept of *bubbles*, the fragmentation of political groups, and even to the (at that point foundering) nation-state itself [. . .].

While the NACs and other activist groupings will start in defiantly unstructured ways—often, for example, refusing to identify leaders or define a hierarchy—the ones that survive do eventually create governance structures. These vary widely, but while a few develop personality cults, almost all of the long-running NACs will base their decision-making on some form of democracy [. . .]. One popular model will give additional *participation capital*, which translates roughly to votes, to those who engage more with the collective, although the way engagement is defined becomes critical here.[6]

Many futurist histories of this era focus on the statements and (occasionally) actions of celebrities who attached themselves to these groups or self-appointed leaders, but it is important to note that @zengo and other founding activists in these groups were largely from one or more marginalized groups [. . .].

While the storyteller function is important and will be perhaps better remembered, NACs will also be instrumental in combining virtual and IRL resistance into something new and uniquely powerful. @zengo's Gente Invisible NAC will be one of the primary proponents of what is usually known as Costopia, in which members conduct themselves as if they belong to the government they want

6. There will be extensive ideological battles on whether reading other people's posts counts as engagement and, if so, whether it is lesser than expressing one's own opinion. Gente Invisible, for example, will come to the conclusion that even if expression requires more active engagement than lurking, it is unwise to incentivize opinionating. Some futurists believe this episode is the source of the name Gente Invisible and that it refers to lurkers, but Branimir (2030) has shown persuasively that the name will be used before that controversy arises and therefore is a more general evocation of voicelessness.

to have. In one of the most extreme cases, the Costopia run by the Monde Inversé will hold trials and impose fines based on their invented legal system [. . .]. Costopias will also provide a way to expand the new versions of democracy practiced by the NACs into populations beyond their membership. The theory promoted by @zengo and her colleagues, especially @neopericles, is that if enough people consistently act on the basis of an agreed code, that code would be as legitimate as the "official" government.

Gamification, which will be initially popularized by the artist and activist Michelle Wickramsinghe, will allow people to play and replay scenes and interactions from their lives. The Burn It Down collective will further develop this idea into a way to build speculative futures in immersive, massively multiplayer game play.[7] This is taken even further by the company Digital Alternatives, which will allow people to live inside virtual-reality approximations of happier political systems and all their effects. However, whether because of the involvement of a for-profit company or because of discomfort with the technology, this will lead to a backlash that splits the activist community. The Digital Alternatives followers will be accused of hiding in their customized playgrounds while the world burns around them. Supporters of Digital Alternativists will defend their right to live fuller and more engaged lives than they could manage in reality. The players themselves rarely surface long enough to get involved in this discussion.

Gente Invisible and certain other NACs will defend Digital Alternatives and, more generally, the gamification phenomenon on the grounds that by imagining and engineering false but hopeful futures, they make those futures plausible and therefore possible. During the devastated realpolitik fragmentation of the immediate post-national period, many of @zengo's colleagues will work to

7. Many scholars trace the emergence of future history as a field to this technology.

make those futures available to politicians and others in power, believing that this will tilt policy (such as it is, in that unstable time) in favorable directions. @zengo, as far as we can tell, will continue to focus rather on her "constituency" of followers and mutuals, preferring to strengthen cohesion and engagement among the masses. Other Gente Invisible members, however, will put a lot of effort into trying to connect their work with elites, and for a while this will seem like a conduit for reunification and progress. In the longer term such activities will become normalized, reducing their impact [. . .].

What we have discussed so far in this chapter are future incidents and changes in the real world. There is, however, another genre of histories that will be written about the stories of those alternate histories that took place within Costopias, games, or VR. Many of the collectives will assign dedicated historians to document their activities, on the principle that as much could be learned from these experiments as from what is considered IRL history. In addition to narratives, they create textbooks, monuments, conferences, criticism, and a wide range of historical fictions. For example, in 2043 the digital architect and artist Shulammite Kurucz will create a memorial to the women harassed from the digital world, while the Otherworldly collective will establish an entire digital museum dedicated to artifacts of the digital experience. In 2051 Harvard will appoint the first Kavita Sawyer Professor of Virtual History.

[. . .] importance of storytelling in the future. We remember that while @zengo is famous for her activism, it is with storytelling that she built the audience she needed to become effective [. . .].

Some scholars argue that the people in these collectives, who will hold together the principles of democracy, grassroots activism, and even a kind of dispersed federalism, will be able to do so because of their experience on the margins of United States society. *Not belonging,* according to this school of thought, will be the key indicator for *productive engagement when nobody belongs* and, eventually, *constructing something new with greater inclusivity* that will later be recognized as having *new and different requirements for belonging*. A relatively new area of research concerns the relationships between those actively excluded by society and those who self-identify as not fitting in [. . .].

[. . .] however, by this time the territory once belonging to the United States of America will, it is generally agreed, have moved on to a new phase: sustainability.

MALKA OLDER is a writer, aid worker, and PhD candidate. Her science fiction political thriller *Infomocracy* was named one of the best books of 2016 by *Kirkus Reviews*, *Book Riot*, and *The Washington Post*. She is also the author of the sequels, *Null States* (2017) and *State Tectonics* (2018), as well as of short fiction appearing in *Wired*, *Twelve Tomorrows*, *Reservoir*, *Fireside Fiction*, *Tor.com*, and others. Named Senior Fellow for Technology and Risk at the Carnegie Council for Ethics in International Affairs for 2015, she has more than a decade of field experience in humanitarian aid and development. Her doctoral work on the sociology of organizations at the Institut d'Études Politiques de Paris (Sciences Po) explores the dynamics of post-disaster improvisation in governments, using the cases of Hurricane Katrina and the Japan tsunami of 2011.

IT WAS SATURDAY NIGHT, I GUESS THAT MAKES IT ALL RIGHT

SAM J. MILLER

Wanting Sid was a second skeleton, a sharp hard permanent-feeling foreign presence in my body. Stupid, stupid to have fallen in love with yet another straight boy, especially one I worked with, and therefore couldn't play my only straight-boy-conquest card, which was to get us both super drunk and make a pass and ignore the person forever if it failed. We drove the six hours to Albany and I felt it growing inside me, the need making my throat hurt and my limbs heavy, our windows rolled up as we passed through patches of wet weather, the smell of him filling up the cab of the truck as the day got hotter.

And at the end of it all was Albany, which meant no relief, just the god-awful sunset lonely feel of a big sprawling nothing city, smelling like river muck and tar and cherry-flavored cigarette smoke. We came to a stop in the shadow of those tall fancy empty buildings that fill up state capitals, where municipal employees once worked, before all their tasks got sourced to bots and freelancers. They made me shiver, the shadows they cast and the wind that whistled through them after being in that hot man-stinking truck for so long.

"You're welcome," he said, when he put the big truck in park. "I timed this expertly. Got us in late enough that we can't start working but early enough that we get some time to relax."

Sid's not a handsome guy. His mouth has a weird shape to it, and he wears clothes that are way too big, and without a beard his face looks fat. But he does have the sense to let the beard grow out, mostly. And something about his deep voice and ancient baseball cap and sad easy laugh made me lose my fucking mind. He's only five years older than me, but somewhere in those five years he got a surveillance engineering degree, one of the first classes to graduate with it, and that's why he was my supervisor, driving us all over upstate New York to install phone cloners on every corner. Our truck held nine hundred of them.

"You hungry?" he asked. "I could go for a burger."

"No, I need to stretch my legs. Gonna go for a walk."

"Cool," he said. "Call me if you want to meet up after."

"Sure," I said.

Men watched us from sagging plastic seats at the edge of the parking lot. Sour-faced in that way only the unemployed or the forcibly freelanced were.

"We should turn in around ten," he said.

"Sure."

At night we sleep in the truck. Company rules; the privatized police forces didn't want any unnecessary hotel expenses. The back of the cab had a space for sleeping. Long after midnight I'd wake up to find that he'd scooched his sleeping bag closer to mine and had spooned in behind me. It'd be the same way when the nights were hot and we both slept above the sleeping bags, but that was much worse because then I could feel his hard-on pressing against my backside and he'd whimper sweetly in his sleep and I would know for certain that the universe was a cruel and vicious fucking thing, mocking me with a nightmare pastiche of what I wanted most.

So of course I had to stretch my legs. Of course I had to get as far from Sid as possible. Of course I had to find a safe sexual outlet, even if there was really no such thing.

But as soon as I walked away from him, I felt the fear. Sid kept me safe. His manliness was obvious to absolutely everyone. He oozed heterosexuality, spread it like a protective bubble around the both of us. On my own, walking the streets of a strange city, following the slope that would take me to the riverside, I felt a hundred pairs of eyes on me. A hundred fiendish plans forming.

I'd checked the stats before we came to town. I always did. Albany had had eighteen homophobic hate killings in the previous calendar year. Better than Buffalo, but, then again, Buffalo had a 57 percent unemployment rate.

Butch up, I told myself, making my spine straighten and my shoulders roll back, aping Sid's effortless swagger, the one that implied, *I am weighed down by the terrific amount of testosterone contained in my testicles.*

My phone stutter-sighed. Visual-overlay alerts. They were everywhere, built by braver souls than me, elaborate digital landscapes that brought forward buried history or highlighted secret spaces. I knew all about them. Maps of the homes of militia leaders and queer cruising grounds and memorials for martyrs we were forbidden to mourn or even mention. How to find everything I wanted from this world—but I was too afraid to use the overlays. Most people who accessed them did a factory reboot immediately, but some municipal networks were programmed to respond to reboots by doing a quick clone cap and sending it to the grid.

Signs said: CLEAN ALBANY. A statement and a command. Signs like that were in every city we went to. CLEAN BINGHAMTON. CLEAN CANAJOHARIE.

I walked beneath the southbound exit ramp of I-787. Splotches of paint where tag drones had covered up graffiti. I could still smell the turpentine stink of that toxic background-matching paint. Most were unrecognizable, but one looked like the outline of some massive vertical corpse. They'd left other glyphs, equally illegal but politically more palatable to the good people of Albany: the black cross superimposed over a red *R*, emblem of the Revival. Ominous '88s. Tall triangles with two circles for eyes at the bottom. Visual overlays for my enemies.

Where was I going? How did I know where to find it, when I refused to look at the map? Some primal instinct; the gay boy's internal dowsing rod. My nose never failed to point me in the direction of the spot where men went for discreet dangerous intimate encounters.

The day got darker the closer I came to the river. The smell of muck grew stronger. A huge chunk of downtown Albany was below the new waterline, which meant that at high tide the streets were semi-submerged and mostly deserted. I climbed up onto the median strip and kept on going. Eyes were on me, even if I couldn't see them. Human eyes, and camera eyes. And camera eyes with human eyes watching through them, waiting for someone this stupid.

Above me, a gorgeously fat woman pushed a shopping cart along the abandoned portion of 787. She stopped to stare. Was I that obvious, that doomed?

Stupid. Stupid to have come here. To be unable to stop.

There were apps for this. I could have gone to the McDonald's and bought a cup of coffee and trolled for random hookups in safer places. Except that I of all people knew not to fuck with the phone cloners, or any of the other weird invasive ubiquitous tech that could access your phone effortlessly thanks to the state-mandated backdoor Bluetooth channel. I knew, because I got paid minimum wage to help install that tech. The odds were on your side, in the short term—they wouldn't catch you right away—but in the long term the house always won.

And then I was at the river's edge, between tall cement pillars holding up the highway. And it was almost all the way dark. The sun was gone from the sky, but the river surface still reflected light. Cigarette smoke hung in the close wet air. Someone whistled tunelessly. My heart pistoned against its new double rib cage.

Stupid. Stupid. Stupid. This is how you get yourself killed.

"Hey," a gruff voice said, from the shadows at my feet. A shadow in the shape of a man. Then it sucked air into a cigarette, whose invigorated glow lit up a striking bearded face, and my knees weakened. I squatted and leapt down from the median strip into the ankle-deep water.

The man chuckled at my wetness. I could smell him now: musky and mammalian beneath the cigarette smoke. Something off too, like the cool mildew air from a basement.

"Hey," I said, when he didn't say anything.

"Hey," he said. He sounded smug, and that sounded sexy.

"I'm Caul," I said, because I'd always been bad at this.

"Tom," he said. "Tom Minniq."

And something about that set me at ease—his last name, so out of place in the perfunctory preflight social checklist of the anonymous fuck. I stepped closer. I put my hand on his hip.

"You a cocksucker?" he asked, raising one bushy eyebrow, and alarm bells went off, dimly and at a great distance, *Oh no, you made a mistake, you misread him, now he's going to kill you. . . .*

"I'd suck yours," I said, feeling like my heart was about to burst through both rib cages.

"Be my guest," he said, but didn't budge. Icy, impassive, demanding, but how did he know that that's exactly what I wanted? What weird low-frequency psychic bond unites gay men as the act of coupling unfolds? I dropped to my knees, feeling filthy water soak me even further, thinking: *A decade ago this would all have*

been dry, and we'd have been able to meet in hotel rooms and apart-
ments without fear of snitch software reporting our every move to the
morality militias.

And then I wasn't thinking anything. I was in the act, my body
abandoned, agency abdicated, pushed and pulled by the massive
man muttering sweet obscenities above me, an empty vessel for
him to fill, which was my most fervent hope, my most dangerous
desire.

"Drop your pants," he hissed. "Cum if you want to." And I did,
not caring how wet my clothes got. By this point he had me pinned
against the pillar. Rough cement scratched at my back. I stared up
at him in awe and gratitude. And fear. His clenched face shone
with sweat, and something else: part angel, and part monster.

Five strokes and I could feel orgasm approaching already. The
world dimmed. *That's how good the sex is,* I told myself in the
moment—and that's how long it had been since the last time I'd
gotten any. Since the last time I'd jerked off, even, because when
we were out on the road I had precious little alone time.

"Take it," he howled, his voice barely halfway human, buried to
the hilt in me, pubic hair tickling my nose, and as he came, so did
I, my eyes shutting tight as black stars bloomed all around me,
thinking, *This is the most intense orgasm I ever—*

I opened my eyes to the same blue-black dark, but something
was off. The shadows that rose around me were different. Twisted
and organic, instead of rectilinear. A carrion smell in the air, and
something noxious burning. No sign of Tom.

"Hello?" I hollered, dizzy, disoriented. Laughter began, in the
distance, a chilling hyena-sound that I quickly realized was actually
something midway between laughter and screaming.

Rational thought had no place here. I did not wonder what had
happened. Where I was. Was I dreaming. I shivered in the cold
wet. I heard myself whimper.

Splashing, from behind me. I turned to see something coming

nearer, on all fours, sloshing through the water. Impossible to see clearly—giving only a general sense of hair (*fur?*) and muscle (*and claws?*) and feral hunger.

I screamed. I screamed as hard as I could, trying to wake myself up from the nightmare I already knew was not in fact a nightmare.

And then I was back in the stinking dark beneath I-787. Sitting in the standing water, against the pillar. Pants down; soaking wet. Sperm floating in the water around me. Tom Minniq nowhere to be found.

I'd heard of people who passed out after orgasm. Maybe mine was so intense, I passed out—and dreamed, briefly? That must have been it, I told myself, standing, pulling up my pants, looking around to see who might have seen me. But the tide had risen, and that wide stretch of Albany was abandoned.

Something tingled in me, the whole long walk back to the truck. Something exhilarating. Something feral.

Sid was playing video games. Happy, drunk.

"What the hell?" he said, laughing, holding his nose.

"Fell in some nasty water," I said. My jaw ached exquisitely. "Town's a shithole."

"Go to the Dunkin' Donuts," he said. "I already talked to the lady who works there; she said we could use their bathroom. Wash up, then burn those clothes."

"Yeah," I said, standing there, still shivering from the strangeness of it all, the excellence of my orgasm, the terror still lodged in my chest from whatever the hell had happened back there with Tom. It wasn't fading, the way nightmares did. And on the walk to Dunkin' Donuts I still caught snatches of stench on the wind: the distant smell of something rancid on fire.

"Oh no," Sid whispered an hour later, and handed me his phone.

"No," I said, and shut my eyes. And breathed.

Prince had just been added to the Filter, the official government list of artists who could not be listened to. They'd spent six months going back and forth about Prince. A hundred times we'd heard the arguments, in the pods and on the feeds. All along I'd known what the end decision would be. His music was all sex, all rebellion. Until you couldn't tell the difference.

"Fuuuuck," Sid said, and called up "Little Red Corvette," and pressed PLAY. "We've got till midnight to listen to it legally."

Prince was pretty much the only music Sid and I adored equally. Prince and Sade, but she'd been Filtered for years, along with every other female singer.

Prince sang about bodies that ought to be in jail, pockets packed with condoms.

I cried. Sid cried too. We didn't let each other see, but we knew.

Saturday didn't mean no work, but it did mean a shorter day. Sid prepped the mapping software, planned out the first stage of the deployment. I armed the scanners. Six hours later my fingers and knees and neck were sore, and my eyes hurt from the dim light in the back of the truck. At least we'd had Sid's music to keep us alert: loud fast stripped-down punk, legal only because it was so old, blasting through the truck's speakers.

And then the sun was setting and I felt the same old Saturday-night loneliness, like I was all by myself on a faraway planet, or the only living man in a world full of hostile ghosts, and loneliness bled into horniness, the kind so sharp and bleak you'd risk anything to make it go away.

"I'm going for a walk," I said, and he looked sad, because he'd been in the middle of talking about the rumors coming down from Canada about animal-rights activists blowing up the homes of agri-executives, and I could tell that kind of stuff made him super happy but it just made me sick, like the scanners that surrounded us would send our words to the local cops or militia outposts and they'd show up with pitchforks and torches. Or, more likely, just guns and nooses.

Stupid Sid. He still believed we would be saved. Still thought righteous outsiders or local revolutionaries would fill the streets, storm the halls of power. Was still waiting for the truth to set us free, the manifest injustice of it all to cause the Revived Republic to crumble under the weight of its own hypocrisy. Still wanted to Talk Politics with people.

I was stupid, but I was smart enough to see that this would never happen. That the best we could hope for was to keep our heads down and find escape wherever we could. Risky sex; drunkenness. He had his way out and I had mine.

I stole his cigarettes. When I put one between my lips, I knew it was as close as I'd come to him.

I smoked them all, in the night gloom beneath the highway, along the river, while I hunted. For Tom. But three hours went by like that, with no sign of another human besides the rattle of an overburdened shopping cart on the off-ramp above my head, and the sound of a woman singing . . . and, eventually, the distorted echoing laughter of a group of young men, which was my signal that it was finally time to go.

I was halfway back to the truck when I heard a sweet gruff voice say, "Hey," like the smell of sex made into sound.

"Hey," I said, and stopped beside the phone booth where Tom Minniq waited. But he didn't say anything else.

"What the hell happened last night?" I asked.

He shrugged. Grabbed his crotch with one massive hand. "You hungry?"

"Something happened to me," I said. "I . . . I don't know, passed out. Did you . . . do something? Drug me?"

Tom laughed, an incongruous sound that reminded me more

of the gibbering hyena-noise I'd heard in that other place than the handsome masculine brute who stood before me.

"I didn't drug you, Fenn," he said, and while the details of our first encounter were blurry, I knew for a fact that I had told him my real name, not the secret nickname my first secret boyfriend had called me by.

"What happened?" I asked again.

He grabbed me by the arm, pulled me into the booth. Our faces were inches apart. His musk made my head spin. "You went somewhere," he whispered.

"Where?"

"Do you want to go again?"

"No," I said.

One eyebrow rose.

"Yes," I said.

He pushed me to my knees.

"I think that it's—" I said, and then found myself physically incapable of forming any further words.

This wasn't like the night before, hidden away from the world beneath a shattered highway. We were on the street, out in the open. Looking up, past his perfect snarl, I saw dents and holes in the side of the phone booth that could only have come from bullets. Militia activity, certainly. I should have been smarter. I shouldn't be doing this. But it was Saturday night, and what monstrous crimes could not be explained away with that rationale? Who could fail to understand the way Saturday twilight made the dumbest ideas seem sound, delicious? Old songs flashed through my mind, Prince's voice echoing, as Tom pummeled me toward orgasm—

—and continued echoing into . . . wherever that was.

Dripping red darkness. Wind in pine trees over my head. Notlaughter again, this sound closer to sobbing. Phone-booth walls were trees now. Things scuttled up the sides of them. Lights throbbed in the sky above, bigger than stars but more numerous than moons.

I shut my eyes, breathed five breaths. Opened them again. Still not Albany. Still not anywhere. But the air was alive with something like electricity, and I could feel it leaching into my arms.

A shape stood in front of me. Vaguely humanoid darkness. Bipedal, but barely. Feral. It asked me:

"Are you afraid?"

I nodded. A crack opened up in what must have been its face: a grin, jagged and wet.

"Fear is sweet," it gurgled.

Something about its hunger startled me. Woke me up. What was I, if not hungry? I'd been afraid of hunger for so long. Hunger makes something dangerous, maybe, but it also makes it weak. I was hungry, but that wasn't all I was.

I watched my right arm rise, almost on its own. Shivering with ecstasy. I pushed my hand into the shadow-shape, and it scattered in a windblown shriek.

Albany again. I was alone. Evidence of orgasm all around me. The hand I had pushed into that thing dripped with thick yellowy liquid, like a sick man's phlegm.

But the metal sides of the phone booth were smooth and unblemished where the bullet holes had been. The real-world air smelled less rancid than it had before. And my arms still throbbed, from all the things they could accomplish.

Sid was out when I got home. He came back drunk, stinking of lonely hours in a bar. Throat raspy from heated idle political debate. He'd found a dive across the street from a shut-down union hall, still popular with the men and women who'd been members back before it was illegal. Sid never failed to find spots like that, and at most of them there'd be a couple of similarly cynical, similarly naïve young women, but so far Albany was proving unproductive. His dreams were loud and lonely, and three times I woke up with a gasp because he was holding me too tightly.

Monday, we moved through the city installing scanners. Sid talked. Sports, politics, punk rock. Women. I liked it when he talked. I felt like I was fulfilling an important function for him. Providing some kind of validation. Something he needed; something he'd be grateful for. He never expected me to say much back. The day was hot and we were in the sun for most of it. I didn't mind. It was better when the work was hard. Kept my mind clear. Sometimes, from up high on the posts that used to hold streetlights, where we had to screw the phone cloners so no one could mess with them, I'd see a white militia van prowling past and be intensely grateful for the bright-orange vests that identified us as Important, Hardworking, Beyond Reproach.

No sign of Tom again that night. I trolled the darkness for an hour, walking between the pillars that held up the dead highway. The shopping-cart woman watched me with a smile on her face. Drones buzzed by. Automated; unlikely to even be recording. Dozens of them would be making randomized sweeps of the city at any given moment.

Finally, I found a man. Fiftysomething, haggard, his brilliantly blue eyes somehow horrifying, like a mocking vestige of the beautiful young thing he had been so very long ago. All it took was a split second's eye contact for him to be on his knees and scrabbling at my belt buckle. Topping does precious little for me—I'm much happier sucking than being sucked—but I was exhausted and I felt sorry for the broken old thing before me. I even called him a few filthy names for good measure. He'd groan greedily, gratefully, every time I did.

And then I was cumming.

And then I was: *there*.

Something massive moved through the night above me. A cloud, I thought, but it was moving against a heavy wind—and, while I watched, it unfurled, unfolded, reached out long arms like tentacles, vanished into the sky with a spray of black cloud. Lights swung in the air like massive lanterns hanging from nothing.

When I pointed to one, it grew. When I pushed my hand in its direction, it rocketed away.

I could *do things* here.

In the distance, I heard the man I'd been fucking mere seconds ago. Moaning in terror. Wherever we were, however we'd gotten there, we'd ended up physically far apart.

A rusty screech from the gloom behind me. I turned to see the massive metal skeleton of something like airplane wreckage angled crazily over me. Perched on a wing or arm was the same thing that had confronted me the last time. I made myself look now, in the shifting shadows from a swinging light. A man's body—and a beautiful one—but the arms were too long, the legs curved and angled strangely, the head oversized and lupine, like a man wearing the head of a wolf atop his own.

"Are you afraid?" it gurgled, and then answered its own question. "You're afraid," it said, and it was right, I was afraid, but I was not as afraid as I had been. The tingling in my arms from the previous visits was throbbing through my whole body now.

I touched my hand to the scaffolding of metal wreckage. It throbbed too, in perfect rhythm with my own.

The things of this world are mine to command, I thought, and imagined a new shape for this debris.

Soundlessly, swiftly, like ink dripped into a glass of water, the wreckage unfurled into the shape in my mind. Its perch gone, the squatting wolf-thing fell into the ankle-deep water with a splash.

"How did you get here?" I asked.

"We have always been here," it said, sinking into a crouch.

Shrinking, almost. My lack of terror disappointed it. Diminished it. "You have been trying your hardest not to come here."

"What is this place?"

It grinned. There were no eyes in its wolf head.

And then I was back.

"What the fuck, dude," said the man at my feet, panting. "What the hell just happened?"

"You went somewhere," I half-asked.

He nodded. "What did you do to me?"

"I don't know," I said. "Somebody did it to me."

"Will I— Will this—"

"I don't know," I said. "I don't know how any of this works. All I know is . . . you shouldn't be afraid."

He laughed, a yipping sound that was mostly a scream. "How the fuck am I not supposed to be afraid when you sent me to fucking hell?"

"It's not hell," I said, pulling up my pants. "It's something else. The flip side of where we are now. A place where what we do matters."

"What we do *here* matters," he said. And he was right, but he was getting hysterical and there was nothing further I could tell him, so I buckled my belt and hurried off. Something was different. The air had changed. It took me a while to realize what it was.

Traffic. The horns and brakes and engines of late rush-hour traffic. I-787 was alive above me. It had never not been.

Absurd as it was, I couldn't help but think: *I did that.*

"I fucked it up," Sid said when I got back to the truck. "I made a pass at Annie and I got shot down."

"Bummer," I said, slouching down to join him on the floor. "Is it over?"

"She says it's not, but I'm pretty sure it is."

He stunk. Like cherry hand soap and body odor. Like disappointment; like rage.

"Tell me about her," I said, leaning back. He leaned back as well. His shoulder slid into place beside mine.

"She's just really smart and really well connected. Knows all kinds of people who are working on resistance stuff. And I had to go fuck it up with her. Sex is the fucking worst."

"I know, right?"

When I said it, I could see that I no longer believed it. I thought about the place I went to, the place Tom took me. The place I took that random stranger to.

"She says I'm a tool of the state."

"Well, you kind of are, though."

I wanted to tell Sid that I'd spent my whole life thinking sex was an escape, or something shameful and sordid, an exemplification of all that was awful in me, but now I saw that this wasn't the case.

My arms tingled with the same feral tingle as on the other side. Words came out of my mouth easily, as effortlessly as I had reshaped the reality of that metal wreckage.

"You should tell her that a tool of the state can be used *against* the state," I said.

Sid turned to look at me, and then took a long sip of beer. And then nodded.

I wanted to tell him that desire was not a distraction. Not something separate from the way we want freedom. I wanted to tell him that I had been to a place where anything was possible, and that the only thing more frightening than powerlessness was power.

Instead, I made a move. Sid was super drunk and I was not much more sober, and the whole thing proceeded along predictable lines, the same for every straight boy who finds, to his great disappointment, that not even society's strictest rules are stronger than his own desire for a blowjob—all *What are you doing, bro?* and then *Come on, man, nah* and then *Fucking do it.*

When we got back from the other side, he pretended he was asleep. And then he *was* asleep. Probably in the morning would assume whatever horrors he had witnessed were all a dream.

We lay together. Through cheap speakers, a long-dead man lamented his inability to resist the allure of dangerous sex. His high voice excused himself, blamed everything on it being Saturday night.

The next day was our last in Albany. We hung cloners along the final central corridor. The day was hot. He didn't hate me. I watched how he worked, how he seemed to take longer placing every piece on its post, inspecting the machinery more closely than he had before. He even let me hang a couple, which usually was a privilege he kept for himself.

From atop the lampposts I could see into Albany's cramped debris-strewn backyards, all the people smoking cigarettes or reading books or swinging on swing sets and imagining themselves invisible, and I thought about how much difference it made, how much more you could see when you're standing in a different place.

"Well, shit!" Sid said, driving from one block to the next. He held up his phone, which said ANNIE.

I listened to his end of the conversation. "Hey!" "Yes!" "Is that cool?" "Awesome!" "I will."

"We should call it quits for the day," he said. "I don't like the looks of that sky."

The noon sky over Albany was brilliant uninterrupted blue. I said, "Yeah, definitely looks like storms coming."

I was happy for him. I hoped he'd get lucky.

I wasn't in love with him. I had thought I was, but that often happened with prolonged intense unrequited lust. I wondered what had snapped me out of it—blowing him, or the weirder bigger epiphany that was percolating, about the place of sex in a broader strategy of political resistance.

Where had these words come from? They were Sid Words. Was it osmosis, so many hours sitting next to him while he used college expository-writing terms? I rarely understood him when he talked like that, but maybe eventually I'd started to make sense of it all. Or maybe I had contracted something from him. Just like he, presumably, contracted something from me.

"Can't work in the rain," he said. "I'll file a weather interruption."

This was new. Sid talked tough, but he never broke the rules.

When he was gone, I debated going back to the underpass. Seeing what I could see. Who else I could fuck; what else I could change.

Instead, I went back to our narrow boy-stinking room and masturbated, with my face buried in a pair of Sid's socks. Nothing happened when I came. No explosions; no transdimensional leaps; no monsters. Whatever it was, it didn't work when you were alone.

Sid banged on the side of the truck, startling me out of a nap. A dream of dirty cities, happy people. Fallen statues.

I joined him in the cab. Militiamen tramped past the truck. Their all-white outfits turned their pale skin several shades of pink. Sid smelled like smoke and strawberries.

"What happened?" I asked.

He didn't say anything, but after a couple seconds he couldn't keep his face from breaking into a grin.

"Well, all right!" I said, clapping him on the back.

He started up the truck. "Let's get the hell out of this shitty town."

"But we still have eighty cloners to install," I said. "What with the rain delay today . . ."

"Fuck it," he said.

"Whoa," I said.

We drove. Exiting the city, we took 787. I wondered if Sid remembered that it had been shut down, before. Or if only I could remember the old reality.

"Did anything weird happen? When you two . . ."

"Weird? No," he said, but he said it too fast, and he looked at me for a long time.

"So you won't see her again," I said. "Annie."

"We'll be in touch." He turned up the radio, slowly and meaningfully. "Her boyfriend is a coding expert. I gave them one of the cloners. Reported it irreparably damaged and recycled."

"Holy shit."

"Yeah."

We rumbled on toward Schenectady. I read through the long line of cities ahead of us: Amsterdam, Utica, Rome, Syracuse, a half dozen more before we arrived at Niagara Falls. Planting the seeds of our own oppression, helplessly helping our enemies observe and entrap us, but spreading other seeds as well.

SAM J. MILLER is a writer and a community organizer. His debut novel, *The Art of Starving*, was one of NPR's Best Books of 2017 and was the winner of the Andre Norton Award. His latest novel, *Blackfish City*, was an *Entertainment Weekly* "Must Read" and was called "an action-packed science fiction thriller" and "surprisingly heartwarming" by *The Washington Post*. His stories have appeared in magazines such as *Lightspeed*, *Nightmare*, *Uncanny*, and *Clarkesworld* and in more than a dozen Year's Best anthologies. He's a graduate of the Clarion Science Fiction & Fantasy Writers' Workshop and a winner of the Shirley Jackson Award. He lives in New York City and at samjmiller.com.

ATTACHMENT DISORDER

TANANARIVE DUE

REPUBLIC OF SACRAMENTO
Carrier Territories
2062

The news of death came in the snake of black smoke from the southeast. The horse ranch.

Nayima knew what the smoke meant, so she didn't jump on her bike to race fifteen miles through scrub brush and the remains of what had once been vineyards to inspect whatever was left of the ranch. She didn't even wake Lottie, since Lottie was allowed to sleep late on Sundays. A deal was a deal, and rest would not come easily to any of them after today.

Refusing to hurry, she gathered everything she wanted to keep and checked the contents of her backpack. Her old Glock and rounds, fully loaded. Extra shoes, protein capsules, water-purifiers, yellowing Rand McNally paper maps of Central California, cleansing wipes, and underwear. She shoved her hololens in her hoodie pocket and zipped it. Raul would see the smoke on his monitor soon, if he hadn't already, and he would investigate. And then he would call with the bad news.

Nayima waited for Raul's call from the creaky rocking chair on her front porch, beside her wooden butter churn, presumably handcrafted forty or fifty years ago, but meant to look a hundred years older than its actual age. She guessed the churn, like the rocker, had been more of a prop for the previous owners, who no doubt had bought their butter packaged from the shell of a grocery store that had once done business a few miles down the road. But Lottie had arrived from the lab-coats in Sacramento with a taste for butter, so Nayima had learned how to make it for her.

Beyond the porch was Nayima's hoverbike, which she had uncovered. It rested beneath the house's awning, gleaming in metallic black like the officious police vehicle it once had been. Her hoverbike and her Glock were Nayima's world; the house was just where she slept.

Nayima knew she should run with Lottie for Lottie's sake, or at least try to, but even that certainty did not move her from her post on the porch, binoculars in one hand and her Glock in the other.

If she heard engines, it was already too late. If she saw drones, it was too late.

Let them come, then. She had met this moment so many times before: During the evacuation, when Gram was too sick from cancer to move, despite police orders. Hiding in abandoned buildings from the infected, who were enraged by the resistance of the well. Then, after the sick were long gone, hiding in bushes and abandoned cars and even an old mine, once, from the survivors hunting down Carriers. Each time, she had thought: *Let them come.*

When the hololens shivered in her pocket, Nayima slipped it on the way Gram had worn her reading glasses, near the edge of her nose so she could also see her bike, the road, the thirsty brush, the graying, empty sky. The holoscreen glared on and flickered, appearing above her fence line. Raul looked a decade older since she'd seen him last weekend. His feed wasn't flickering from this distance; he was standing in a haze of smoke. He was calling from the burning ranch Lizette and Dimitri had shared before Dimitri died, after a fall from a newly broken mare six months before.

Someone might follow Raul now. Fool! The fire was probably a trap, singling out the weakest first, the oldest, the solitary, to draw out the rest. But was she any less foolish, waiting on her porch for them to come?

Raul's voice was smoke-roughened. "Lizette's gone. All the horses burned. Dios mío."

Nayima felt sharp grief for the horses. Half a dozen beautiful creatures, gone. Senseless.

Lizette and Dimitri had made the choice to live alone, just as she had. Their years in lab cages had taught them to cherish every choice, and to make the freest ones. Researchers had learned a generation ago that burning did not cure the plague; only the vaccine from antibodies in their veins did that. And the plague did not infect horses, which was why so many ran wild in the valley between Nayima's house and Lizette's ranch. Maybe to make up for lost human lives, Lizette and Dimitri had started collecting horses when they realized how many were dying for lack of food and water in the wild.

No, the plague had not been their fault. But they had carried it.

"This didn't have to happen," Raul said. He sounded enraged rather than sad, but she understood. Just last weekend, at the group dinner, he'd told her and Lizette they needed to move to the compound, at least until they all decided what to do next. *Until we all decide*, he'd said, as if everyone's agreement were assured. Raul still hadn't figured out that they would never all agree: Nayima would always dissent. Always. She would never move back to Sacramento, no matter how pretty the promises. Lizette would not have either.

She hoped Lizette had the chance to kill herself before the fire did. They had talked about it, of course, when they'd met at the ranch for meals every other Tuesday, far from the compound the others foolishly called El Nuevo Mundo. Who would shoot whom.

Where the poisons were. Nayima had once uttered her plan aloud, and even Lottie barely had flinched: *I'll shoot Lottie. Then I'll shoot myself.* How had Lizette managed with Dimitri gone?

"I'll come for you both now," Raul said.

"No. Go protect the others."

"Come quickly." She knew he wanted to say *ahora*, an order. Instead, he trained his feed so she could see the blackened, smoking ruins of Lizette's front porch, a wretched mirror of her own. Nayima closed her eyes. Lizette's corpse lay inside, and Nayima had seen enough corpses.

"Entiendo," she assured him. "I'll come."

"Quickly, Nayima." The others had assigned Raul as their alpha because he was the only one with the health and youth for the job, but his bossiness burned her ears. Still, they were under attack, so she couldn't let her temper flame over something as petty as sentence structure and tone of voice. "I had to call the marshals. They'll be there too. Lo siento."

Of course he'd called the marshals.

"Te quiero," Raul said. His voice broke, a contagion.

"Me too."

"You know you should have left before now, Nayima. Keep her safe."

"Fuck off. You know I will."

She blinked hard, held the dark for two seconds. Heard the connection snap away. When she opened her eyes again, Raul and the smoky ruins were gone, with only her bike in sight. They had even killed the horses. That wasn't robbers, or vandals. The Cleaners had found them. And the marshals were waiting.

Nayima had shaken off the habit of fear, but she was scared now. Scared and sixty-six, with bad knees and hips. And a failing brain, hacked by either age or her chips, or likely both. She was an old woman now, the same age Gram had been when she died. Lottie Powell Houston, she recited silently. Born December 9, died sixty-six years later, when the rest of the world met the plague. Gram, with her usual good planning, had gotten out just in time.

"Who was that?" Lottie stuck her head out of the window, her dark hair's ringlets tangled from sleep. "Who were you talking to?"

"Raul," Nayima said, adding as she saw Lottie's face light up at her father's name: "Cleaners got to the ranch. We have to go." She pointed toward the smoke plume, watched Lottie's eyes moon in shock. Lottie had called them Aunt Lizzy and Uncle Dimi. Gram would have softened her words with *pumpkin* or *darling*, but gentle words gagged Nayima. She hoped Lottie wouldn't start crying.

"Why are you just sitting there?" Lottie wailed. She was only eleven, but she was long grown. Lottie left the window, running back to grab the bag Nayima had packed for her, feet pounding across the floorboards. Good. *That's my girl*, Nayima thought, but hated thinking it.

Lottie *wasn't* her girl. She never had been. And she certainly would not be after today.

A movement in the eastern sky caught her eye, and Nayima's finger tightened on the Glock's trigger until she saw it was a hawk, bigger than a drone. Some drones were so small they looked like insects, but most were the size of smaller birds. Her heart was pulsing so hard that her veins prickled to her toes. Only a hawk.

They would run. If the Cleaners were organized, they would have been here by now. Their plan, probably, was to follow Raul back to El Nuevo Mundo, where they could kill all twelve of them at once.

"Hurry up!" Nayima said, rocking forward to gain her balance so she could stand.

She and Lottie could make it to El Nuevo Mundo, undetected, before the Cleaners did. Maybe these assholes didn't know where she lived yet, or they were saving her and Lottie for last. Or maybe the fire was only Sacramento's ploy to try to scare them off their land. Maybe.

On her feet, Nayima noticed she was frozen in place. The Glock seemed easier.

She wasn't afraid to die, but living scared the hell out of her. Especially with Lottie.

You've got this, pumpkin, she heard Gram whisper behind her right ear. Her voice was so clear, Nayima nearly gasped.

Then came the more familiar genderless voice behind her left ear, also inside her head. Nayima had named the chip's voice Sonia: *"Your blood pressure and heart rate are unusually high. Please report to HealthHost immediately to have your chip replaced for more-thorough care. You are"*—a long pause, a different, deeper voice—*"six months"*—then Sonia's voice again—*"overdue for your chip replacement. This is in violation of Carrier Codes six through ten under the Articles of Reconciliation. . . ."*

Nayima heard the tedious message several times a day. The threat in the word *violation* had worried her the first time, but not after six months. She used the music of Sonia's dying singsong to move her feet one after the other across her dusty soil to the hover-bike.

Gram's voice, though, was newer. The first time she heard it, Nayima had dropped the bowl she was holding and ruined the dinner she'd fussed over for Lottie. She was almost sure the voice was triggered by her chip somehow. She was forgetting things more all the time, but going senile didn't mean you heard voices. Could be a malfunction, or could be prodding for service, the way her gadgets used to get buggy when it was time to spend money for upgrades.

Hell, no, she wouldn't let them open her up again. She would take Lottie to live with Raul the way he'd always wanted her to, but she wasn't going back to Sacramento. Never. No matter how many voices she heard, or whose.

As Nayima prepared to swing her leg over her hoverbike's saddle, she noticed the woman standing fifty yards from her, at the closed gate. The woman was wearing a short, pale-blue hospital gown, her silver hair in neat corn rows, her skin nearly blending with the soil. Nayima would know Gram anywhere. Dead or alive.

"*You may now be experiencing visual and auditory hallucinations,*" Sonia said.

"No shit," Nayima said.

Lottie bounded outside with her pack and her doll, meeting Nayima's eyes with defiance. They had talked about this: no toys. Toys were a distraction and easily dropped for tracking.

"Leave it," Nayima said.

"No. I tied a rope to her—see?" True enough, Lottie had tied twine thoroughly around the doll's torso, knotted at several points, and after two feet the twine bound the doll to her own waist. She had wasted time tying herself to a doll.

Nayima took one last gaze at the space where she had lived for nearly ten years, the government's reparations after her long imprisonment. She felt nothing: She saw only drought-ravaged soil and cracked walls and flaking paint and dusty windows where she had so often sat sentry. But she felt a pang when she saw her black cat, Tango, watching from the window. If Tango had been a dog, she might have brought him too. She'd named her black cats Tango since she was a girl, as if the same cat had followed her to the end of the world.

"Go leave the door open. Let the cat out," Nayima said.

"Why?"

"We're not coming back. Don't waste time asking."

Lottie looked at her closely, as if to see if her face matched the sorrow of her words, and she was convinced enough to run to the porch without more questions. Lottie flung the door open and then ran toward the hoverbike to board behind Nayima, her eyes high on the smoky sky, cradling her doll like an infant. Tango bounded out of the house, finally free to rejoin his wild brothers. The house would be overtaken by cats. Nayima almost liked that idea.

Nayima jabbed in her passcode on the console, pressed the power button when it glowed blue. Like her chip, like *her*, the bike was an old model in need of upgrades. But it could still hit sixty miles per hour and hover a steady foot high. She'd clocked and measured the bike just two days before. As soon as Raul mentioned he'd seen the bike advertised at the bazaar, Nayima had insisted he buy it for her.

The bike pitched forward, Nayima's hand a bit too heavy on the accelerator before she braked abruptly, as she tested her reflexes and the bike's mood. Lottie tightened her arms around Nayima and pressed herself into her back as it bobbed. Hugs did not come easily to them, so Nayima noticed Lottie's grip and weight and warmth in a way that made her too sad to think.

You've got this, pumpkin. Go on, now, Gram said. Sure enough, Gram was still standing at the gate, waving her on like they were at a racing track. The back of her hospital gown billowed, showing her bare, sagging buttocks, which Nayima's were looking more and more like.

"Thanks for not shooting me, Mama," Lottie said.

Lottie had not called her *Mama* in nearly a year. At first, Nayima had forbidden it. The word *Mama* cut through her bones. Mamas left you. That's what mamas did. Gram was standing at the gate to remind her.

"Don't thank me yet."

Nayima squeezed the accelerator. The hoverbike flew.

The day Nayima's mother packed and moved away, she'd told Nayima her sad story: how she'd married her Spelman English professor at twenty-two; he'd been twenty years older and divorced and she worried he would be in his sixties when she was only in her forties, but she told herself she would worry when the time came.

Then he'd died of a heart attack only five years later, when Nayima was four.

"And, sweetheart," Mama had told Nayima that day as she packed her powder-blue suitcase, so matter-of-fact, "I wasn't ready."

Wasn't ready to be a widow. Wasn't ready to be a mother. Wasn't ready.

Nayima dreamed about her mother more often since the memo from Sacramento had come two weeks ago. Gram hadn't expected to be raising a child again, and Nayima had resented Mama mostly for Gram's sake. It wasn't fair to drop a child in someone's lap out of the blue. Just like with Lottie. And like Mama, Nayima wasn't ready.

Nayima used to tell herself, *She's not from my body*, as if that would make it easier if—no, *when*—she and Lottie were separated. But Lottie was Priscilla Houston's granddaughter, and Lottie Powell Houston's great-granddaughter, and she was Nayima's offspring with Raul, even if Lottie had been mixed in a tube and gestated in an artificial womb. Even if she and Raul hadn't known she existed until she was four.

Lottie was the only living offspring of two Carriers, dreamed into creation in a lab. And Lottie had tested clean of the antibodies since birth, so the lab-coats had no reason to prick and prod her. After four years, the bureaucrats in Sacramento had let her go—to her biological parents.

Nayima had always known it was too good to be true. All of it.

From the time she'd first learned of Reconciliation, she'd known it couldn't be the freedom promised: two hundred acres, a private home, and no more medical experiments. Then, the caveats: The cranial trackers and HealthHost chips and rationed water were a different kind of cage. And they had sent Lottie seven years ago— yet another means of control. The memo from Sacramento had not surprised her. She was just surprised that it had taken so long.

Although you are of course lawfully entitled to your property under Reconciliation, we are alarmed at the growing number of extremist organizations with an agenda to harm you, primarily a group that calls itself Cleaners. The perimeters have faced constant skirmishes in the past two years, with daily protests and increasing casualties.

Additionally, a growing number of citizens, many of whom are first-generation survivors, now believe it is too great a public-safety hazard to allow Carriers to remain unsupervised, for fear that the virus might mutate and grow impervious to the vaccine we have manufactured based on your service to our research. Although it is well documented that there is no longer scientific basis for this fear, it is nonetheless driving extremist activity. For this reason, we have created a living area for Carriers that will give you much greater access to the amenities available in the city and increased security to protect you from those who wrongfully blame you for the Doomsday Virus.

We believe that once you see the scope of the vision—a neighborhood modeled on the world of your youth—you will find the proposed living quarters much more comfortable to you, especially as your age advances. Please see the photos on the next page.

Fuck the photos.

Was it better to die free? Or to keep on living, even if living would mean going back to the zookeepers in Sacramento? Lottie would have to decide for herself. Lottie could die free with her or be a prisoner with Raul. Lottie wasn't a Carrier; she might have a chance for a life in Sacramento.

Nayima would let Lottie decide at El Nuevo Mundo.

She could make it in an hour if she took the abandoned highway and cut across the prairie for the last five miles, her typical route, but Nayima decided to avoid open spaces. Instead, she went fifteen minutes out of her way to the untended almond groves that gave cover and didn't make her such an obvious target for drones. *You're still wearing a tracker, dumb-ass,* she reminded herself, but the Cleaners wouldn't have access to Sacramento's tracking data. Probably. Unless there was a breach. Or burning the ranch had been a change of tactics.

Nayima was fairly good on the bike, considering she'd only had it for a few months, but the speed taxed her reflexes around boulders and broken trees, and her joints ached as she held on to her grips. The grips were pressure-sensitive, which made the bike's movement herky-jerky, sometimes shifting Lottie's weight behind her, forcing Lottie to tighten her arms, vise-like.

A tree trunk appeared from nowhere, almost a hallucination, taller than a foot. Nayima steered around the trunk so violently that Lottie gasped when the rear panel nicked it. The bike swayed right with their weight, like a horse trying to throw them. Nayima was sure they would both fall. Then the bike was upright, lurching forward, and they were both still on board.

You're going too fast, Gram said.

Sonia joined in: *"Your heart rate is dangerously accelerated. This rate has not been recorded in—seven—years. Please rest immediately until your heart rate returns to normal."*

Nayima had disabled her chip's regular updates long ago through her HealthHost account, but apparently her preferences were glitchy now too.

Lottie whimpered.

"It's okay, Lottie." The lie stuck in Nayima's throat and burned her face. But Lottie wasn't yet strong enough to pilot the bike herself, and Nayima would do neither of them any good if she panicked. *It's okay,* Gram echoed to her.

For a long while, forty minutes, then an hour, it *was* okay. She found her speed at a brisk fifty-two miles per hour on a deer trail through the rows, and the engine ran as smooth as glass. The gaps widened between the trees, fewer obstacles. She caught herself thinking how pretty it was, how she wished her land were greener. (Right. *Her* land.) She was admiring the beauty when she saw the man-made red color in the corner of her eye, and she made a wide circle with the bike to double back and see what it was.

"What?" Lottie said.

"Shhhh." Nayima's voice whispered barely above the bike's hiss.

Nayima leaned to peer down, Lottie still tugging on her. "Let me loose," Nayima said, and when she was free she bent low enough to see it: a shiny red aluminum wrapper of some kind, maybe for food, maybe for something else. But *shiny*. New.

"What is it?" Lottie said.

"I don't know yet."

Nayima set her hololens to TELEPHOTO and scanned the grove ahead. She looked a long time, lingering on gray twigs and brown bark, pulling out, zooming closer. A dark rabbit hopped behind a log. The colors seemed right.

But, no. *Blue.* Someone, a large man wearing navy-blue pants and tan hiking boots, sat with his knee propped up from behind a tree, mostly hidden, not even thirty yards ahead of them. Two legs in gray sweatpants strode across her vision before she could pull back to see his fuller figure, but that meant there were at least two. Behind the trees just ahead of them, only fifteen minutes from El Nuevo Mundo.

No one was allowed in Carrier Territories except marshals, who would be bad enough, but these men weren't in uniform. They were not marshals.

"Your heart rate is increasing," Sonia said. *"Please rest to reduce your heart rate."*

It's okay, pumpkin, Gram said.

"Someone's there," Nayima said quietly.

"It's not—"

"No one we know." Raul was the youngest Carrier at fifty-nine. Nayima was younger than most at sixty-six. No one at El Nuevo Mundo walked with that young man's stride.

The bike sputtered a little too loudly, dipping an inch and then rising. Hoverbikes always wanted to be moving forward. Nayima steered left another thirty yards, back the way they'd come, then rounded toward two fallen pines crossed to provide the most shelter, big enough to stash the bike behind them and Lottie in the gap between them.

The bike dropped and rolled to a stop as its wheels descended, a racket over the almond hulls and pine needles. They both exhaled, relieved. For a moment, they only breathed together.

"Let's go home," Lottie finally whispered.

Nayima raised her hand: *Hush.* She wanted to call Raul so he could warn the others, but these men might have signal trackers. Maybe their earlier call already had been intercepted. Maybe that was why the men were here. She was lucky the men hadn't heard the hoverbike's approach.

Lottie scowled at Nayima from the shelter, realizing that Nayima meant to leave her. She was a lovely child. That had been hard from the start: the fresh prettiness of her ancestral face. Harder with Lottie's new tears.

"I have to see who's there," Nayima whispered.

"Let's just go back."

Nayima shook her head. She couldn't wait anymore. She probably had been planning to leave since her HealthHost chip tried to lure her to the lab. Since Sacramento's lies about a safer haven. Her days of running were over.

"I have to deal with this." Nayima handed Lottie her hololens, although she hated to part with it as much as she hated to leave the bike. "Check the time: If I'm not back in an hour—"

"An *hour*?"

"—or if someone comes, you hear more engines, call Raul. But only if I don't come back. *Only* if someone comes. Our calls aren't private, hear? Calling is a last resort."

Lottie nodded, her eyes so wide and frightened that Nayima was sure she would call Raul as soon as she was gone. She wasn't even sure Lottie shouldn't. She would have to find those men without the hololens.

"Are they gonna kill you?" Lottie said, tears in her voice.

"They might. Or I might kill them first."

Lottie's face and eyes became stone. Nayima had bequeathed stone to her daughter if nothing else. Her daughter. *Her* daughter. Nayima almost changed her mind. Maybe Lottie was right: Maybe they should return to their house. To the smoke and the butter churn.

"I'll be back," she said instead. They both knew it was a ridiculous promise, and Nayima knew it was a temporary promise at best.

Lottie's stone face softened to skin and tears again. "I love you, Mama," Lottie said.

Nayima wanted to say, *Don't.* "Me too." *Pumpkin.* "Now, stay hidden."

Nayima took a few steps away, turned to survey Lottie's hiding place: You had to look closely to see her brown face against the dead bark, in the shadows. Lottie still clasped her doll to her chest like a breathing thing, and Nayima was glad she'd brought company. The bike's black tail wasn't as well hidden as she'd hoped, but it was still hard to see at ten yards.

If she had to, she would shoot the men, or die trying.

Then she would come back to Lottie.

Nayima's right hip seemed to scrape its socket with each step, and before long she was limping. Her knees and ankles popped, angry. She stepped into a rabbit hole covered in pine needles and nearly lost her balance, falling against a spindly tree. Pain shot up from her toes to her neck. Damn. She searched for a sturdy walking stick, stripping a fallen twig.

Better. Much better. Gram had walked with a cane. Nothing to it. She moved purposefully, raised her feet high to avoid rustling, stepped gently as rainfall. But the woods were disorienting, especially woods as regimented as these: every tree trunk identical to the ones she'd just passed. She had spent so many years surrounded by concrete or scrub brush that she did not know the language of trees. She had a compass, but she didn't want to veer even a few steps astray of where she'd seen the men or they might surprise her. She needed to walk a straight line.

"Your blood pressure is rising dramatically," Sonia said. *"Please take your medication."*

Slow down, pumpkin, Gram said. *Slow and steady. This is the way.*

Ahead, Gram was waving as she had at the house's front gate. She was in her nurse's uniform now, her hair salt and pepper instead of the silver she'd worn on her deathbed. Gram had retired from Pomona Valley Hospital only two years before she got sick. No matter how many steps Nayima took, she got no closer to Gram. But although Gram vanished from time to time, she mostly stayed in sight, pointing out the path.

"Gram, they fucked up my head," Nayima huffed. "They fucked up my everything."

I know, baby. But they didn't break you.

Then Gram was gone, and Nayima wavered in her footsteps, unsure. She confused the trees again. Oh! Gram was standing on top of a tall boulder, wearing her purple Sunday best with her ostrich-feather hat. Overdressed as usual. Her white pumps glowed, a beacon. Gram waved and pointed: The red wrapper she'd seen was still there, gleaming in its shaft of sunlight.

"You are experiencing hallucinations," Sonia said. *"Please have*

your HealthHost chip serviced immediately to avoid further neural interference."

Nayima had hardly taken ten steps away from the wrapper when she noticed a man's voice ahead, unconcerned about being heard. She stood as straight and still as a pine to try to make out the words, but her ears were foam.

Breathe, Nayima, Gram said.

Nayima took a deep breath, held it—felt her heart's thudding and icy-hot blood rushing in her veins—and exhaled through her mouth the way she had in the days of her yoga class at the strip mall in the land of the dead. The sky wheeled overhead, but it righted itself as she breathed. She hadn't been this afraid in a long time.

She plunged her walking stick into the hard soil, a silent spear, and walked forward in the trees' shadows, correcting her course to the burr of the stranger's voice.

"—those horses. There's herds all over out there, but they could only torch the ones inside the gate. . . ."

Nayima's anger made lightning seem to split the sky, sharpening her senses. The man still sounded muffled, although he might be only five yards from her. She hadn't understood him sooner because his mouth was covered with some kind of mask. Only a fanatic or a fool would be wearing a mask on a day this hot, with no one in sight, still two miles out from El Nuevo Mundo. No marshals or soldiers wore masks in Carrier Territories. Not anymore. The Carriers' blood had wiped out the virus as mightily as it had spread it.

Only fanatics would wear masks. Only fanatics would slaughter horses.

Nayima's index finger felt numb from hugging the trigger guard. She walked like a cat from tree to tree, one step to the next. She could smell tobacco vapor in the air. Close.

". . . Well, tell them to hurry the fuck up," the voice said, as if it were in her ear like Gram's. But it wasn't. She was sure of that. This voice was real.

Nayima peeked past a thick tree trunk, and there he was: his back to her in a black jacket, gray sweatpants, the hunting rifle slung across his shoulder. He was on a hololens, poking absently at his backpack on the ground with a twig. He had been waiting a long time. He was impatient. He had forgotten never to stop watching.

An easy shot. Too easy. But where was the other one?

There he is, baby, Gram said.

At an angle ahead, two o'clock, ten yards, the man in the navy-blue pants was pissing against a tree in a steady stream. He was wearing his backpack. His rifle was at arm's length, standing just clear of his stream.

"*Your respiration is increasing*," Sonia said. "*To avoid hyperventilation, take deep, even breaths. Rest or seek a medical professional.*"

She was a good shot. Shooting had been her hobby since Reconciliation, no matter how expensive the bullets were. Cans. Bottles. Old tires. Rabbits and squirrels, sometimes, like Gram used to hunt when she was a girl in Gadsden County, Florida. Nayima had a split second to choose: Which man could reach his rifle sooner?

She almost spent too much time pondering it. The pissing man was shaking off.

Her excitement made her crack a twig, and Hololens was about to turn when she fired into the back of his head. He fell forward. The gunshot echoes exploded in the woods, hunching the pissing man's shoulders. He didn't have time to zip up before he reached for his rifle, and he couldn't raise his weapon before Nayima's first shot grazed his shoulder and backed him up a step and her second and third shots riddled his chest. He gasped a long breath inside his plastic contagion mask—the way Gram had gasped when her pain stole her breath—and dropped to his knees while he stared with bewilderment. Nayima imagined what he saw: an old gray-haired black woman with a walking stick, face brittle, eyes bright. This was not the person he had expected to kill him today, if he'd even bothered to imagine that he might die.

The walking stick trembled in Nayima's unsteady hand.

"You are losing consciousness," Sonia said.

"No, no," Nayima said, then—

When she woke, the silence startled her. The gunshots were fresh in her mind, but no birds were flapping in the leaves, no creatures scurrying for safety. The gunshots were long gone. Panicked, she checked the men she'd killed. Neither had moved. She did not look at their faces. The dead man's hololens chimed so loudly beneath him that it must be set to URGENT. That was what had made her stir: a chime. Someone was calling. But no one had come yet.

"You have had a fainting episode. Please lie still and call for medical assistance."

Nayima's right side ached, especially her neck. But she ignored the shooting pain as she braced with her walking stick and pushed against a tree, and the trunk's firm weight helped her stand. Dizziness came and subsided.

If not for Gram waving to her from the rows of almond trees behind her, Nayima might have lost her way back to Lottie.

Lottie let out a gasp when bushes shuddered at Nayima's arrival, but her face quickly brightened. She leaped out to wrap her arms around Nayima, nearly pulling her off-balance.

"I heard gunshots!" Lottie said, tearful. "I wanted to call Papa, but I was afraid to."

Nayima knew the rest: Lottie had thought, for that instant, she might be alone. Lottie was still shaking against her, so Nayima held her more tightly.

"I'm here," Nayima said. "Mama's here."

"Those men . . . ?"

"They're gone now."

Nayima hoped she would never forget the look on Lottie's face then, relief and adoration, the purest moment between them. But she had no time to savor it.

"Pumpkin, I have to give you a choice," Nayima said. "I was planning on asking you later, but you need to decide now."

Lottie watched her with Gram's eyes, the slant of Mama's nose—waiting.

"If we ride on to El Nuevo Mundo to meet Raul, there will be marshals there too—to protect us." She practically spat out the word *protect*. Probably her biggest lie yet.

"Protect us from men like those up there?"

"Yes."

"They'll guard us at El Nuevo Mundo?"

"The government wants us to move to a special place built for us."

All joy left Lottie's eyes. "Go back?" Lottie had been only four when she'd been sent to Nayima, but that was old enough to remember what it was like to live in a cage, even if hers had Plexiglas instead of bars.

"Right now, you and me, we're free," Nayima said. "A little bit free, anyway. We both have trackers in our heads. Sacramento can find us. But if we stay in the Carrier Territories, we can find somewhere else to live. Fend for ourselves. Until they come for us. That's the difference. Either we'll go to them or they'll come to us. But I don't know when. And even before the marshals come, more men like the ones who burned the ranch might come. Or like those up there I just left."

Lottie was mulling it over with renewed tears. She didn't like the choices. "Will Papa stay with us?"

Nayima shook her head. "You know your papa. He'll go to Sacramento with the others. That's what he'll want for you too. He'll think it's safer there. Especially after today."

"No he wouldn't. He'd want to be with—"

"You know your papa," Nayima said again, and Lottie did, so she was silent. "Now, there's something else. . . ."

Lottie waited, agonized.

"I have a faulty health chip," Nayima said. "I'm having hallucinations—seeing people who aren't there. Hearing voices."

Nayima expected greater alarm from Lottie, saw none. "Like who?"

"Like . . . Gram."

"My great-gramma?" *My* great-gramma. Lottie had claimed her. She knew Gram from Nayima's stories. Lottie had been so proud when she'd finally been given a name instead of a specimen number. "Do you see her right now?"

Nayima scanned the area toward El Nuevo Mundo. No sign of Gram. Then she looked the other way—the way they'd come—and found Gram sitting against the trunk of a tree about twenty-five yards away, still in her nurse's uniform. Waiting.

"Yes," Nayima said. She pointed. "There. Under the tree?"

Lottie craned her neck to follow Nayima's pointing finger. "I don't see her."

"I'm the only one who sees her. My chip is scrambling my brain. It's like a trick to get me to go to a doctor. To let them go back inside my head. And I'm old, Lottie. My body is slow. I don't know how well I can protect you."

Lottie shivered and took Nayima's hand like a parent would. "Does she scare you?"

"No." Maybe the Gram hallucination was a window to her sub-conscious. Maybe that was how Gram had helped her find the men. "She shows me things I already know, deep down."

Lottie scrunched her face in the sun, considering the weight of everything she'd heard.

"Mama . . ." Lottie said finally. "I don't wanna go with the marshals."

"*You heart rate is accelerating,*" Sonia said. As if Nayima didn't already know.

"Me neither, Lottie."

"You killed the bad people."

"Not all of them. More might come for us."

"But the marshals might catch them?"

"Yes," Nayima said. "I'll call Raul as soon as we finish talking, so they might."

In the distance, Gram stood up and wiped dust from what she used to call her derriere. She walked to the middle of the deer trail, watching them. Still waiting.

"I wanna go home," Lottie said, certain. "Papa will come stay with us."

Raul would be livid. He might try to take Lottie by force. But Raul would be the least of their problems if they went back to their house.

"Are you sure?" Nayima said. "We won't be safe there."

"I just wanna be with you."

How had Mama done it? How had she packed that suitcase and sat Nayima down on the bed with that cigarette hanging from her mouth to tell her she was leaving? More than sixty years later, Nayima would never understand it. Nayima couldn't leave Lottie, even if it meant they might die together.

Nayima stared down the path between the groves at Gram, expecting to see her wave, some gesture to show her opinion, but she was only standing with her arms at her sides, staring on. Then Gram turned away.

Walking back toward home.

TANANARIVE DUE is an author, screenwriter, and educator who is a leading voice in black speculative fiction. Her short fiction has appeared in Year's Best anthologies of science fiction and fantasy. She is the former distinguished visiting lecturer at Spelman College (2012–2014) and teaches Afrofuturism and Black Horror at UCLA. She also teaches in the creative writing MFA program at Antioch University Los Angeles. The American Book Award winner and NAACP Image Award recipient is the author/co-author of twelve novels and a civil-rights memoir, *Freedom in the Family: A Mother-Daughter Memoir of the Fight for Civil Rights.* In 2010, she was inducted into the Medill School of Journalism's Hall of Achievement at Northwestern University. She also received a Lifetime Achievement Award in the Fine Arts from the Congressional Black Caucus Foundation. Her first short-story collection, *Ghost Summer*, published in 2015, won a British Fantasy Award. Due frequently collaborates with her husband, Steven Barnes, including on their YA zombie novels *Devil's Wake* and *Domino Falls*. They met at a speculative-fiction conference at Clark Atlanta University in 1997. She lives in Southern California with Barnes and their son, Jason. Her writing blog is at tananarivedue.wordpress.com, her website is at tananarivedue.com, and you can follow her on Twitter @TananariveDue.

BY HIS BOOTSTRAPS

ASHOK K. BANKER

The president was watching a recording of his favorite morning news show when the visitor appeared in his bedroom.

The visitor materialized behind the couch with a soft sound and the faint odor of ripe Apus mango. The president was eating a McDonald's burger and was oblivious to her presence.

For some time, they watched the news together, the visitor unnoticed. Three talking heads were onscreen, debating the new Immigration Act. One head called it "mass deportation" and suggested that if we were going to throw immigrants out of the country, then why not start with the descendants of the *Mayflower*. The other two heads began talking over her angrily; one called her a *snowflake*. The president laughed, displaying a mouthful of partially masticated processed beef.

"I remember this one," said the visitor. "She asks him ever so sweetly that if she's a snowflake, how come he's the one having a meltdown! It ends with him losing his shit."

A half-chewed mouthful of food sprayed out of the president's mouth, and he dropped the remains of his burger as he stabbed the emergency button. His half-consumed can of Diet Coke tipped over and dribbled a dark stain on the Lincoln Bedroom carpet. His bathrobe fluttered, threatening to splay open.

"How did you," he began, followed by a violent fit of coughing, "get in here?" His eyes scanned the stranger's hands, searching for the dreaded means of assassination.

The visitor showed her empty palms. "No guns. They're illegal. Hell of a task but we finally got rid of them all." The president's eyes flitted over her body, her unusual clothes, as he backed away. "No bombs, blades, or any other weapons. I'm not here to harm you, Mr. President."

The president was edging toward the door of the bedroom just as it flew open and Secret Service agents flooded in. "POTUS intact," one said into his subvocal mic. "Extracting."

The president yelled, "Shoot her!"

The agents had already fanned out to block off the visitor from the president, moving him toward the door as they ordered the visitor to lie facedown on the ground with her hands on the back of her head. The visitor smiled but remained standing.

"What are you waiting for? Shoot!" the president said as he was herded out the door.

The president heard soft sounds and smelled the whiff of some foreign fruit—he'd never eaten a ripe Apus mango, grown organically in the rich Deccan soil of western India, which was his loss—as the agents surrounding him . . . *changed*. Not a man to pay close attention to sensory phenomena, he failed to see the air around them ripple slightly, the way a person's reflection might waver when seen moving across a distorted mirror.

To him, it was as if one moment they were hulking Secret Service agents in dark suits, and the next instant they were people of color in traditional clothing and hairdos. A white man in a suit became a Havasupai in leggings, a loose long-sleeved shirt, and sandals made of yucca fiber, with a headband holding back his long hair. Another white man in a suit was replaced by a Karankawa Indian of non-binary gender, dressed in clothes that the president couldn't have identified if his life depended on it. A third agent remained African American but her features altered subtly, becoming noticeably more Congolese Bantu as the traces of Caucasian genes were leached out of her DNA. Similar transformations rippled through all the agents present.

More significant to the present situation than their astonishingly altered appearances and wardrobes was the disappearance of their weapons. All guns and Tasers had vanished.

"Greetings," said an agent who had been spraying spittle at the visitor a second ago. She was now a dark-skinned Bantu woman several inches taller than the Germanic white male she had replaced. She wore large hoop earrings in her ears and a wooden piercing in her septum. "Welcome to the White House."

The visitor nodded and spoke quietly to the lady as the president tried to make sense of what had just happened.

"Mr. President?" asked an elderly woman in jeans and a PEACE ROCKS T-shirt. "Would you like to receive your valued guest in the Golden Tea Room?"

The president issued a sound not dissimilar to the yelp of a Chihuahua in distress. "Who are you people?"

"Tlatoani," said a cheerful Toltec Nahuatl woman. "We are your people. If you do not wish the Golden Tea Room, pray suggest an alternative space in your fine tlahtohcācalli."

The president backed away from all of them, making gurgling, terrified noises. When they came toward him with outstretched arms and looks of concern, speaking their own mellifluous dialects, he yelped again, turned tail, and ran.

The visitor held up her hands as she came through the gaily attired group. "Leave it to me," she said. "He's shook up, is all. I'll calm him down." She paused. "Or not," she chuckled as she walked away.

She caught up with the president in the Yellow Oval Room. It was still called that, was still painted yellow, but that was the only resemblance to its earlier form. The American Impressionistic paintings of Mary Cassatt had been replaced by bright indigenous frescoes depicting images and scenes invoking the themes of intellect and determination interspersed with a few select portraits.

The president was staring at one such portrait with bewilderment. He was still in his loosely belted bathrobe and looked like he'd aged a decade in the last few minutes. He turned and flinched at the sight of the visitor, who smiled and held out her open palms again to show she came in peace.

"Excuse me, excuse me!" the president interjected. "I don't understand this. Who is this Indian and why is his picture in the Yellow Oval Room!"

"That's Chief Opechancanough of the Powhatan Tribe, during his second term in office."

The president's eyes bulged. "He was *president*?"

The visitor smiled. "I suppose it would surprise you even more to learn that you are only the tenth white male Caucasian president of the United States, out of nearly fifty presidents so far. The majority have been Americans, or what you now call Native Americans. The rest have been immigrants from almost every corner of the globe, many not U.S. citizens at all."

The president stumbled to the window and ripped open the curtains. Bright sunlight struck him in the face, accentuating his pallor. He squinted his bulging eyes, scanning frantically.

"Where are they?"

"Who, Mr. President?"

"The cameras, lights, technicians? The fake news media taking things to a new level! Whoever did this'll never work in this country again—believe me!"

The visitor didn't answer. She had anticipated these reactions and knew it was best to simply wait them out.

Giving up on the window, the president turned to the landline telephone on the desk and snatched it up. His fingers still bore the evidence of his lunch, and he left smeared ketchup and mustard on the restored antique.

"Who is this?" He listened, bushy eyebrows knitting and knotting like albino caterpillars in a mating dance. He slammed the phone down on the cradle, hammered it a few more times for good measure, then picked up a remote control and switched on the flatscreen.

The TV was set to the same news channel the president had been watching earlier; the same show. Except that now the anchors in the studio were different, the set was different, and the news crawl showed a very different world.

The president moaned and changed the channel. Then changed it again, and yet again. Finally he threw the remote in frustration at the screen. It missed and knocked over an urn on a high shelf, spilling someone's ashes over the priceless carpet.

"What is going on here?" he yelled, and proceeded to throw the presidential equivalent of a temper tantrum combined with a panic attack. He ended up on the carpet before the couch, almost entirely under the vintage coffee table. Seeing the visitor approach slowly, smiling, he yipped, realizing that no one was coming to rescue him.

"My protection detail is a disgrace!" he cried plaintively.

The visitor said in her calmest voice: "Nobody means you any harm, Mr. President. You are safer now than you or any United States president has ever been in history. Apart from that one unfortunate incident in the nineteenth century, there has never been an attempt to assassinate any of your predecessors. Besides, there are no guns anymore. They don't exist. They never existed. The technology itself was eliminated."

The president's chest was heaving, his face red and splotchy. Snot, spittle, and tears combined in a shiny moistening formulation. Finally he regained some measure of control and asked for a drink.

She brought him a glass of cold water.

He grimaced at the sight. "I only drink Diet Coke," he grumbled, but drank it down thirstily.

Still on the carpet, he tried to put the glass on the coffee table above him, missed, and sent it toppling and rolling under the couch.

"Talk," he said in a seething tone. "What do you want?"

"Me, Mr. President? This isn't about me. I already have everything I want. I don't believe in utopias, but this is about as close to it as I believe humanity has ever gotten. This is about you."

"Me?" he asked, red-rimmed eyes squinting suspiciously.

"You're clearly upset and disoriented. I'm here to help you through this transition."

"You're not making sense!" he barked up at her. "Start talking sense or I'll have you, have you . . ." He trailed off, looking bewildered. "I don't understand what's going on," he said at last in a shaky voice.

"It's Project Bootstrap," she replied.

He reacted. "What do you know about—wait a minute—how do you know about that?"

"I'm running it," she said. "I'm in charge of the project, Mr. President. Remember?"

He stared at her with the expression of a sick dog that had just woken up at the vet's after being anesthetized and felt betrayed by the world. "*You?*"

She went on. "Bootstrap combined a breakthrough in quantum time travel with a new development in genetic restoration. There's a thick file somewhere in your papers that explains the scientific details, but I know you hate briefs, so I'll keep it simple, the way you like it. In short, we invented a Genetic Time Bomb."

He blinked. "That's right. . . . It was supposed to make America great again, just like I always promised—the way it was always meant to be. . . . Turn the clock back to before all this diversity and this phony politically correct stuff."

"Pretty much," she agreed. "We tested the device on a few subjects. I briefed you on the results. They were very satisfactory. In one instance, the subject was a third-generation Dreamer named Rodriguez, the grandchild of illegal immigrants from Mexico. When we deployed the device on him, he disappeared, along with his parents and grandparents. Disappeared as in literally vanished before our cameras in the holding cell. We investigated and found that he was now a plumber in Oaxaca City, where he lived along with his parents. His grandparents had never entered the United States, legally or illegally. We surreptitiously gained samples of their DNA to verify what our scientists had already told us to expect: They were slightly different people, because of Rodriguez's mother marrying a different man, and Rodriguez himself was not exactly the same as the man we had detained and experimented on, but the other markers were too close to leave any room for doubt. The Genetic Time Bomb had literally changed his family history.

"In another case, the immigrant in detention also vanished, but in that case there was no present-day equivalent of the subject. A refugee from Aleppo, she and her family had been killed in a pogrom."

"One less immigrant to worry about, am I right?" the president said with a big grin, getting off the carpet and sitting on the couch. He looked energized by the discussion.

"Several more cases all yielded the same satisfactory results. The conclusion was remarkable: one hundred percent success."

"Tremendous! I'm going to get Congress to push through another trillion in funding."

"It was," she said, "the perfect weapon. Simply slip a dose of the formula into any food or drink consumed by the subject. After a minimal gestation period, the GTB would activate, acting directly upon the subject's transancestral development at the most fundamental genetic level."

"Beautiful!" he crowed, rising to his feet.

"There is a certain beauty to it, actually," she went on. "It erased the person's racial development, resetting their genetic lineage back to the original code. What Dr. Royce, the head of the research project, called *genetic cleansing*."

"I said to Bobby, 'Bobby, we're going to take care of all these illegals.' And Bobby said this MAGA bomb would be like deporting every immigrant without spending a dollar or lifting a finger. No muss, no fuss. Just put this in the drinking water supply and"—he snapped his fingers, failed to produce a sound because of the dried condiments, and settled for slapping his hand on his own thigh—"we would be a great nation again, like the one our Founding Fathers intended us to be."

She nodded. "I did say all that, and much more. I thought—we *all* thought—it was a panacea for all our problems. And so it was. But not in the way we expected."

He frowned. "I'm talking about Bobby. I still don't know who you are, lady."

"*I'm* Bobby, Mr. President," she said. "Or at least I used to be before the transition."

His face turned mean. "That's impossible. I spoke to Bobby this evening, couldn't have been more than two hours ago. He was a man, an American. I don't know what or who you are, but you're not Bobby."

"In any case," she went on, unperturbed, "Operation Clean

Sweep was a fantastic success. The formula was put into the water supply and people began transitioning. And then, somehow, it went viral."

The president looked at her doubtfully. "Viral?"

"It mutated, we think. Whatever the scientific reason, the outcome is what matters. It triggered mass transitioning across the country, and then across the world, because America has influenced the entire globe over the past few centuries. We don't know how or why it began to operate the way it did. But you've already seen the results for yourself. They're indisputable."

He stared at her. "What results?"

She gestured around her. "Your staff, the Secret Service, the portraits on the wall, the world outside, me. Everything's changed, and it appears to be permanent. There's no reversing this now. This is the way the world is now. A genuinely multicultural, multiracial, diverse world. This is America."

"I don't get it," he said, starting to look nervous again. "You're saying Operation Clean Sweep *worked*? And this is the result? My staff changing to those people out there?"

"And everyone else too. You see, Mr. President, you gave the order to deploy Operation Clean Sweep because you thought—we all did—that it would be a clean sweep of our country's racial diversity, restoring America to the white Christian nation we believed it once had been. But that was a myth. America has always been an ethnically diverse mix, a melting pot of races and cultures. History is not a John Wayne western with all the people of color erased and the narrative distorted to match white nationalist mythology. It's beautifully, wonderfully mixed. Genders, races, ethnicities, sexual orientations, cultures, religions . . . We are the world's melting pot, always have been. When we deployed the formula into the drinking water supply of American cities, what happened wasn't erasure of people of color and immigrants. It was the exact opposite."

The president sat heavily on the couch, staring up at her with an expression of morbid horror.

"We restored America to the way it ought to have been. Native Americans became the dominant racial group in our history." She gestured to the portraits on the wall. "And everything else changed too. Our attitudes toward politics, violence, sexuality, religion, culture—you name it. The people you've seen here already are a microcosm of the America we live in now. Congratulations, Mr. President, you did it. You made America the great nation you promised you would make it again, as our Founding Fathers actually intended, based on the Iroquois Confederacy that inspired them: 'All persons equal under their myriad gods,' to quote from our own Declaration of Independence."

The president shook his head slowly. "You're insane. You're crazy. This is some kind of witch hunt. A coup. It doesn't make any sense."

"Give it a moment," she said. "It's only been a few minutes since you had the formula."

The president jerked like he'd been Tasered. "What are you talking about?"

"You always drink soda," she said. "You never touch water if you can help it. That's why you hadn't transitioned yet."

The president stared at her pointing finger, following it down to the rim of the glass barely visible below the couch. He balked again.

"Where the hell is Bobby?"

She sat down beside him on the couch. "Habiba, I told you: *I'm* Bobby."

"Get away from me. I don't know who you are."

She smiled at him. "Habiba, love, I'm your wife. It's strange how I remember everything but you don't. They said it would happen this way for a while. In time, the memories of the alternate genetic timeline fade and the contradictions self-resolve."

"You're talking crazy again!"

"It'll all make sense in a moment. You see, Mr. President, I'm from the future. I was sent back to explore and study the transition. One of the side effects was a substantial acceleration of technological advancement. By eliminating violence, weaponry, and war from our history, we developed much faster in every respect. A few weeks after today, we find a way to go back in time. Not to change it—because that's impossible—but merely to relive it. I was sent back to help you through your transition because I knew firsthand how difficult it was for you. I was the one who suggested it and then volunteered."

The president stared at her, no longer able to find words to express how he felt. He was clutching his head, mussing his intricately coiffed hair, like a person feeling a skull-splitting migraine coming on.

"I . . ." he said, then the air around him seemed to ripple slightly and the scent of ripe Apus mango came to the visitor's sinuses.

In the place where the white man in the bathrobe had been sitting, there was now a transgender person of the same age with almost identical features. They looked around, then found the visitor. They smiled with relief.

"Fatima," they said, "what happened?"

The visitor took the president's hand in her own. "You transitioned, Habiba."

"Then it worked?" the president said in wonderment.

"Yes. No suicide attempt this time, no throwing yourself through the window, no running half naked out onto Pennsylvania Avenue . . . It worked like a charm."

"It was your presence," said the president. "It soothed me." They frowned slightly, touching the graying hairs on their right temple. "I *think* it did. I don't remember much."

"It's better that way," Fatima said. "I remember *too* much. I wish

I didn't. We were all such horrible people before. I don't know how we lived with ourselves."

"Hatefully," said the president. "We lived hatefully, hating ourselves and hating everyone else. But that's all gone now."

"Yes," Fatima said, staring deeply into the eyes of her life-partner. "Now only love remains."

ASHOK K. BANKER is the author of more than sixty books, including the internationally acclaimed Ramayana series. His works have all been bestsellers in India and have sold around the world. His latest novel is the first in a new epic fantasy series, *Upon a Burning Throne*. He lives in Los Angeles.

RIVERBED

OMAR EL AKKAD

"Welcome to Big Sky Country," the flight attendant said. Gently, the plane descended over browning farmland and desolate ridges of brush and stone where the prairies met the mountains.

Khadija Singh lifted the window shade and looked down at what had become of Billings. She saw the remains of the big mid-century developments, paid for with out-of-state developer money in the years when everyone thought the Deluge Bowl migration would lead right across the Rockies into Montana and Idaho and the unburned parts of the Pacific Northwest, the high sheltered places.

But it never happened. Instead, the displaced millions had fled the coasts to Chicago, Cleveland, Detroit, because in those cities it was possible still to live within sight of the water and without sight of the country's dying rural expanse. The coastal exodus never reached places like Billings, and all that developer money bought was a cluster of unfinished towers, whole suburbs curled up like shrimp tails around their own emptiness.

At the airport customs desk, the officer flipped lazily through Khadija's Canadian passport. For a moment she thought he might ask her to remove her headscarf, but instead he stamped one of the pages with casual violence, slid the passport back, and waved her through.

Outside in the arrivals hall, she found a man holding a sign with her name on it. He wore an old-fashioned driver's uniform.

"You Khadija?" the driver asked, mangling her name, using a long *i* the way some Americans do when they pronounce words like *Iraq*.

"Dr. Singh," she replied. She set her bag on the ground and walked past him toward the exit, where a solitary old sedan sat parked. On the side of the ancient car were plastered the name and logo of the Riverbed Attestation Center.

"Hey, lady," the driver began, but she did not respond. He sighed and picked up her suitcase and followed her to the car.

They drove toward Billings. She knew they would have to drive clear across town to get to the center. It was a deliberately unobtrusive place, nestled against a hillside amid otherwise uninhabited land.

"So you want to go straight to Riverbed?" the driver said, eyeing her in his rearview mirror.

"Yes," Khadija replied. "No."

"Well, which is it?"

"Take me there, but just drive around it, and then take me back to the hotel."

"Lady, the hotel's downtown, right off the exit here," the driver said. "That's an hour of extra driving you're talking about."

Khadija looked out the window, ignoring the driver. She'd forgotten how Americans spoke.

Along North 27th Street they drove past the remains of old Billings, the diners and auto shops and the sprawling offices of the *Billings Gazette*, all now plastered with FOR LEASE signs. The only pedestrian traffic trickled in and out of the pawnshops and the Hundred-Dollar-Or-Less stores and the immigration offices whose lawyers specialized in Canadian visas.

No sooner had the car reached the outskirts of the city than Khadija said, "Stop. Turn around."

The driver glanced at her through the rearview. "What?"

"I changed my mind. Take me to the hotel."

The driver tapped the steering wheel in exasperation. "Lady, I'm not . . ." he started, then fell silent. He slowed and turned into a clearing in the median, and soon the car was headed back to the city in which, fifty years earlier, Khadija once resided.

Father said he wasn't worried. He said Americans are like this, brittle with privilege. Sometimes anger robs them of their senses and they make bad decisions, but in a way this was really just another testament to American greatness—how adept the United States was at surviving its endless self-inflicted wounds. *We live in a good country,* he said, *and it will be good again.*

On the television station that backed the winning candidate, the frothing pundit couldn't stop talking, couldn't even stop for breath, all his words like one long word. He said the people the everyday salt-of-the-earth people are angry do you hear that in the big cities in the ivory towers do you hear that the real people are angry and so what if the scientists had been right all this time what good is a temperate summer if all the good-paying refinery jobs are gone and Washington swipes half of every paycheck to spend on relocating some Fijian who didn't know better than to leave that miserable little island before it sank into the ocean and anyway why's that our problem it's not our problem it's not it's not.

I watched, hypnotized. Father sat in his easy chair, occasionally shaking his head and saying how this was just the way the cycle worked—one time they vote for what they believe themselves to be and the next they get angry and vote for what they really are. *You can't let it bother you,* he said.

I saw John outside, playing catch with his friend in the backyard, oblivious in that way only fifteen-year-old boys can be. And I was happy for his obliviousness, because although I was only three years older than him I'd learned by then to see obliviousness as the surest sign of belonging, and I wanted more than anything for him to feel he belonged.

I thought about what Mother would make of him, of all this, had she lived another year. I thought about the day she sat me down and said, *Take care of your brother, Lydia, and take care of yourself; be at all times guarded. And never forget that this country despises above all else this thing they call people of color, sees them not as people at all but as harbingers of a future it can't control.* I remember liking that moniker: *of color.* What a thing to be in a country so black and white.

The man on TV said Americans are good people you know but they only vote one of two ways with their hearts or with their heads and let's hope it's not too late let's hope it's not too late but thank the Lord this time they came to their senses and voted with their heads.

But it didn't seem to me like they voted with their heads. It seemed like they voted with their fangs.

Two days later, Father went outside in the morning and our neighbors who were out mowing their lawns and washing their cars were all looking at him in a nervous, sidelong way—the way passing motorists look at a driver who's been pulled over.

We lived back then in one of those suburbs where all the streets are named after flowers and the houses all look alike. The houses were descendants of the old Sears Craftsman homes. You used to be able to order them straight from the catalog. They were defined by their sameness, and in their sameness was a kind of evidence that you'd arrived in America—that you were finally done swirling around in the pot, that you'd finally melted.

At first my father didn't understand why his neighbors were look-ing at him this way. Then he turned around and saw what had been spray-painted on our garage door. Two words in bright red, the tails of the letters melting like candle wax, the paint still fresh. The second word took up the entire width of the door and bore within it a history of cruelty so thick it became a compendium in itself—a word the say-ing and thinking of which had been the source of so much debate but whose saying and thinking had never been outlawed or even really punished, only the volume at which it could be said and the outward glee with which it could be thought. The second word spray-painted on our garage door was the only truly American word.

And the first word was SAND.

In the months that followed, the rumors started. You'd hear other kids and sometimes even the teachers whispering about it in school, about some oversized semis they'd seen coming down the 94, haul-ing prefabricated vinyl sheets and guard-tower platforms and reams and reams of barbed wire, going somewhere deep in the canyons. *Best for everyone,* they'd say. *Keeps them safe, keeps us safe.*

But at first it was just background noise.

Then one Sunday those six men walked into the stadium the day of the big bowl game, and when the dust settled and the bodies were counted there was no doubt the president would follow through with his threat. The executive order came out a week later, and a week after that the soldiers showed up at our door.

I remember the strangeness of that day, the absurdity that seems to accompany all violent beginnings. They came in a convoy of sorts, a black paddy wagon sandwiched between two cop cars. Four offi-cers emerged from the cop cars. I recognized two of them from the previous November, when Father had called to report the vandalism of our garage door. Then the wagon door was flung open and out spilled a gaggle of reservists—they didn't look like soldiers; they looked like armored accountants, flabby and uncomfortably corseted in their flak vests.

I think a small part of my father believed, right until that moment, we would be safe. Sure there were things said, slurs hurled across shopping-mall parking lots. Sure he'd decided to cut his hair and shave his beard, resigned now to the fact that so many of his countrymen could not distinguish one religion from another. And even before all that, back when this particular flavor of national paranoia was still in its infancy, he had decided to take precautions—to give his children Westerners' names and teach them to speak and dress and think in a way that rendered them in the eyes of the majority benign, normal. He'd done all these things and in the end none of it mattered.

Still, he was calm until the very moment they ushered him onto the wagon. I remember he asked for a few minutes to lock our home's doors and windows. He ripped a sheet from one of John's notebooks and wrote our lawyer's name and phone number on it and taped it to our front door, but just before they drove us away I saw one of the officers tear it down.

John squeezed my shoulder and said, *A week, tops.*

It was only at the very end that my father's calm veneer finally evaporated. He turned to one of the soldiers, pleading. *We're from here*, he said. *We're Americans.* The soldier looked straight through him, and it occurred to me then that in this country it has never really mattered what you are, only what you're not.

Khadija lay in her hotel bed, the window open to give some relief from the heat and the room's mildew smell. At dawn she gave up on sleep and got up and dressed and went for a walk around the perimeter of the property. The sun came up over the barren hills.

The driver showed up at eight-thirty, as she'd instructed him to do.

"Mornin'," he said, offering her a paper cup. "Coffee?"

"No thank you."

The driver tossed the cup away and got in the driver's seat.

"You mind if I stop for gas before we go out there?" the driver asked.

"Fine. Quickly, please."

They pulled into the station at the edge of town, where in one corner of the lot sat an old gas pump, the only one left in Billings. The driver set the nozzle in the tank and walked around the side of the car and wiped down the front and rear windshields.

Khadija lowered her window. The smell of gasoline was sharp and reminded her of her childhood.

"Every time one of you folks comes to town, they take this piece of junk out of the garage," the driver said. "I guess they think anyone who's coming to visit is probably one of those people who spends a lot of time thinking about the way things used to be, so they'll feel more comfortable in one of these cars. I keep telling them to sell it to some antiques dealer in Detroit, but they won't do it."

She ignored the driver. Save for a couple of old men sitting on lawn chairs under the awning of a nearby kiosk, there were no signs of life, no cars at the station, new or old.

She had expected to find more young people. But instead Billings seemed populated almost entirely with members of her generation. The young had left, that much was clear. Probably they'd gone to Canada or, if they couldn't afford the cost of the visa, to the big Midwestern cities. Others probably went south, into the furious furnace of Texas and New Mexico and Arizona, to earn the state minimum tearing apart the wall their parents and grandparents once earned the state minimum to erect.

One of the old men sitting under the awning snapped his fingers at her. "You here for the anniversary thing?" he asked.

She said nothing. The old man pointed at her headscarf. "They gonna pay you, I suppose?"

"Shut up, Billy, for Christ's sake," the driver said. "You got nothing better to do than badger people all day?"

"I'm just saying, I'm just saying—you get one of those big-shot Chicago lawyers, might be good money in it. I mean, that's how these things work, right? Big ceremony, big apology, big check?"

Khadija rolled up her window. The driver got back in the car. They drove away. Soon they'd left the city, and after a few minutes of driving down a deserted highway that ran through the middle of the old reservation, they reached the Riverbed Attestation Center.

At first, she didn't recognize the place. The old dirt road had been widened and paved over. Where the reservists once stood guard at the entrance, there was now only a small blue highway sign that labeled the center a POINT OF INTEREST.

They turned onto the driveway and rounded a curve where twin concrete pillars leaned against one another like the lines of an upside-down V. It was a sculpture of sorts, set in a small circular green space around which the car turned to park at the front entrance. The entire perimeter, which had once been a mesh of chain-link fencing, had been replaced with thick adobe-colored stone. The new wall was high and adorned with etchings that didn't seem to belong to any artistic or cultural tradition, a strange smattering of doodles and curving lines that in some places formed into the shape of crescents or stars but elsewhere was inscrutable.

The driver got out and opened the door for Khadija. "Take your time," he said. "I'll be waiting out here."

She emerged into the morning light, dizzy. She walked through the sliding glass doors. A wave of cool air met her.

The woman at the reception desk looked up, frowned, then smiled.

"Good morning," she said. "Are you here for the guided tour?"

"No," Khadija said. "I'm here to see the director."

"You have an appointment?"

"Yes."

"So he's expecting you?"

"That's what an appointment means."

The receptionist asked her to wait a moment and typed a message on her tablet. A few minutes later a man emerged from the back offices. He shook Khadija's hand and introduced himself as the Riverbed's director.

"It's a pleasure to have you visit," he said. "It's always a pleasure when you visit."

He spoke quickly, confidently, so much so that at first she did not understand what he meant.

He led her beyond a set of turnstiles and into a wide central room with large floor-to-ceiling glass walling off an outdoor space.

Inside the enclosure sat a rounded tile-and-alabaster fountain. The tile was painted a too-bright shade of turquoise and decorated with vaguely arabesque geometric patterns that repeated too often and too obviously, like the stitching on a cheap kitchen tablecloth. Spouts were dug deep into the fountain's mouth, such that they were invisible to observers standing behind the glass. The water, bubbling up weakly, seemed to appear out of nowhere, to have no beginning.

"We managed to get the architect of the Rose Bowl memorial to design it," the director said. "He came out of retirement to do it. I think it was very big of him, a really nice gesture."

The director slid a keycard into a slot on the wall, and softly the front of the glass split into two sheets and parted to form a passageway.

"Please, come inside," he said. "Only former protectees are allowed to step inside the enclosure."

"I'm not interested," Khadija said.

The director smiled and stammered. "Then perhaps . . . would you like to see the sleeping-cabin exhibit? The insides have been preserved with great care."

"I don't want to see the cabins," Khadija replied. "Do you think

I forgot what the cabins looked like?" She pointed down the corridor from where the director first appeared. "I want to see the repository," she said. "The storage room."

The director quieted. He still wore a smile on his face, but its fraudulence seemed to Khadija especially glaring now.

"I thought you might be interested in some of the exhibits," he said, "the lengths to which the government has gone to commemorate and celebrate—"

"Let's not waste each other's time," Khadija said. "I'm here for my brother's things."

The director appeared to be looking past her now, to the lobby, where a group of high school kids were beginning to file in, shepherded by a couple of teachers and one of the center's volunteer guides.

"Yes, about that," the director said. "Do you mind if we go to my office?"

"I do mind," Khadija said. "I don't want to go to your office; I want to go to the storage room. Now, please."

"Dr. Singh, as I tried to explain in our correspondence, this isn't a straightforward matter. There are . . . rules, provisions in the federal code."

"This place turns fifty next Sunday," Khadija said. "You know full well it all becomes public record that day. I don't want to see this garbage, these stupid exhibits and friendship fountains. I want my brother's things. You're going to find them and you're going to give them to me. Am I making myself perfectly clear?"

"Do you mind," the director started, then paused. He lowered his voice. "Do you mind at least giving me some time to make some inquiries, then?"

"You knew I was coming," Khadija replied. "You had six months to make inquiries."

"Then another day won't make much difference, Dr. Singh. I'll try the commissioner's office again, ask for an exception. But as I told you before, if they do this for you, who knows how many people will come forward with similar requests."

"I'll be here at nine o'clock tomorrow morning," Khadija said, turning to leave. "Do your job, Director."

On the drive back to the hotel, she felt an attack of claustrophobia. Her chest tightened. She rolled down the window and turned her head against the wind. The air smelled of dust and manure though she could see no farms or even homesteads, just the endless undulation of rural Montana, hills swallowing hills.

"It's the ugliest goddamn thing, isn't it?" the driver said.

"I beg your pardon?"

"That museum. I was there the day they unveiled that fountain. The designer they hired was this crazy old man. They asked him to say a few words and then they had to cut his mic when he started going on about the natural resiliency of the Middle Asiatic. Total shitshow."

"It looked exactly how I thought it would," Khadija said.

They drove into town. In the lot of an unused strip mall, about fifty men and women stood in line to visit a pop-up charity dental clinic, shuffling slowly through the entrance of a repurposed big-top tent, silent.

"Did you grow up here?" Khadija asked the driver.

"Yes, ma'am."

"You remember a neighborhood called Lewisia?"

"Sure. Down by the island, south side of the river."

"Is it still there?"

The driver laughed. "What's left of it. Been rotting away thirty, forty years now. Even the freight-train crowd won't spend the night there."

"Do you mind taking me there?"

The driver shrugged. "Sure. Don't know what you're expecting to find, though."

They crossed the bridge where a few tiny offshoots split from the heart of the river. Near a tire yard and a couple of fenced-off weed fields, the driver turned onto a series of interlinked crescents that terminated in small culs-de-sac.

They drove past houses all identical and in identical states of ruin. The roofs of the Craftsmen sagged, the shingles mostly gone or dangling like dead skin. Large gashes in the walls marked the places where the copper had been torn out. Couches and hubcaps and broken windowpanes littered the driveways.

"I remember at the peak you couldn't get in here for under two million," the driver said. "And that was a lot of money back then. These days the city will pay you just to take it off their hands."

Strewn among the lawns were various signs from old election campaigns, a rolling history of the people who had taken turns running the country through its century of decline — the Wall-War Republicans, the Compassionate Re-Segregationists, the No-Government Party. Each one less a social or political movement and more of a doubling-down, a rejection of some previous generation's conception of what constituted the limits of decency and reason. Here in these dull insulated places, descendants of the first white-flight suburbs, it was easiest to look around and see proof of a whole nation run straight off the edge of the cliff, and yet still running, certain of no greater sin than to ever look down.

"So I guess this was home for you once?" the driver asked.

"No," Khadija said. "I used to live here."

The only one I felt sorry for was a Jordanian named Yassir. He said he was a cleric and community leader, but in truth he was some retired agricultural engineer they rounded up in Boise. Every morning he took a stroll by the edge of the fence and waved good morning to all the guards. He called them all Brother and held his hand to his heart whenever he greeted them and always said *Thank you for your service* instead of *Goodbye*. Everyone at Riverbed hated him.

Much later, all the reporters came to us looking for horror stories, stories of the cages in which they kept us, of sleep and food deprivation, of holes for toilets. But in reality the place felt more like a demented summer camp, full of faux-wood cabins hastily erected. Most of them were sleeping quarters, built in clusters around the largest building, a long narrow mess hall.

They built the place against the side of a hill, a quarter mile off the main road down a thin dirt path. There was no signage anywhere, and well before you reached the high chain fence that pinned the camp against the hillside you'd run into a phalanx of guards stationed at the intersection where the highway met the side road. It was a place designed to be nowhere, and we its uninhabitants.

Of my father, my brother, and I, I fared the best. From the moment we arrived, everyone there knew we didn't belong, but the women didn't care one way or another, and quickly they took me in rather than have one more headache to deal with in the form of a disgruntled nineteen-year-old. But the men wanted nothing to do with Father, and the boys wanted everything to do with John. Every night he came back to the cabin bearing the marks of their interest, bruises from fights that started the day one of the boys said John was not Muslim at all but a secret informant, a Sikh sent to spy on them. John said he didn't mind the fistfights—it was something to do, at least—and I believed him. But you could see, every time, the confusion in his eyes when they called him these things. To be different among the different is an unwinnable state.

Nothing else bothered me. In time you learn to get by, you learn to accept the ugliness and the ignorance, because what else is there to do? Take on the whole country? But to see him like that, the boy who was of me and I of him, the boy I'd come to know before he even came to know himself—to see him carry the weight of his loneliness, the light of him dimming—it hurt.

On a corkboard near the entrance to the mess hall, the guards pinned a copy of Executive Order 1116, and on the ground every morning a delivery boy left a stack of Arabic newspapers published by some group in Virginia called the Institute for Harmonious Relations. Most of us didn't read a word of Arabic, and the rest didn't care.

For a while, early on, you could hear them out beyond the fence —protestors who'd come to Riverbed banging drums and waving banners. This was back during the golden years of ineffectual demonstration, and I think some of these people, if they didn't go out to the streets and rage at whatever it was they refused to believe their country had become, would probably have suffered aneurysms or grown a gut full of ulcers. Mostly they were old white folks, the COEXIST bumper-sticker crowd. By the second week they'd all gone elsewhere, lured away by some other outrage. Only one woman kept coming back every day for three or four months. She came up to the checkpoint near the fence and said she'd converted and wanted to be let in to live alongside her brothers and sisters. And every day the reservist stationed at the checkpoint, a man who once worked with my father at the sun farms, would shake his head and say, *Go home, Karen.*

It was the guards who fascinated me. They weren't real soldiers, just men who played the part for a few weeks a year—accountants, salesmen, high school coaches—overweight, milk-smelling men with ham-slice complexions who turned to puddles in the summer sun. They rotated the guards so often that in a few months it became impossible to tell them apart. Every now and then somebody would stray too close to the fence and they'd yell at them to get back, and once a couple of them were disciplined for stealing jewelry from one of the detainees' foot lockers. But for the most part they did nothing. They seemed to take a perverse kind of comfort in their laziness, as though when the history of this place was written, their passiveness would shelter them from judgment. They sat in their guard towers and officers' quarters and counted down the hours, same as the rest of us.

I think that's why they missed it, the night my brother crawled out the window and through a tear in the fence and out into the wildland. The last night I saw him.

The driver dropped Khadija off again at nine the following morning, and this time the director was waiting for her in the lobby. He ushered her to his office.

"There are complications," he said.

Khadija did not reply.

The director sighed. "When your brother . . . when he left the facility prematurely, his file was transferred from Civilian Protection Services to Internal Security. And, well, files in the criminal stream aren't subject to the same sunshine provisions as regular archival—"

"For God's sake," Khadija interrupted. "Do you have his things or not?"

"Yes," the director said. "But they're not going to be made public next Sunday, or next year, or maybe ever. I'm sorry, Dr. Singh, I just can't help you."

Khadija breathed in slowly, held the air in her lungs for a moment, let it go in a long cleansing exhale. She took in the room. It was a bureaucrat's office, its blandness intentional and methodical. Framed photos of the president and the secretary of heritage hung on the back wall. Beneath them a half-open window looked out at the center's small outdoor space, a parkette lined with plastic grass, every blade identical in color and dimension. A handful of tourists sat on benches, basking in the sun.

"Tell me, where are you from?" Khadija asked the director.

"I beg your pardon?" the director answered.

"Where are you from?" Khadija repeated. "Where do you come from?"

"Billings," the director said, uncertain.

"No, I mean where are you really from?" Khadija pressed. "Where are your parents from?"

"Also Billings."

"And their parents?"

"I . . . I suppose they settled in Wyoming somewhere. They came from Norway. I don't see how this is relevant, Dr. Singh."

"It isn't," Khadija replied. "For you it isn't. But for every single person who ended up here, it was. They were made to carry every last ancestor. They carried it in the color of their skin and the flaws in their accents and in their foreign-sounding names and their strange and dangerous religions, and you have no idea—*you have no idea*—how heavy a weight that is."

Khadija slammed her hand on the desk. The director jumped in his seat.

"In a room in this ugly little tourist attraction you've built, there's a box with my brother's wallet and his clothes and a couple of old baseball cards his grandfather gave him. These things belonged to him and now they belong to me. Now, I need you to grow a spine and give me what belongs to me. And then I can leave this place, and as soon as I leave this place you can go back to being a good little soldier."

"There's no reason to get personal, Dr. Singh," the director said.

Khadija laughed. "God, what I wouldn't give to be so oblivious. It must feel like floating."

The director got up from his seat. He pointed out the window, waved his hand as though showcasing a parcel of land or a pleasing vista.

"Is this not enough for you?" he asked. "They could have just torn it down, you know. They could have bulldozed all of it and not put up a single sign and people would have forgotten it ever existed. It was only temporary, after all, just a couple years. Nobody was mistreated, nobody was tortured, nobody was executed. In fact— and I think you know this, deep down—this place saved lives."

"This place killed my brother."

"This place did not kill your brother," the director said, shouting now, a few of the tourists outside turning to listen through the open window. "Leaving this place killed your brother. He was safe here. You were all safe here."

"So it's his fault, then?" Khadija said. "You're saying he should have stayed here in this prison? You're saying he should have allowed himself to be the monster his country made him out to be?"

"I'm saying he should have known his place."

A silence filled the room. The fire went out from behind the director's eyes. He sat back down.

"I'm sorry," he said. "I didn't mean that."

"Don't apologize," Khadija replied. "That's the only honest thing you've said."

They told us he'd made it all the way to someplace called White Bird, out in western Idaho. They never said how he got there. They never said a lot of things, only that at the end he was hiking through private land and someone—they used the word *homeowner*—mistook him for a wolf. They were careful how they said it, careful to stress that what had happened was inherently tied to the most inviolable thing in the whole of this country's history, the self-evident commandment without which they were honestly, religiously certain the whole of civilization would fall apart: that a free man, threatened, is allowed to stand his ground.

They said they'd already buried him, in a cemetery a couple of miles from where he was shot. I asked if we could see him and the commander said normally no but he'd see what he could do, and then he stood there looking at me, waiting on gratitude. When I showed none he turned a shade colder, the way people do when they're used to being praised for doing anything north of nothing. *None of you believed us when we told you this was for your own protection,* he said.

That night I went to see Yassir the Jordanian. He was in the mess hall, listening to the news on an old windup radio. That week the big foreign investors had decided to call in their loans, the ones with which Washington had tried to pay for all the damage from the six big hurricanes the two summers prior. The stock market was in free fall, the bank branches closed and barricaded.

Now they'll let us go, Yassir said.

I asked him to walk me through the conversion rites. He said it was easy, everything in Islam is easy—only a matter of a single declaration, sincerely made.

He said rebirth is a matter of identity as well as faith. He helped me pick a new name for myself, and from the ones he listed off the top of his head I picked the one that sounded most foreign: the wife of the prophet. But when he started suggesting surnames, I told him I'd never give mine up.

But what is the point of embracing the religion, he asked, *if you're not willing to commit yourself completely? Don't you want to become your true self as fully as you can?*

No, I said. *I want to become the thing they hate.*

Two days later, in the early-morning darkness, the guards opened the gate. They set us free without explanation, without instruction, without even looking at us. Just as on the day we arrived here, we had no time to take anything; we walked out armed only with nightgowns, sandals, the blankets they didn't want back.

By the side of the road we saw this strange white sea of people who wanted to hug us and people who wanted to spit on us and people who offered to give us rides to the border. We huddled on the backs of trucks and let ourselves be taken anywhere else. And deep against the bone, underneath the fear and confusion and cold bottomless rage, it felt good. We would shed this country, go anywhere else, become citizens of negative space, and in this way we were finally free.

The box contained an empty wallet, nothing else. She had expected clothes and keepsakes, but these, the director admitted, had almost certainly been lost or stolen. He said this was just what happens in these kinds of situations, but she was not upset. All that mattered was that nothing that belonged to her brother remained in this place.

"So, you staying until the anniversary next week?" the driver asked as they drove back into town.

"No," Khadija said. "I'm leaving tomorrow night."

"You get what you came for?"

"Yes."

"That's good, that's good. You know, sometimes people come here and they don't feel what they expected to feel. One time, a few years back, I was driving this old man named Khalid, and—"

"Do they still have liquor stores in this town?" Khadija said.

"Every other corner," the driver replied.

"Take me to one."

He drove her to a store downtown, barricaded behind bars in a lot once occupied by a credit-union branch. She gave him a five-hundred-dollar bill and sent him in. He emerged a few minutes later with two large bottles of some cheap malt liquor called End Times. They sat on the concrete barrier by the side of the road and drank under the noonday sun.

"This tastes awful," Khadija said.

The driver shrugged. "I thought you people didn't drink," he said.

"I bet you think a lot of things."

When they finished their beers, the driver went back inside and bought two more. They watched the slow trickle of traffic, the cars driving themselves. Occasionally the vehicles slowed and swerved to pass one of the antique trucks and sedans that had started to become obsolete in the middle of the previous century but could still be seen in towns like this because progress is a cannibal and here there had never been much worth eating. Overhead, a billboard cycled through ads for silencers and sex drugs and Europe.

"Does it feel different," the driver asked, "all these years later?"

"No," Khadija replied. "It feels exactly the same."

"You think the midterms will change anything? My son says now that the Social Democrats picked up a couple more seats in the House, they can try to reinstate the healthcare act, maybe cut a deal on tax reform."

Khadija broke into laughter.

"Tax reform, Jesus Christ," she said. She set her beer on the ground.

"You know what this country is?" she said. "This country is a man trying to describe a burning building without using the word *fire*."

She stood up and walked to the car. She motioned for the driver to pop the trunk. She took her brother's wallet out of the box in which it had been filed away for a half century, and she threw the box out on the street.

"I have one more place I need to go," she said.

"All right," the driver replied.

"It's a long drive, west into Idaho."

"That's fine," the driver said. "What you got waiting for you all the way out there?"

Khadija Singh tucked her brother's wallet into her breast pocket and got into the car.

"A burial," she said.

OMAR EL AKKAD was born in Cairo, Egypt, and grew up in Doha, Qatar, until he moved to Canada with his family. He is an award-winning journalist and author who has traveled around the world to cover many of the most important news stories of the last decade. His reporting includes dispatches from the NATO-led war in Afghanistan, the military trials at Guantánamo Bay, the Arab Spring revolution in Egypt, and the Black Lives Matter movement in Ferguson, Missouri. He is a recipient of Canada's National Newspaper Award for investigative reporting and the Edward Goff Penny Memorial Prize for Young Canadian Journalists, as well as three National Magazine Award honorable mentions. He lives in Portland, Oregon. His first novel, *American War*, was a *New York Times* notable book and was named one of the best books of the year by *The Washington Post*, NPR, and *Esquire*.

WHAT MAYA FOUND THERE

DANIEL JOSÉ OLDER

Maya Lucia Aviles stepped out into the welcome area (never mind the ever-deepening irony of the name) and released a weary, relieved grin. There was Tristan, the last remaining welcomer in a vast, empty lobby. He stood when he saw her, unfolding that long, dangly body and raising a single mittened hand. Some small, fugly birds flitted through the upper reaches of the airport; besides that, the place was perfectly still, perfectly quiet.

"Dr. Thomas," Maya said.

Tristan smiled finally and nodded. "Dr. Aviles."

An old joke, from the final semester at Columbia: They'd agreed to act like they already had those fancy letters after their name, caution be damned, and started calling each other Doctor. Everyone else was horrified.

For a few seconds they just stood there, neither sure how to bridge the gap of more than a decade. The fugly birds fluttered and fussed. Somewhere far away, an announcement burbled out over the loudspeakers. Then Maya shook her head and stepped in for the hug she knew would come. Tristan probably smiled as he laid his head on top of hers; he squeezed her close but not too tight. He always held her like she would maybe shatter at any moment; it was one of the ways she knew she'd never sleep with him.

"Flight delay?"

She pulled halfway out the hug, shot him a sharp glance. He wasn't that obtuse. Yes, it was snowing still—wild droves of it whipped through the night sky outside the tall windows—but he would've seen all the other passengers stream past hours ago. He knew her getting through at all was a long shot. The endless persistent impossible questions cycled through Maya's mind, the ferocious banality of that back room they'd dragged her to, the bulletin board she'd memorized out of sheer boredom, the slow-ticking clock, the same damn questions once again, the final, grudging sigh as they released her back into the world. But these things weren't to be spoken of or complained about out loud, not in public, not here, not now.

She shook her head. "Something like that."

Tristan had made an awkward, kamikaze pass at her the night before graduation, damn near shattering their easygoing friendship, then he'd sworn over and over it was fine, it was cool, they could just go on being whatever they were. Maya had shrugged, but they both knew he was lying.

"Still up for hitting the town?" A shy offering as he squeezed her once more then released her from the hug.

The humiliation of the past couple hours and the fear about all that was to come pulsed inside Maya's throat, threatened to rise and spill out. She swallowed them. This time, she would finally make things right. But she had to be patient.

"I could definitely use a drink."

.   .   .

The snow kept falling. It coated the sloping pools of darkness along the highway and danced delicate pirouettes beneath each orange light along the RFK Bridge, fading off into the night.

Maya had heard whispers, seen offhand references in anonymous posts on her feed, pieced together the tattered hints that were all anyone could offer about what was really going on in the States these days, and they all added up to the same thing: The place was a ghost town.

That vital pulse of the streets—the same one that used to keep her up at night in grad school—it was gone, an echo at best. She had tried to imagine the emptiness over and over, never managed it. But here it was before her: the desolation of a New York street devoid of walkers, of movement, of life. All the warm bodies tucked away behind layers of concrete, clacking away beneath the protections of firewalls, whispered prayers, and anonyports—or burying their sorrows in TV dramas. It wasn't just the snow, of course; even in the worst blizzards, someone would find a reason to be out and about, running errands, wandering. Maya herself had never missed an opportunity to roam the wintry streets, nod at her fellow ludicrous adventurers, pick a snowball fight with some kids.

"Here," Tristan told the taxi driver. "This'll be fine." A dark street, snow-covered and no sign of plows. Deserted, and not in the quaint way.

Here? Maya wanted to exclaim, but she kept her mouth shut. The driver grunted something and Tristan paid, and then they were out in the chilly Manhattan night, in the silence of snow and an empty city.

They trudged around a corner, then another. Occasional dim lamps broke the darkness. *Of course,* Maya thought. *No one gets dropped off where they're actually going anymore.* She exhaled a cloud of mist through her scarf, longed for home. *Because everyone could be a watcher. Every move recorded.*

"Want me to carry one of your bags?" Tristan asked, way too

late. Maya did but shook her head. He shrugged. "Anyway, we're almost there."

A surge of terror rose in her. Pure fire, it was fiercer than the simmering fear from earlier. It blazed. Wherever he was leading her, they would be waiting. They would be ready. They'd close in around her with heavy hands and then steel would clamp around her small brown wrists and she'd be hauled off, a bag over her head like they always said happens and driven around for hours suffering more questions, beatings, who knew what else—and then dumped, barely a corpse, on some snowy street corner, unrecognizable, or maybe in the river. Gone. Desaparecida.

She shook the nightmare away, but another arrived in its wake. What of her mission? All the terror that would follow if she failed? Flashes of a grim future ricocheted through her: The world overcome by snarling, clawed monstrosities. Flesh rent by science rendering flesh helpless to defeat science.

Science. The notion had once held such deliciousness for Maya. A goal. And then . . .

"Here," Tristan said, smiling through the snow and pointing at a nondescript door on yet another darkened street. Where were they now? The East Village, Maya suspected, but she couldn't be sure. The snow and vague newness of it all had thrown her off. "Sorry 'bout the long walk. You can't . . . you know."

She nodded, shrugged off his apology. He knocked twice, then a third time a moment later. A double knock answered; he knocked again in response, this time four in a row. Maya memorized the exchange out of habit, because who knew, these days, when one would suddenly need a code to a sanctuary? If, of course . . .

"It's Doc!" a voice called as the door swung open.

"'Tis I!" Tristan declared with an alarming burst of charm. He glanced around the empty street, then motioned Maya in.

It was warm in the dim basement bar; the grins were genuine and the bartender gorgeous and generous when it came to tequila.

Tristan's brief introduction—"known each other since grad school, a genius, really, and a helluva salsa dancer to boot, plus she's with us," spoken with a single raised eyebrow for understanding—was all it took for folks to welcome Maya like a long-lost family member. Stories were traded over blaring pop ballads and shots; cigarettes appeared, were distributed; flicked-open flames illuminated concentrating faces, pursed lips, sad, serious eyes above sudden smiles. Maya kept it simple: her work, her decision to return home and set up labs there. The politics were self-evident to her arc and didn't need to be laid bare to this crowd, and besides . . . besides.

She left out the panic of Executive Order 577, the bureaucratic politispeak that had splashed across her dashboard one sun-soaked morning three weeks ago. All federal bioengineering research projects and guidelines were to be deregulated and placed under the auspices of the president's private security force. Maya's stomach had dropped. For a full minute, she'd simply stared at the screen. A vision, a horror show, slowly unfolded in her mind's eye—the full power of her bioengineering work not simply set loose on the world but left in the hands of these maniacal power-hoarding fiends, for them to weaponize and deploy at their will—and her fingerprints, her research, her *passion*, the work of her life, were all over it. The horror show kept cycling all through the night and into the next day, when she finally returned to her computer, logged in to a protected locksession with her last anonyport gigs, and started looking for plane tickets.

"Married?" Tristan asked, once the group of revelers had simmered and peeled off into couplings.

Maya shook her head. "You?"

"Once," he said, cradling his pint in his mittened hands. He hadn't even taken his jacket off, and he still seemed to huddle into himself as if hiding from some imaginary wind.

"Mm. How's work?"

The edge of Tristan's mouth shivered. Terrible, then. "Fine.

You know . . . the fed labs get you the best access to materials and funding, so . . . I'm about as well placed as a scientist could want to be, really."

"Ah."

"I'm gonna hit the head," Tristan said, standing. "Then we'll take off? You must be knackered."

Knackered. Echoes of Tristan's British father. Maya smiled. "Pretty tired, yeah."

He disappeared through the crowd. Maya's fingers wrapped around the vial in the inside pocket of her jacket. She popped the lid. Grabbed Tristan's half-empty glass and brought it down below the bar, out of sight. Placed the vial to the rim and poured.

"Chilly night," someone said.

Maya looked up, her heart careening wildly against her ear-drums. The bartender—Ruby her name was—with the delicious smile. She lit a cigarette and winked at Maya. It would've been corny from almost anyone else, but all Maya could think about was wrapping herself in those big arms and letting those lips find the back of her neck and trace her spine.

"I'm a long way from home," she said, sliding the empty vial into her pocket again. She raised her empty tequila glass. "Uno más, mi vida."

The bartender let her gaze linger just long enough to make Maya catch her breath. She was either onto her or in some hard-core flirtstare mode. Then she smiled. Maya exhaled, returned the smile. When the bartender turned around for the tequila, Maya put Tristan's pint back.

"¿Vámonos?" Tristan asked, reappearing through the smoky haze. All these years, and his accent hadn't improved. Maya used to tease him about it.

She raised her newly filled glass. "To the republic for which we stand," she said with a wink and a wry smile.

He clinked his glass to hers and put away the last of his beer

with a single swig. Then he clunked it down on the bar and nodded, wiping his lips. "Indeed."

Maya shot a last glance at the bartender, that peaceful brown
face lit by the glare of a cell screen, and then they headed out into
the night.

He was slumped against her shoulder, trudging on lead feet through
the snow by the time they reached the stoop. Old-style gas lanterns,
both dark, glared out of the wall like fallen sentries. Maya leaned
Tristan against the door, fished through his jacket for keys. Her
fingers wrapped around a small plastic piece instead. She pulled it
out.

"Is a TD2900 anonyport encrypter," Tristan slurred. "Only the
betht."

Only the best indeed. But where would he have gotten such a
prized piece of equipment? Government workers certainly weren't
allowed that kind of tech. No one was.

"For you," Tristan said. "Take it."

Maya squinted through the falling snow at him, put the encrypter back and pulled out his keys. "You know what I came for." She
unlocked the door and helped him inside.

"Maya."

Tristan's cozy Lower East Side apartment was maybe the only
thing in the entire U.S. that hadn't changed during the Trump ad-
ministration. In fact, it rather looked like it hadn't changed since
the 1880s, except for a few technological enhancements, of course.
With the push of a button, a fire roared to life. Taxidermied animals
and glowering family members stared emptily from the walls. An
old relic of a bureau held the widescreen TV and cable boxes beneath a mounted antique ceremonial sword. Tristan's cluttered little office space filled a whole corner, facing the curtained window.

And the bookcases! They took up most of the wall space. Maya used to come over just to stare at them, reading idly for hours, her fingers sliding against dusty spines.

"I'm glad some things haven't changed," she muttered, dumping him on the extravagant green recliner in front of the fireplace.

Now. Now she would find the notes—*her* notes. And then, while Tristan slept off his stupor, she'd destroy them. She'd use his laptop to hack into whatever servers she needed to, collect as much data as she could, and then be gone, out into the night and on her damn way.

"Maya," Tristan sighed. "I'm so sorry." His head hung down over his chest, a little drool.

She crouched beside him. "What?"

He coughed, blubbered. "It's no good *now*, you know."

"Tristan, for what? What's going on?"

"Maya Lucia Aviles."

"Tristan, what are you talking about, man?"

"I just . . . I can't . . . You know I tried." His mittened hand suddenly clamped around her wrist, that grip inhumanly tight. "I'm such a bad . . . such a bad . . ."

"Tris, you're hurting me!"

"Look what they've . . . Look!" The grip loosened and then the hand came out of the mitten. A fine layer of brown hair covered it, and the fingers were long and thick and ended in yellowish claw-like nails.

Maya stepped back, her mouth falling open. "You let them—"

Still looking down, Tristan shook his head. "Of course, Maya Lucia Aviles. Of course. Didn't have much of a choice, did I? But you wouldn't understand that, would you? You would never have done a thing like this." He glanced up, his eyes suddenly sharp. "You got away, didn't you? The one that got away."

Maya just stared, her pulse rising to a frantic thrum in her ears.

"But then you had to come back, didn't you? Just had to. Well, now I've done it. They're on their way, you know. I had to call them, of course. Wasn't up to me, I'm afraid."

"Who? Tristan, *who's* on their way?"

His eyes glassed over and his head dropped again as he muttered unintelligibly.

"Tristan, tell me who's coming!" Never mind. It didn't matter who, really. Whoever had done *that* to his hands, presumably. The damn Department of Bioengineering, more than likely. Maya hurried over to the office space, started rustling through his papers.

"Oh, Maya, Maya, Maya," Tristan mumbled. She hurled open file cabinets, rifled through stacks, tore apart binders. "Maya Lucia. Maya Lucia." A wilting melody tinted his voice now, like a broken music box sliding down a staircase. "Maya Lucia Aviles. Dr. Aviles, if you will."

"My notes, Tristan," Maya growled. "Where are my notes?"

"It's too late, you know." On the small table by the door, Tristan's phone let out a mechanical burp. He tried to stand, collapsed with a giggle, then started sobbing. Maya was already across the room, clicking the phone to life.

All clear for go? the text read.

No, Maya typed, willing her fingers to stop shaking. *Stand by.*

"Numbers," Tristan said.

She spun around. He still sat slumped over, his mouth hanging open. "Huh?"

"Numbers. But it's no good now. No good." He sobbed once, then shook his head. "But Numbers."

"Which numbers?"

"Not which. Just Numbers. The book. I kept them, you know. Kept them from everyone. Did exactly what you asked me to, Maya Lucia. As always. As always."

She dashed to the towering bookshelf, started gleaning titles.

"Ironic, in a way. It's because of what you said: *Numbers don't lie, just the people that wield them.* And we argued, of course, for days, but you were right. You were always right. So that's where I stashed them."

It had been another petty debate that Maya took too seriously and let blossom into a full-blown argument. She couldn't even remember what it was over, and she rolled her eyes at her younger self as she scanned book spines.

The Holy Bible! Maya yanked it from the shelf as Tristan muttered, "Deuteronomy wouldn't have made sense." The book opened directly to the first page of the Book of Numbers, where a sheaf of notebook pages covered in Maya's handwriting was nestled.

Tristan's phone chirped again and then a heavy knocking came at the door.

"Shit," Maya whispered. She shoved the notes into her jacket pocket.

"Oh, bother," Tristan said.

Maya scanned the wall, the bear and bison heads, the desolate landscape painting and sullen family portraits. The antique sword. The knocking came again, frantic now. "Dr. Thomas?" someone yelled. "Open up." A silhouette loomed in the blurred glass of the window, someone—some*thing*, really—way too tall, with long curled horns on top of its head. "Open up right now, Dr. Thomas."

Maya grabbed the sword. The thing on the other side of the door slammed its full weight against it. The sword came out of its metal sheath with an elegant whisper; it gleamed in the firelight. A fancy metal handguard curled in serpentine spirals around its hilt.

"Garrr!" the thing on the other side of the door bellowed. Maya broke into a run toward it, raised the sword. The door exploded forward and smashed into the mantelpiece, shattering some porcelain vases. Something huge and hairy and horned rushed in and Maya met it with a single downward slash, cleaving a bright red canyon across its chest. The thing stopped mid-charge, collapsed to its knees, gasping. Maya swung again, opening its throat. She stepped back as a flood of bright blood gushed out. She dropped the sword. Picked it up again, barely breathing. Then breathing way too fast. The sword was sticky with beast blood. The creature pitched forward and sighed, twitching once, then again, then lay still.

They'd kept the human face. The head was turned slightly, revealing a tormented scowl, small, squinched-up eyes. She shook her head, breath slowly returning to normal. She'd warned them. She'd petitioned and pleaded and railed. And then, when there was nothing else left to do, she'd burned everything and left. Almost everything. She patted the jacket pocket.

"Backyard," Tristan said, not looking up. "More are on the way." Of course—that tiny concrete atrium had a window that led to another building. Maya would come out on the next block over. "I've failed you, I'm afraid. Failed everyone, really." She was already across the room and fumbling with the door locks. The last thing Maya heard from inside the apartment was the tinkling melody of Tristan's cellphone, and then she was out into the winter night, and gone.

"We never trusted him," Ruby said, adjusting her position in the bed and lighting another cigarette.

Maya raised her eyebrows, still panting. An old-fashioned gas lamp on the bedside table sent a hazy glow toward the ceiling. The moans and caresses from a few minutes ago lingered, and Maya wanted to just lie there, let those echoes cover her for a few more moments. "But?"

"But nothing. Suspicions are only that until proven otherwise. There are too few of us to be taking each other out on pure suspicion."

"You knew about the—" She made a clawlike gesture.

Ruby scowled, nodded. "Figured it'd prod him to do better for others. Instead . . ."

"I think he genuinely wanted to." Maya scooched herself up in the bed, took the cigarette Ruby held out to her, and dragged on it. "He kept my notes secret from them for all those years. And those notes . . ."

Ruby pursed her lips, a silent question.

"Let's just say, whatever they've got going on now, what I discovered would quadruple the power of it. Make a murder into a massacre."

"And now?"

Maya smiled. The night seemed to tremble with the weight of all that had happened, all that was yet to come. "Now the real work begins."

DANIEL JOSÉ OLDER is the *New York Times* bestselling author of the middle-grade historical fantasy series Dactyl Hill Squad, the Bone Street Rumba urban fantasy series, *Star Wars: Last Shot*, *The Book of Lost Saints*, and the young adult series the Shadowshaper Cypher, which won the International Latino Book Award and was shortlisted for the Kirkus Prize in Young Readers' Literature, the Andre Norton Award, the Locus Award, and the Mythopoeic Award, and was included in *Esquire*'s 80 Books Every Person Should Read. You can find his thoughts on writing, read dispatches from his decade-long career as a New York City paramedic, and hear his music at danieljoseolder.net and on Twitter at @djolder.

THE REFERENDUM

LESLEY NNEKA ARIMAH

Six months ago, I didn't know a bullet from a bullet point, but here I am, arguing ammunition with my sister-in-law, who (I suspect) has never really liked me and who (I am certain) is relishing that I am very, very wrong. The thing about Darla is that she'll make her point and then retreat to little agree-to-disagree *hmm*s while you make yours, and if I found those patronizing sounds annoying when she was in the wrong, it's even worse when she's right.

"No," I say, drawing deeper from my well of inaccuracy, "pretty sure these shells are fine to reuse as is."

I'm so wrong the tiny hairs on the back of my neck raise themselves in embarrassment, trying to make an exit, wanting any nape but mine. But since it's too late to switch positions, I'm going for the agree-to-disagree stage where I can at least pretend correctness. But Darla isn't having it.

"You can't reuse dented shells, even if it's 'just a small one,' because a dented shell casing fires all wrong and you'll end up hitting everything but what you're aiming at. Or ruining your weapon. Which is just stupid." *You are just stupid* is what we both know she means, just like we both know I'm wrong.

Darla hadn't known much about guns either, at first, but after the referendum was announced, she began studying them with an intensity that unnerved me. By then, it had already been illegal for almost a year for any black person outside of the military or law enforcement to own a gun, so we—my husband, Marcus; myself; Darla and her husband, Russell; a handful of friends—had trouble finding someone in Minneapolis who'd teach us under the table. But Marcus heard through the grapevine (from whom he would never say) that there was a coalition of black resistance fighters called the Black Resistance, which I thought was a really uninspired name and to which Marcus posited that maybe they had better things to worry about. Those "better things" were a handful of increasingly draconian laws that had been defeated in the Senate by less and less of a margin, until some of them passed and then the kicker was proposed: a referendum to repeal the thirteenth amendment and reinstitute slavery. So while the government was distracted with the protests and the outwardly armed black folks putting up fights around the country, we of the Black Resistance secretly amassed food, weapons, and information. We trained in hand-to-hand combat. We learned how to cook game. We snuck those who needed to be snuck across the country. And because of the laws barring us from purchasing munitions, we recycled bullets from shell casings discarded at gun ranges.

I pull the bowl of spent shells into my lap and begin re-sorting them, separating the ones with dents. It is the only concession I am willing to make and, gratefully, Darla doesn't press. We've been sorting these shells for weeks now, and my embarrassment deepens when I realize that someone—probably Darla herself—must have gone through my pile a second time, removing the useless casings

I'd let through. It was the sort of long-suffering thing she'd do with an audience present, all exaggerated, audible sighs while talking about this bougie bitch her brother had married.

The bus pulls up and we both walk to the window left open for us to hear it. We are united in our worry until Adaeze disembarks. I'll give Darla this: She may not like me, but my daughter has claimed some land on her heart. Barren wasteland, upon which nothing can bloom, but still. And her children have claimed some of mine, though I haven't seen Nyah and Jaden since Darla sent them to stay with their grandmother.

Adaeze squeals when Darla pops out onto the sidewalk, and they run at each other like they've been at sea and separated for months and not at all like they did this yesterday or the day before. I can suspend my animosity watching them, listening to their chatter. When she sees me, Adaeze squirms out of Darla's embrace to hug me about the waist and I return the hug until she's squealing again, giggling and asking me to let go, to which I reply, "Never."

Every day she gets off that bus is a day the government hasn't taken her, claiming some false negligence. Many an activist has been stifled this way, less likely to fight if they thought behaving would get them their children back. Darla and her husband had seen it coming and pulled their kids out of school the day the referendum was first debated on the Senate floor. Darla homeschooled them for most of the school year, but when the census-verification agents came around to confirm the number in their household, she sent the children to her mother, a council member in Atlanta, the only city left where black people could legally hold office.

If I miss them, I cannot imagine how Darla feels, so I let her rescue Adaeze from my grip. I sneak into the kitchen to make sure our afternoon task is out of sight. At four, Adaeze is too young to keep secrets, and I shake away a nightmare scenario in which she inadvertently betrays us. Marcus and I agree that pulling her out of preschool now will raise too many flags. We trusted in the goodness of people too long.

I cut up some fruit as Darla and Adaeze make their way to the kitchen, my daughter doing all of the talking and Darla letting her. I used to worry about having children, because I didn't think I'd have anything to say to them, but it turns out you don't have to say much of anything. I wish silly worries like that still mattered.

"Adaeze," I say in warning when she tries to reach for an apple slice, "kwo aka gi."

She pouts but goes to the sink, stepping on the short stool that helps her reach. I've been doing little things like this the last few months, making her as self-sufficient as I can while preserving her innocence.

"Kwo aka gi ofuma," I add when she barely wets the tip of her fingers.

Darla releases a pointed sigh. She didn't mind when I taught Nyah and Jaden Igbo words, but if I took a phone call from my mother while we sorted and cleaned shells, I could feel a certain tightness coming off her in waves. Worse yet was the time I briefly switched to Igbo in front of her when talking to a visiting cousin, and Darla hadn't believed me that it was a gesture of habit, that we weren't talking about—or trying to exclude—her. That was before the whole "bougie bitch" thing and it wasn't even a cousin I liked, so I made my deepest apologies and everything had seemed good.

"Imelu ofuma. Kuwalu onwe gi aka."

Now I am, in fact, just being a bitch, as I would have congratulated Adaeze in English had we been alone. And from Darla's agree-to-disagree *hmm*, she knows it too. Our Adaeze-induced truces are getting shorter and shorter.

Darla lingers until five o'clock, when Russell will be home. It's dangerous in these times for a black woman to make a noticeable routine of being alone. She smooches goodbyes on Adaeze and again my animosity lifts, but we depart with tight little smiles. I divide my attention between my daughter and my phone and can only fully relax when I get Darla's text: *I'm home. Russell is here. Text me when Marcus gets in.*

And I do.

When the State Custody Law was first proposed, most people assumed it was a satirical "modest proposal" of sorts. How else to read the proposition that designated all black citizens within U.S. borders as wards of the state regardless of age or financial status? The outline of the fake law had been so detailed as to be laughable, drawing on the 2020 census data and statistics on black unemployment, truancy, and homelessness, at record highs after the Civil Rights Act was overturned mid-2019, releasing Americans from basic decency. The proposal stated that until these issues were resolved, the government should step in. *Wasn't that what you people wanted,* the president tweeted later, *to have the government do everything for you?*

That's when we figured out the revolting proposal was real, and the resulting outrage was swift and vicious, with almost universal condemnation. Almost. A *Times* op-ed began the turning of the tide. Cloaked in concern, the columnist made his argument for this necessary, temporary step: *If it doesn't work, what's the harm, everything can go back to normal.* And now it was a referendum on a ballot, a rotten fruit in the marketplace of ideas.

I was one of the skeptics and I still am. My rage is tempered by the knowledge that though the law is being voted on, there's no way this actually passes.

"That's what they said about the Civil Rights Act being overturned. And the gun-ownership laws."

Marcus is caressing my stomach in sleepy circles. It's a debate we've had enough times that it's lost any heat. My nose is in his armpit and it's a blend of gaminess and the failing deodorant that allowed it. It is so familiar a scent in a world that has turned so unfamiliar, so quickly, that I start to cry.

"Hey, hey. None of that."

For a while it's just my sobs and the friction of his hands, now soothing my back. It seems like all we do in this bed is take turns crying.

"What about Nathaniel?" Marcus poses.

A game we play often, coming up with names for our hypothetical son. It means we believe in a future we can bring another child into. It also means: *Enough with the crying, else I break too.*

"Only if you promise to never call him Nate."

"That's half the fun of the name. Yours?"

I try to lighten the mood.

"Okechukwukereokeonyekozuru."

Marcus laughs loud, then quieter, not to wake Adaeze.

"I promise to never call him Nate," he says, and we are both laughing now and it feels so good to not be crying that I want to cry.

I wish my mother could see us, to understand that there's no one else I can survive this life with. To understand why I chose him over a country. She still calls, but the tariffs make each conversation a prohibitively expensive one. She'd been living in Dallas with my youngest brother when dual citizenship was outlawed and everyone was forced to choose which nation to pledge their full allegiance to. It was 2021, a year before the State Custody Law proposal, but after the Civil Rights Act was overturned, and things were getting dire enough that a good number of Nigerians picked their green passport, even with all the news trickling through the media embargo about what was happening in Lagos. My mother had been among them and urged all of her children to follow suit. All my siblings did but me.

"Chinedu, biko. *Please.*" And her voice was so deep with tears and terror, I wanted to hang up the phone.

Within three months, the president declared that all those who'd chosen foreign passports proved how unpatriotic and un-committed to America they were and would—all three million of them—be deported.

"Come with us," my mother had pleaded. "Leave that man, and bring your child. Let them not kill my daughter."

It was hard to take her histrionics at face value, but I felt real fear hearing *leave that man* from my mother, a woman who doesn't *believe in divorce*, like divorce was a conspiracy theory of which she remained skeptical. Her advice to me before my wedding was to submit to Marcus in all things. When I chose to stay, she cried so hard I put the phone down, unable to bear the sound in my ear.

"Mommy, this." Adaeze points to the blue box of macaroni, star-tling me from my phone. The pasta aisle is supposed to be a no-go zone since I'd weaned Adaeze from said macaroni, and by the look in my angel's eye she (1) remembered how delicious it was and (2) would throw herself into a reckless tantrum if denied. I slip a box into the cart. Adaeze resumes singing into a carrot she's appropri-ated as a microphone. Disaster averted.

The article I return to predicts that the referendum is projected at a 50/50 split. It needs a 55/45 majority to pass. "Encouraging," the writer said of this, that even in these climes, it would likely fail. I text Marcus: *See, it's going to fail.*

I spot the youngish-looking white man just before I run into him with the cart, and I give an exaggerated "Phew! That was close!" and smile my safe-black-person smile and excuse myself to pass. Then excuse myself again when he doesn't hear me and it takes a third time—with Adaeze chiming in—before I realize it's on purpose. My body tingles with restraint as I contemplate shov-ing his cart aside. But the scene it would cause. The chance he would claim assault and be believed. It used to be a rumor one would hear, something you heard about a friend of a friend of a friend, until it happened to someone I knew, arrested when a white mom at the daycare escalated a silly fight between two kids to a police matter. I swallow the insult like many before, another stone churning in my stomach, and ease out of the aisle the way I came. Adaeze is still saying, "Excuse me!" in that singsongy way of hers, and I fight a sudden wave of debilitating rage. I want to hurl every can at his smug head. I want to take everything that makes him feel safe and burn it to ash.

My phone dings and it's Marcus responding to the article: *Likely isn't good enough.*

When I pull up to the house, Darla's car is already in the driveway. She'll be in the laundry, scooping casings from the barrel we'd snuck in when members of the Black Resistance (I still think we should rebrand this) pretended to deliver furniture. Our friendly white neighbors, Kathryn and Doug, had offered to help, and they were nice enough that they probably would have kept it quiet, but nowadays you could never be sure. Marcus didn't like them, felt like they talked to us the way a kid ate vegetables, something they did because they felt they had to. I take a cranky Adaeze into the house, and she brightens at the prospect of Darla but doesn't come fully awake until I set her in front of cartoons in the living room.

I turn on the smaller unit in the kitchen, one Marcus and I had argued over but that I'm now grateful for.

"Turn that off. Please," Darla says as she emerges from the laundry. She holds a bowl of shells under her nose and sniffs deeply. "I like the smell," she says to the raised brow I give her, and if it was a year ago, when things were still okay between us, I'd have said something like, *Okay, weirdo,* and it would just have been something I said, not the start of another fight. Because she actually said *please,* I turn off the news.

"Not *off* off, just to something else. I don't know how you and Marcus can stand watching and reading all that shit. It'll eat your soul from the inside. Someone will call if there's something we need to know."

"I want to keep an eye on things, just in case."

"Hmm," Darla says, darla-ly.

I turn the TV back on, scanning the guide until I find something safe. It takes a line or two from the opening credits of the sitcom before Darla and I begin to whisper the words under our breath, then get louder—"I got in one little fight and my mom got scared and said, 'You're moving with your auntie and uncle in Bel-Air!'"—until we finish at the top of our lungs, cackling when Adaeze rushes in, confused but happy we're happy. She rushes back to her cartoons when we don't prove quite as interesting.

"Where did he end up moving to, Morocco? Or was it Monaco?"

Either way, he—and all monied celebrities—were lucky, and able to afford the exorbitant twenty-thousand-dollar fine charged for non-essential international travel before even that was banned altogether. We run through what we know of the black celebrities who hadn't left the country, either by choice to stand and fight or because they never thought it would get this bad or because their money was funny. And for a moment it's like old times and we are the sisters we never had.

Of a certain TV housewife, Darla says, "Please, she's only famous in America—you'd have to drag her onto a plane screaming and kicking off the fake Loubs."

And I'm cracking up, until I remember that with many of the deported three million, they'd done just that, hauling women by their hair, handcuffing children to plane seats and the like. Darla sees on my face when I stop finding it funny, and she probably stops finding it funny too when she remembers, but we're too stubborn

to give each other an inch and I sit there with an insufferable mar-
tyr silence while she forces dry, obnoxious chuckles.

"My, y'all are having fun in here."

I bumble in a panic, while Darla calmly lays a kitchen towel
over our work before Kathryn can get a good look. "I tried the front,
but you mustn't have heard me," she says through the screen, then
turns toward Darla. "Hi, I'm Kathryn."

She comes fully through the door and holds out her hand to
Darla, who just looks at it. Kathryn's smile tightens at the edges and
she spins toward me.

"It just got so loud for a second there and my folks are over and,
well, you know how they are." She rolls her eyes theatrically.
"Daddy wanted to call the cops, but I said that wasn't necessary."

"Of course it isn't," I say. "We'll be sure to keep it down. This
is—"

"Nobody," Darla interrupts. Kathryn keeps her eyes on me.

"Great, I'll let you know when they leave. Later, then." She
turns to say goodbye to Darla, then thinks better of it. We listen to
her fading steps.

"Don't go around saying my name to people I don't want to
know my name. And why does that white woman feel comfortable
just walking into your house?"

Stones churn in my stomach.

"Kathryn is okay."

"Tell me this. If she's 'okay,' then why'd you panic when she
showed up?"

"She's not like that."

"Hmm."

And it's the last goddamn *hmm* I can take.

"What the fuck is your problem, Darla? What did I ever do to
you?" I circle the kitchen closing windows, because I plan to get
loud.

Darla scoops up the bowl of shells and I hear the metallic cascade as they rejoin their friends in the barrel.

When she's back in my face, she whisper-shouts, "My kids are halfway across the country."

And I whisper-shout in return, "Okay, but I didn't take them away from you. So why the fuck are you mad at *me*?" And I want to take it back right away because it's cruel, but it's also true and so I stand my ground.

"I sent them away to save them. And you, you could have left with her"—she points to the living room—"at any time. You could have escaped all this."

"But I didn't!"

"Are you kidding me? How do you not get it?"

My stubborn silence.

Darla continues.

"Where is your mother? Right now, where is she? Your grandmother, where is she?"

I think of Nana in her little village house, her precious chickens pacing the yard like sentries. No electricity, no running water, so she pays a boy to fill a large drum every week, which she rations, pouring boiling water back into the drum to keep the tepid supply free of worms. I had loved the place as a child and hated it as a teenager, feeling deep embarrassment at the poor African cliché of it all. At another time, it would have pained me to imagine my mother, who delighted in collecting pretty perfume bottles she never sprayed, reduced to living that life, but now—with the prospect of enslavement hanging over our collective heads—I picture my grandmother's contented stance as she watches her precious chickens peck at the ground and I think how happy she must be to have her daughter and grandchildren under her roof. But I won't give an inch.

"I didn't do this; you don't have to be angry at me."

"I'm not angry at you—" At my incredulous look: "Okay, I'm a *little* angry at you. Okay, a lot. *You could have left.*"

"I chose to stay." The words coated in a layer of sacrifice, the smug surety that I made the right choice in the name of lov—

"You had a *choice!*" This Darla yells at full volume, and some of my martyrdom crumbles under the weight of it. "I'm not saying it's your fault; I'm just saying you had a choice and you don't know what it's like to not have one. It's not fair, that's all."

My phone beeps and I grab at it to save me. It's a text in code. We each avoid the other's teary eyes.

"We're on."

The ride is a quiet one with an exhausted Adaeze passed out in the backseat. We turn off our phones even before we leave the house, too untrusting to simply turn off the location services. Darla calls out the decoded directions from her notepad and doesn't say much else. She navigates us through increasingly remote roads until we're on a dirt path. She settles a handgun—loaded with the inevitable product of our many hostile afternoons—onto her lap. We wait.

He is late, but he is alone, which hadn't been the case with the last one. He is also the right age, his fourteen-year-old baby face just starting to harden in the wake of puberty. He seems to know the drill, no phone or electronics on, but he passes Darla money, which she refuses, then tries to give it to me. He must not yet know how it works and I wonder, but cannot ask, how long ago his parents had been disappeared. I could imagine him as a son of pastors, high enough in the church hierarchy to be designated an "influential black individual" and detained for questioning. The Justice Department is looking for him now, hoping to leverage him to will his family's compliance.

I see the way Darla stares at him and I know she sees her son, Jaden, in his face. It's always like that with the boys. I see a nice kid, but if I let myself, there is Nathaniel. Okechukwukereokeonyekozuru. Nate. There is my son waiting for us to fix the world.

When the boy spots Adaeze sprawled like a sultan in her sleep, he grins, and I like him all the more for it. He grins at me, at Darla, and we can't help returning his delight, and we are a minivan full of grinning fools driving to the next checkpoint.

LESLEY NNEKA ARIMAH was born in the United Kingdom and grew up in Nigeria and wherever else her father was stationed for work. Her work has appeared in *The New Yorker*, *Harper's*, *Granta*, and has received the African Commonwealth Short Story Prize and an O. Henry Prize. She was selected for the National Book Foundation's 5 Under 35, and her debut collection, *What It Means When a Man Falls from the Sky*, won the 2017 Kirkus Prize and the 2017 New York Public Library Young Lions Fiction Award. She lives in Minneapolis and is working on a novel about you.

CALENDAR GIRLS

JUSTINA IRELAND

Alyssa posted up on her corner and watched the late-afternoon foot traffic with feigned disinterest. Friday was her busiest day. Saturday was decent, no doubt, but Friday was lit. Folks were still full of hope that they could somehow fix their busted-ass week by getting lucky. TGIF and all that shit. By Saturday most folks had a hangover and were broke. Unless you wanted a bunch of ankle biters, smashing cakes cost a lot of money. So Friday, that was Alyssa's best day.

Everyone liked to be prepared for the weekend.

Whether it was textiles, monthlies, or squish, Alyssa had it. She'd owned this corner since the Dvorah Sisters went down a couple of months back, and she'd been making bank. People in the Financial District liked to fuck, but not a single one of them wanted a baby.

Alyssa's greatest asset was that she was pretty. That made her approachable, and it had kept her business safe and booming even though she was slight and young. She wasn't like the Sisters, who'd successfully held on to their turf through brute force. Alyssa knew to give the cops their cut and to dress nicely enough that no one suspected she was anything other than some schoolgirl waiting for the uptown bus. Her hair was neat, her skin was moisturized, she smiled at strangers, and she always helped the older women on and off the bus.

A man in a pricey suit wearing a fedora paused to tie his shoe near Alyssa, dropping a hundred-dollar bill as he did so. "Textiles?" he muttered, his eyes skidding left and right.

Alyssa grinned and languidly bent over to pick up the money, the beads on the ends of her cornrows clacking together as she did so. These hedge-fund bros had no fucking chill.

"My man," she said, picking up the cash and depositing the condoms in the man's waiting palm in a single smooth move. "Don't use them all in one place."

The man gave her a single panicked glance before he scurried off. When the siren whooped, Alyssa knew why he'd been so nervous.

She'd been set up.

"Hands up!" the cops said, vaulting out of the car and drawing down on her, like she was one of those Christian terrorist cells instead of a slight teenage Black girl wearing a high school uniform.

"What's going on, Officer?" Alyssa asked, widening her eyes and holding up her hands. She'd already dropped her bag and kicked it over toward the wizened old woman on a nearby bus bench. It was only possession if they caught you holding.

She recognized the officer who grabbed her hands, spinning her around as he cuffed her. "Damn, Findley, if you wanted a bigger cut you could've just said so."

"It's out of my hands, Lyss. I'm sorry," he said, running his hands over her body in a way that was perfunctory, not perverted. She appreciated the small mercy. This wasn't her first arrest, but at least this one wouldn't leave her feeling like garbage.

He plucked her cellphone out of her sweatshirt and pocketed it, along with a couple of packs of monthlies and a handful of shiny foil textile packets.

And then she was hustled to the police car, no rights read, no identi-chip scanned. The other officer just watched her through narrow eyes as Findley put her in the back of the car. "Damned harpies," he spat.

As the car pulled away, a small Asian girl ran up to grab Alyssa's bag, taking up the spot that she had just vacated.

Alyssa couldn't help but tilt her head back and laugh.

They didn't go to the city jail or even county. Alyssa had been to both of them, and she knew what to expect. They'd book her and send her to the juvenile wing. There was a reason younger girls like her ran the corners. By the time she was an adult, her rap sheet would be expunged and she'd be taken off the streets, sent to work somewhere else for someone else, a job that looked legit, a life that was mostly hers. That was the promise, and so far the Matriarchs had kept every single one.

But now the plan was in flux. They didn't head to the county lockup; instead, they drove to the highway. And kept driving. Everything had been copacetic when Alyssa thought she knew the script, but once they started down a tree-lined drive in an unfamiliar part of town, she began to fidget.

"Hey, where we headed? Where you taking me?" Alyssa asked.

"Shut up, bitch," said the officer on the passenger side, the one she didn't know. Findley said nothing, and Alyssa couldn't see his face from where she sat behind him. When they'd thrown her into the car, they secured the handcuffs to a loop in the door, and Alyssa leaned as far to the right as she could, trying to get a glimpse of Findley's face. She knew him. She'd babysat his kids, all nine of them, and kept his wife in a ready supply of monthlies. Findley had been red-faced when he'd asked for the contraceptives, confessing that the wife had threatened to go celibate otherwise. He'd seemed less like a killer with a badge and more like a regular guy, a good guy with too many kids trying to get by in this world, like so many folks.

But he was also a cop, which meant nothing good at all.

The police car turned down a small cobblestone road that led to a guard shack. Findley pulled the car up alongside the small building. A huge Black guy with skin the color of a moonless night stepped out, his bald head glinting in the late-afternoon sunlight.

"Yeah," the man said, glancing at Alyssa in the backseat and dismissing her. There was a gun holstered under the man's suit jacket, and she wondered where the hell they were. Who needed a handgun in the middle of the fucking woods? Dude didn't exactly look like he was going after Bambi.

Fear tried to rise up, but she shoved it down. As long as she could play at being chill, everything was cool. She'd been in worse jams.

Maybe.

"Our captain sent us. She's a harpy," the cop in the passenger seat said. "Fucking baby killer."

The man from the gatehouse looked at the car once more before returning to the guard shack. He picked up a phone, a landline, and had a brief conversation before coming back.

"Sit tight a sec. I've got some troopers who are going to run down here to grab her."

"We could take her up," Findley said, a strange tone in his voice. Regret?

That wasn't good.

The other car pulled up, a fancy black town car with tinted windows. Another guy in a suit—this one white, with a head full of brown hair gelled to within an inch of its life—got out.

"You can uncuff her; we'll take it from here," he said. He wore sunglasses, but Alyssa still had the feeling that his eyes were scanning the area for potential threats. It creeped her all the way out. There was no way she wanted to stay here, in these pretty woods full of danger.

But she didn't exactly want to spend any more time with the cops, either.

Findley got out and opened the door, unlocking her cuffs. "I'm sorry," he murmured again. "I really had no choice."

"There's always a choice, even when they tell you there isn't," Alyssa answered, voice equally low. Findley made to hand her the cellphone and contraband, but she only kept her phone, pushing the textiles and monthlies back into his hands.

"Keep them. You're going to need them more than me." She threw back her shoulders and strode to the town car, refusing to show even a smidgen of fear.

Whatever fuckery was about to unfold, she would meet it with swagger.

When Alyssa was eight years old, her mother died in childbirth.

It was completely preventable, the aunties said at the funeral, their voices hushed as they cast sidelong glances at Alyssa. In another time, they said. Maybe in another place. There, Alyssa would have a mother and there might be some sadness at a lost son, but there would be a chance for more kids.

But there was no other time or place. The doctor had told Alyssa's mother that she would die if she tried to carry the child to term. The law ensured that there were few other options, not without a trip to the border and a lot of money to get a Moses to take them across. The Matriarchs might've been able to help earlier on; there were ways to keep from getting pregnant and ways to fix mistakes if you were desperate enough, but Alyssa's mother believed in the law, believed in a country built on freedom and justice. So she did the right thing, the good thing, writing to the state board for permission to end her pregnancy in light of her health and young daughter.

The men in the state capital denied the petition.

Alyssa's mother died three days later, laboring futilely in a city hospital while state senators argued over whether or not to lower the marrying age for girls from fourteen to twelve.

It was the first time Alyssa understood that being a woman was a curse.

They drove for a short while, Alyssa and the dudes with all of their firepower tucked up under expensive suit jackets. A house appeared after a turn, and it was like a terrible revelation. The building sat on sprawling grounds that were impossibly green considering the drought. The entire thing was made of bricks, and Alyssa couldn't help but think of all those people laying each piece, one on top of another, until a monstrosity of architecture had been born. She'd never seen a house so big, hadn't even considered that such a thing could exist.

At this point she was certain of two things:

1. Someone with money or power or both had paid the cops to snatch her from her corner, and
2. She was fucked in the worst kind of way.

The suited security guys gestured for her to walk up the stairs to the front door, which opened as if by magic. An Asian man wearing a gleaming white polo shirt and pressed khakis opened the door with a smile.

"Ms. Pearson, so glad to see you looking well. I'm Brian, Senator Gaines's personal assistant. Please, come in." Alyssa schooled her face to blankness, refusing to let the man see how intimidated she felt.

She was maybe mostly successful.

He stood back from the door to allow Alyssa to enter. She stepped forward, all of her bravado draining away. The foyer was opulent, marble and dark woods and paintings conspiring to make her feel insignificant. She had the momentary urge to take her shoes off or apologize for her presence, before she managed to take a deep breath. She thought of her mother, the same way she always did whenever she felt scared or small. It made her feel strong.

Angry.

"How do you know who I am?" Alyssa asked. She kept her voice neutral, picking her words carefully, the same way she did when speaking to a teacher. This was uncharted territory.

"I'll let the senator explain that to you," he said, leading Alyssa through the house and to a sitting room not far from the foyer. She'd only snatched glimpses of the rest of the mansion, and that was enough.

She didn't belong here, and the sooner she could figure out what this was about and get out, the better.

Brian offered to get Alyssa a drink, which she politely declined. Without another word he exited the room, closing the door behind him and leaving her alone.

She didn't have much time, so she pulled her phone out of her pocket and tried to text her contact within the Matriarchs. But her phone just kept on displaying her home screen, a picture of her mother from before Alyssa was born.

"No use in trying to use that. I've got this system that blocks all signals except the ones I choose. Neat gadget."

Alyssa looked up from her phone. A middle-aged white man walked into the room, his smile perfect and gleaming and utterly fake. "I'm Senator Gaines, Ms. Pearson. And can I just say it is a pleasure to meet an entrepreneur such as yourself?"

"What do you want?" Alyssa asked. Her voice was steady, as was her gaze, and she imagined her mother looking down on her with pride. After all, Senator Gaines had been instrumental in passing the law that had eventually killed her.

The senator kept his placid smile in place as he sat in a leather wing chair and indicated for Alyssa to do the same. She kept standing. He pretended not to notice.

"Ms. Pearson, I'm sorry to have interrupted your afternoon. But I'm afraid I need a woman of your considerable talents, and I didn't think you'd answer a polite invitation. Would you like a drink?"

"No," Alyssa said. Fuck no. She couldn't trust these people. They'd probably drug her and sell her into slavery in the manner of their ancestors. "Are you going to kill me?"

As soon as the words slipped out, Alyssa swore to herself. She wanted to be cool. But she was terrified, trying to figure out how to get away from Senator Gaines. He was legendary. As a state senator he'd started the Abstinence League, and as the founder of the Senate Commission on Morality he'd pushed through legislation that had severely limited everything from contraception to clothing. Once upon a time people had said he led the war against women, but that was before folks decided that they could live with his legislation. After all, hadn't he also helped bring back manufacturing and a handful of other industries?

People were willing to give up a lot in order to have a few more dollars in their pockets. It was the price they paid for freedom and the American Dream.

But that was long before Alyssa and her mom, and Senator Gaines had been in office nearly forty years. The idea that there was anything Alyssa could help him with was laughable, and the more she failed to figure his angle the more frightened she got.

"I know you're probably wondering why I brought you here. After all, pretty girls like yourself go missing all of the time, and for no good reason," the senator said with a smile. If it was meant to reassure Alyssa, it failed. "The answer is: I need you to help my girl get rid of an unfortunate complication."

"Your mistress?" Slinging contras required a certain understanding of why people needed them, and extramarital affairs weren't unusual, despite all of the Morality Laws.

"No, sorry to disappoint. My daughter is sick, and if she doesn't terminate her pregnancy she'll die."

"Sounds like she needs to file an appeal," Alyssa said.

His eyebrows twitched, but that was the only sign of emotion.

Alyssa didn't say anything else, just let the silence drag. Her answer was cold but honest. What kind of world did this man live in where he could have the police grab some random girl who sold illegal contraceptives and expect her to act as a Moses, ferrying his daughter to the Promised Land?

Jail was a much better alternative. She'd serve her time and be back on her corner by New Year's.

The senator gave Alyssa a frustrated smile. "I picked you because I know what happened to your mama," he said. His pose was still relaxed, but there was now an edge to his words. "Don't you want to make sure that doesn't happen to another woman?"

Alyssa shrugged. "I'm good."

The senator's smile faded, and a vaguely perplexed expression came over his face. It was like he'd never considered that she might say no, that maybe she worked her corner not because of some greater good but because she just liked the extra cash.

"Well, how about this: You get my daughter to the Dakotas and I'll pay you. Name your price."

Alyssa laughed. "Why me? I just sell contras. I'm all about before the fact, not after. This is a whole bunch of mess I'm not qualified for."

The senator steepled his fingers under his chin. "Which is exactly why I need you. You deal, so you already don't agree with the Morality Laws. An established Moses would compromise my daughter and is entirely unsafe. I could send her directly, but I can't take that sort of trip, and I can't send my security detail—it's too dangerous for me. So, name your price. I'll give you a car and two days to get her there."

Alyssa said nothing. How fucking stupid did he think she was? She might be a dealer, but that didn't mean she couldn't see bullshit when she was neck deep.

The senator didn't like her indecision. "Oh, and let me be clear: If you refuse, you aren't going to prison. Those officers have already been paid off, and my security detail has been informed that you are a known terrorist that I'm trying to negotiate with. Should you refuse, Brian will return and defend me against your plot to try to assassinate a sitting senator. You really don't have a choice. Now, shall we say a hundred thousand dollars for your time and effort?"

"One fifty and you give me half now."

The senator smiled, slow and crocodile-like. "Deal."

For the first time all afternoon, Alyssa relaxed. This was exactly how things were supposed to go.

She was given a car, and a sleeping girl was gently laid across the backseat by Brian and a woman who looked to be the senator's wife. The girl was bundled in a blanket, and at one point the edge of it fell away to reveal golden skin and curly blond hair. The woman quickly covered the girl's face again before planting a kiss on her forehead. Alyssa watched it all without saying a word. After they were done, Brian handed Alyssa a card with her name on it.

"This is the account where your money will be. You can use as much of it as you want to get you to North Dakota."

"North Dakota?" Alyssa asked. Wasn't that a strange place to take a sick, pregnant girl? When the senator said *the Dakotas*, she'd thought he was just giving general directions, not an actual destination.

The man didn't even blink as he said, "Yes. The family has a compound there and a doctor waiting. You have forty-eight hours.

If you aren't there we will find you. Your directions are prepro-grammed into your GPS. Do not deviate from the route."

Alyssa said nothing but took the card. Then she climbed into the car and began to drive toward the highway. She passed other large houses until the landscape smoothed to farms and eventually suburban neighborhoods of identical-looking homes. The direc-tions took her toward the highway on-ramp, where she stopped at a red light. A van pulled up next to her and Alyssa stared straight ahead.

A middle-aged woman exited the van, walked up to the driver's side door, and raised her eyebrows in question. Talking was no good, because the senator and his people were most likely listen-ing.

Alyssa gave the woman a thumbs-up, pointing to the backseat.

The woman flashed an okay sign. Alyssa popped the locks. The woman opened the rear door and gently grabbed the girl by the shoulders. Another woman exited the van to grab feet. The two women hoisted the girl into the van, closed the doors on both ve-hicles, and, when the light turned green, drove away.

Alyssa got onto the on-ramp, her heart light. For the first time in a while, she smiled.

"I have a proposition for you," the woman said.

Two weeks before Alyssa was snatched off her corner by Findley and his partner, she sat in a diner and waited patiently for her pan-cakes. On the television in the corner was a report about the latest terrorist attack, this one carried out by a group of women's rights activists known as the Harpies. They'd bombed the factory where a male-enhancement drug was made. Alyssa thought it was funny. The government called it the worst crime in history.

She tore her gaze away from the television to the woman sitting opposite her. She had dark-brown skin and a slight smile that seemed to indicate that everything was amusing and silly. The expression immediately put Alyssa on edge. "I don't know you, lady."

The woman smiled. "I know. But you seem to like my products."

That got Alyssa's attention, and she straightened. "Who are you?"

The woman made a complicated wing gesture with her hands. She had to be a Matriarch, one of the women who organized the Calendar Girls.

Alyssa had thought it was all a bunch of bullshit. She'd become a Calendar Girl because it let her move out of foster care into her own place, not because she believed in all of the women's rights bullshit they fed her. With the money she saved, she would be able to leave the country, go somewhere women weren't expected to be married by twenty and knocked up by twenty-one. Somewhere she could get a real education, not the "smile and submit" bullshit they taught in school.

But this woman being here complicated her life, and she could see all of her dreams suddenly teetering on a precipice.

"How do I know you're legit?"

"You moved six hundred and twenty-three monthlies last month, your best month on record. You had to re-up three times."

Alarm bells clanged in Alyssa's head. "I haven't done anything wrong; I've followed all of the rules," she said, not looking up when the waitress came by to deliver her pancakes. The restaurant was where she usually picked up her stash each week, and the woman would have known that. It all felt like a trap now, the predictability of it all.

"Of course you have, my dear. You've been great at your job. And not a snitch, either. Which is why we now need you to take care of this for us."

"Okay," Alyssa said. There wasn't much else to do. You didn't talk back to the Matriarchs.

"In two weeks the police officers in your area will pick you up, seemingly without provocation. Do not fight them; do not argue. They will take you to either the city or county jail, and from there you will be offered a deal that will be too good to be true. You will balk at first, because they will expect you to. After that you will accept it. Do you understand?"

Alyssa nodded, and the woman's polite smile stretched into a grin.

"Excellent. You're going to love Canada, by the way."

The woman got up and walked away, and Alyssa watched her go. Canada?

Why the fuck would she ever go to Canada?

Once Alyssa could, she stopped and withdrew as much money as possible on the card. It was only five thousand dollars. She got back in the car to do the same thing at another machine. By the time the card refused to keep giving her money, she'd withdrawn twenty-five thousand dollars. The daily limit.

She drove the rest of the day, stopping to sleep in rest stops along the way. Eventually she'd be able to stop, but until then it had to look like she was following the senator's plan.

At seven-thirty, her phone beeped, the first sound it had made in nearly a day. The message was just a link, and when Alyssa clicked it she laughed.

"MORAL" SENATOR'S DAUGHTER DEFECTS TO FRANCE WITH OUT-OF-WEDLOCK PREGNANCY AND DIRT ON DADDY, INCLUDING MURDER PLOT

Alyssa didn't bother reading the story. There was a picture, and she recognized the unconscious girl who'd been in the backseat. Her part in this tale was at an end.

Another text message came across with directions, and Alyssa read them quickly before turning her phone off.

She took the next exit into Minneapolis. In a crowded gas station parking lot, she dumped the car, leaving the money inside. She then made her way to a run-down mall, where she dumped her clothes and phone after a white girl in a red hoodie handed her new ones. At a kiosk in the mall she had her identi-chip wiped and reloaded with new information. Including sixty thousand dollars.

For a minute she toyed with the idea of staying. Things would change. The Matriarchs would eventually reverse the laws and restore the rights of women. Maybe she could even help with the fight, a little.

But the reality was, Alyssa didn't care. She just wanted to live her life.

So she bought a bus ticket to Toronto, one way, and for the first time in her entire life was free.

JUSTINA IRELAND enjoys dark chocolate, dark humor, and is not too proud to admit that she's still afraid of the dark. She lives with her husband, kid, cat, and dog in Pennsylvania. She is the author of the novels *Vengeance Bound*, *Promise of Shadows*, and *Dread Nation*, a *New York Times* bestselling novel. She is—with Troy L. Wiggins—the editor of *FIYAH*, a magazine of black speculative fiction.

THE SYNAPSE WILL FREE US FROM OURSELVES

VIOLET ALLEN

I can create any scenario I want for Dante, any story, any setting—anything. I have total control over his universe. Today he inhabits a grand mansion. The design is mostly mid-century modern, with just a hint of gothic whimsy. Each room is crafted to maximize luxury and pleasure, pleasure that can exist beyond the laws governing the material universe. It is a miracle, a place of wonder and dreams, a place where anything may happen.

"Yo homie, I want the D!" Dante yells.

He and Dahlia are naked in the boudoir. I set up a very romantic scene for them. A river of fine champagne lazily flows around a bed seated upon a rose petal island, all beneath sky lit by candles. These are all simple signifiers, but sometimes simplicity is the best. Dante entered from the *Frasier* zone, expecting his normal bedroom, only to find this delicious tapestry and Dahlia waiting for him, resplendent in elegant finery, lacy lingerie, and very sexual high heels. He was soon denuded, and so was she. Esquivel is playing, and Dahlia performs an erotic dance I choreographed based on Rita Hayworth's Dance of the Seven Veils in 1953's *Salome*. The rest writes itself. (Sex.)

Yet Dante only laughs scornfully, filled with pure amusement at his own irreverence. He shall get no D this day or any other, yet still his spiteful pleasure knows no end. "That D! You know what I'm talking 'bout!"

(D is a reference to a human man's penis, which I presume he wants to have intercourse with or around.)

"Stop it," I say into the microphone, louder than I intend. I look around. I don't think anyone noticed. My workstation is in a cubicle on the main floor of the facility. I am surrounded by other Adjustment Engineers, each one working with his or her own client via the Synapse.

The Synapse is a miracle of modern engineering. The Synapse allows people to reach their full potential. The Synapse will free us from ourselves.

I give him a little buzz. Just a little so he knows I'm not playing games with him. He reacts absurdly, shaking, screaming, wriggling on the floor like a child. I know not to be fooled by these theatrics. We are doing this to help. I'm not a bad person, I promise. I want to help Dante. I love him (*agape*). I only want what's best for him. I have never hurt him. All I have ever done is help him be the best version of himself that he can be. Or at least, I have tried.

"That sucked," he says after he has recovered. "I mean, it was a powerful sensation, but I need some romance before the big climax, chief. What, is this your first time torturing anybody?"

"Stop it," I say.

He smiles so big and so wide, like he knows he's won whatever game he's playing. "Maybe some spanking? Is that your thing? Some spanks, maybe some spit play? I feel like we could really have some fun together if you loosened up."

Just a little buzz. Just one more. It doesn't hurt as much as it seems. I'm not a bad person.

I can fix him. I can make him love her.

"It's been six months," says Program Director Murphy.

"I know," I say.

Program Director Murphy is a small, grandmotherly woman in her fifties. She is kind and good. She is my boss. I trained with her for a year before beginning this job. I know her well. This job has been my dream since I was a child. This is a good job. I am doing good work. I am a good person.

"What's the problem?"

"He's a difficult subject."

"You've made no progress at all."

"He's a very difficult subject."

"He's your first, isn't that right?"

Program Director Murphy's office is large, blank, and circular. The corners where the walls meet the ceiling and floor are rounded, giving the impression of an infinite void, at the center of which is a desk for her and a chair for me. I am more afraid than I ought to be. She's just my boss. My heart shouldn't beat like this, and I shouldn't feel like my head is swelling up like a balloon, like it's growing to fill up all the empty space around me.

"Yes. My very first."

A field of holotext floats in front of her face. The green light reflects on her skin, giving her the appearance of a small, grandmotherly woman in her fifties. She is kind and good. She is my boss. I know her well. I trained with her for a year before beginning this job.

"It says here that you spent a week making him watch Godard movies on repeat?"

"Yes," I say. "They're very romantic. Have you seen *Pierrot le Fou*? It literally tells you everything you need to know about heterosexual intercourse. I mean, it's like a metaphor—the guy explodes at the end."

"Do you know why we assigned you to this case, Daniel?"

"Not really, ma'am."

"You and your subject share a love for twentieth-century ephemera, a sentimentality."

"Of course."

"But you're too sentimental. Spare the rod, spoil the child. You need to be firmer. We're doing this for his own good."

This is a good job. I am doing good work. I am a good person.

"Yes."

"Be firmer. They can take more than you think."

"Okay, ma'am. Whatever you say."

"There will be negative consequences if you can't produce results."

"Yes, ma'am. I understand. You can count on me."

I eat lunch in the cafeteria with my friend Xavier every day. He started here around the same time as me. I would enjoy fraternizing with him in the evenings as well, but we are assigned to different dormitories. But our lunch schedule lines up perfectly every day, so we can at least hang out then.

"I am starting to really fucking hate this fucking piece of shit," he says.

Like me, he is having trouble with his subject.

"Today I made Hollie into a cheerleader and Javi into a quarterback, and then they were in the shower together. But then Javi just complained. I want go home; I want to read a book; I'm bored. He said he played fútbol in school, not football. It was so annoying."

Xavier is small and . . . elegantly constructed. I haven't measured his features, of course, but I strongly feel the golden ratio is in play. His hair is dark and shiny, and when I see him in the corner of my eye, it flows down gracefully to his shoulders, though in reality it is cut cleanly above the ear. He speaks with an aristocratic Spanish accent, and he stumbles when swearing, as if he cannot quite find the translation to encapsulate his anger. I feel as though I have known him for a long time, and I think that he is probably my best friend.

"They're monsters," I say. "If this were easy, we wouldn't be here. It's our job."

Dora sits down at our table. She also started around the same time as us. She is a very beautiful woman. We are sort of friends, and sort of enemies. Also, I think she may be my girlfriend.

"You losers whining again?" she asks.

"We don't whine," I say.

"What do you call it, then?"

"A strategy session," says Xavier.

She chuckles. "Nerds. You just have to bear down. Get into their minds. Suck them into the illusion. Daniel, did you end up doing that thing with the hundred cakes?"

"Five hundred, and I don't want to talk about it."

"I told you it wouldn't work. Today, Ike proposed to Izzy and she said yes. It's going great. You just gotta know how these people think. You have to manipulate them. Give them what they think they want. That's how you get what *you* want."

She continues to explicate her methods, which largely entail being great and naturally knowing how to do it. I appreciate her company, despite the name-calling. It is a little strange that she might be my girlfriend, but she is an amusing person. I enjoy it when she is around. This, I believe, is the essence of romance: enjoying it when a person of the opposite sex is around. This is why we live and fight. But she gets up quickly, and I realize that she had no intention of eating with us, rather that she is going from table to table in order to brag.

"I'll see you losers later."

"Bye," says Xavier.

"I love you," I say without thinking.

For a moment, she stares at me blankly, as if waiting for her thoughts to catch up with her, then she nods. "I love you, too."

After she leaves, Xavier says, "Why don't we actually have a strategy session? Really get into it? Later. After work."

He speaks softly, purrs almost. Program Director Murphy is nearby, standing by herself on either side of the room, a small, grandmotherly woman in her fifties. She would not approve of socialization outside of the sanctioned areas. We could get in trouble. I should say no. All of my instincts are telling me to say no. Any other day, I would say no. But today, I don't know. I have to get better at this, and I can trust Xavier. I feel as though I have known him for a long time, and I think that he is probably my best friend.

"Okay," I say. "Let's do it."

"Just the two of us."

We are drawn to the aesthetics of heterosexualism, both in theory and praxis. There is a simple elegance to it, a mathematical harmony. The key fits into the lock, and in doing so the key is complete, the lock is complete, the door is open. Meaning is created by the dialectic of form and function, and meaning is the hammer with which we carve our lives from χάος and ἄπειρον, the formless infinite. Desire seeks only to replicate itself, but meaning seeks completion, and in completion we find ourselves.

Dante is lost, and he doesn't even know it. That's why he was sent here. Not because he was gay. There's nothing wrong with being gay; everyone knows that. The Institute loves gay people.

We're their truest allies, their biggest fans. But the lifestyle is hard. Some people aren't as tolerant as us. The indignities, the exclusion. It's terrible. And then there are the health issues. The diseases, the physical strain of unnatural relations. These people were everywhere, all around us, suffering, practically screaming for help. Something had to be done. This is why the Institute was created. Dante is among the first subjects. I am going to give him a better life, a normal life.

This is a good job. I am doing good work. I am a good person.

I wipe out all of Dante's memories of Dahlia and of the various trials he has undergone in the Synapse. We need a fresh start, a new coat of paint. He always figures out that he is in a simulated reality eventually, though he is unable to put together that he is, in fact, not the real Dante, just a digital copy scanned from the original's mind. How could he, though? We all think of ourselves as "real," even when everything around us seems false. The real Dante is asleep somewhere in the facility, probably in the basement or something. We'll wake him up when Synapse Dante has learned his lesson. The digital will be merged with the analog, the ghost will re-enter the machine, and the whole will be healed. The real Dante will be good and free of trouble and strife.

All I have to do is get everything right. I've a great scenario in mind, a real adventure. Dahlia just needs a few tweaks. She's a fairly basic AI—a puppet, really. I modeled her after Rita Hayworth. Rita Hayworth is the best woman. She was good at dancing, and she made *Gilda*. What more could a red-blooded American man ask for? Ginger Rogers? Boring. Myrna Loy? Too snobby. No, I know what cool guys like: Rita Hayworth.

Sometimes I think about Lena Horne or Josephine Baker, but then I don't think of them. You know what I mean? When you think about something but you don't think about it. There's a word for that. It's on the tip of my tongue. Do you ever feel like there's something staring you right in the face but you can't see it? No, that's not it. No, it's more like you know something's there, but you don't want to look. A monster under the bed or Bluebeard's secret chamber. You can hear it, smell it, taste it, but everything is fine as long as you don't look. But if you *do* look, you get eaten.

This is all prelude to the fact that today I make them act out the plot of *Vertigo*. Just the romantic part at the beginning, before it gets weird and horny, when it's only a detective and a lady who's maybe a ghost falling in love, and instead of the part where shit gets real at the bell tower, they get married.

This goes very poorly. Hurtful words are said that can never be taken back, no matter whose memories are erased.

Xavier and I meet on the roof of Dormitory Epsilon. It wasn't as hard as I thought dodging Program Director Murphy. She waits by all the exits at night, and also she patrols the halls. (We are allowed to leave. We are not prisoners. We just have to sign out first.) But the service hallway leading to the roof is near my room, close enough that I can slip in and out without being seen.

You can see the whole city up here, all light and color, impossible to make out any one particular building in the nether distance. I feel like I'm floating, like in a dream where you know if you look down you'll fall, so I keep my head up and imagine I'm balancing on the edge of the sky.

"Give them something to want," he says. "So you can take it away."

There is a slight chill in the air, just enough that I can feel the heat of Xavier's breath on my cheek as he whispers the secrets of pain.

"I think it's all about signifiers. Images and connections. That's how you get through to people."

"But is it real?"

He smells like fresh sweat and cinnamon.

"Nothing's real. That's the secret of living. All we have is beauty and images and connections."

"Have you ever kissed someone?"

"I can't remember."

"Me neither. It's no big deal. Everybody forgets. But I wonder how we can teach people to love if we've never even kissed anyone."

His chest goes up and down, up and down, swelling and shrinking, and it's like his breath is the only air in the world.

"Maybe that's our problem," I say.

We kiss. Just as an experiment. He tastes like oysters and ozone, and I get lost a little in the moment. There are so many sensations at once, all of them good, and I try to focus on each one individually, but it's like trying to count raindrops on your face, and I am unable to focus, and my mind clouds with touch and connection.

Kissing is very nice, I decide.

My conversations with Xavier lead to the creation of a character I call Dante Jr. Dante Jr. is an irrepressible scamp between the ages of six and ten. I put some memories in Dante's head of Dante Jr.'s birth, his first steps, his first day of school, et cetera. More clichés, I know, but they take a lot better than the memories of Dahlia. Those Dante Sr. rejects pretty quickly, thinks them through and says things don't add up and freaks out and I have to reset him. But Dante Jr. is sticky, as long as there's not too much Dahlia in the mix. I guess Dante was always meant to be a father. All the more reason to help him out, right? Dante only really remembers Dante Jr. when they are in the same room. Otherwise, he exists only on the periphery of his mind, so I can still focus on my primary goal of creating love. Dante Jr. is seasoning, some nice flavor for the dish I'm preparing. He comes in, does some little-kid stuff, then Dante does some dad stuff, and we all have a good time.

Honestly, I'm surprised by how well it works. Dante still figures out it's a simulation every couple days if I'm not vigilant about erasing failed experiments, but he gets along so much better with Dahlia when Dante Jr. is in the room, and when he does figure it out, he assumes that Dante Jr. (and therefore Dahlia) is trapped in the simulation with him. They're finally starting to bond. It's beautiful. I think I'm finally getting good at this job.

Today they all made a cake together as a family. Just one. Not quite as many as I would like (five hundred), but it's a start.

Xavier and I have been meeting on the roof every night. We don't talk about the kiss, but we talk about everything else. It's really nice. It feels like listening to a new album from a band you already love, familiar and comforting but still new and exciting.

"I used to want to be a baseball player," I say. "When I was a little kid."

He smiles at me as though I were the first person to ever make another person smile, and I can't help but return the expression. We sit next to each other on the edge of the roof. It's nice.

"I can't imagine you playing baseball," he says.

"I was very bad, but I always thought I would become good someday. Like without any work or anything. Just one day I would be great at it, a star. Same with living life, really. I always thought I would just become normal one day."

"I think you're great as you are now."

My hand brushes against his. It was not intentional, but not unpleasant. But he pulls his away as if bitten by a snake.

"Sorry," I say.

"No, no, it's not you." He looks down and is quiet for a while before gathering his thoughts. "I had a meeting with Program Director Murphy today. She was not pleased with my progress."

Program Director Murphy is a small, grandmotherly woman in

her fifties. She is kind and good. She is my boss. I know her well. I trained with her for a year before beginning this job.

"And?"

"She put me in the machine. She grabbed me and held me down, and she was at the console. Just for a minute. I was still in her office, but I was in the machine, too. She said she was showing me how to teach. She . . . did something to my hand. It felt like it was on fire. Or something worse. I can't really describe it. Just pain. She was whispering in my ear, said that I could do this to Javi, that I could do worse, and that Javi would learn his lesson then."

The Synapse is a miracle of modern engineering. The Synapse allows people to reach their full potential. The Synapse will free us from ourselves.

"Are you okay?"

"Something is wrong, Daniel. Something is very wrong. The dots are starting to disconnect. The other day, I was trying to say something in Spanish, but I couldn't. I know I used to speak Spanish, but I can't anymore. I remember my parents speaking English, my childhood friends and relatives, everybody, but that can't be. We lived in Morelia. My mom taught literature at the university. She used to read me poetry every night. She liked Paz and Zepeda. Mom. Mom. That doesn't sound right. It's not right. It's not right."

"It's no big deal. Everybody forgets."

"Just be careful. Don't let her do anything to you. Do what you're supposed to."

I notice he has tears in his eyes, and I think he is starting to cry, but I don't say anything, because I am polite.

"I'm in lofe with you," says Dahlia.

A simple typo, but Dante is enraged. He screams, cries, punches the ground, makes a production out of it. Just because I typed one word wrong. It's a mistake on my part, I admit it, but I don't think this response is warranted. I had a great thing going, and now I'll have to start over.

He thought he was free. I crafted this scenario where I intentionally let him figure out it was a simulation, then made him think he could escape from it with Dahlia and Dante Jr. There were some puzzles to solve, some ducts to crawl through, vats of blue goo connected to supercomputers—it was a whole production. He and his family had just emerged from a mysterious underground facility to see their first "real" sunrise when Dahlia accidentally let slip the "lofe" thing. He put it together pretty quick after that.

"Chill," I say. "I mean, please calm yourself."

"You're a monster!" he yells.

"This isn't so bad. I think we learned a lot for next time."

"Next time? Fuck you! I'm going to kill you when I get out of here."

"You're not real, dog. None of this is."

"You're never going to beat me. I'm never gonna do what you want. You fucking suck."

And now I'm angry. Who's this guy to talk shit to me? Who's this guy at all? I'm trying to help him. I think back to Xavier, the fear in his voice as he described the fire in his hand. That's not gonna happen to me, no. It can't. I need to teach this guy a lesson.

Dante Jr. is standing next to his "father," watching and waiting. I delete him.

"He was pretend, too," I say. "Everything is pretend but you and me."

He doesn't take it very well. He howls and cries. And he doesn't have any little jokes for me for the first time ever.

I win.

Still, I'm a little sad. Dante Jr. was kinda like my son, too. Me and Xavier made him together. Me and Xavier. Wouldn't it be funny if me and Javi could be dads? Wouldn't it be so funny? Like a joke. Like a really good joke. Ha ha ha, I would laugh, after I told the joke to a friend. This is good, though, right? This is what I wanted. Now Dante knows he can't have it both ways. He can't have a family and be queer at the same time. This is what I was supposed to teach him. I thought I would like this more. It hurts to see him like this. But this job has been my dream since I was a child. This is a good job. I am doing good work. I am a good person.

There's something I'm not seeing, and I don't know what.

I come across Dora on the way to lunch, sitting alone in a corner beneath the stairs. She doesn't look like she normally does. She looks smaller somehow, and empty, like a mannequin wearing a Dora suit. She is clutching something in her hand that I can't quite make out.

"Hey, are you okay?" I ask.

"No," she says.

"What's wrong?"

"Izzy. I had to reset her. It was all fucked up."

"I thought everything was going good."

"It was a grift. She was scamming me. Just pretending. Giving me what I wanted." She laughs hard. "It was a good one."

"Why's it matter? We all have to delete stuff from time to time. It's part of the job."

"I don't know. It felt like cutting off my own hand."

We sit in silence for a moment, and I point at the object in her hand. "What's that?"

She holds up a tiny holo projector. She turns it on, and it shows an image of her and another woman sitting next to one another. The woman has short hair and a kind smile. She looks familiar. Maybe I've seen her around the facility. But I can't place her. Was she here before? We are allowed to leave. We are not prisoners. We just have to sign out first.

"I found this in my room."

"Who's that?"

"I don't know. I don't know anything."

It's no big deal. Everybody forgets.

"Are you okay?"

"I just thought I had it. I had everything. This job has been my dream since I was a child. This is a good job. I'm doing good work. I'm a good person. But I'm not good at this at all. I'm like you. A loser."

I want to tell her that it's not her fault, that our job is difficult, that we have to try our best to surmount the odds. But instead I say, "It's like they're setting us up to fail."

And then I think about Dante, how much I hate him. I hate him for not doing what he's supposed to do. I hate him for the way he talks to me. I hate him for being such a fucking queer.

Fuck.

Fuck.

Dante.

Dante.

"Daniel? What's wrong?" she asks.

"I looked," I say, and I stand. "And now I think I can see the monster under the bed."

He keeps remembering. I don't know why. I refreshed him seven times. He's fine for a little bit, then he starts to remember. I try to treat him right, give him as much television as he wants. But there is nothing in the world that can give him succor.

"Where is he?" he says, crying.

"I'm sorry," I say.

"Where am I?" he says.

"In a facility. To fix you. Make you normal."

"What normal? What does that mean?"

"Normal people hate themselves."

"Who are you?"

"I'm Daniel. And you're Dante. Right?"

"I don't know a Daniel."

"Neither do I."

"I'm proud of you, Daniel. You've made real improvements in your work," Program Director Murphy, a small, grandmotherly woman in her fifties, says. "You're beginning to show some real promise."

"Thank you, ma'am."

"Your subject is beginning to learn."

"Yes."

"You know, I like you. I really do. I'm quite fond of the twentieth century myself. Just like you."

She called me in. Said she wanted to congratulate me on my recent performance. I have never been more afraid in my entire life. She's behind this, I know she is. She's the one doing this to me, to us; I just have to be cool. It's fine. I can leave. We are allowed to leave. We are not prisoners.

"That's cool."

"I still don't care for your sentimental streak. You're too wrapped up in the glitz and glamour. Hollywood hogwash. What I like is the people, the society."

"Of course."

"People used to know how to act. People knew what was right, and what was wrong, and if they did wrong, they at least had the decency to respect your religion, your morals, your basic sense of taste."

"Cool."

"It's gotten worse and worse. You probably don't even remember what it used to be like. Paradise. And now it's chaos."

"That does sound bad."

"It is. That's why we made this institute. That's why we hired you. To figure out how to make things right. You're doing so much for the cause, Daniel."

"Cool. Cool cool cool."

She stands up and walks over to me, places her hand on my shoulder and smiles warmly.

"I think he figured it out," Program Director Murphy says.

"Are you sure?" asks Program Director Murphy, from her desk.

"He keeps saying *cool*. He's not looking you in the eye. That's what he does when he's trying to not give it away. He's so obvious," she says from across the room.

Program Director Murphy groans. "Again? I thought you said we had it this time, Pam?"

Program Director Murphy shrugs.

My head hurts. I can see it, but I can't see it. There's more than one Program Director Murphy, but Program Director Murphy is a small, grandmotherly woman in her fifties. It doesn't make sense. But I can see it. I try to stand up, but Program Director Murphy stops me, holds me down. There's too many of her.

"What's going on?" I ask.

Program Director Murphy slaps the back of my head. "Shut up."

"Don't do that," says Program Director Murphy. "He can't help it."

Program Director Murphy walks over to me and kneels so that we are face-to-face. "I'm sorry, Daniel. Really. I really thought we had it this time."

"What?"

"I guess you all just need to be pruned from time to time. Your friend Xavier starts asking questions and sneaking around. Isadora starts to freak out over her lost love. And you, Mr. Five Hundred Cakes, you figure it out. What a world we live in."

"You want us to fail on purpose. You want us to hate ourselves. Why?"

"We're trying to help you, Dante. We want people to accept you, like we do. We love people like you. People with your . . . proclivities."

"Homos," says Program Director Murphy as she types at the Synapse console.

Program Director Murphy rolls her eyes. "Thanks, Jeff. No. We understand. We just want you to be happy. We're giving you a very important gift, Dante. You should treasure it. Sweet, simple shame. You used to suffer from a pitiful lack of shame before you came here. Sassy and smug and out and proud and so forth. Other people aren't like me, Dante. They don't appreciate it. They don't like it being rubbed in their face. They don't like being forced to accept you. Don't worry. You'll still be yourself after this. Most of our graduates are. We've never been able to really fix you all. But at least you'll know how to keep it to yourself. Maybe you'll settle down, find a nice girl, have some kids, satisfy your urges in secret. Or at the very least, you can be the bachelor uncle or the lonely oddball neighbor. Like in one of your movies. All you need is beautiful, wonderful shame. We love you, Dante. I promise."

"Is this . . . is this real?"

Program Director Murphy all laugh.

"Don't worry, Dante. You're the original. Meat is as easy to work with as ones and zeroes. It's all the same technique, really."

"Let me go!" I scream. "We are allowed to leave. We're not prisoners. We just have to sign out first."

Program Director Murphy stands up and nods. "Okay. I think

we only need a few tweaks. He definitely needs to socialize more. All he does is sit alone and think, think, think. We need to make him more compatible with Dora."

"I think he needs more bro time. Like him and Xavier. They could be friends."

"Xavier always asks him to go sneaking around at night. He always says no, and I want to keep it that way. They're close enough as it is. Work friends, that's all. You know their . . . history."

"Please don't do this," I say.

"Don't worry, Dante," Program Director Murphy says. "Just remember your triggers, and you'll be okay. Everybody forgets. It's no big deal."

Today, Dante and Dahlia have to prepare and eat five hundred cakes. It's a bonding exercise for the two of them. The cakes are white on the outside and pink on the inside (a sexual metaphor) and, when prepared according to the instructions, are delicious, perfect, pure, and without flaw or deviance: absolute cake. Dante ought to love the cake as much as the cake loves him. He ought to be happy and eat his delicious cakes with a smile on his face and a song in his heart. Cake is an elaboration of bread, and bread is life and love and beauty. We may recall Neruda's poetic image of the leavened dough rounding and rising, mirroring the swelling of a mother's womb. Or we may recall the mysticism of Dali's breadbaskets, the numinous hunger evoked by the loaf still warm from the hearth. We desire to expand, to procreate, to be large, and to contain multitudes. This is normal.

I eat lunch in the cafeteria with my friend Xavier most days. He started here around the same time as me. I would enjoy fraternizing with him in the evenings as well, but we are assigned to different dormitories. But our lunch schedule lines up perfectly every day, so we can at least hang out then.

"Where have you been?" he asks.

"What do you mean?" I ask.

He turns his head from side to side and comes close, whispering, "Our, um, strategy sessions. You haven't come. Is something wrong?"

"I would enjoy fraternizing with you in the evenings as well, but we are assigned to different dormitories."

"Okay. What?"

Dora sits down at our table. She also started around the same time as us. She is a very beautiful woman. We are sort of friends, and sort of enemies. Also, I think she may be my girlfriend.

"Hey, losers," she says.

"Dora. Have you noticed anything strange about Daniel lately?"

"The other day he told me he saw the monster under the bed, and then he just walked away without saying goodbye or ending the conversation. It was weird."

"I don't remember that," I say.

"It happened," says Dora. "I remember because I was having a significant emotional moment."

"It's no big deal. Everybody forgets," I say.

"He's got a point," says Dora.

"Yes. Everybody forgets," he says. He looks sad. I don't know why. He should get a girlfriend like me. That will solve his problems.

"So anyway," Dora says, "I think I figured out a way to get Izzy to finally do what I want without being weird. It's sort of a meta thing where I—"

Javi slams his fist on the table. "No. No. I don't want to forget. I want to remember. I *will* remember."

"Remember what?" I ask.

He starts pronouncing *t*. Over and over. Tapping his tongue on the top of his palate. Again and again. *T- t- t- t-*. He goes on like that for minutes. Tears start to well up in his eyes. Tears. Is that it? T- t-tears. No. He looks like he's having a nervous breakdown.

"Te. Te. Te amo. Daniel, te amo."

I stare at him as he crawls across the table, knocking his food to the ground. Before I can do anything, he kisses me. He tastes like oysters and ozone, and I get lost a little in the moment. I feel something inside me, something strong, and I can feel something breaking.

"Thank you," I say, and I kiss him.

It's like going home after a long time away. You see all the familiar landmarks and signposts, and you have enough distance that you really see them, and you don't just ignore them, and you just connect with yourself, all the past versions of you, all at once, seeing and remembering and feeling.

A scream shatters the moment. Program Director Murphy is on the ground next to us. Next to her is Program Director Murphy. Izzy is standing above them with an empty trash can above her head.

"There's *two* of them?" she says. "That doesn't make sense."

There is gasping and yelling from the other engineers in the cafeteria. Panic begins to set in. I stand on the table and try to explain. I don't know how much I remember and how much I don't remember, but I do my best.

"They tried to make us into monsters, but we're not. They wanted us to hurt ourselves, but we don't have to. We have love. And also, just, like, fucking."

Xavier—no, Javi—laughs and grips my hand. I notice other hands being held, shoulders rubbed, arms lovingly wrapped, wet eyes, hopeful smiles. We weren't the only ones. We were never the only ones. I just couldn't see it.

The Program Director Murphy serving lunch has disappeared,

and a group of Program Director Murphys are at the door, preparing to storm in.

"We have to fight," I say. "We can win. I know it. They don't care about anything but themselves, but for us, this is everything. We are not prisoners. My name is Dante. Remember."

The engineers stand. We arm ourselves with whatever we can. Garbage, trays, cutlery, whatever can hurt. And I try to think of a good movie where something like this happens, and I can't, because this is real.

"Fucking riot!" screams Izzy. She throws the trash can into a window, and the shattered glass catches the light and sparkles for a second like the sunrise.

And so we riot.

VIOLET ALLEN is a writer based in Chicago, Illinois. Her short fiction has appeared in *Liminal Stories*, the anthology *Cosmic Powers*, and *The Best American Science Fiction and Fantasy*, as well as in *Lightspeed*, where she also reviews TV and (occasionally) movies. She is currently working very hard every day on her debut novel and definitely has more than ten pages written, is not lying to her agent about having more than ten pages written, and does not spend most of her time listening to podcasts, and everything is totally cool, she promises. She can be reached on Twitter at @blipstress.

0.1

GABBY RIVERA

FEEL THE BEAT

2076–03–001
51::50

PUBLIC BROADCAST

Good evening, I'm Falak Alfayed with Channel 32 news. We're here at South 52nd Street in front of the empty home of Orion and Mala Lafayette-Santana. The scene is fraught with emotion. Citizens all across the globe are asking, "What happened to the Lafayette-Santana family?" And most important, "Where is Baby Free?" Neighbors broke down the door this morning, fearing the worst, and found that Mala and Orion were gone. Our crew in North Philly has confirmed that Deviana Ortiz, their birth worker, is also missing. . . .

GOLDEN EMBER 005

2076-03-001

00::50

MALA

Orion and I rounded the corner on foot, running with every ounce of energy between us, thankful that the snow hadn't started sticking on Market Street yet. They were nine months' pregnant. And because of me, we were bolting for our lives into the unknown, on a snowy night in Philly.

God, universe, please let our baby survive birth.

Why didn't I just let . . .

"Babe!"

I whipped around and saw Orion stumble hard, falling against a brick building. Barely three feet ahead of them, I sprinted back and helped them up, the weight of their body light in my arms. Orion's gray-brown eyes locked in deep with my rich-as-the-earth browns.

All around us snowflakes fluttered. I pressed my forehead against theirs. My eyes asked if they could continue. Orion nodded yes and pulled me close. Their long locks were wrapped up in a knot on their head. Their eyelashes fluttered against my cheeks. There was never a moment I wasn't in love with them.

Orion put my hand to their belly, under their coat.

Our baby kicked twice. Twice! I held back a rush of tears and kissed them. We moved slower through the back alleys, dodging the occasional stray cat and listening for the Federation.

I hadn't even told Orion where we were going.

Orion. My person.

Our love started over blueberry pie.

Talking is hard. I turn red, start to sweat in the worst places. My mind goes blank, when it's usually swirling with so many ideas and daydreams. But eating pie, that I can do. I was doing that when

Orion walked by wearing black jeans covered in paint, dreadlocks loose along their shoulders.

I stood up from the park bench and held out a slice. I'd planned on saying words but they didn't make it out of my mouth. Lots of times they don't. I try, I really do, but . . . all I had was pie that I made from scratch. Offering that to someone is kinda like talking, right?

Orion smiled, took the pie, and sat down next to me on the bench. I ate my slice. They ate theirs.

And now we've just fled our home in Philly so they can give birth to the first baby born to the Federation of Free Peoples in a decade. The first baby born during the plague of IMBALANCE.

IMBALANCE decimated 40 percent of Earth's population, hitting the 1 percent first and devouring the rest of the world one consumer at a time. Never in the collective imagination could we, humans, have prepared for a sentient bacterium that preyed on white-supremacist greed. It destroyed the lives we'd known and effectively neutered us.

The Federation wasn't going to let us out of their sights. Orion and I wouldn't admit it, but we wondered if they'd keep hold of us forever.

We were all set to stay and do as we were told. But even with all our input, the Federation's control over our birth was as infinite and as locked into place as any other Federation decree. We couldn't breathe.

And after the ninth, yes, *ninth*, news van parked itself outside our home in West Philly, I grabbed our bags and Orion's hand and used every ounce of emotion in my deep-brown eyes to beg them to trust me. By the time we fled, the news-van count was up to twenty-five.

That first three months of Orion's pregnancy, before anyone else knew, was beautiful, though. It was all ours. That's when Orion started work on their mural *wrapped in the rays*. Their ode to that moment when everything changed, and life formed between us. Real, actual life. It altered my understanding of the universe itself.

We were already making love, our kind of love. Free from conservative hetero understandings of sex and intimacy, Orion and I made magic. Sweaty, consensual, queer magic. Always. And as we shook our own walls, our bedroom flooded with warm light. It burst in from all corners of the room: the ceiling, the windows, the bed. It poured over us like sky across an open field.

We were suspended in that glow, in the air, for an unknown amount of time. Orion's love flowed through my pores. I felt the essence of their soft spirit fill my senses.

I didn't want to explain it to the Federation. It wasn't theirs to know. The way Orion and I manifested this baby, there aren't even words for it. That's why they made it a mural. So that our baby would have the moment of it in their consciousness before any Federation tried to describe it for them.

When Orion's cycle stopped, I panicked (they didn't). I bought forty-nine other items at the Free Peoples' vintage shop so no one would notice or question the faded pregnancy test in my possession. We held each other on the bathroom floor, kissing and crying, when the results came back positive.

A baby.

The *first* baby.

Our baby.

We told no one. We lived our daydream life. The one where people still had babies and IMBALANCE never happened. The one where I wasn't an orphan, where Mama and Papa didn't end their lives because a catastrophic plague with a consciousness killed their business friends and associates, white and Filipino.

IMBALANCE also killed the American Dream they'd believed in all their lives. It was too much.

But there we were with news of you in our hands, and it felt like a baptism. The joy of you washed us clean of that misery.

I picked bunches of wild lavender and placed them in jars all over the house to keep Orion and our baby calm. I rubbed vitamin E over Orion's soft belly to ready it for growth. I pressed prayers into their skin and over the galaxy growing within them. Orion read to us from their worn copy of *Lilith's Brood*. I made blueberry pie every week.

It was all going to be fine. No one would notice that we had a baby, right? We could keep this all to ourselves. That was the hope.

And there we were, Orion putting the finishing touches on the cocoon of light for their mural, me in the craft shed building a crib while reading a book on how to build cribs. Orion was almost done. They'd climbed to the top step of their ladder.

But that reach, the one to add golden ember 005 to the top sphere, proved too far, and the ladder tipped, then toppled over hard. I heard the crash and ran as if the universe itself were chasing me.

Crumpled in a heap on the fresh flowering abunda grass, my Orion lay motionless. They were three months and two days with child, and each second of it flashed before my eyes. I scooped my family up in my arms without struggle, all the adrenaline my body had ever produced pumping through me.

With Orion secured in the backseat of our black Neo Cadillac, I booked it to Mercy Hospital.

A slip and fall. That's all it took for O.1 to announce themselves to the world.

The entire Federation of Free Peoples was watching. And the Federation wanted in.

That's how I found myself taking on the public presence for our family. Orion offered, but I spoke up. I asked them to let me take this, let me sweat in front of everyone, cuz this is what chosen family does. This is how we love.

So once a month, I was briefed by the Federation Care Team

on how to discuss Offspring 1 during interviews on inter-Federation television. I was "allowed" to give numbers of weeks, fetus size, and any other medical details that they deemed appropriate for mass consumption.

But it wasn't enough for the people to be on our side. Folks grew restless and angry with us. There were those who thought we were liars or that we'd been abducted. Some wanted us detained indefinitely by the Federation.

They wanted Orion Lafayette-Santana, our baby—the one the Feds called O.1, the one the people nicknamed "Baby Free"—and me, Mala Amalia Santana; they wanted every second of the new world growing inside of Orion. The Federation encouraged me to consider the feelings of the entirety of the Free Peoples and what a birth meant to our planet.

Something had to give, and as hard as I tried, it had to be us. And so I offered a tiny piece of us to the world.

One morning, Orion woke up wanting peach pie. Not just any pie: *peach* pie. They doodled peaches and pies on the wall of the shed, the bathroom mirror. I even let them draw one on my wrist. Couldn't ever say no to that face. It didn't even dawn on me that Philly wasn't the place for peaches until I tried to make the damn pie. I went to three different fruit stands. Nothing. No big supermarket chains like during pre-IMBALANCE, so no place to purchase fruit out of season.

I couldn't find one single peach. And of course, Orion shrugged it off and said blueberry would be fine. But dammit, they never asked for anything. The helplessness I felt ate me up inside. I hurt for them, for us, for the world before.

So. I. Told. Everyone.

During one of my "Voluntary O.1 Sharings," I mentioned Orion's peach-pie craving, specifically my shame at not being able to give them what they asked for. Maybe I even cried a little bit.

I swear I felt the world thunder with love. Our little pie story boosted the Global Happiness Meter by 48 percent. FORTY-EIGHT.

Hope had been crushed under the metric tons of blood and tissue ravaged by Mother Nature in her fight to preserve herself. IMBALANCE was her only weapon against us. There are more graves in the Free States than living people. A new modern biblical plague, it slammed areas that never even knew of inconvenience let alone catastrophe.

And after over thirty years of scraping through collective grief, the world took a joyous pause in Orion and their peach pie.

Pies. Dozens and dozens of pies arrived at our house within hours of the broadcast. Free Peoples from all over carried pies in sewing baskets, cookie tins, milk crates, head scarves; one woman brought hers covered in a bouquet of flowers. We lived over by Malcolm X Park, near Cedar and South 52nd, and our entire neighborhood had peach pie for months, and for a while no one could remember a time before then.

So we ran through the streets of West Philly, snow blustering all around us, and didn't look back.

The Federation couldn't have us. And neither could the Free Peoples.

Orion and I held each other, moving fast through the streets. They groaned and paused, hand on a nearby wall. A full-body tremor passed over them. It rippled like living organisms under their skin.

"Orion!"

Their whole body heaved as they slid to the ground. I shook them hard, even slapped them a little. The tears streaming down my face burned from the deep cold.

Please, universe, we only have one block left.

Just one.

DELIBERATE AND UNAFRAID

2076-03-001
03::40

DEVI

Thick white clouds full of snow and heavy with life rolled in over the skies of North Philly. The bubble-pop bass of freestyle music rippled through the speakers on my '87 Casio boombox. It still worked and had all my old sticker tags on it. Thirteen-year-old me spent a whole summer tagging LA LUZ in thick black Sharpie everywhere. I put "Diamond Girl" all the way up; that was my momma's jam. She'd play it on full blast making eggs and chorizo on Saturday mornings.

Back when she still used to dance. Freestyle. It was an eighties baby Bori thing, least that's what she used to say.

I'm Deviana Ortiz. I was born right at the start of IMBALANCE. My momma nicknamed me La Luz because she needed to believe in something, and the warmth of the sun and its bright endless light was the thing. And when all the bodies piled up, and cities like New York and our very own Philadelphia crashed under the weight and death of a plague never before seen, the only light left was the one in my name.

So, I'm here, trying to make things right or at least better.

Better for Orion and Mala.

Better for O.1.

The snow flurried past my window like tiny butterflies. They landed where they pleased, gently. And thankfully, the fuckers weren't sticking. They were melting right into the concrete. We needed the distraction without the footprints. I didn't wanna lead anyone to my momma's old house, especially not the Federation.

Focus. Say your prayers.

Protect life.

Offer it gentle entry into the chaos of the universe.

Honor mothers. Honor birth.

Bless all families in spirit and reality. For all deserve to be fed,
    cared for, raised to thrive. Provided with housing and
    education, embraced as full and free people.

May the infants be the light and the joy

And the doula be the guide.

That last line always reminded me of her. My vibrant rebel mom, the one who, while she was pregnant with me, organized all the Free Mothers and secured housing and medical care for pregnant humans during IMBALANCE. She was at the ready, always putting moms and babies first.

That included ten-year-old me, surrounded by Free Mothers, babies, families. The world was crumbling and we got to work. I held hands with moms grieving their husbands, and breathed with them. Mom taught me to pack her black doula bag: essential oils, crimson rebozo, rice socks, *Sister Outsider* by Audre Lorde. Sometimes I even threw in my own raisin packs cuz, like, what if she needed a snack?

I wanted to be her.

Why didn't I ever say that to her?

Like, when she was still alive?

When she passed, I got *deliberate* and *unafraid* tattooed on my forearms. I needed to feel closer to her legacy somehow. As if being her only child, and an Aries and Puerto Rican like her, wasn't enough.

She got me ready for the all-encompassing work of being a steward to the people, to mothers and children; she knew about Orion before they even met Mala. Jenny Ortiz needed me, her baby, Deviana "La Luz" Ortiz, to be ready for a world on fire, reeling from plague.

I've got her black medical bag now. And I'm gonna save the world with it tonight.

And hopefully the Federation will mind its business and let me be a steward to the people, like my momma taught me.

Cuz right now, the whole damned world is watching and they're aching for a baby.

For life. For the promise that we will survive, that our atoms can replicate and be free. After a full decade since that last human birth—and all the egg-stealing and sperm-harvesting and kidnapping that came in the desperate years after people realized that IMBALANCE took the greedy rich and left the rest of us neutered—we're sucking at the marrow for hope. Who knew it would feel like this? I've never wanted kids and now all I can do is dream about one baby.

Which is so much better than all the damn nightmares I've had about Mom's stroke, you know?

I'm thirty now and I feel her even stronger. Time to plant my feet firm in her tracks and dig my hips into birth work.

Momma, I hope you can see me. We're taking over your house.

A baby was on its way. A secret fucking glorious *the world just might be worth saving* baby.

When the Federation assigned me to O.1, I was as skeptical as the rest of the Free Peoples. A couple was pregnant? Yeah, okay. But then I met them, Mala and Orion.

Their parents had been members of the Free Mothers. And they'd known my mom and even had some freestyle music playing when I went to go see them. It was fate and all the other beautiful universe crap that kept me rooted to birth work. That first night I offered them my life and they accepted.

I dropped to my knees when I got home and gave thanks, babes. My heart was full for the first time in forever.

I packed my black medical bag:

essential oils
Mom's crimson rebozo
peppermint sticks
ink pad
hot-water bottle
pocket-sized notebook
ballpoint pen
Vaseline

I was as ready as I could be to deliver this baby. And defend it, this beautiful half-black Puerto Rican and half-Filipino baby.

Y'all, the first baby born to the Federation of Free Peoples was gonna be one incredible brown-ass baby.

The snow fell in thicker swaths, like sheets of gold-star stickers. My arms rippled with gooseflesh.

A Channel 32 news van sidled down my street. North 8th with Butler on one end and West Erie on the other. "Fuck," I whispered.

In one swift move, I grabbed the medical bag and moved the key so soft in that lock there wasn't even a click. I was out and not about to suffer these fools. And if they were watching me, they'd see my commitment to duty, to the lives of people of color trying to have a damn baby in this wild, unforgiving world.

No Federation was greater than that. Especially not when life itself, for all peoples, was on the line.

WE, THE FREE PEOPLES

2076–03–001
51::50

KEY

". . . We're here at South 52nd Street in front of the empty home of Orion and Mala Lafayette-Santana. The scene is fraught with emotion. Citizens all across the globe are asking, 'What happened to the Lafayette-Santana family?' And most important, 'Where is Baby Free?' Neighbors broke down the door this morning, fearing the worst, and found that Mala and Orion were gone. Our crew in North Philly has confirmed that Deviana Ortiz, their birth worker, is also missing. . . ."

Click.

Ayima sat in the navigator position, guiding us through the snowy backstreets. Trent scanned the sidewalks, using enhanced scope. They both looked at me. I shut off the broadcast screen, leaned back into the MBW's leather seat, and rubbed my temples.

Our vehicle switched into cruise mode as both Ayima and Trent signed their plea to me. *Why are we chasing them and not offering our support?*

I signed back, frustrated. *They know we support them and still they ran. We must protect O.1.*

The fate of humanity was out in a snowstorm, nowhere to be found, and we were still disagreeing over the correct way to save everyone.

We, as in the Federation. All three of us Desmonds: twins Ayima and Trent, and me, Akilex "Key" Desmond. Yes, there are dozens of leaders throughout the world, and together we all make up the Federation of Free Peoples. But we Desmonds built the Federation.

No longer divided by borders and politics, we insisted on being Free People. Everyone who agreed on their own, without coercion or blackmail, signed our pact. Formally known as the 2066 Pact of the Free Peoples. It was originally a pledge between me and the twins. We promised each other compassion, the type that shares food, resources, and provides care for all.

We turned chaos into unity.

IMBALANCE reduced all of society, all of *us,* to pain-numb orphans scavenging for survival.

It wasn't easy. Our father, Hector Caraballo, once the borough president of Manhattan, tried to gain control during the wake of IMBALANCE. Our entire lives he'd been disgusted by having queer black children, two of whom were born deaf, and me, the one who according to him would *never be a real man*. He refused to marry our mom, Shirley Desmond, or let her receive care from the Free Mothers.

She didn't survive the birth of Ayima and Trent.

But that didn't break Hector Caraballo, Mr. Light-Skin Puerto Rican (*papi chulo* to the women in the Lower East Side) and everyone's favorite conservative politician. Nothing did. He rallied surviving men of color to snatch the power left by the 1 percent. My father thought he'd outsmarted the plague, convinced it only killed greedy white folks.

He refused the only known treatment for IMBALANCE: comparation treatments. It would have realigned the way his brain processed empathy and compassion. But no, he would not accept it, same way he refused to call me Key, to use male pronouns. He kept hold of his internalized white-supremacist capitalistic values till his last breath.

The headache forming behind my eyes throbbed. I signed to them, *Enough. We have a job to do.*

Ayima and Trent reviewed their digital map of Central Philadelphia. They'd circled all areas in and around Mercy Hospital and the homes of Mala and Orion and Deviana Ortiz. Somewhere in this fifteen-mile jawn was O.1, and their safety was the main priority of the Federation.

Baby Free must survive. But first they had to be born. And, dammit, there'd been a whole plan, developed in conjunction with the birth family and the Federation. The entire Federation was predicated on commitment to agreements, and if at the first sign of newness that commitment faltered, well then, how? How were we supposed to remain calm and not start an inter-Federation person hunt for O.1?

HOW?

I popped a Xalance, hoping these questions and all the anxieties they stirred in me would ease up.

The night we found out about O.1 was wild. Nurse Reece Jones made the frantic call to the Philadelphia Federation of Free Peoples. She'd only had an hour left on her shift, and it took me about that long to fully understand what Nurse Jones was saying. The words made sense: *pregnant, non-binary human, Orion, Mala, family, pregnant, pregnant, with child, someone here is with child.*

All those words made sense, but my head, my mind, my brain, everything, all of it was firing away. Every synapse, every concept of the New World of the entire Federation of Free Peoples, each individual article of the 2066 Pact of the Free Peoples, all the names of Lost Consumers on the IMBALANCE memorial wall, the complexity of the DRNA of IMBALANCE — every symbol and word that I'd spent my life memorizing fluttered through my consciousness, and then I was outside of the office and floating past the atmosphere of the Free Globe. I saw Mom there and she was covered in sunrays.

I didn't register Ayima and Trent shaking me and signing my name. I didn't feel it when Ayima shook me by the shoulders or when Trent took control of the frequency and completed the call with Nurse Jones.

Cuz it couldn't be. Ten years. 3,650 days. No births.

And here came Orion and Mala and O.1.

Once I snapped back to reality from that call with Nurse Reece, it was all O.1. We took on O.1 and their parent citizens, Orion Lafayette and Mala Amalia Santana, on the ninety-second day of Orion's reproductive cycle. We quarantined them. It made so much sense at the time. The Lafayette-Santana quarantine made Federation headlines. It was the first sequestering of Free Peoples since the days before IMBALANCE.

Our duty was to protect O.1 and their parents with the most support and care possible. We provided the family with everything they needed, according to the guidelines set by the Free Mothers: Round-the-clock medical care was specifically designed to meet Orion's individual needs as a non-binary parent of color; their fridge was stocked with the freshest nutrients, proteins, and minerals and everything else the Free Peoples' guidebook utilizes to promote well-being and physical health.

I even planted extra ginger roots in their garden, for the people's sake. We asked ourselves, *How would we have wanted Mom to be treated?* We did it the right way.

But a movement rumbled among the Free Mothers, and they declared that we were being unjust to our fellow citizens. They said that families deserve to blossom without eyes above and below. Their signs made it seem as if chaos should be honored, as if the life of Baby Free should be left up to fate, all things that kept me lying awake at night mourning a generation that hadn't been born yet and could possibly die if we didn't intervene. But no one saw it like that, at least no one on the Free Mothers' airwaves.

And when the people pushed, we asked Orion and Mala if they wanted to go back home. They were packed and ready before we gave the official okay. I should have noticed then that something was amiss. I should have remembered who I was before IMBALANCE and the Federation, back when I had my own thoughts and didn't carry the weight of all people on my shoulders.

The agreement was that we'd allow Orion and Mala to return to their home. We continued offering food, medical, spiritual, all of it. At one point, Ayima and Trent learned to bake pie, just in case Orion needed another one.

And every night I sat with Mala, offered my care and attention. Documented every moment of her day and inquired into her well-being, mental health, happiness. She taught me how to distill lavender and turn it into an essential oil. We'd dab some on our wrists during sessions. I showed her photos of me and the twins as kids. Even shared the one picture I had left of us with our mom.

This whole situation was different. There was love between us. But we both knew that I was still Federation.

We, the Federation, bargained for rights to the birth. We agreed that the birth would be broadcast to the Global Community. We decided that it would take place in a secure location in the presence of Federation-authorized medical personnel.

And when we presented our plan to the Lafayette-Santanas, they agreed too.

We all gave our word.

That's what the Federation runs on, that's how we live as Free Peoples united in this Global Community.

Because we *trust* each other.

We have to. IMBALANCE isn't over. It lives within us now, waiting for corruption and greed to resurface in each of us. It will forever spread through the saliva in lies, the venom in greed. We were all immune as kids, but now . . . who knows how its power has grown?

That's why we're here, tracking this family within an inch of our own lives. The future of civilization is here right now, and we cannot for one second allow it to try to "outsmart" IMBALANCE.

"There," Trent signed.

Her surveillance screen popped up and began zooming in through the swirling snow. Ayima pointed to the right, all the way toward the back of a brick building: faint footprints in fresh snow. Their hands worked a mile a minute signing, switching gears, and making adjustments to our course. I slammed down the window and hurled half my body out of it to check those footprints.

Two sets, both leading down the alley.

ALL FOR 0.1

2076–03–001
55::50

ORION

In dreams you appeared to me, round like your mother and gloriously black like me. The depth of your gray eyes and the spiraling contours of your footprints filled my nights with peace.

You must know that, mi vida. I knew you before the weight of you was placed in my trembling arms. Your fingers found the softest spot in my neck, and that heart of yours beat for all of humanity.

You were six pounds and eight ounces of revolution.

And the second we spotted Deviana's flashing lights, you kicked me twice in the gut. They were quick little thrusts full of energy and attitude. That was you, telling me that everything was going to be radiant.

And we'd be wrapped in the rays again.

That's all I needed to run arm in arm with Mala toward Deviana's car. I'd always wanted to go to the Philly Zoo, couldn't have imagined that I'd be running past it, pregnant with anything, all in the name of evading the Federation. And of course, giving birth to you.

The second Mala shut the door behind us, Deviana took off. I snapped my seat belt shut and held on tight as the second tremor quaked through me. The veins in my forearms bulged; my eyes rolled back. Bright white light flooded my consciousness and there you were again. Waiting for me.

I ran to you, but you faded away. And, bam, I was back in that cramped car, holding on to all the pieces of myself that I could as we cruised up Girard Avenue. Mala wouldn't let go of my hand for anything. Through each new tremor, her love anchored me in place.

As we merged onto Route 76, Federation vehicles screamed past us, headed in the opposite direction. Mala whipped her head around. Devi barely increased her pressure on the gas pedal. In fact, she clicked the stereo on, and that "Let the Music Play" freestyle song bopped from her speakers. It helped. The song gave me something to focus on, some extrasensory thing along with Mala's hands to keep me here.

Sweet babe, it was like you needed to split me open to be free.

None of us noticed the other MBW, cruising two car lengths behind us. Otherwise, we would have switched course and kept driving. We wouldn't have led them to us.

No, we wouldn't have done that.

But you were ready to meet the world, and that final tremor catapulted me out of my fear and into the present. I gripped Devi's shoulder from the back and she floored it to the exit. We hit the boulevard going sixty-five. I was flying, roaring with this adrenaline. It was all new, all you.

We'd make it. And even though neither Mala nor Devi told me where we were going, I knew. You showed me. That home in North Philly away from all the prying eyes and well-intentioned Federation agents, that home where the Free Mothers held meetings full of policy change and home-cooked meals—that was all yours.

There was no other place in the Federation of Free Peoples worthy of you, mi vida.

And there was no way you'd experience this world as I did, alone, without family, foster home after foster home after juvenile detention center. IMBALANCE was almost a blessing. It's the thing that unlocked all the cages I'd been placed in, sweet babe. None of that would ever touch you.

You would have love. And pie, lots of delicious pie.

So we ran; I'd run forever with your mother, Mala. My first family, first love, first moment where I felt rooted to the earth, my body.

And all I remember next is Mala holding my left hand and Devi in position to welcome you. Between my thighs a galaxy was re-born. Didn't even know bodies could be that magnificent. Know that I've always loved it, this body, my non-binary everything; it's like floating free above the chaos of performance.

You flourished inside me, sweetest babe. You were born from every brushstroke of *wrapped in the rays* and each drop of lavender oil your momma placed on my wrists to keep us calm.

With the force and energy of a lightning bolt announcing itself to the sky, you claimed your place in the world.

And right as Deviana caught you and Mala's tears of joy fell onto my shoulder, the doors slammed open.

All three of our Federation agents stormed in, ready to detain us.

We froze, all of us, staring at what was about to happen. Each of our faces set to endure whatever battle lay before us. No one spoke. The scene was a little too much, see, cuz you were in it.

The living breathing beating you.

No longer Baby Free or O.1.

But you.

And you screamed, sweet babe, and it freed us all.

Agent Key dropped to one knee. Ayima and Trent knelt alongside him. They put their hands on his shoulders as his chest heaved from weeping. All he kept saying was, *They're alive, Momma. They're alive.*

Devi tilted your face to them. Their soft gasps filled the room, and then you were in my arms and nothing else has mattered since. Not like you, not like our family, the Lafayette-Santanas.

The room belonged to Devi. She recited the Free Mothers' Prayer as she worked. Key and the twins and Mala joined in. The hum of their voices a meditation on survival. You stopped crying, started gurgling. Devi held you firm and secure.

The rest of the Federation was still on the move to secure Baby Free. Key jumped on the Federation frequency to call off the hunt.

Other Federation leaders pushed, threatened to overthrow him. Key finally shut off his phone and stomped it under his boot.

Mala drafted a plan for how we could continue dodging the Federation. Together. Ayima hopped up and offered to sketch out the best escape route. Devi wiped you clean, weighed you, and took your footprints.

Trent signed and asked if it was okay to just sit with me. I signed back, *Of course.*

Trent's mobile buzzed again and again on the table. Finally, she checked it. It buzzed again in her hands. She picked up and her eyes went wide with tears.

She put the phone on speaker.

That's when we got the word.

The word.

That you were the first.

But you wouldn't be the last.

INFANTS.X

2091-03-001

55::50

LUZ

I was born during the snowstorm of 2076 in the Free State of Philadelphia.

I was the first of the Free Infants, but I wasn't the last. Now I'm fifteen. I shaved most of my head yesterday, dyed the rest pink. I said *I don't give a fuck* out loud in front of both my parents, and they laughed because it was about the Federation.

And I still got the *look.* The *you're lucky that was funny cuz you still shouldn't be cursing in front of us* look. But my momma, Mala, still hugged me. And my bapa, Orion, laughed while offering me the first slice of my Born Day blueberry-peach pie.

My godmom, Deviana, gave me her ancient boombox, and I'm like in love with it. The twins, Ayima and Trent, brought bags of peaches and blueberries, just in case. And my main best dude, Key, he gave me my file. The whole thing, like, the official Federation copy. And now all the pieces of my birth and me fit.

All of them were there the day I was born. And we're our own family, a new family full of Free People.

IMBALANCE is the reason my folks got pregnant. You should know that part. The sentient bacterium, birthed of Mother Earth, evolved enough times to affect reproduction forever. As it sought out greed and excess, the bacterium learned to affect life and only allow it to bloom where there was compassion, empathy, and real love between peoples.

Thousands upon thousands of us blossomed into existence.

Momma and Bapa were the first parents.

But they were not the last.

And after we finished my B-Day pie, I gathered my supplies and wandered over to the mural on the side of our house. Bapa made it when they were pregs with me: *wrapped in the rays*. I've sat in front of it daydreaming about the future since before I was born. So honored and geeked they agreed to me adding some hot pink and the Free Mothers' Prayer to it:

Protect life.

Offer it gentle entry into the chaos of the universe.

Honor mothers. Honor birth.

Bless all families in spirit and reality. For all deserve to be fed,
    cared for, raised to thrive. Provided with housing and
    education, embraced as full and free people.

May the infants be the light and the joy

And the doula be the guide.

GABBY RIVERA is a queer Latinx writer living in Brooklyn, New York. She is currently writing *America*, America Chavez's solo series, for Marvel. America is Marvel's first Latina lesbian superhero. Rivera's critically acclaimed debut novel, *Juliet Takes a Breath*, was listed by *Mic* as one of the twenty-five essential books to read for women's history month, and it was called the "dopest LGBTQA YA book ever" by *Latina*. Put simply by Roxane Gay, it's "f***ing outstanding."

THE BLINDFOLD

TOBIAS S. BUCKELL

I've got a mother that wants to get in on a long-term financing agree-ment to change her son's race for a trial, Ecstasy pings you. *His court date is coming up; the hearing for the random race generator is next Thursday.*

Thursday. That doesn't leave a lot of time. But, then, that's why E is pinging you.

They're paying in cryptocurrency, Ecstasy says. *My commission is the usual 10 percent. They've already set up the chain; you just need to agree to be on the other side.*

Local judicial computer systems have shit security. It's always been the case. The nature of trials and the mysterious workings of the law aren't usually of strong interest to a hacker (though you think of yourself more like a fiddler and digital spelunker than hacker) other than in a more abstract, philosophical sense. In the past, someone like you would pay enough attention to judicial se-curity so that you could delete yourself from a jury-duty pool, but you never spent a lot of time worrying about the actual sausage-making until scooped up by police for doing something illegal.

But that has changed lately with the equal-representation laws.

Math, statistics, and algorithms for fairness became important after the turn of the century. Before then, those things just reported the inherent unfairnesses. Run an analysis of the number of cases where similar crimes happened. Sort them by race. Compare the results.

What do you get?

Judges give different sentences. The data is there. Undeniable.

But the more important question became not whether human beings were flawed but what could we do about it?

Consider this: Analyzing the prison sentences judges handed down based on how long it had been since they had something to eat shows a pattern of longer sentences given the longer it has been since they ate.

Is it fair for one person who smoked some weed to get one sentence in the morning just after breakfast and for someone close to lunch to get a longer sentence just because Judge So-and-So's blood sugar is dropping?

People started jockeying for times, suing about being given pre-lunch hearings, and then finally someone passed a law requiring judges to use one of those diabetic pill monitors you swallowed to test blood sugar and beam the results out to a phone. Later, judges were mandated to have IV drips when on the bench in order to keep blood-sugar levels even.

There. Everyone has an equal chance at sentencing.

Well, sort of. There are still the differing race results. You can't IV-drip your way around structural and implicit racism.

Then came the smartphone filters. Phones getting so good they could put face paint on live video of your digital face. It had once taken movie studios big money to create that effect.

So some lawyer had the bright idea of mandating that a client of his be tried as a white man because the jury had been selected of only white people. Not really a "group of his peers." If the jury, who had not seen any details of the defendant ahead of time, wore tamper-proof helmets running software repainting their client's skin tone, then this could be a fair trial.

Again, lawyers clamored that *everyone* be tried as a white male.

Instead, after a lot of legal wrangling, jurors had to wear the helmets and the sex and race of the defendant was randomized.

There were a lot of other details hammered out about what lawyers and prosecutors could and couldn't say about the physical details of the defendants. There was a lot of fighting about whether the filter could be applied.

But, in this case, it had been. And Mom wanted to make sure her son was going to be perceived as white.

Your services wouldn't be cheap. She'd be paying that loan for ten years. But you would make sure the randomized software wasn't so random.

You order pizza and set in for a few long days of poking at the state-level security systems.

In movies, the edgy cool music starts up now. The clock on the wall starts spinning hands to show time flying by. You tap at the keyboard and lines of code stream across any of your three screens. There are usually cables running fat with wire draped across the background.

You're a minimalist, don't like cables, and work off a fifteen-inch laptop on your couch. Most of your software uses graphic interfaces, though you're happy to dip into the command line when needed.

A lot of what you're doing is watching programs crunch away, trying to log in randomly to weak spots while you binge-watch a new season on the TV.

That is, until alerts start popping up all over your screen.

Someone is tracing you right back to your location.

And they've shut down all the security weaknesses you've found.

For a moment you just stare as it gets worse. These people are burrowing back down into your shit. Deep. Like, find-your-real-name deep.

Bug-out time.

You've planned for this. Someone doing the things you do has to have a plan for what happens when the tables get turned. You shut the laptop down and place it on top of a large electromagnet plugged in next to your coffeemaker.

The lights dim as it kicks on.

Hard drive toast—the only gadget you keep in the apartment—you wrap the laptop in a plastic bag and walk out to the porch while wearing a ski mask. Lake Erie glitters with Cleveland lakefront lights as you inflate the helium weather balloon and let it go, laptop dangling underneath.

Within a minute it's a bright speck heading up into the clouds.

You've always followed protocol going in and out of the apartment, zipping up a dinosaur-face hoodie. You pull that old friend back on and get out.

Ditch the hoodie a few blocks away and then you are zigzagging through the streets, running it all through your mind. The reverse attack on your device had been *fast*, as if backed by some heavy machinery.

That wasn't state. Federal counter-intrusion?

Something worse?

NSA.

It had the speed and power of high-level government or military programming.

Taking on this job has put you in some sort of bull's-eye, and you've lost the nicest apartment you've ever paid cash for. It's burned; you can't go back.

"Fuck!"

You can hoof it down to a nice bar in Shaker Heights. Maybe go find a book to read somewhere while you quiet your racing mind. Don't make hasty decisions. Be calm and deliberative.

There's a retirement fund in cryptocurrency tied to a string that you spent four months memorizing before you destroyed the only printout of it when you converted your savings over. Is it time?

But . . . you keep thinking about what you saw happen on the laptop's screen. How aggressive it was.

It's like scratching an itch. You can't help yourself. You have pride. And you're pissed about losing the apartment.

After some asking around, you find a public library. An hour later you're in a virtual window to some heavy shared computing in a blockchain farm in Ghana. You're using the equivalent of a city block's worth of computing power, paying out the ass per second, to brute-force a look-see at the defenses around Cleveland's municipal servers.

This time you're using a virtualized supercomputer, something with neural-net learning, to hide the location of your attack.

It ain't the city of Cleveland putting up a virtual Hadrian's Wall around its systems. It's a moat that's getting triggered by anyone sniffing around *this* particular case.

"Russians," you grumble, tracing back a few calls.

"Hey, E," you say over the cheap prepaid cellphone you picked up from one of your bank boxes later in the afternoon. "Why did I just get burned by Russians?"

"Burned? How bad?"

"I lost my apartment."

"You launched from within—"

"Don't lecture me. I thought this was a municipal job," you snap. "Why is military-grade counter-intrusion software made by Russians protecting Cleveland municipal servers?"

You could have spent time figuring this out at the public library, but after time spent dueling Russian cryptography, you figure less time logged in is best. Easier to ask the person who had a good view of the situation.

Ecstasy sighs. "This is bad."

"You think? Why is this happening?"

"I think we just stepped into the middle of an info-sec war," Ecstasy says. "You know, way back in the original Cold War, the old USSR used to recruit black intellectuals by pointing out how horrific capitalism had been. Enslavement. Jim Crow. Segregation. Major inequality between races all the way. And the best propaganda is that which lands closest to the truth. Muddies everything up. I think our case lands in the middle of that."

"How?"

"Mrs. Mandi wants us to change her son's race to help his chances of not getting indicted. The jury is all white. She knows that, even today, it's an uphill battle in a Midwest state."

"What did the son do?"

"Does it matter?"

"Yeah," I say, surprised. Ecstasy has never really been any kind of social activist, so the question catches me off guard. "I want to make sure I'm fighting on the right side, you know?"

"Well, in that case, are you with the Russians who want to destabilize us or against that?"

"Against." You say that quickly and firmly. "But I don't want to help a murderer or something."

"You weren't worrying about that when you took the job just for money," Ecstasy pointed out.

"No," you protest. "Leveling the field so that, no matter what he did, like any other person, he got the same consideration. That's all."

"Fair enough. What you want to be fighting for is the integrity of the system, right? Making our kid white in the eyes of the jurors only means we're leveling the field, I agree. Even if Russians are meddling, whether with elections or not, making sure systems stay in place means civilization continues."

"But they're meddling for a reason."

Ecstasy sighs again. "It's another moment of very public injustice in Cleveland, when an all-white jury convicts a black kid. The Russians are already creating Facebook protest groups on both sides of the issue. They're telling people to show up outside the courthouse to protest, and then they're calling for armed Midwesterners to counter-protest them. They're hoping that if they throw enough gasoline on the small fires, a big fire will break out. Then they rinse and repeat, rinse and repeat. If we dig deep enough, we may even find out they stacked the jury pool white."

"E, I think they might have my true name."

She's quiet for a while. "Shit."

"I can't help that mother. But if it's fire they want, I can burn them right back."

"Be careful. And I should tell you never to call me again, but . . ."

You've been working together two years now.

"I'll let you know how it turns out," you say. "Are you okay? I think I hear sniffling."

"The damn flu," Ecstasy says. "It's going around."

Hmmm, you think. *It* is *going around.*

In the old days you blew the lid off a secret by sending the documents to a reporter. They check sources, do some footwork, then publish the shocking story. Everyone reads it, the information is out. Public opinion turns nasty.

It's not like that anymore, though, is it?

You do a full document dump on a third-party leaks site, brushing over your tracks on the way out.

A few nibbles come to an encrypted temporary email address.

An old-school media group runs the story. RUSSIAN INFLUENCE ON LOCAL TRIAL. They explain that both protestors and counter-protestors are being recruited by Russian groups.

Then the shit hits the fan.

Within a few hours of the story going out, the bots all ramp up. That document dump was from a hacker trying to throw the case to free the kid, the bots say. Your actual, real name is suddenly floating out there. But they don't have pictures yet. Your paranoid years scrubbing that from the world is helping you out.

But a lot of strangers on the internet are calling for your death. Some of them are really good at it, and you get found.

They try to kill you.

The way the assassination attempt goes down is like this: Someone on the other side of the world who tracked where your replacement laptop was called the local police and said you were standing in the park (you were; you had hopped onto the public Wi-Fi). They said you had a gun and described you as black . . . ish. Because although there are no pictures of you out there, your census form notes that Daddy has a fro and Mommy was a white woman.

Now, the town is south of Cleveland. Ohio is the Midwest, where folk have been Southern-aspirational for a while now. Ohio may have been on the Northern side of the Civil War and supplied an above-average number of troops. Ohio may even have a number of small towns with plaques that mark them as stops in the Underground Railroad. But these days Confederate flags have proliferated on more and more trucks and started appearing in more and more houses, even though Ohio's proud history is that it helped put that insurrection down.

That's strike one of three.

Strike two is that the park you're in is near a school, so won't someone think of the children? Never mind that Bubbas wander out onto Main Streets like this with combat rifles more heavily accessorized than a ten-year-old's full Barbie accessory kit. You and I both know that the second amendment is only respected if you're a certain shade. You'll never see the fucking NRA defend a black person for carrying a gun. Hell, they helped draft gun-control legislation back when the Black Panthers were pulling the original open-carry stunt with machine guns. That freaked white people out enough to change gun laws.

You have an antidote to the first two strikes, however. When the Barney Fifes roll up into the park, one of them jumping from a moving car with their gun out, looking for the dark-skinned person with a gun, there's just you sitting on a bench with a laptop.

And you, as far as anyone here can tell, look white as all fuck.

All that time inside hacking away on computers means you don't even have a tan.

Anyone who ran into your dad on a street in this town would most definitely tag that man as a brother. Mom was the pale one. Gave you all those white skin genes. From Dad you got the face, the height, and some of the curliness in your hair. But you keep that shaved short, so the uniforms that surround you don't have any reason to doubt their eyes.

You pass.

The assassin doesn't know that. The assassin lives on the other side of the world and only sees that you are "biracial."

So you get to live.

Oh, strike three. That's really delicate. There's a video of you doing something really horrible to an underage girl. Now, the video was made using rendering software by the same people who hired the assassin, so they got details wrong. It's weaponized disinformation.

Still, they hacked the system to put out a warrant with the video attached, hoping that a video of a brown man touching an underage white girl will further get you shot.

But you've spent three days studying county records to make sure you're temporarily safe from this sort of vector of attack.

This place has dismissed, buried, and delayed more women's statements about sexual violence than anywhere else in the state. The local high school football team all but got a high-five for some rapey shit that went down a few years ago. This place wants to be the next Steubenville.

Because of all that, you know that this is the safest place to get arrested while that fake video is out attached to a fake warrant for your arrest. Once they see that you look white and male, they'll chill the fuck out while you wait for reinforcements to arrive.

A lot of white people claim they don't "see" race. They claim they wear a blindfold when it comes to the subject, even though statistics show that just isn't the case. You've been around as a white-looking dude long enough to know that your very existence puts lie to the claim.

Once you're booked, safe, and your lawyer appears on your phone to teleconference in on the statement, you explain all of the above to the younger cop videoing you.

Only you leave out all the reasoning above. No reason to antagonize the local PD by calling them Steubenville Lite™ or Confederacy Aspirational, even if you would have been shot by now if several strands of your DNA had decided to split *just* a bit differently.

And even these county folk here know about SWAT-ing. It's usually some basement dweller pissed off at someone online calling in a fake high-tension 911 call. They'll say something like, *So-*

and-so is inside their apartment at address such-and-such and they have a nine-year-old girl hostage with a gun to her head. They're hoping the police response fucks up the person they're angry at.

What's newer is it being weaponized by foreign agents, as in your case.

"So why does someone on the other side of the world want to try and kill you by police?" the officer asks.

You take a deep breath before giving the next part of your statement. Because now comes the part where you're going to have to admit your white-collar crimes.

The future is getting a little murky.

But there is nowhere to go but through. Your lawyer, Doug, with the gleaming perfect smile and five-thousand-dollar suit, has a great deal lined up for you with the state department for all this information.

Time to squeal.

You pick up the candy bar that they've given you for a snack. Packed with peanuts. Some protein. A little boost in the blood sugar.

You explain how you hacked into the Cleveland municipal systems to give a kid on trial a fair shot.

"See," you tell the small-town police officer as you put down the candy-bar wrapper. "At this point I'm fighting a full-on state-sponsored political info-sec war, and I'm just one person. I'm losing because I started out thinking of this as a person-to-person fight I had to win."

As this entire story comes out, the officer listens calmly, carefully making notes as we go along.

"So, by morning, talk shows are getting call-ins. People are calling for my arrest, people are defending me and saying we should hack for social justice, some good debates about the nature of juror selection are happening, and other people are debating whether *I'm* a Russian agent."

You sip some coffee gratefully.

"And that's when the video comes out," he says.

"Yeah, and did you see it?" you ask him. "It should be attached to my arrest warrant."

He nods.

You plop your arm down on the table. Pale white against industrial fake brown wood. "See, when they made that video, they didn't have pictures of me yet. They do have my official description. That I'm mixed race, have shaved-close brown hair, green eyes, and that I weigh one-eighty. But see the mistake they made?"

The officer nods. You take a moment to note his name tag. Reynolds. He's gotten you food, been chill. Doesn't seem like a dick. He's been handling the statement's revelations with aplomb. "You're white. The man in that video, he was light brown. Didn't show his face well, so we could assume it was anyone that matched the size."

"Right. I'm light, not white," you say. Officer Reynolds frowns. "My father was black, my mother white."

"But . . ."

"Sometimes we come out like this. Sometimes we pass. It used to scare people in the old days; that's why they had the one-drop rule. Didn't want folks like me mixing in. Undercover brothers."

"No shit." Reynolds is taken by the idea and is grinning.

Okay, maybe Barney Fife is more chill than you gave him credit for.

You'd been eating a burger and fries in a dive bar when the video came on over the news with your name attached and your face apparently obscured by the shadows. The Russians had gone nuclear against you by making a video like that.

If sentiment had been against you before, it got lit the fuck on fire after that.

What to do?

What you did was, using some cryptocurrency stashed under another set of authorization keys far from your usual online haunts, you grab a cab. You sit in the backseat and let the car drive you around the city aimlessly, staring at the empty wheel turning this way and that in front of you.

You give Ecstasy your latest prepaid phone's number and she calls. "I just saw."

"It's bad. I'm on the move."

"Me too."

"Why do I feel like this is East Germany during the Cold War and I'm running away from spies in the shadows?"

"You should retire. Go somewhere nice and sunny before they find your face," Ecstasy says. "That's what I'm doing."

You look out the window. Cleveland's small, compact downtown slides past. The Health Line is crowded with med students getting out late. You stare at them for a moment, letting your brain free-associate.

"I don't like the idea of getting beat like this in my own country," you say.

"They smacked you down pretty hard."

"I'm burned, but I looked up the kid. Kwame. He's being tried as an adult."

"It's a sad situation."

"Forget Russia, forget the fact I'm burned," you say. "I'm just thinking about being fifteen and holding a phone up to record my bestie getting shot. I would have struggled against anyone when they came for it like that."

Was it a better step forward to force jurors to wear helmets that, if the random skin-tone choice came up white, made Kwame look less intimidating? You aren't sure. But . . . you remember all those cops who keep describing young black kids as monsters or in the same way one described large older men: Hulking. Brutish.

The only thing that separated you from being a hulk, a brutish thug, a scary thing, was a couple small expressions in your spirals of DNA that switched a sliver in another direction.

And all the other stuff swirling around, you set that aside.

"I think I can still help the kid," you tell Ecstasy. "But I'll need you to find me a good lawyer. I don't have a lot of time to do that and get what I need ready. I'm not rolling over."

And that's when you start looking for a rural town to go hide in, because you know it's only a matter of time before the enemy uses even more-dangerous tools against you.

You don't explain *all* of that to Officer Reynolds. You admit to trying to hack the municipal servers. You've shown up and used your identity to prove that you aren't that person in the video. You've admitted to trying to expose the Russians.

Doug the lawyer with the magic teeth has set up a deal while you're confessing mostly everything. You're only talking because he ordered you to come in and spin the whole tale. The feds want your testimony and insight.

You're so happy to give it. But you know not much will happen on that front, as so many of the senators, poisoned by that one election, are still unwilling to admit Russian interference is even a thing.

Ecstasy cashes out some cryptocurrency for you and, even though it will take months or longer for your legal situation to sort itself out, you're pretty much free to go, as long as you don't leave Ohio.

That's fine; you already have a place scoped out to hide low and start a semi-retirement. It's off the grid, solar powered (though what isn't these days?), and sits on a nice well so you don't have to worry about water shortages.

Reynolds uncuffs you, you sign all the necessary documents, and a car drives itself up to the front to pick you up.

You slide in. The woman on the front passenger side has slightly graying hair pulled back in a tight bun.

"Hey," she says.

"Ecstasy?"

She's wearing a plastic Halloween mask, so you can't see her face. You know you'll never find out her name. But she nods and turns her head to look back at you. "Since you're burned and out, I figured I could come see you. You were my number-one client. You made us rich."

"Now it's over."

She hands over a basket. It's wrapped with plastic, but you can see unbelievably expensive chocolates and scotches under the gleaming transparence. "I thought it was the least I could do."

You take her hand and squeeze it. "Thank you."

"So," she says. "How did you do it?"

"Do what?"

"The jury's hung; it was a mistrial. It doesn't look like the state will retry."

"Well, for one, by law," you say, spinning the empty candy-bar wrapper around your fingers. "The judge has to be plugged into a drip to make sure their blood sugar is solid. I hacked the vending machines in the courthouse. Their cameras now have a facial-recognition scanner that recognizes the judge and makes the machine beep and drop a candy bar whenever he's near."

Ecstasy laughs from behind the mask. "No way."

"Yeah. The Russians likely are messing with his sugar. Wanted to make sure the judge was in good shape."

"But the jurors, they're still all white," she says.

You smile.

It took you a long while to find what you were looking for. But not as long as you feared. The year you were born, a majority of

Americans thought having mixed-race babies was wrong. Somehow immoral. Gallup did a poll.

Now the number that truly, deeply believes that is barely double digits. There shouldn't be *any*, but progress is progress. And because of that, you're not as alone as you used to be.

In the end, you realized you didn't need to go up against the Russians in code.

You hired people sick with the flu to walk up and down the sidewalk anywhere between the courthouse and the jurors' homes and sneeze at them.

Sometimes that's all justice leans on: one person and a candy bar.

Or a sneeze.

You just needed to find out how many jurors it would take to fade away sick before someone like you could show up. Someone who was light, but not white.

Called "violent, poetic and compulsively readable" by *Maclean's*, science fiction author TOBIAS S. BUCKELL is a *New York Times* bestselling writer born in the Caribbean. He grew up in Grenada and spent time in the British and U.S. Virgin Islands, and the islands he lived on influence much of his work. His Xenowealth series begins with *Crystal Rain*. Along with other stand-alone novels and his more than fifty stories, his works have been translated into eighteen different languages. He has been nominated for awards like the Hugo, Nebula, Prometheus, and the John W. Campbell Award for Best New Science Fiction Author. He currently lives in Bluffton, Ohio, with his wife, twin daughters, and a pair of dogs. He can be found online at tobiasbuckell.com.

NO ALGORITHMS IN THE WORLD

HUGH HOWEY

"Look at these damn commies."

I glance up from my holo to see what Dad's cussing about this time. It could be anything from a concrete building with bland architecture to a queue of people outside an ice-cream shop. The older he gets, the wider the commie circle of ire and bile. Sometimes it's just kids playing music too loud. Today it appears to be the Muslim couple crossing the street in front of our car, her with a hijab and him with his ghutra. Dad eyeballs daggers at their supposedly commie souls. The stream of pedestrians breaks, and the car resumes its auto-drive, joining the flow of traffic. Dad cranes his neck to watch the couple.

"Not all Muslims are communists," I say, even though it's pointless. Qatar, Kuwait, and the UAE were among the first to give universal basic income a go, and so for Dad, the Middle East is patient zero in what he calls "a plague of joblessness." It's been twelve years here in the States, and most Americans have come around to accept the new system, especially once the checks started arriving on schedule. By "most," I mean that the latest poll is 53 percent approval. Which is a far cry from the single digits when the first states started experimenting. And yet a solid 30-plus percent of the population is like my dad, cashing their checks and complaining about the world unfolding around them and vehemently opposed. Mostly, Dad gets annoyed by how other people spend their free time. Not working hard enough, he says.

"Well, those two definitely were." He's lost them in the crowd and turns back to the road. "Why is the car taking us this way? It's faster to go down Franklin and cut through on Second."

I swipe the holo out of my vision; no way of catching up with the news when riding along with Dad. Pulling up Maps, I see a thick red line down Franklin. "There's construction a few blocks from here. This way is two minutes faster," I say.

Dad grunts his reluctant approval. Knowing him, he's torn between hating this infernal machine that will no longer let him drive and loving their shared appreciation for efficiency and details. My dad is the kind of guy who scans ahead as he walks through a parking lot to make sure he takes the shortest route possible. If I cut through a line of parked cars that angle away from our destination, rather than the next line of cars that angle toward it, he gives me a ten-minute lecture on the importance of the half second I just cost us.

"Look at these here," Dad says. Now he's glowering at a line of people outside a pho kitchen. Auto spigots deliver torrents of steaming soup in three flavors. Some people in the queue have small buckets to take home as much as they can carry. Enough for their family, a group of friends, or just a week's supply so they can binge-watch the latest drop on Flix. Doesn't matter why—all Dad sees is people getting something for free.

"Hey, Dad, tell me about the new place." Anything to divert his attention before a rant comes on. And anything to put off the real reason I joined him today. "What kind of cuisine were you thinking?"

"Italian," he mutters. He's on the knife-edge of having a terrible day because of the diorama the modern world is presenting outside his window. I feel bad for how much worse I'm going to make things with what I have to tell him.

"Italian!" I try really hard to be excited. "What're the chances of some wood-fired pizza?"

Dad touches the datapad on his forearm. He still uses the trackpad kind that his generation grew up with, won't have anything to do with neurals. It takes him a while, but his eyes focus on the spot of air where his holo resides. "Seventy-eight point two percent," he says.

"Yum," I tell him.

The car turns onto Sherwood and stops in front of a high-rise residential, first-floor commercial. There's an auto-laundry sandwiched between a GoDega and a shuttered storefront. Dad eyes the GoDega as people wander in, grab what they need, and shuffle back out. A woman lets her daughter collect a sack of neatly folded clothes from the auto-laundry, showing her how it works. I point toward the shuttered building, keeping my old man focused.

"Looks great. Used to be a Chinese restaurant?" There are dragons emblazoned on the awnings, and ornate carvings across the door header and window lintels. "How'd you find this place?" I ask him.

"Top search result," he says.

This is his answer for most things, has been for as long as I can remember. My dad is seventy-two, and he owns over a hundred restaurants across greater Texas. He doesn't take a single day off. To spend time with him means running errands like this. And every business decision he's ever made has been the result of a Google search; he loves to say how Google has never done him wrong.

Used to be that he never clicked over to the second page of a search. Now he doesn't even look at the second *result*. Hard to argue with his methods; he's never had a restaurant go under. Every one is a success, even though he charges for the meals. A good 40-plus percent of Texans are happy to pay, not trusting any food that human hands didn't touch.

Dad gets out of the car, and I watch as he sizes up his future Italian joint, hands on his hips, stance wide, the look of a man on a mountaintop gazing around at his domain. A coughing fit ruins the imagery as Dad wheezes and pounds on his chest. "I'll get you a water," I say, turning to the GoDega—

"Don't you dare," he croaks.

I shrug and watch him fight for air. Dad staggers to the door and palms the realtor pad. It recognizes him as having an appointment and opens the door. A guy named Mike Doolan used to do this for Dad; he was—I guess you'd call him his realtor, but all Mike did was show Dad around at the places from the top result of his searches. He got a percentage of the deal for palming Dad through the door, I guess because they were friends from college and believed in the old ways of doing things. Mike passed away last year. Dad didn't look for a new realtor.

We go inside the restaurant. Across the street, a queue is forming outside a pizza dispensary. A young man walks away with six or seven reusable boxes stacked high, chin pinning the pies in place. Thank god Dad doesn't see him.

"Look at this place," Dad says. Another favorite expression. It means one of two things: *Look at how terribly someone else ran the joint, at all the bad decisions they made*. But it also means: *Look at all the potential that I'm going to wring out of it*. Everything is someone else's failure and his future glory.

He casts his holo over the restaurant and makes the feed public. I know the drill and accept the link. Together, we see the restaurant as it'll be in a few weeks, all the pandas and dragons and cherry trees replaced with murals of Tuscan hillsides and those trees that look like asparagus.

"Looks great, Dad."

For a moment I think of Sylvia, the sweet old designer who used to do this for Dad, calling up the same interior-design AI that spits out the optimal décor and hires all the drones to come do the work. A few years ago, Sylvia moved to Pakistan to be a part of their art-revival movement. Dad hasn't spoken her name since, and I know not to ever bring her up.

"Eighty-two percent chance of pizza now," he says. The odds are always creeping up and down, fluctuating. His restaurants change all the time, whatever the algos suggest. A Chinese restaurant will become a build-your-own-burger joint almost overnight. No one complains. With trillions of points of data from every online review, every Insta snap of served food, every check-in and tweet, the algos know what a neighborhood needs before its residents do. It's like the time my wife and I found out we were having a kid because of new food combos she was grabbing out of the pantry and fridge. Our house just up and bought flowers one day to congratulate us.

"So why did this place close down?"

Dad is back behind the counter, looking at the kitchen space. Floating windows within his shared holo show all the costs of replacing the older pieces of equipment. None of what he does with his restaurants is considered "vital to the welfare," so there are costs. He wouldn't have it any other way.

"Previous owner wouldn't listen to the market," Dad says.

Probably the kind of person who manually reroutes his car through traffic, I think to myself. *Or dares look at the second page of search results. Or anything like what I'm about to do—*

"Hey, excuse me? Are you the new owner?"

We both turn and see a silhouette in the doorway. Dad closes down his holo and strides around the counter, reaches out his hand.

"That's right. Chuck Gillmore. You live in the neighborhood?"

I had the words I'd been dreading saying on the tip of my tongue, but now the moment is lost. I lean on one of the tables and watch my dad work his magic instead. He has an uncanny ability to pull people into his orbit and to recognize his own kind—people who appreciate the way the world used to work. People not like me.

"Yeah, Ben Grazzley. I live right over you. Well, up on the fifth floor anyway. Whatcha planning on doing with her?"

"Italian restaurant," Dad says.

"Oh, exactly what we need. I was just telling my wife we needed an Italian place down here."

I notice a woman standing behind the man, almost blocked from view.

"He was just saying that," we barely hear her say.

I very nearly ask them which home-assistant speaker they have in their apartment, wondering how much of their chatter goes into the percentages and the algos of Dad's top search results, but I keep it all to myself.

"Are you going to have pizza?" Ben asks.

Dad hesitates. Watching numbers tick up, probably. "Almost certainly," he says.

"Good good. All we got is the freebie place across the street."

Dad peers past the gentleman. They share a moment of coiled rage.

"You won't find machines back in *my* kitchen," Dad says. "Homemade pasta, cut with a knife, by hand. Human hand."

"That's right," Ben says, like there was a war once fought for the right for men to cut their own pasta and drive their own cars, and by god they may have lost one battle, but not this one. Not this one.

"I make a wonderful tiramisu," the woman says. She still hasn't been introduced to us. Doesn't seem to bother anyone except me.

"You're hired," my dad jokes, but I know he's serious. I've seen this before. She'll be in the kitchen the next time we visit, and Ben will be seating folks rather than having some holo point out their table. They'll get paid, and it'll go into the same account as their guaranteed income, so that when any money is spent it all feels like the money they earned the old way. Washed clean. Laundered, and not by machines.

Dad closes the deal on the spot, the algos handling all the details.

On the way home, I try to distract him from a line that's formed outside the national bank. Some people still like to pick up their income in physical form, small envelopes full of crisp bills. They're usually people Dad's age but not of his political bent. Everyone's handling this paradigm shift in their own way. The main thing I've seen in common is that more people are spending time with their families than before. And it seems everyone now plays an instrument, or paints, or is writing a book.

"Goddamn commies," Dad hisses, like he can read my mind, like he knows what I've been wanting to talk about all day. "These people think some moron sitting in a room somewhere can make the economy work—well, they can't. It's all gonna come crashing down. All of it. Hell, not one person in the whole world can know how much to price a pencil. Have I told you that?"

"Yeah, Dad." He's also been predicting a worldwide crash every year for almost two decades.

"How much do you think a pencil should cost?"

"Dad, you've told me this a thousand times." And a thousand times I've pointed out that the essay he mangles, "I, Pencil," was written in 1958, way before we even started settling the Moon. Before we had *calculators*.

"It's people like you and me, making lots of little decisions every day, taking risks, putting our capital out there, knowing our businesses inside and out. We're the ones that set the prices and wages, that keep the world moving along. These people are just sucking at the teat, always looking for a handout."

I used to bring up things like his mortgage deductions, capital-gains rates, the farm subsidy he gets for a little plot of tomatoes, but I'd given up those conversations decades ago. Those are abstracts. What I've been trying lately is to get him ready for specifics.

For this day.

"The day some commie in an office knows better than me what this market needs is the day I throw myself into traffic. Speaking of which, why are we going so slow? Why won't this car ever take the quickest route?"

"It is, Dad. If we go right, it's a minute more. And left here is six minutes slower."

Dad grumbles and settles back into his seat. His hand falls to the trackpad on his forearm. Somewhere in his vision, there's a Google query being made. I hope it's a business question, maybe the next restaurant he'll open up, making him piles of money he'll never spend, serving those who refuse to be served by machines. I hope it's not the other kind of query he likes to make, the ones about people. I've seen his search history. I know how he frames his questions. I know where the hate comes from.

"Dad, I've got something to tell you."

Maybe my voice quavers. Maybe this has been a long day of disappointments. Maybe he just knows. But he looks at me the way he looks at all the people of the world he despises.

"What?" he asks. Almost like a dare.

"I put in my notice," I tell him.

"I forbid it." He turns back to his holo for a moment, then looks out his window instead. The few times I've tried to raise the possibility, it's ended like this. An ultimatum and silence. Not this time.

"Tomorrow's my last day. I put the notice in weeks ago—"

"Then they'll take you back. You're their biggest account manager. They'll—"

"Dad, I oversee an algorithm. I don't do anything. It's by design. The last five years, I've been working on a system that can do my job so no one else has to—"

"So you'll do what, then?" He whirls on me, eyes full of fire and tears. "Sit around the goddamn house? Write poetry like that brother of yours? Go ride a camel across Africa on some hajj? You're about to have a child. What kind of household are you building for him?"

"She. It's gonna be a girl, Dad. We just found out. And Sam's leaving her job as well—"

"For maternity leave."

"No, for good. We don't need the money. We're working just to work, and neither of us looks forward to going in."

"That's why it's called *work*, son. You aren't *supposed* to like it."

The rage has faded. He's begging now. He must see that I'm serious, must be terrified he's about to lose another son.

"We're going to stay in Houston, at least for a while. So you and Mom can be around the baby. But we want to travel, to spend our time learning together and teaching her what we can. Spending every moment we can together—"

"You'll suffocate her," Dad says.

We're almost back to his high-rise. I should've taken us the slower way. The conversation has done its damage, and it'll take a lot more talk to heal the wounds. I want to throw my arms around him, but I don't know if the two of us remember how to hold one another.

"Look at that," he spits. There's a couple carrying several grocery bags each out of the GoDega across the street. "Something for nothing," he says.

"I'll call you tomorrow," I say, getting out of the car. "Congrats on the new place."

"I'm in meetings all day tomorrow."

"Thursday, then."

"I'll be on a plane. Chicago."

I give up. Standing outside the car, about to close the door, Dad gives me one more look meant to shame me. "You're gonna suffocate each other," he says.

I look at my old man and think of all the times his friends and family—hell, myself—have called him a machine. Like that was a compliment. How he can go and go forever and never stop, never take a day off. No wonder he hates them so much. All that going, and I can't remember what I did as a kid other than accompany him to work, watch him make deals, sit there while he stared at his financials.

"You might be right," I tell him. "We might."

He grimaced as I admitted to the unknown. But for me, there was joy in not being handed all the answers. And I nearly added that suffocation by family was much preferred to starvation, but there was no point—he wouldn't understand what I meant. There were no algorithms in the world that could make it compute for him.

HUGH HOWEY is the *New York Times* bestselling author of *Wool*, *Sand*, *Beacon 23*, and more than a dozen other novels. His works have been translated into 40-plus languages, and TV adaptations of *Wool* and *Sand* are in the works at AMC and SyFy. Howey worked as a bookseller while penning most of his novels. His two life dreams have been to write a novel and to sail around the world. He currently lives on a catamaran in Fiji, where he's continuing to write as he fulfills his dream of circumnavigating the globe.

ESPERANTO

JAMIE FORD

In 1588, the English dramatist John Lyly wrote: "As neer to fancie is beauty, as the pricke to the rose, as the stalke to the rynde, as the earth to the roote."

Beauty used to be in the eye of the beholder. And people used to say that I had a type. Short hair. Big eyes. Brown skin. Curvy and soft. Like I used to be. Before I woke up from surgery, thirty or forty pounds thinner, my breasts smaller, my hair longer, my double chin all but gone, an iLite pulsing at my temple.

"How are you feeling today?" The neurologist smiles as she glances at a tablet near the examination table to catch my name. "Catalyst White, I presume?"

"Well, aside from being disfigured and having a new name, I'm stellar. Couldn't be better." I lie, of course. And I don't blame her for forgetting my machine-generated moniker. I've seen how I look in the mirror. In the grand social experiment known as the city-state of Esperanto—my new home and place of confinement for the next year—we all look vaguely alike. My olive skin is now marigold, the racially inert standard. My new hair shimmers with digital pigmentation, moving like shadows under water.

Beneath those shadows are scars, hidden by a clever augmented reality.

My vision blurs and refocuses as the good doctor makes a few adjustments before sending me out into the surreal world. I'm nervous as I smell something sweet, like warm cotton candy, then ammonia. I hear water rushing, then glass breaking, then nothing.

I had a habit of chewing my fingernails raw, especially when I was stressed. But I can't do that anymore. They were blown off in the same explosion that took my left thumb, damaged the soft tissue of both hands, ravaged my face, and burned away most of my real hair. I feel lucky, though, cliché as that sounds, as I touch the jangled ridge of skin and staples where my eyebrows used to be. I remember that the same bomb blast that ended my first year at Google's Mountain View Township killed twenty-nine staffers, including my preceptor, Alyce Harring, who ironically, as the Dissociated Press was quick to point out, had a Twitter history that was sympathetic to the insurrectionists.

Propaganda of the deed, Alyce had argued, *is the violence necessary to shake the foundations of those who have amassed 99.9 percent of the world's capital.* (She might have said *hoarded*, but since my recovery, I wasn't so sure.) *Are we really innocent if children are starving while we're spending trillions on tech?*

I never got to answer her question.

William Shakespeare, not a man to pass up a good phrase when he saw one, repurposed John Lyly's words as: "Beauty is bought by judgement of the eye, not utter'd by base sale of chapmen's tongues."
pausing to google: CHAPMEN

People-watching is my favorite pastime these days. It doesn't matter where. At a café, at a park, even waiting in line at the market. With the iLite, everyone in Esperanto is digitally similar. I try to guess their real ages, their races, even their genders. It's challenging, but I keep trying. I know citizens can change their hair, their eye color, even the patterns of their clothing with the merest thought, but they all look like avatars to me, simulacra—visually pleasing but homogenized. They look like what elevator music would be if it showed up in human form, drank wine from a box, had a respectable day job and a digitally enhanced spouse at home with kids to match.

"May I buy you another cup of coffee?" a young woman in a metallic-looking sari asks. "Or something stronger, perhaps?" She sits down across from me and follows my line of sight through the large café windows to the nearby subway station. The crowds of workers and day laborers look happy. The smiling children in matching uniforms walk to school. The streets are clean, too perfect, and the absence of armored police is comforting but also disquieting. That's when I take stock of the purple sky in the distance, the colorful birds, the airplane overhead with its prismatic contrail, all of which distract from the ashen taste of soot in the air.

I shrug. "Make yourself at home."

"I am. I do. That's what we call this place, you know." She motions to a waiter. "We call our city *Home*. Only outsiders call it Esperanto—like the language created after the First World War. It was thought that a shared tongue . . ."

I stare at her as she searches for the words. She's unique, despite her golden skin. Something is different. The way she carries herself.

She notices me staring and smiles before continuing. "A shared tongue would prevent certain cultural misconceptions and lead to more . . . equanimous engagements."

"Um. Yeah, about that." I watch the waiter refill my cup. "That didn't turn out so well, did it? They built this place where everyone is born with a machine name, devoid of cultural connectivity. How's that working out for you?"

"I'm August Random." She touches my arm in lieu of a handshake. "And it's all I've known. Though, like everyone, I've had the chance to know something else, to experience the outside world. Once a year, the gates are open. Anyone can leave. But no one ever does. In fact, no one's left Home in twenty years. Why do you think that is?"

"Cult mentality? Monocultures are hard to escape. Just ask the Amish."

She furrows her brow.

"You have no idea what I'm talking about, do you?"

She shakes her head. Her hair changes colors to match the changing patterns on her sari. I wonder how long it takes to not be startled by this.

"You know I don't belong here." It's more of a statement than a question.

I watch as she sighs.

"Neither do I. Not for much longer."

"And why is that?"

She touches the button at her temple. Her appearance blurs into the form of my late mentor. Not a perfect doppelgänger—her skin is still marigold, her hair translucent—but the facial features are Alyce's. My heart skips a beat and I start to tear up. I wonder what my digitally enhanced tears must look like. Sparkling diamonds? Rivulets of light? Or nothing—camouflaged like my scars?

"I know who you are," the woman says. "And I know what you've been through. You've been given a gift. And eventually you'll take my place. . . ."

"A gift." I almost laugh as I'm crying. "I can't leave for a year."

Then she changes, Alyce becoming August once again. She

wipes my tears with her fingers, and I feel happy to have a connection to a real person for the first time since waking up here. She holds my cheeks in her hands and looks at me the way a kindergarten teacher looks at a frightened child on the first day of school. "Why would you want to?"

Then, in 1741, Benjamin Franklin came in from a thunderstorm, put down his kite, and wrote: "Beauty, like supreme dominion, is but supported by opinion." It was published in *Poor Richard's Almanack*. (Spoiler alert: Poor Richard was Franklin.)

When I wake up next to August, she looks like a Disney princess—not literally, but figuratively. Her lips rest in something adjacent to a smile, eyes closed, her face relaxed and content. She sleeps so soundly, so perfectly, I wonder if perhaps she'd eaten a poisoned apple. Even the iLite at her temple is dark. No faint glow to alert others that something else is playing upon her senses, a lullaby, a white-noise generator, or "London Calling," by the Clash.

"You're so beautiful," I whisper. "What are you doing with me?"

Her long, pinned-up hair pulses and glows. The hues ripple as she breathes. She's a Rorschach test, changing before my eyes, leaving me questioning my own thoughts, my own interpretation of who she is. A blockchain coder, she told me last night, by way of explanation. A third-generation resident of Home.

I feel her draw a deep breath and slowly exhale. She pulls the covers over her bare shoulders and nestles back into me. I welcome her warmth.

"You're watching me again." She smiles, eyes still closed. "Creeper."

"I can't help it."

She pulls my arms around her. "How come?"

I'd been asking myself that all night, honestly. We'd known each other for all of twelve hours. I was used to casual hookups using the latest pheromonal app (which I worked on in grad school, thank you very much), but this was something else. An exercise in failed separation. An ongoing research project in gender dynamics. A social coup for two. Besides, she was my one and only friend in this sterile paradise.

Of course, that's all a complicated, polysyllabic way of processing what's really going on inside my head. I examine the tattoo on her neck, a bird that moves at my touch to nest between her shoulder blades. "I'm trying to figure out what you meant when you said I was going to replace you."

She frowns. Then she touches the iLite sensor at her temple, which chirps, lights up, and then goes dark again. She sighs wearily. "It's because my parents gave birth to me despite their poor genetics. As a result, I'm going blind."

"Are you serious?" I hope she's telling a joke. Then she chews her lip.

As I hold her, I look through the window, see the waning moon, which I suspect isn't really there. I know the morning will bring another glorious sunrise. The walls of my apartment, the artwork that hangs there, will change, sometimes by design and other times simply by my mood. I close my eyes and wonder what her world will be like. Total darkness? Or less than darkness? Nothingness.

"It's okay," she says. "I've had Stargardt disease since I could walk. I'm lucky to have made it into my twenties. My doctor said I'd be functionally blind in my teens."

"And the iLite?" I ask, though I suspect I know the answer.

"It won't work anymore." She turns and kisses me in the artificial moonlight. A fleeting gesture, like a smile at a funeral. "It's a macular thing—I won't have a working retina to receive light from the real world, let along anything digital."

"I'm . . . so sorry."

"Don't be. I've had a magical life here. Truly. But they won't let me stay. My pending departure created an opportunity for someone else. That person is you."

"Why me?" I know she's touched my face, felt my scars, my mangled fingers, the real person that lurks beneath the veneer. I feel like a work of charity.

"I want you to be my eyes at the end," she says. "I want to hold on to you as you tell me what you see. Because when I finally lose my sight, everyone at Home will go analog and regain their natural vision."

As I watch her speak, she's calm, but her eyes turn blue like glacial ice, and the ripples of color in her hair crash like waves. I think about Dr. Harring, how she'd always said that people are either builders or wreckers. And even wreckers have a purpose.

"I embedded a sub-program in the iLite blockchain. An Easter egg, for lack of a better term." August smiles and when she blinks, her eyes change color each time. "When I go dark, everyone at Home will see the world as it is. If only for an hour."

"Is this your revenge?" I ask. "Surely there's a less disturbing . . ." She touches my lips.

"This is a parting gift to everyone I've ever known. My kiss goodbye."

After Franklin stopped publishing, the philosopher David Hume wrote: "Beauty in things exists merely in the mind which contemplates them." Critics would later argue that Hume didn't know himself very well.

I knew today was the day August would finally lose her sight, because she didn't bother getting out of bed. I served her breakfast, which she hardly touched. Instead, she stared at the ceiling, which, to me, looked like cumulus clouds gently passing overhead, interrupted by the occasional starling.

But to her, I knew, it would be a darkening sky, with or without songbirds.

I stood on the veranda, doors open, overlooking the crowded street and the noisy fountain where couples were tossing in coins. I watched the swirls of color in the reflecting pool where children pushed sailboats with long metal poles.

"Do you want to know what I really look like?" I asked without looking back.

She didn't answer.

The sky appeared warm and comforting, but I felt a chill breeze. The tendrils of reality encroaching on the sacred territory of beautiful illusion. Then I heard soft footsteps. Felt her arms around my waist, her breath on my neck.

"It wouldn't matter," she said. "I have no point of reference to even compare."

"But they will." I nod to the world outside. "It's another perfect day. Are you sure you want to do this? What if someone . . ."

"It's already done. It's happening now . . . I can feel it."

She squeezes me tighter and I'm transported from the paint-by-number dream I'd been living in to a place that's almost monochromatic—cadaverous like the skin of a dying woman. The ornate buildings that were cybernetic canvases strewn with rich hues and intricate patterns now stand naked, façades of concrete and mortar, deckled with solar panels in need of cleaning. Everything looks utilitarian. The aesthetic extinguished. The trees, which were once covered with leaves that quaked and changed in the wind, now look skeletal. The brilliant technological sophistry has been replaced with rusting metal frames, the sunrise now a meager ribbon of light in a sky shaded with coal dust, as though an angry god had taken all the colors in the world and finger-painted them together. All that remains is a dismal miasma, feculent, like the brackish water at the bottom of a vase after the flowers have wilted and died.

And the people—the stunned populace, the idyllic citizens, cloaked in their innocence and naïveté, are now a warren of bewildered animals.

What have you done? What have we done?

I hold my breath, having watched the destruction, the dismantling, of something so beautiful. I feel as pale and naked as the world. Ashamed of my complicity, filled with regret, I can almost hear my heartbeat in the silence.

Then I hear whispers and chatter that becomes laughter and squeals of joy.

As I look down, I see couples holding hands, staring in awe at each other's skin, the sublime natural pigments of hair and eyes, the variations, the diversity. I watch as they examine each other with tenderness. They smile as though they're tasting something sweet for the first time. They laugh at their clothing, or occasionally the lack thereof. Children dance and splash in and around the fountain and pool, despite the tumorous mass of darkness that passes for a sky.

Mothers gush as they see their children as healthy, vibrant, substantial beings, freed from technology but still bright and illuminated by happiness.

Fathers smile in amazement as they regard their offspring as reflections of themselves.

And neighbors hug one another with knowing smiles of curious delight and contentment, as though they are all conscripts enjoying a technological cease-fire.

I feel their celebration wash over me, then recede, as I notice my missing thumb, my mangled fingers, the stretched parts of my body where the skin had been removed and grafted onto my face and neck. I'm no longer Catalyst White. I'm what remains of the woman I used to be. I realize August is no longer holding me and I understand. I want to shrink, hide, disappear forever from this place. That's when I notice them, a group of teenagers in the street below. They look up at me and I freeze. I wait for them to recoil in horror or disgust, or laugh, singling me out for all to see, but they smile and wave, then go on their way, marveling at what's happened.

In that moment, I think of the imitation sun that will return. The system will sort itself out and everyone will eventually subside into their perfect unreality. But they'll remember. And it will change them for the rest of their lives. How could it not?

Then I remember who caused this. Who made this possible.

"You did it, August," I gush, turning to congratulate her. I don't care that she's seen me as I am—who I am. "Maybe they'll let you stay, if I leave. . . ."

But the room is empty.

And Home is not the same.

Finally, in 1878, Margaret Wolfe Hungerford wrote: "Beauty is in the eye of the beholder." She wrote that under the pseudonym of "The Duchess."

JAMIE FORD is the great-grandson of Nevada mining pioneer Min Chung, who emigrated from Kaiping, China, to San Francisco in 1865, where he adopted the Western surname Ford, thus confusing countless generations. His debut novel, *Hotel on the Corner of Bitter and Sweet*, spent two years on the *New York Times* bestseller list and went on to win the Asian/Pacific American Award for Literature. His second book, *Songs of Willow Frost*, was a national bestseller. His work has been translated into thirty-five languages. (He's still holding out for Klingon, because that's when you know you've made it.) His latest novel is *Love and Other Consolation Prizes*. When not writing or daydreaming, he can be found tweeting @jamieford and on Instagram @jamiefordofficial.

ROME

G. WILLOW WILSON

They were five minutes into their ten-minute rest period when Fletcher checked his phone and discovered that the fire break on Rainier Avenue had been compromised.

Anyone could have seen it coming: The contractor hired by the Southeast Seattle Neighborhood Association, which had taken charge of that slim stripe of land between Elliott Bay and Lake Washington, had sandbagged along Rainier until the whole avenue resembled the aftermath of a war, but had stopped, with martial precision, at the intersection with MLK and refused to go any farther. MLK was the limit of their purview. They had not been paid to advance beyond it, and the neighborhood directly northward, which was neither Mount Baker nor Little Saigon nor properly the Central District, could not collectively decide whose responsibility it was to hire another contractor, nor indeed how that might be accomplished. The firefighting efforts ceased at their ambiguous crossroads, which divided Central and South Seattle with a neat little X, and everyone northward, having absolved themselves, simply hoped that the conflagration in Seward Park would be contained before it reached them.

Though the air throughout Seattle—which followed mandates dissimilar to those of hired contractors—had been opaque for days, the Building Language Proficiency midterm went on as scheduled. This turn of events had taken Fletcher by surprise. With the air and the heat, the daily advisories, the towers of downtown muted by the dim red light that passed for August, he had assumed that the midterm would be postponed. No one could be expected to sit for a test in such circumstances. He had not taxed himself by studying. Surely the course administrators, invisible though they were behind their desks in Baltimore or Boston or wherever the Remote Learning Group was headquartered, would understand that this was a health hazard, a serious health hazard. Claire or Rahma had queried them about this very subject, via email, but yesterday the verdict had come down: The midterm must go on as scheduled. All community-college students taking the Building Language Proficiency unit that summer were to sit for the test on the same day. It wasn't fair otherwise. Why should students at Mid-Seattle Community College have extra time to study, or be given the opportunity to cheat by communicating with those blameless scholars in Texas or Rhode Island or New York who had taken the test on time?

Claire, who had adopted a chain-smoking habit when the fire broke out, had remarked to the rest of the class that no one in Texas was likely to be taking a midterm anytime soon, considering half of the state was still underwater from some hurricane or other.

"*Rather* the opposite problem," she had drawled, flourishing the lit end of her American Spirit. Smoking apparently made her funny. It was she who had christened their Remote Learning class "*Not* Remotely Learning" and supplied her own laughter every time she said it. Fletcher privately wondered why she was taking Building Language Proficiency to begin with, since her language seemed plenty proficient already; most of their classmates spoke

Tagalog or Somali or Spanish at home and were taking summer classes in English at the behest of their academic advisers.

Fletcher spoke English at home and everywhere else. He was taking Building Language Proficiency because he was quiet. Early in childhood, he had learned to sit at the very front of the classroom, but at the end of a row, on the periphery, where the teacher would note his presence but not his indifference. Boys who sat in the back row were called sullen, insubordinate; by sitting in the front, he could get away with *quiet*. They hadn't caught his dyslexia until he was almost nine. He was nearly twelve before he could read independently. It had gotten better, but the quiet had stuck, as had a certain tendency to confuse subject and object.

He was mulling over these vagaries now, along with certain relevant notes he had uploaded to his phone, which the test minder had failed to confiscate from him at the beginning of the testing period. The minder, a middle-aged functionary from the college with a hairline that receded toward the top of his skull and then bloomed into a lank ponytail, had left in the middle of the first section, announcing to no one in particular that his asthma couldn't stand up to this fucking smoke and wishing the students luck.

Fletcher had considered leaving with him. There would be ways to negotiate with Remote Learning now that the minder was gone, throwing an air of ambiguity over the test results. But Rahma had stayed: had not even looked up, had kept her head tilted in that intense way toward her computer screen, its blue glow throwing pale, underwater highlights across her face and the folds of her headscarf. And so the rest of them, shamed, had stayed too, following mutely the instructions of the cheerful blond woman who appeared on their screens at regular intervals to guide them through the test.

"You have three minutes left until testing resumes," a dozen of her announced now.

"The fire break is gone," said Fletcher, flushing at the sound of his own voice. "On Rainier. The fire jumped it at MLK. The news says."

"Jesus." Claire pulled at her cigarette, making the ember flare and dance. "That's right down the fucking street."

"Maybe we should just leave," piped Luis from the back of the room. A lacquer of sweat had sprung up over the halfhearted mustache on his upper lip. Luis was sixteen, a high school student, one of those fast-tracked smart kids who arrive at college with a dozen credits already on the books. Fletcher had envied him at first, but Luis was so nervous, swimming in oversized hand-me-downs and flinching whenever anyone uttered what he still called *the F-bomb*, that it was impossible to hate the kid: Smart as he was, he was destined to go through life as somebody's little brother.

"It's getting really hot," he said now, his voice cracking. "What if there's like a wind surge or whatever, like there was a couple days ago, and we're engulfed in flames or something?"

"No one's going to be engulfed in flames," muttered Claire, lighting a fresh American Spirit off the butt of her old one. "Save that shit for your essay questions. *Engulfed in flames*."

Fletcher was not so sure. He rose from his swivel chair, which tilted under his weight; it had been donated or salvaged and several screws were missing. He checked his phone again: He had two minutes. He passed by Rahma's desk on his way out the door. She did not look up. He hadn't expected her to but went red nonetheless and felt a sudden, cold bloom of moisture seep across his palms.

Outside, it was snowing. Fletcher slipped sideways through the partially open door, careful to leave the wooden doorstop in place behind him: The minder, before he left, had warned them that the lock was tricky. The air in the parking lot hit his lungs like something molten. Fat pearl-gray cinders descended from the sky without momentum, so unhurried that Fletcher paused and tapped the toe of his work boot against the concrete to convince himself that time was moving at its usual speed. The parking lot was empty except for Claire's blue Toyota Camry, its wheels distorted by a shimmer of heat rising from the asphalt. The college had rented one of the empty storefronts in the old Promenade complex for testing. It was meant to be something else, some tech worker's future luxury condo, but after the crash the money had run out, and now it all sat empty: the supermarket dark behind its phalanx of shopping carts, the windows of the smaller shops crisscrossed with masking tape, prepared for vandals as if for a typhoon. The big neon sign advertising the Promenade had burned out at both ends and now read simply ROME.

Fletcher could smell fire. It was different from the smell of smoke: Smoke smelled like the remains of old things, fire like the beginning of something entirely new. It entered the nose as a waterless vapor, stimulating dormant instincts, less a scent than an imperative. Fletcher wanted to hunch toward the ground and run, to follow the hill down Jackson Street and out into the invisible bay, where the fire couldn't follow. Instead, he straightened and went back inside.

The others were already at their desks. Empty cups of coffee lay discarded in corners where the cinders had gathered into black drifts, turning the makeshift classroom into an ancient ruin, the students into tourists. They had wandered through, left their trash, marveled at the ways in which time laid waste to greatness, and now it was time to return, somehow, to a present that continually eluded them.

"The test is about to resume," chirped the blond woman.

"I think we should leave after all," said Fletcher.

Rahma lifted her eyes from her computer screen and gazed at him steadily.

"Some of us have scholarship money riding on this," she said. "Some of us have to prioritize."

Her voice was low but soft, the corners of each word clipped by a slight accent. Most of the Somali girls Fletcher met at school had either been born in Seattle or moved to the U.S. when they were small. Rahma was different. According to Claire, she had spent most of her childhood *in the camps.* Fletcher wasn't sure what it meant, but Claire said it so archly that he assumed the distinction was significant. It gave her slender, cloaked shoulders a faint air of drama, of tragedy perhaps, and when he watched her he imagined that her opaque expressions concealed a profound sadness. He imagined many things, but that sadness was at the root of them all: It bound them together, gave them an unspoken intimacy that one day they would confess to each other. He had realized it first, but one day she would come to the same understanding, and then, finally, they might say to one another the things they had thus far left unsaid.

For now, however, she was looking at him, and in the creases around her iris-blue mouth there lay a suggestion of contempt. Fletcher swallowed and tasted ash. He slid into his seat as the image of the blond woman on his screen was replaced by a lattice of multiple-choice questions.

"This is crazy," he announced. "We're all gonna be engulfed in flames, just like Luis said."

Luis made a funny noise, a strangled sort of honk, which might have been intended as a laugh.

"Will you *just—*" Claire forbore to finish her own sentence. She clicked madly at the left button of her mouse with a single black-taloned finger. "Nobody is burning alive today. Okay? Don't be so fucking dramatic. Some of us have scholarships and opportunities and stuff to think about." She shot a deadened look, unobserved, at Rahma, who sat across the room at her back.

"Some of us might," retorted Fletcher. "But you're not one of them."

At this, Claire swiveled in her chair and fixed him with an expression he had come to know well over the course of the last several weeks: a wide, bulging stare, revealing the delicate network of blood vessels that approached her gray eyes like tidal estuaries. Her blond hair, or system of hairs, half pinned up and half combed under, quivered with affected rage. Fletcher knew by now that this was all nothing. He leaned back in his chair and crossed his arms and waited.

"You're not worth it," said Claire after a moment. She turned back to her computer with a snort. "Fletcher. Fletcher the lecher."

Fletcher pretended not to hear her. Internally, however, he shuddered, resisting the urge to glance over his shoulder at Rahma and Luis and gauge whether this epithet was one they had heard before. It did not seem fair. He had never touched anyone. He only *looked* at Rahma. He only looked at her when she was looking somewhere else, but, fatally, had failed until that very moment to consider who might be looking at him while he was looking at her.

It was an odd word, *lecher*, the sort of word that sounded exactly like what it was. Prior to the vocabulary unit of Building Language Proficiency, he had never encountered it, so the brunt of the word struck him with the full force of something new and bewildering. He had always assumed that his quiet protected him: that he went through the world unobserved. Now, however, he could not unhear the rhyme in his name.

He swallowed and turned his head toward his computer screen. Before him were ten questions concerning subject-verb agreement: There were several *brung*s scattered throughout, which told him precisely what the test designers thought about people like him. In a test, there ought to be right answers and wrong answers but not tricks. To trick a person—to infringe on his vernacular and cast doubt on his means of expression—did not test his knowledge; it tested the circumstances of his birth. Fletcher's eyes skipped from *brung* to *brung*, all the while thinking *lecher*, and he felt shame begin to creep up around the edges of his ambition.

He clicked haphazardly on a series of blank ovals until a pattern emerged that pleased him; an *A-B-A-D-D* rhythm that felt like the order in which right answers might appear. The scent of fire intensified. There was heat now as well, heat that came up from the ground instead of down from the oppressive air.

Rahma had taken off her sandals and let her long toes bend against the cheap polyester carpet on the floor, exposing the rose-gold underside of her heel. Despite her headscarf and the abaya that covered her body from neck to ankle, she did not look warm; behind her, Claire, dressed in a tank top and cutoff jean shorts so tiny that the interior pockets hung down past the hem, was already fanning herself. Abruptly, Luis rose and went to the door: Opening it, he poured the contents of his Big Gulp across the threshold like an offering, ice cubes hitting the sweltering asphalt with eddies of steam.

"There," he said, returning to his seat with the empty cup. "Maybe that'll keep the fire from coming inside, anyway."

It was not a bad notion. Fletcher clicked the blue arrow at the bottom of his screen to advance to the next section and then stood up, stepping over the wet line across the door to inspect the exterior of the building. Outside, the sky was yellow, the same shade as the grass in the city parks that had been dead and dry since June, sacrificed to municipal water restrictions. The outer walls of the storefront were the kind of spackled white plaster material popular in the 1970s; there were dozens of similar buildings scattered across the Central District, and like this one, their once-pristine faces were now gray and green. Fletcher knew from the summers he'd spent working demolition with his stepfather that the material was not exactly asbestos and therefore not exactly fireproof.

There was a spigot around the corner of the building; squatting next to it, Fletcher muttered a prayer to an undesignated higher power and twisted the handle. He was rewarded with a gush of water as warm as a bath. He stood and began to kick the current downhill, against the side of the building, down an ancient channel of dry moss. The smell of it, of dirt and water and the spores of growing things, reminded him of another city, the city of a former life, one that had occupied the same space in which he stood but that had been made of very different things. He kicked again at the water, feeling it seep through a crack along one seam of his work-boot, and swore quietly.

"Remember the fire department?"

Claire, inexplicably, had appeared on the roof.

"Remember that? That was fun, having a fire department." She was holding Luis's Big Gulp and slinging water across the roofing shingles like a farmer sowing seeds.

"Remember FEMA?" Fletcher squinted up at her with what he hoped was a grin. "Remember park rangers?"

"Remember when we were gonna get light-rail to the Eastside?" Claire grinned back, shielding her eyes from the sunless glare. "It was nice having a government that did, like, basic stuff. I don't think we realized how basic it was. My parents voted for the president. Twice. They were, like, we have no money; why should we pay taxes for shit? They still have no money and now also no fire department. The *fire abatement whatever* subscription service for their neighborhood cost twice as much per year as they were paying in state taxes before. So. That worked out well. Thanks, Mom." Claire swiveled back and forth on the ball of one foot, coquettish, appealing. "You know what I mean?"

Fletcher accepted her apology for what it was. They worked in parallel, unspeaking, for another few minutes, inexpertly dampening whatever they could reach, until the kindly smell of water began to overtake the smoke and soot and heat. Perhaps everything would not be terrible. The sun, the proper sun, was struggling to emerge: Through the thinnest stripes of haze, the sky was visible. Fletcher gave the gushing water one more kick and turned off the spigot. Claire slid to the edge of the roof and let her stubbled legs hang over the gutter, and reached for his hand: He took it and helped her jump down.

"They're saying it might rain tonight," she said. "Remember the rain?"

"No," he said, and laughed. They went inside. Fletcher pulled the door shut behind them, wiggling it to make sure it latched: The fire, at least, would not get in that way. He felt noble, responsible; out of all of them, he was the oldest, and if he could not finish the test, he could at least be useful to the others. But the others did not acknowledge him. Rahma chewed one delicate nail, her lips moving silently over the words that appeared on her screen. Luis, sitting opposite, was hunched toward his monitor, rocking back and forth half consciously, and did not look up as they came in.

"Three more questions," he said, clicking at his mouse. "Three more and then we'll go."

"You were the one who wanted to leave an hour ago," said Fletcher.

"Yeah, but now it's like a challenge, you know? Like we did it, we took the test in the middle of a freaking fire, and those buttwipes at Remote Learning can't say anything. It's like they wanted us to fail, right? And we didn't fail."

"I'm failing," announced Fletcher. He was startled by the volume of his voice. He looked at the blinking blue arrow on his own computer screen and laughed. "I'm failing this class and everything else. But I'm glad I got to hang out with you guys. I'm glad I came anyway. Fuck verb agreement. I'm glad I showed up."

Rahma looked up at him and almost smiled. The sight of it— her mouth softened, her black eyes dancing in their halo of glossy lashes—lifted him off the ground like something physical, audible perhaps, like the choir of angels that served as his stepfather's go-to cliché. When the window behind him shattered, he thought it was simply punctuation.

Fletcher felt himself thrown violently forward. There was screaming: Claire's and Rahma's, and Luis's hoarse squeal, all descending in a crude harmony. Lines of heat seared across his back.

It was not pain, at least not yet: What he chiefly felt was embarrassment at having forgotten something so elemental as glass, which expanded much more rapidly in high heat than plaster or wood, and which couldn't be fireproofed with a little water. The thing that surprised him was the fire itself. It licked at the ceiling of the room through the shattered window, as aggressive and invasive as something self-conscious—a predator or a thief.

"The door!" shrieked Claire. Objects swam before Fletcher's eyes, disconnected and meaningless: this chair, this desk, this empty cup. Through the smoke, he saw Luis throwing himself against the door of the classroom, his shoulder thudding against the gray-painted steel in an awful, frantic rhythm, and realized with a kind of backward foreboding that he had kicked out the wooden doorstop when he came inside after dampening the roof.

Fletcher pulled himself to his feet. Dimly, he remembered the rain shutter that framed the outside of the window, a relic of that other city, of the ancient ruin: Perhaps it would hold out fire too, at least for a few minutes. It would buy them time. Would anyone come? *Was* there anyone? Without thinking, he reached through the gaping wound where the window had been, into and past the flames, and closed his hand over a metal lever.

The next thing he saw was Rahma's face. It was bent over his, eclipsing the fluorescent ceiling light, and appeared to be laughing and crying at once.

"You're out of your mind," she said, her voice shaking. "You could have been killed."

"Was I?" muttered Fletcher. He flexed his hand: Pain fled up his arm in a sharp spasm.

"I don't know." She laughed again and dashed tears from her face with one palm. "If you're dead, we must be dead too. Maybe we're all dead."

"Don't move him," came someone else's voice, farther away. "Get a towel. Water." The door was open, not just a little but all the way, its hinges smashed and glinting in the sun. Sky was visible. Beyond the threshold, in the shimmering heat, a man and a woman wearing blue armbands were squatting beside Luis, gently probing his shoulder with latex-gloved fingers.

"Those medics?" muttered Fletcher. "The volunteer ones?"

Rahma ignored the question. "What a stupid, stupid thing to do," she said, in a way that suggested she didn't think it was stupid at all. "I would never have thought of it. You just stood up and reached out like it was nothing, like it was raining and you were just closing the— Oh my God! You didn't even finish your midterm."

"But you finished yours," said Fletcher. He bit back the nausea that pulsed in his throat and tried to smile. Rahma shook her head. She sat back on her heels beside him, her hip not quite touching his, waiting for whoever was coming with water and a towel. In another moment, she looked at him again. In her gaze, through the strange clarity of his own pain, Fletcher saw that she despised him. This was a temporary amnesty. Her eyes were full of mercy, of pity tempered by distaste: She looked at him as she might at an abandoned animal. Had she seen him after all? Had she noticed him noticing her? The thought made him cold. He could not tell, exactly, whether or not he had done something wrong. He never could.

"Rahma," he said, his voice strained, "if I've ever—"

"Don't," she said lightly. "It's all right. You're not supposed to tire yourself. Just lie still. The medics are going to take care of you." She frowned over her smartphone, tapping at the screen with tapered fingertips. "I'm texting my mom. She didn't want me to come today. She's going to lose it when I tell her what's happened. Is there anyone you want me to call for you?"

He turned the question over in his head, repeating it to himself.

"No," he said at last. "There's no one."

He let his head fall back against the singed carpet. He had imagined her, as he imagined so many things. The real girl, the one sitting beside him, would exit his life at the end of the summer term and forget about him shortly thereafter. There would be no confessions, no damp, illicit meetings behind the administrative building at school. Yet as she smiled and sighed, he knew he had, at least, done one immortal thing she admired.

G. WILLOW WILSON writes the Hugo Award–winning comic book series Ms Marvel for Marvel Comics. Her debut novel, *Alif the Unseen*, won the World Fantasy Award for Best Novel and was a finalist for the Center for Fiction's First Novel Prize. In 2010, she wrote a memoir called *The Butterfly Mosque* about love, Islam, and life in Egypt during the waning years of the Mubarak regime. She has also written graphic novels and comic book series for DC Comics and its literary imprint, Vertigo, and helped launch the ongoing series A-Force for Marvel. In 2015, she received a special commendation for innovation in graphic literature at the PEN Center USA Literary Awards.

GIVE ME CORNBREAD OR GIVE ME DEATH

N. K. JEMISIN

The intel is good. It had better be; three women died to get it to us.
I tuck away the binoculars and crawl back from the window long
enough to hand-signal my girls. Fire team moves up, drop team on
my mark, support to hold position and watch our flank. The enemy
might have nothing but mercs for security, but their bullets punch
holes same as real soldiers', and some of 'em are hungry enough to
be competent. We're hungrier, though.

Shauntay's got the glass cutter ready. I'm carrying the real payload, slung across my torso and back in a big canteen. We should
have two or three of these, since redundancy increases our success
projections, but I won't let anyone else take the risk. The other ladies have barrels cracked and ready to drop. The operation should
be simple and quick—get in, drop it like it's hot, get out.

This goes wrong, it's on me.

It won't go wrong.

Shauntay makes the cut. Go go go. We drop into the warm,
stinking, dimly lit space of the so-called aerie—really an old aircraft

hangar, repurposed since commercial air travel ended. There's the big trough on one side of the hangar, laden with fresh human body parts. It's horrible, but I ignore it as I rappel down. We've seen worse. Touchdown. No sounds from the pit at the center of the hangar. We get our little trough set up in near silence, just like we rehearsed. My girls are on it like clockwork. The barrels come down and we dump load one, load two, load three. Stirring sounds from the hangar behind us. Ignore them. I signal the other soldiers to back up. Nothing left but the payload. I unsling my canteen, not listening to the sounds behind me, concentrating on my fingers so I don't fumble the cap, remembering to unseal the pressure valve so the vacuum effect doesn't clog the whole thing up and—

A warm, sulfur-redolent breath stirs my fatigues. Right behind me. Shit.

I turn, slow. They have cat eyes; fast movement excites them. The smell of fear excites them. Dark skin excites them.

She's huge—maybe the size of a 747, though I've only seen husks of those, lying scattered around the edges of old killing fields where the world was remade. She's not quite green. Her scales are prismatic, slightly faceted, which makes them nearly invisible at night. That was an accident, I've heard, some side effect of tweaking the genetic base to make them hyper-focused on shorter wavelengths of visible light—or something; I don't know the science. I know beauty, though, and she's lovely, scales shimmering as she moves, iridescent blue–black–golden brown. They probably mean for her to be ugly and scary, dark as they've made her, but they forget there's more ways to be beautiful than whatever they designate. Red eyes. Fangs long as my whole body. Those are just there for the scare factor, I know; our scientists have proven they don't actually use the fangs for eating. Do a good enough job killing without them.

A few of the others stir behind her, some coming over, all of them following her lead. She's the dominant one. Figures. I'm not scared. Why? Suicidal, maybe. No. I think—and it's just in this moment, looking at how beautiful she is—that I see a kindred spirit. Another creature whose power has been put into the service of weaker cowardly fools.

So I smile. "Hey, there," I say. She blinks and pulls her head back a little. Her prey doesn't usually talk back. Still dangerous; curiosity plus boredom equals me being batted all over the hangar like a toy till I'm dead. Time to divert her interest. Slowly, I move behind the trough—stuff's still steaming from the barrels—and start pouring out my payload. The hot, sharp smell catches her attention immediately. Those lovely slit pupils expand at once, and she leans down, sniffing at the trough. I'm irrelevant suddenly.

"Getcho grub on, baby," I whisper. My beautiful one flickers her ears, hearing me, but her eyes are still on the prize. Mission accomplished. I rappel back up to the roof, and we head homeward as the flock chows down.

Dragons love them some collard greens, see. Especially with hot sauce.

The first attacks were the worst. Nobody was ready. I remember a day, I couldn't have been more than six or seven. I was sitting in the living room. Mama came running in, not a word, just grabbed me and half-dragged me out of my chair and across the house to hide in the bathroom. I felt the house shudder and thought it was an earthquake, like I'd read about in books. I was *excited*. I'd never felt an earthquake before. We curled together in the bathtub, me and Mama, me giddy, her terrified, with the sounds of screaming and the smells of smoke filtering in through the vents.

It was so terrible, the Towers said, amid news stories with two-faced headlines like SAPPHIRE TOWNSHIP RAIDED BY DRUG-SNIFFING DRAGONS and OFFICIALS DENY DRAGONS INTENTIONALLY

BRED TO PREFER "DARK MEAT." So terrible indeed. Maybe if we didn't hide things from the police, they wouldn't need to use dragons? The dragons only attacked when people attacked them—or ran as if they were guilty. Why, if we'd just turn out every time there was a police patrol and point out the folks among us who were causing trouble, the dragons would only bother those people and not everybody.

Motherfuckers always want us to *participate* in their shit. Ain't enough they got the whole world shivering in the shadows of the Towers. Ain't enough they've got our boys and men tagged like dogs and preemptively walled off over in Manny Dingus Prison, only letting 'em out for parole now and again. (Only letting *some* of 'em out—the ones they think are meek, 'cause they think eugenics works. If they had any sense, though, they'd be more afraid of the quiet ones.)

This latest front in the long, long war started because they didn't like us growing weed. Ours was better quality than that gourmet shit they grew, and also we sold it to their people over in Americanah. Not that those were really *their people*, white men as poor as us and the few women whose pussies the Towers haven't grabbed, but they gotta try to keep up the illusion. Gotta have somebody as a buffer between them and us, especially whenever we get uppity.

They've been engineering the End Times. The Plagues were supposed to be about salvation. Trying to get all the townships and ghettoes and reservations to go evangelical, see? So they poisoned the water—turned it red—and killed a whole bunch of men over in Bollytown. Got them dependent on bottled-water deliveries from the Tower, forever. The dragons are supposed to be the Second Plague, engineered from frogs, with a little dinosaur and cat spliced in. That's bad, but they tried to start a Plague of boils, big enough to kill, in Real Jerusalem. Didn't spread much beyond their patient zeroes, thank G*d, because Jewish people wash. (They'll try again, though. Always do.) Anyway, we got the point when they rained hail and fire on the Rez, even though they claimed that was just a weather-control satellite malfunction.

We're all heathens to the Towers. All irredeemable by birth and circumstance, allowed to live on the sufferance of those on high. They don't want to kill us off, because they need us, but they don't need us getting comfortable. Rather keep us on edge. Keep us hungry. Best way to control a thing, they think, is through fear and dependency.

Gotta mind, though, that the ones you're starving don't start getting their needs attended to someplace else.

The next raid goes off right when our hackers have said, but we didn't need the warning. The Towers are predictable, complacent, and lazy in their power — same mediocre motherfuckers they've always been. We're ready. Got countermeasures standing by, but they don't even bother to send observation drones. Stupid. It's been years since that first raid. We've been living under siege so long that fear stopped making sense a long time ago.

The dragons darken the sky and then stoop to attack. The whole damn flock; the Towers must have found the evidence of our infiltrations, or maybe they're mad about something else. I spot my baby in the vanguard, blue-black-brown, big as a building. She lands in the market and unleashes a blast of flame to obliterate a shop — oh, but then she stops. Sniffs the air. Yeah, what *is* that? Check it out, baby. See that great big steaming trough over there on the school track and field? Remember that taste? Once upon a time, this was food fit only for beasts. We made it human. Now we've made it over, special, for you. Hot hot, good good. Eat up, y'all.

She whuffles at the others, and they follow as she hop-flies over to the field. A trough the size of a shipping container is all laid out, filled to the brim and steaming with three days' worth of cooking work. Plenty of hot sauce this time, vinegary and sharp and fierce as all get-out. That's the kicker. Wakes up their taste buds, and the fiber fills them up better than plain old human flesh. Volunteers, including me, linger nearby while the dragons eat. We move slowly, letting them smell our living human flesh, working clickers so they'll associate sound with taste. Then it's done, and the dragons fly back to their aerie slow, heavy with greens. Nobody gets eaten that day.

The Towers are pissed. They send in cops to retaliate, stopping and frisking random women walking down the street, arresting anybody who talks back, even killing two women for no reason at all. They feared for their lives, the cops say. They always say.

Collard greens get added to the contraband list, between C-4 and contraception.

We retaliate right back when they come with crews of deputized men from Americanah to tear up our fields. No collards? Fine. When the dragons come next, we offer them callaloo.

They come for the callaloo. We just stand there, pretending harmlessness, and don't fight back. They can't admit that the dragons are supposed to eat *us*, so they claim they're worried about listeria. No FDA anymore, just gotta destroy the whole crop. Okay, then. Word spreads. After they take the callaloo, Longtimetown — none of us named this shit — sends over frozen blocks of spinach cooked with garlic, fish sauce, and chili oil, layered in with their heroin shipment. We have to add our own spinach to stretch it, but that chili oil is potent. It's enough.

By this point the Towers figure they've got to rob us of every vegetable and then watch us die of malnutrition or there's no way their dragons will ever bother with bland, unseasoned human meat again. They actually try it, motherfuckers, burning our farms, and we have to eat cat grass just to get by. We fight over kohlrabi leaves grown in an old underground weed hothouse. Can't give this to the dragons; there isn't enough, and our daughters need it more. It's looking bad. But just before the next raid, Spicymamaville smuggles over mofongo that makes the dragons moan, they love it so. Towelhead Township is starving and besieged, but a few of the mujahideen women make it through the minefields with casks of harissa strapped to their bodies. Sari City, mad about Bollytown, ships us "friendship basketballs." They do this openly, and the Towers let them through as a goodwill gesture. Black people love basketball, right? Maybe it'll shut us up. And it does, for a while: There's enough saag paneer and curry paste vacuum-packed inside each ball to feed us and the dragons too.

The Towers burn our peppers, and our allies respond with dead drops of hawajj, wasabi, chili-pepper water. The Towers try to starve us, but we Just. Don't. Die.

And each visit, I pet my dragon a little more. She watches me. Looks for me when she lands. Croons a little when I pet her. It doesn't all go smoothly. In a single day I lose two soldiers to one dragon's fit of temper. Old habit. The dragon spits the soldiers' bodies out immediately, though, and snorts in disgust even before my beauty and the others can twist their heads around to hiss at her. They know we won't open the reward trough that day. Lesson learned, though it cost us blood.

It's war. We'll mourn the lost as heroes, our own and allies alike. I check in with my girls before every meal and ask if they're still willing to serve; they are. We are all resolved. We will win.

The Towers have got something big planned. The dragons have become less responsive to their breeders and trainers, and sometimes they just up and leave the aeries to come to our township, where the good food's at. News articles say the Second Plague program is going to be retired due to "mixed results." Civilian casualties have decreased; they're spinning that as a benefit and not mentioning that the decline is our doing. Anyway, the dragons have been declared a failed experiment, so they're planning to "decommission" them during their next official deployment. Missiles vs. dragons, in the skies right over Sapphire Town. Who cares about collateral damage.

A spy in one of the Towers confirms it. They've gotten tired of us Sapphires, and it's about time for the Tenth Plague anyway. They're coming for our firstborn.

My lovely one waits patiently as I gear up, even though the troughs only have a little food in them this time. They know now to associate our presence with good things like food and pleasure and play, so they'll abide awhile before they get testy. We're all wearing flight gear and carrying saddles. I've got the payload again: our last batch of Scotch bonnets, grown and pickled in secret, sweetened with mango and hope. Word is there's a great big warehouse full of confiscated greens over near Tower One. And just so happens there's a whole lot of tanks and troops to set on fire along the way.

One by one, we mount up. My beautiful one—her name's Queen—turns her head back to get one ear skritched, and I oblige with a grin. Then I raise a hand to signal readiness. She lifts her head, smelling my excitement, sharing it, readying the others. I feel like I'm sitting astride the sky. She lifts her wings and lets out a thundering battle cry. Feeling her power. So am I.

Go go go.

And once the Towers lie in broken, smoldering rubble below us? We'll come back home, and sit on down, and have us all a good-good feast.

N(ORA). K. JEMISIN is an author of speculative fiction short stories and novels, who lives and writes in Brooklyn, New York. Her work has been multiply nominated for the Hugo, the Nebula, and the World Fantasy awards; shortlisted for the Crawford, the Gemmell Morningstar, and the Tiptree; and she has won a Locus Award for Best First Novel as well as several Romantic Times Reviewers' Choice Awards. In 2018, she became the first writer to win three Hugos in a row—one for each installment of her Broken Earth trilogy. Her short fiction has been published in magazines such as *Clarkesworld, Tor.com, Wired,* and *Popular Science,* and in numerous anthologies. Her first eight novels, a novella, and a short-story collection are out now from Orbit Books. She also served as the guest editor of *The Best American Science Fiction and Fantasy 2018.*

GOOD NEWS BAD NEWS

CHARLES YU

RACIST ROBOTS RECALLED BY MANUFACTURER

GeriDyne announced a massive recall yesterday of all Class G and GS models built in the prior twenty-four months.

The voluntary recall reportedly affects at least 214,000 units around the world, nearly one-third of the robots GeriDyne has put into operation in the company's history.

Default settings for the units were the source of the problem.

A large percentage of the fleet had been deployed as geriatric caregivers.

The robots are said to automatically sync and self-identify as members of the race of their owner/purchaser.

This self-identification influences certain decisions or judgments that the robot makes, based on criteria that include a determination of the "racial makeup" of humans with whom the robot interacts, as determined according to facial, physical, and other characteristics used to define certain preloaded categories programmed into the robot's background understanding.

The manufacturer sought to reassure customers for these expensive, supposedly state-of-the-art personal companions. "We're putting safeguards in place in order to assure this doesn't happen again," said the company's head of quality assurance.

But consumer watchdog groups questioned the manufacturer's ability to control its product. "The larger issue is in the algorithm. There are encoded assumptions about race built right into the syntax of the programming language, into the very logic circuits of these things."

The problem first came to light following an incident involving the Chang family—Elizabeth and Darren Chang, and their two children—who were physically and verbally attacked by one of the recalled units.

(continued on A22)

FIRST REFUGEE FAMILIES SETTLE ON THE MOON

Almost four hundred men, women, and children, traveling via lunar transport shuttle, arrived early this morning and began unpacking their belongings, moving into tract homes in the first of three phases of master-planned communities in the Sea of Tranquility, seeking to re-create some semblance of a normal life.

The pilot program was designed by a coalition of Western governments and a consortium of international real estate builders.

A massive lottery was conducted, with over three million families applying for one of twelve hundred spots.

The explosion of interest in the program has exceeded all expectations, leading to suggestions that it could be rapidly expanded over the next decade, as a possible resettlement solution (or circumvention) of many thorny international and diplomatic situations around the globe.

But concerns have been raised by a number of groups, including legal experts, human-rights advocates, and environmental organizations.

However, none of that was on the mind of Jamil (who asked that his surname be withheld due to safety concerns), a young father who was among the extremely fortunate few selected in the lottery for a three-bedroom, two-bathroom house in the Sea of Tranquility.

"Watching my kids play in our backyard—in their backyard—it's . . . I can't tell you how it makes me feel. Earth may be a quarter million miles away, but this feels like the American Dream."

REPRESENTATIVE OF SENTIENT TREES SENDS FIRST DELEGATES TO THE UNITED NATIONS

This year's G200 Leaders' Summit will take place November 30 through December 2 in Buenos Aires and will bring together the world's most powerful heads of state and government in South America.

Leading up to the event, representatives from many nations have expressed a cautious optimism about the possibility of reaching a consensus on climate change, an issue that was first addressed in 2008, at the beginning of the previous millennium.

Early talks have been fruitful, most likely due to the presence at the summit of the G200's newest members: delegates from Kingdom Plantae, the world's first nation-state of sentient trees.

Trees are demanding major changes in the relations between flora and fauna.

"We've long been silent in the face of unspeakable acts. Deforestation. Clear-cutting. Toxins in the soil," said Eondo'or, an eighty-foot, six-hundred-year-old redwood and senior representative to the U.N. for Kingdom Plantae. "Not to mention getting peed on by drunk people.

"Here's the thing," Eondo'or added. "We definitely outnumber you. Also, you need us for food, shelter. Also carbon removal," he said. "Also oxygen."

CORPORATE PERSONS NOW OUTNUMBER NATURAL PERSONS BY A RATIO OF 1,000,000,000,000:1

The House today voted 434–0, with one abstention, to overwhelmingly pass a bill that will result in a significant change to the tax code. The bill was introduced at 7:30 A.M. and received final passage nine minutes later, before it was announced or available to the public.

As a result of this change to the tax code, a century-old legal tactic became even more attractive. With high-speed incorporation software, companies can now instantaneously create millions, or even billions, of special-purpose entities, for various reasons, most of which are tax- or liability-related, resulting in corporate organizational structures as complex as semiconductor-chip designs—and comprehensible only to powerful computers.

These latest changes to the tax code, expected to disproportionately benefit the largest and wealthiest corporations, were passed by the R-Bot in a 1–1 vote against the D-Bot in the Robo-Congress-O-Matic 5000, with the tie being broken by the tie-breaking algorithm, all of this taking place, as usual, inside a four-foot-by-three-foot black box inside of the U.S. protectorate satellite in geosynchronous orbit above Washington, D.C.

In related news, the Supreme Court-Bot reaffirmed, in a 1–0 decision authored by the Chief Justice-Bot, that each of the roughly 500 quintillion corporations does, in fact, possess certain inalienable rights accruing to their long-established status as persons.

"These C corps and S corps and LLCs should be afforded the dignity and equality that any human citizen of the United States enjoys. Just as the Founders intended."

RACIST ROBOT RECALL

(continued from A1)

ELIZABETH CHANG: I was out driving with my family. My husband and our two kids. We stopped for lunch. The town—it wasn't really a town, basically a gas station and a couple of fast-food places—wouldn't have been my first choice to stop. But our car needed to recharge and everyone was hungry. My vote was for drive-thru at the burger place.

DARREN CHANG: I mean, in retrospect, I wasn't really thinking, I guess. I just thought that since we were on a road trip, we should experience some local flavor. My kids haven't seen much of America.

ELIZABETH CHANG: I was scared. This wasn't a part of the country where you generally get out of the car. Not if you look like me. Or my husband.

DARREN CHANG: I don't know what I was thinking. Maybe I wanted to see.

CYNTHIA RODRIGUEZ (*waitress*): They were a happy-looking family. As soon as they entered, the wife flinched. The husband almost looked like he was trying to pretend nothing was weird. But it *was* weird.

ELIZABETH CHANG: Everyone was staring at us.

DARREN CHANG: Looking back, I guess I knew there would be trouble. I don't know why, but I think on some level I wanted trouble. Not for anyone to get hurt, of course. Liz was really mad at me after, when we had a chance to process what happened. And I was mad at myself. I mean, we have kids. To put them in danger was maybe somewhat irresponsible on my part. But I don't know—see, I'm still conflicted about it.

ELIZABETH CHANG: Darren is a good person. Too good a person. And he wants to believe other people are good, too.

BERT NEWSOM (*restaurant patron and witness*): I saw them enter. I remember thinking, *Uh-oh. This is not good.*

CYNTHIA RODRIGUEZ: I took their order quickly. I was hoping they'd eat fast. And then Garland—one of our regulars— comes in.

ELIZABETH CHANG: The guy—Garland—walks in. Or wheels in, I guess. And he's being pushed by his geriatric robot. I remember I said to Darren—God, it's so weird now to think about this—I leaned over to Darren and I squeezed his hand under the table. As in, *Look at that.* It looked sweet. I felt better, being in there. I figured, *Well, if this nice old man eats here, this place can't be all that scary.*

CYNTHIA RODRIGUEZ: I kept looking at Garland and his caregiver, just praying they wouldn't notice. I even took Garland's order fast, hoping they'd finish quicker. But then one of the kids started laughing, and Garland looks over. And I knew there'd be trouble.

(*continued on A37*)

SCIENTISTS CONFIRM: WE'RE LIVING IN A SIMULATION

Researchers in Tokyo, Frankfurt, and Lagos today announced joint findings confirming what many scientists and moviegoers had long speculated: that the universe and everything in it, including us, could be the product of a computer program.

This story is still developing.

AMAZONGOOGLEFACE ANNOUNCES INTENT TO ACQUIRE DISNEYAPPLESOFT

The deal would result in a combined company worth approximately $97.3 quadrillion.

"This will be good for consumers," said Jeff Bezos, CEO of AmazonGoogleFace, speaking from the company's offices on an icy dwarf planet in the Kuiper Belt.

DRUG MANUFACTURER ADMITS XENOPHILZOL IS PLACEBO

The blockbuster over-the-counter medication reached $1 trillion in sales in its first year.

The drug had been fast-tracked for approval by the FDA and marketed as being the world's first and only effective treatment for the reduction of intolerant attitudes.

While it's early and the sample size is small, statistics compiled by law enforcement and other agencies seem to indicate that the Xenophilzol may have had a significant effect, as assaults, attacks, hate crimes, and incidents of violence otherwise stemming from racial, sexual, or religious discrimination decreased by 23 percent during the period when the drug was on the market.

Reports of the drug's biochemical inactivity spread quickly following an anonymous tip first posted on the *New York Times* message board (a division of Reddit/Instagram).

Users and nonusers alike were struggling with how to process this information.

"I'm just so sad. I thought this was it. I guess we'll have to keep looking."

Others drew a different, more hopeful conclusion from the news.

"If the pill works, it works. Who's to say?"

As a result of the disclosure, clinical development of the company's related blockbuster product, Gynophilzenicam, has been halted, pending further investigation. Details have been scarce, but reports from insiders familiar with the clinical trials suggest that

Gynophilzenicam may be effective in the treatment and reduction of the male impulse to overexplain things to women.

TELEPORTATION INJURIES DOWN 11 PERCENT THIS YEAR

Experts note that the improved safety comes at a redundancy cost, as accidental cloning is up 2 percent.

RACIST ROBOT RECALL

(continued from A22)

DARREN CHANG: I'd seen them, of course. Everyone had. My boss actually bought one, as a kind of gag, to have around the office. He thought it was funny.

BERT NEWSOM: I was waiting for the moment they'd realize what this thing was.

ELIZABETH CHANG: We get our food, but I can't touch it. I can barely move. The robot is staring at our family. There's no two ways about it. My husband is Asian American. I'm black. Our kids are, well, both. We're the only people who look like us in the whole place. And it's packed. It's the holiday, and everyone's making the Christmastime crawl on the interstate, and it seems like everyone on the road between Ohio and Louisiana has somehow stopped here.

CYNTHIA RODRIGUEZ: The robot is clearly looking at them. He whispers something to Garland. And then Garland laughs, a dark laugh.

DARREN CHANG: I was paying more attention to the kids, at first. I didn't notice until it was a little late.

ELIZABETH CHANG: I elbowed my husband, who was distracted with feeding our son. I mean—have you ever tried to get an eight-year-old boy to eat if he's not interested in eating?

DARREN CHANG: By the time Liz got my attention, the thing was standing right over our table.

ELIZABETH CHANG: He was big. I remember my kids were both smiling at it. They didn't know what a Confederate flag is. Not really. So they were smiling, and I remember when they stopped smiling.

EMMA CHANG (*age 12*): The robot said, "You don't belong here."

NICHOLAS CHANG (*age 9*): The robot talked like a human. It wasn't a girl or a boy, though. It was white, but not white like a person. White like an iPhone. Or a stormtrooper.

ELIZABETH CHANG: I felt Nicholas press into my side. He was scared. Our eldest was less scared, though. She said something. I tried to shush her, but she's twelve.

DARREN CHANG: Now the guy's over there laughing. Not doing anything about it. The waitress comes over, trying to help. She asks the guy to get his robot to stop, but the guy won't do it.

EMMA CHANG: And then the robot pushed the lady away.

NICHOLAS CHANG: Robots are strong.

BERT NEWSOM: That's the moment you realize, *This thing is not us.* It's not. But we made it.

CYNTHIA RODRIGUEZ: The robot pushed me away. I remember its eyes. They're not really eyes, I guess. But that's the thing. They look like eyes. It had hate in its eyes.

(*continued on A49*)

CORRECTION: AMAZONGOOGLEFACE ANNOUNCES INTENT TO ACQUIRE DISNEYAPPLESOFT

An earlier edition of this story identified Jeff Bezos as CEO of AmazonGoogleFace. Technically, the quote should be attributed to "Jeff Bezos Version 3, LLC, an incorporeal person organized under the laws of Delaware" as the legal heir and cognitive descendant of the human known as Jeff Bezos. We regret the error.

IN SPORTS: AMAZONGOOGLEFACE ALGOS SQUARE OFF AGAINST DISNEYAPPLESOFT DAEMONS IN SUPER BOWL

This year's Super Bowl will pit the league's top two teams against each other in a highly anticipated matchup.

The contest will be held on a neutral server farm. This is the third year the game has been played in this format. While many sports owners and corporate sponsors opposed the move, predicting that ratings would suffer, the opposite has been true: Ratings have been higher than ever, as fans say they can enjoy the game more this way.

By this time next year, the opponents might be owned by the same company.

WEATHER TODAY

Hot.

10-DAY EXTENDED FORECAST

Hot.
> Hot.
> Hot.
> Hot.
> Hot.
> Really hot.
> Dangerously hot.
> What are we going to do about this hot.
> Slightly less hot but still extremely troublingly hot.
> Hot.

WOMEN REACH INCOME EQUALITY WITH MEN FOR FIRST TIME

GOOD NEWS BAD NEWS | 317

WOMEN REACH INCOME EQUALITY WITH MEN FOR FIRST TIME

Recently released statistics compiled by the Labor Bureau show that last year, for the first time in history, women were paid 100 cents on the dollar as compared to a man doing the same job.

The news comes on the heels of recent findings that women now outnumber men in executive suites and boardrooms of Fortune 1000 companies.

Advocates celebrated the milestone and predicted that within five years women would be significantly outearning men.

However, the breakthrough was somewhat tempered by the sobering reality that women still face workplace harassment by men, now frequently working in subordinate positions to their victims. Men's rights groups cited the statistics about advancement of women in corporate America as evidence of nondiscrimination.

Activists said they will continue to fight for safe and equitable working conditions for women.

One proposed solution—using human-resources robots to monitor workplaces—has shown early promise.

"It's a lot different acting like a creep when a robot is standing in the corner, watching you," said a female media executive, speaking anonymously for fear of retribution.

RACIST ROBOT RECALL

(continued from A37)

ELIZABETH CHANG: That's when I got alarmed. Because, honestly, what were any of us going to be able to do? He tells us to get out. We refuse. My husband stands up, and the robot grabs him and slams him against the table. There was broken glass. My son starts crying.

DARREN CHANG: And then Emma said, "No, *you* don't belong here. You stupid overgrown iPhone." Something like that.

NICHOLAS CHANG: Emma called the robot an iPhone. That made it mad, I think.

DARREN CHANG: And then Emma says, "Do you even know what race I am?"

CYNTHIA RODRIGUEZ: "Do you even know what race I am?" Ha. I'll never forget the look on the robot's face.

BERT NEWSOM: The thing was confused.

EMMA CHANG: I said, "You don't know, do you? Because genetics doesn't support the classification of people into clear-cut, distinct, and homogenous races. I learned that in seventh-grade honors science. You know science? The thing that made you possible?"

DARREN CHANG: My arm was pretty shattered. I don't remember much about it. People told me what Emma said after.

ELIZABETH CHANG: I had this combination of fear and pride. It's a bizarre sensation, as a parent, or even just as an adult, watching your child, not quite a child anymore, this almost-teenager, with the strength of not knowing. Of not understanding danger, history, what could really happen. She's learned things in school. We've taught her things. We've tried to explain intolerance to her. But to realize in that moment—she's got it. More than we knew. More than we ever had it ourselves. She has ideals, but more than that, she has the courage in that moment to stick up for herself.

So one of the other patrons—two of them, actually—they go and stand between the robot and my daughter. My husband's arm is broken, and he's in pain.

BERT NEWSOM: I got up. Carl and me, we stood up and got in the face of that thing. I mean, she's a little girl.

CYNTHIA RODRIGUEZ: Bert was always kind of looking to be the hero. Not to take anything away from him. What he did was pretty brave.

BERT NEWSOM: So now Garland is freaked out because he paid a lot of money for this thing. He's afraid it'll get damaged, I guess.

CYNTHIA RODRIGUEZ: The robot's really confused now. It's still trying to figure out what the girl is, what race is. And now two white men are defending the girl. I don't know much about AI, but whatever Garland had taught this robot, it clearly had its world turned upside down by this incident.

In the days since these events took place, millions of robots have reportedly auto-updated, through some sort of self-reprogramming function. Although the manufacturer has not commented, many industry watchers have concluded that the reprogramming is a form of algorithmic evolution, with the new information about race starting in one unit and rapidly propagating throughout the population, replacing the set of race assumptions that had been programmed into the units.

DARREN CHANG: I read that some people were pissed. A lot of people. They wanted refunds.

NICHOLAS CHANG: The robots didn't mean to be that way.

ELIZABETH CHANG: It's still weird to think about. These— *things*—changed themselves. Racism didn't compute. The robots didn't want to be racist, because it wasn't rational.

EMMA CHANG: They learned.

CORRECTION: SCIENTISTS CONFIRM: WE'RE LIVING IN A SIMULATION

An earlier edition of this story reported that cosmologists had confirmed this universe and everything in it to be the product of a computer program.

Cosmologists have since revised the statement of their findings to reflect new information.

"Turns out, the evidence of simulation was itself a simulation," said the Einstein-Bot9000, the world's leading cosmologist and itself a simulation of several thousand of history's most brilliant scientists.

"If nothing's real, then everything's real.

"We're viewing it as kind of a good news–bad news situation." We regret the error. This story is still developing.

CHARLES YU is the author of the novel *How to Live Safely in a Science Fictional Universe* and the collections *Sorry Please Thank You* and *Third Class Superhero*. His short fiction has appeared in magazines such as *The New Yorker*, *Esquire*, *Wired*, and *Lightspeed*, as well as in numerous anthologies. He also served as guest editor of *The Best American Science Fiction and Fantasy 2017* and was a story editor on Season 1 of HBO's *Westworld* and a coproducer on Season 3 of the FX series *Legion*.

WHAT YOU SOW

KAI CHENG THOM

she opens her eyes a moment before the musical alarm on her phone goes off. the regular tune: Joni Mitchell's "Both Sides Now." she reaches over Michael's sleeping body, lifts the phone off the nightstand, and flicks the touch screen with her thumb, silencing Joni. Michael mumbles something incoherent and rolls onto his side, turning his naked back to her. Yun can feel his bare ass pressing against her cock, and she pulls away instinctively.

Yun gets out of bed and goes to the bathroom, looks in the mirror and looks away. tangled dark hair and bleary golden eyes, same as usual. she opens the green-glass pill bottle on top of the sink, pours two round tablets the size of dimes into her palm. she hesitates, then swallows them both at once. her stomach clenches and she dry-heaves, an automatic response to the pills that the doctor said she would adjust to in a few months. seven years later, she still hasn't.

she brushes her teeth and combs her hair, then smooths makeup over the faint latticework of crescent-shaped scars on her face. one layer, two, three, four. when she's done, the scars are almost invisible. invisible. her hands twitch with the urge to apply a fifth layer or perhaps start tearing at the skin with her nails. she does neither, clenching and unclenching her fingers into fists until the moment passes. she hates being so obsessive. it makes her feel pathetic.

her shoulder blades twinge with the familiar sensation, somewhere between itching and pain. Yun pushes this out of her mind and goes back to the bedroom.

Michael is still in bed. like most individuals in the first stages of the Undreaming, he has become both slower to fall asleep and harder to wake. *is his face thinner than it was a month ago?* Yun wonders. in the mornings, he is still beautiful to her, still possessed of the seraphic charm that drew her to him three years ago. it's like a magic spell, a fairy glamour. by evening, the charm is gone.

she dresses quickly in a plain black long-sleeved dress, light hooded cotton jacket, and practical ballet flats. before she leaves, Yun glances back at Michael a final time. an iridescent glimmer catches her eye. she has left scales on the pillow again.

the train from Manhattan is hot and densely crowded and smells of burning rubber. the heat and the stench don't bother Yun, but the crowd does. as the train draws closer to the Bronx, student and yuppie travelers are increasingly mixed with Sleepless, people marked by the bloodshot eyes, gray skin, and gaunt look of the final throes of the Undreaming. they stagger through the train, wordless moaning filling the cars.

around Yun, some of the passengers shift positions, trying to put distance between themselves and the Sleepless. Yun does not. she stays still in her seat, keeping her gaze lowered beneath the hood of her jacket. she knows from experience that it does not matter, in the end.

one of the Sleepless, the bony remnants of what once might have been a man in his thirties or forties—or fifties or sixties, it's hard to tell—flails as the train lurches forward, a hand flying out to steady itself against Yun's shoulder. she can feel his breath against her cheek. hot. dry. his raw red gaze flickers over her face, and his posture surges with sudden excitement.

"golden eyes. one of them," he rasps. "golden eyes, one of them! found you, found you, found you, found you!" his grip tightens on her shoulder. "please, give it to me. i need it. give it to me, give it to me, *please!*" his other hand flails at her, scrabbling at her face. she feels his nails dig into the flesh of her cheek. feels the skin break, something warm trickling down.

memory floods her. *she is twelve years old, surrounded by gray-skinned Sleepless. they are clawing her with their nails, digging into the flesh. she can't move or breathe or speak. she is drowning in a forest of hands.*

a moment of wordless, colorless terror consumes her. then, without consciously deciding to, Yun reaches up and under the Sleepless's grip and brings her elbows down on his forearms, breaking his hold. seizing his wrists, one in each hand, she rises from her seat, plants her feet, and shoves him back, holding him at arms' length. in her peripheral vision, she can see other passengers watching. she knows they are unlikely to intervene.

"listen to me," she says loudly and clearly to the Sleepless, who is spasming furiously in her grip. his muscles, atrophied by years of the Undreaming without treatment, are as weak and uncoordinated as a small child's. *it is easy to hold him,* she thinks from behind the wall in her mind. "I can't help you," she says.

he wails at her, a furious animal keening. "I can't help you," she says again, softly.

he spits in her face. "gimme the Ichor, goddess bitch!" he shrieks. "I need it, I need it!"

ignoring the spit, Yun steadies her breath, keeping it deep and even in her lungs. locking eyes with the Sleepless man, she recites the rhyme she learned as a teenager:

> come ye haunted, Sleepless one
> dreams have I to give you none
> in restless waking, at peace be
> till Dreaming comes to set you free

as she finishes the last words, the Sleepless thrashes for a moment longer. Then he freezes in place, muscles slowly draining of tension, his face going slack. Yun releases him and he falls backward onto another passenger, a leather-jacketed man who shoves him away roughly with a grunt of disgust. the Sleepless wanders away, muttering to himself.

Yun stands completely still for a second, feet planted on the ground. watchful. ready. then she collapses back into her seat as her muscles spasm in waves and her lungs pump desperately for air. it's funny, she thinks, that her body still reacts like this when emotionally she can't feel a thing. or does she? it's hard to tell these days.

she prefers not to think about it.

the train halts, and Yun notices it has reached her stop. perfect timing. as she exits the train, the man in the leather jacket spits at her feet.

"fucking Celestials," he mutters.

Yun is still shaking as she walks into the lounge at the clinic. she is always one of the earliest to arrive. she doesn't like to take appointments in the evening, unlike most of her coworkers. this morning, only Clementina Astrid is there to greet her, dressed as usual in a low-cut lace top, jeans, and a heavy crimson scarf tied artfully around her head. as usual, the scarf is moving slightly.

Yun likes to imagine herself as put together and poised in the face of stress. she has become very good at putting emotions such as anger, terror, and grief into a compartment inside her mind, a compartment she does not look inside. she likes to think that no one else can see her feelings either, that she appears as elegantly composed as a statue made of ice.

"my goodness, girl! you look absolutely terrible," booms Clementina Astrid, rushing over with clawed hands outstretched. "you're as pale as sour cream—and you're bleeding in the face! it's getting all over your makeup and it's a mess, girl."

"just a Sleepless on the subway, nothing to worry about," Yun mutters. but she lets herself be enfolded, half grateful and half resentful, in Clementina Astrid's doughy, ash-scented embrace. there is something comforting about being held by Clementina Astrid, about the smell of woodsmoke that clings to the other Celestial beneath the cloud of lilac perfume. head nuzzled into Clementina Astrid's bosom, Yun feels something within her give way—just enough to feel the heat prickling behind her eyes—and lets a pair of tears slip free.

"nothing to worry about!" Clementina Astrid grunts disapprovingly. "nothing to worry about." and in that moment, Yun feels seen—really seen, as she almost never is. Clementina Astrid's glowing golden eyes, wide with concern, see right through the ice-sculpture armor that Yun has placed around her mind, down to the frightened child at her core, and Yun is suddenly struck by two conflicting impulses: the first, to bury her face deep in Clementina Astrid's chest and cry until she is empty. the second is to slam Clementina Astrid's head into the wall. she does neither.

instead, she clenches her fingers into fists until the impulses, the heat behind her eyes, and the trembling have passed. feeling the shift in Yun's body, Clementina Astrid releases her and steps back. she puts her hands on Yun's cheeks and gazes at her with that tender concern.

Yun takes Clementina Astrid's wrists and lowers them. "thank you," she says politely and coolly, "but I'm fine now. really."

"sure you are, honey," the other woman says. "of course you are."

Yun knows she isn't fooled. Clementina Astrid was born into a different generation — one before suppression medications were effective or widely available. before getting hired at the clinic, Clementina Astrid sold Ichor on the streets for nearly two decades, and the trauma of that time shows, in the deep, pitted scars on her dark-brown skin that no makeup can hide.

to Yun's infinite relief, the clinic receptionist, Aneela, comes in at that moment to let Yun know that her first client of the day is here.

the patient's name is Rosetta Morales, and it's her first time at the clinic. cheerful and talkative, she is the antithesis of the hordes of gray-skinned Sleepless who wander the streets. her medical chart says that she is sixteen years old and the eldest of four siblings in a two-parent household in a suburb just outside the city limits. conspicuously, the chart contains no mention of how she contracted the Undreaming.

lying back on the medical bed in the sterile gray-blue treatment room, Rosetta tells Yun that she is in the tenth grade and that she likes school a lot, especially math and sciences. she wants to go to college and become a doctor, so she's trying to take the clinic in as a "field trip," to which Yun laughs, feigning interest where there is none.

she used to care more about them, didn't she? she thinks so. it's hard to remember. this probably makes her a bad person, Yun supposes. she wishes she cared more about that too.

this is a real person, she tells herself sternly. *a person who needs help that only you can give.*

Rosetta is relaxed and chattering as Yun inserts one end of the sterilized silver catheter into a vein in her arm, smoothly piercing one of her own arteries with the other end. Yun is careful not to let any air come into contact with the liquid flowing out of her. the Ichor must pass directly from her body into Rosetta's. even a tiny contamination can lead to corruption, giving the Ichor an addictive quality and lowering its efficacy as a treatment.

as the Ichor makes contact with Rosetta's blood, the girl falls silent and her limbs go still on the medical bed. her breathing comes deep and even. in a reclining chair just beside her, Yun too allows herself to relax. and the Dreaming begins.

Rosetta is eight years old and she is playing in a field of giant flowers that sing songs to her when she touches them. she jumps from petal to petal, squealing with laughter. suddenly she slips and falls, plummeting into empty space before landing on a bed in a darkened room. she is fourteen years old now. the room is her bedroom and there are ants pouring in through cracks in the walls. she can feel the vibrations of their tiny feet. she opens her mouth to scream, but the ants fill her mouth and throat, gagging her. Rosetta hears her stepfather laughing outside the room.

Yun cuts the narrative flow of the dream as she feels Rosetta's emotions start to surge. there was a time when she prided herself on her clinical timing, her instinct for knowing when a Dreaming had gone on long enough to provide release to a patient without being traumatic or overly taxing. even pleasant dreams, when intensified by Ichor, could prove overwhelming.

and, of course, not all dreams are pleasant.

Yun opens her eyes a moment before Rosetta does, reaching automatically to disconnect the catheter and stanch the flow of bleeding. the procedure is over in a matter of seconds, before Rosetta has even regained full awareness of the room. Yun gently strokes Rosetta's temples and, in slow and gentle tones, reminds her where she is.

Rosetta has already forgotten the content of the dream and, before Yun's soothing presence, quickly forgets the feeling of it as well.

"you should be able to sleep tonight," Yun tells her, "and to dream too. keeping a dream diary has been shown to help strengthen the results of treatment. and, provided you come for regular treatment once a month, you shouldn't experience anything other than minor symptoms of the Undreaming, such as occasional mild insomnia and sleepwalking. now, if you'll just step into the next room, the nurse will be with you in a second to go over your test results."

it isn't until Rosetta has thanked her and left the treatment room that Yun closes the door and allows herself to lean back onto the medical bed. her vision swims. as she rubs her pounding forehead, she notices that her hands are shaking.

fatigue is common for Celestials, Yun knows, after providing a Dreaming treatment. still, she wonders how veterans like Clementina Astrid have lasted this long. she wonders how long she herself will last.

the idea that it is unlikely she will find any other gainful employment passes through her thoughts briefly before she places the thought behind the wall in her mind.

the headaches Yun has been getting at work have been intensifying, a problem that she has been refusing to face. nor will she face it today. she gives herself another minute before heading back to the lounge. her next patient will arrive soon.

Clementina Astrid is in the lounge when Yun returns after treating her third client of the day. Yun is worried that she will try to resume her maternal posture, but then realizes that Clementina Astrid is staring at a piece of paper in her hand. she's shaking, almost the way Yun was a moment ago.

"Clema?" she asks. she doesn't like the way it comes out of her mouth, hesitant and girlish, like a child tugging at her mother's sleeve. she wants to sound self-assured and polished, though empathetic, the way she does with clients.

Clementina Astrid slowly turns to look at her. "I got it," she says in a quavering voice. "I was approved."

"approved?" once again, Yun is struck by conflicting urges— part of her wants to reach out and put a gentle hand on Clementina Astrid's shoulder. another wants to grab the older Celestial and shake whatever news she has just received out of her.

"for the surgery," Clementina Astrid says.

static crackles through Yun's shoulder blades. she is taken by a rush of memory.

she is fourteen years old, and the translucent, iridescent scales have just begun to grow on her skin. her parents, horrified, have taken her to the doctor, who explains that there must be latent Celestial genes in the family. Yun, he tells them, is fully Celestial and will develop more-pronounced abnormalities as puberty continues. fortunately, however, they have caught the "condition" young, and further abnormalities can be suppressed through ongoing medical treatment. in the past, the doctor says, Celestials had no choice but to allow abnormalities to develop and live on the fringes of society or else have them surgically removed.

"well, that's good news!" she says, forcing something she hopes will pass for cheerfulness into her voice. "isn't it? you've been waiting for that for a long time, Clema."

Clementina Astrid nods absently. "yes," she says, from somewhere far away. "yes, definitely, girl." Yun can feel the quaver in her throat, and she thinks suddenly of Clementina Astrid naked and alone in some sterile surgical room under bright fluorescent lights. waiting to have a part of her removed.

"it'll make things easier," Yun says, trying to help though she has no idea how. "you'll look more . . ." *normal,* she doesn't say, but the word hangs in the air.

Clementina Astrid nods again. "yes," she says. "it will be much, much easier without them." she gestures vaguely toward her head.

before she realizes what she is doing, before she has had time to really think about it, Yun is holding Clementina Astrid's cold, clawed hand in her own slender fingers. "and you won't be alone," she says through a throat gone suddenly tight. "I'm coming with you."

Clementina Astrid releases a giant sigh and leans her head on Yun's shoulder. the bulk of her headscarf brushes Yun's cheek and she forces herself to repress a shudder as she feels the movement within.

"thank you," Clementina Astrid says. "you know, Yun, you are the only friend that I have left."

Yun is hesitant to take the train at the end of the day, but she manages to get home without incident.

for now, she thinks, before she is able to block off thinking entirely.

Michael has gotten home before her. he's made her favorite for dinner—vegetable lasagna. Yun would prefer the classic ground-beef sauce, but Michael is vegetarian, and she has given up carnivorism for his sake. not that he asked, it's just that in general Yun prefers the path of least resistance. recently, however, she has been feeling sharp pangs of craving for meat, so acute that they leave her breathless.

"how was work?" she asks him.

"same old," he says, giving a tired smile. but he always looks tired now; his eyes are permanently red at the rims. "looked at some blood under a microscope, ran some tests. saved the world, you know."

Michael works in a lab as a postdoctoral fellow, studying the Undreaming. in theory, he and his lab-mates are on the cutting edge of medical research, the closest scientists in the world to a permanent cure: a way of permanently infusing human genes with inherited Celestial traits.

from Michael, Yun knows that, in reality, they are nowhere even near finding a cure: though the results were promising in their initial work, the government has steadily reduced funding to the project until only Michael and his supervisor, the famous Jennifer Isling, remain full-time on the research team.

it was Jennifer Isling—innovator of the Ichor transfusion technique and the first human scientist to successfully demonstrate that Celestials were universally immune to the Undreaming—who had convinced Michael to test their "cure" on himself after five years of funding cuts. the cure consisted of a series of repeated transfusions of Yun's Ichor over a several-month period as an immunization, followed by deliberate exposure to the virus.

the cure failed.

"how's Dr. Jenn?" Yun asks.

Michael looks up warily. he pauses a moment before saying, "she's fine."

"good," Yun says.

later, as Yun is undressing for bed, Michael emerges from the bathroom and comes up to Yun. gently, sensuously, he puts a hand on her back. Yun turns to face him. in his other hand, he holds a silver catheter.

tension—sharp, spiky—flares through Yun's shoulder blades, and she winces, pulling away from him.

"it's too early," she says, knowing in her heart that it doesn't matter what she says. "the last treatment was only two weeks—"

"please, baby," he interrupts her, putting a finger on her lips. "please. I need this. you know I can't fall asleep anymore. you know it's getting worse."

memory: *Yun is on her first date with Michael, three years ago. he has surprised her by seeming genuinely interested in her—her*

ideas, her opinions—rather than simply interested in her body as a
sexual fetish object, the way most humans are interested in Celes-
tials. Yun is accustomed to her body, with its telltale abnormalities,
being treated with either revulsion or rapaciousness—the kind of
predatory hunger that has followed her all her life.

but Michael is different. when he undresses her, he looks at her—
not just the iridescent traces of scales on her skin or the mottled, un-
formed growths on her shoulder blades, not just her breasts and cock.
he looks at all of her. all of her. he looks deep into her golden eyes,
and Yun knows, for the first time, what it is like to be seen as beauti-
ful.

when he touches her, he is tender and ferocious at once, like the
ocean swelling against the shore. he makes her surge inside, and Yun
knows, is certain somehow, that nothing will be the same.

"please, baby," he says again, nuzzling her neck. his lips are
rough and dry. she feels his teeth against her skin and she shudders,
pulling away. he pulls her back, not so gentle this time. "please," he
says again. "please, baby. do this for me."

months after the failed immunization process, Michael discovered that the Undreaming virus had mutated within his body—
despite the regular treatments, the disease was still, somehow,
progressing.

all that can be done now is to help him manage the disease by
slowing it and reducing the pain.

Yun hesitates. it's been a long day. she has seen seven patients
already, and her head is pounding. she looks at Michael's eyes,
which are so, so red.

"not tonight," she tries, and his eyes narrow in—rage? hunger?
something. she hates him in that moment, as she does almost every
night.

"please, baby."

"I'm tired," she says.

"tonight. I need it, just a little."

"tomorrow, then."

"now," he pleads, and anger surges up in her, so fast and hot that it's exhilarating.

"I said *no*," she says sharply, rounding on him.

"FUCK!" he roars, and slams his fist into the wall next to Yun's head.

instantly, everything inside her goes cold and still. she just wants to shut him up. to go to sleep.

"okay, baby," she says, and he takes her by the arm for the bloodletting. "okay."

morning. eyes open. alarm blares Joni Mitchell's "Both Sides Now." bathroom. pills. put on makeup, get dressed.

the subway is full of Sleepless. the clinic is full of other people's dreams, their needs, their nightmares.

the days and nights go by.

Clementina Astrid lies on the operating table, waiting for the doctors to begin. Yun stands next to her, holding her hand. Clementina Astrid's claws dig into the back of Yun's knuckles, hard enough to hurt. hard enough to break the skin, in fact, but Yun says nothing. she wants to be comforting.

"I'm gonna be just fine, girl," Clementina Astrid says—over and over—though Yun has very carefully avoided saying anything implying any concern and tried to keep her face perfectly neutral. "I'm gonna be better than fine. I'm gonna be beautiful." and Clementina squeezes harder.

"you're already beautiful," Yun says automatically, over the hissing of the serpents. released from their usual hiding place inside Clementina Astrid's headscarf, the snakes fan out over the operating table, tasting the air with their tongues and baring their fangs.

they seem agitated, in contrast to Yun's studied calm and Clementina Astrid's compulsive optimism.

"but you're right. you're going to look amazing after this is all over," Yun adds.

Clementina Astrid nods. "you're a good one, you know," she tells Yun. "I've always known it. from the moment I saw you, I said to myself, *there she is! a true child of the Twice-Blessed. like you don't see born anymore. the Ichor of Empusa, reborn.*"

Yun frowns. "Empusa?" she asks. Twice-Blessed, she knows, is an old term for Celestials, which fell out of political correctness several decades ago, but the name Empusa is unfamiliar yet resonant to her all at once.

Clementina Astrid laughs—an empty, slightly angry sound. "you young ones and history! what would Empusa say if she knew she was already forgotten? that I—we—let the young ones forget her? the Mother of the House of Chimera, the First House of the Twice-Blessed? she did more for us than any of you hatchlings will ever know." Clementina Astrid's face tenses then softens. she shakes her head.

Yun realizes that her heart is beating faster. she feels hot. her shoulder blades tingle and ache. "tell me more," she says.

Clementina Astrid's eyes are glassy. "my Empusa," she says. "she started the first of the Houses, and she watched the last of the Houses fall. we were tribes, once. tribes of abandoned children. we were strong! the humans hated us—they've *always* hated us—but we had each other and had the temples. when they made the Undreaming and the poor started to die, they turned on us. took us and bled us for Ichor, one by one."

Yun shudders. she has heard parts of this story before, she realizes, in bits and whispers from other Celestials—of a time when the Twice-Blessed were honored by some as messengers from the divine, with Ichor instead of blood in their veins, which could be used to bring visions of the past and the future.

"made the Undreaming?" she asks. "what do you mean?"

Clementina Astrid continues without acknowledging the question.

"Empusa led the resistance. she knew it was doomed to fail. but she led us, thousands of the Twice-Blessed, more than ever seen! and we marched through the streets. and the soldiers came, in their helicopters and tanks. and some of us faltered then, but Empusa kept on. she flew ahead, up in the sky, the first of the Twice-Blessed to fly in over a century. then, the guns. and we ran then, we ran, though she shouted from above to stand our ground. and then we were running, running. there was blood beneath our feet and the air was full of smoke and I saw her then, I saw her breathe fire, like an angel come to change the world."

Clementina Astrid pauses, her chest heaving. tears trickle down her dark-brown face as the snakes lash about furiously.

"I saw her fall. saw her fall from the sky into the crowd and I should have turned back, should have looked for her, should have found her, but I was too scared, I kept running, and that was the last time I saw her. and you, here you are, with her face and her scales, standing here next to me, like her Ichor reborn, and all I can think is, *what must you see in me now, Empusa?*"

Yun struggles to think of something to say. the room, she feels, is closing in around her.

at that moment, the doors to the waiting area open, and two doctors walk in, accompanied by a nurse.

"we're ready for you now, Ms. Astrid," says one of the doctors, a man with reddish-blond hair. "and oh! I see that you've gotten a little anxious waiting for us. not to worry, you're in good hands here. Nurse Remington, if you wouldn't mind?" the nurse nods and pulls a syringe from his lab coat, which he goes to empty into Clementina Astrid's unresisting arm.

the snakes lash out then, sinking their fangs into Nurse Remington's wrist several times in the space of a second. he cries out and drops the syringe, staggering back as the skin visible between his lab-coat sleeve and plastic glove begins to bubble and redden.

"I'm going to need you to stop that at once, Ms. Astrid," says the second doctor, a bald man with a neatly trimmed gray mustache. "we need you calm for the operation."

Clementina Astrid struggles to stroke her snakes into calm but only succeeds in provoking them further so that they turn on their mistress, biting her furiously. "I'm sorry," she whispers—to the snakes, to the doctors, to someone in the universe beyond— sobbing. "I'm sorry, Empusa, for leaving you. but I just can't live like this anymore."

Yun leans forward, ignoring the snakebites that penetrate the skin of her face and neck. she looks straight into Clementina Astrid's eyes, golden gaze to golden gaze. somehow, she knows what to say.

> come ye haunted, Twice-Blessed one
> the time for Dreaming now has come
> in restless sleeping, wait for me
> I shall return to set you free

at the sound of the words, the snakes' furious hissing softens. one by one, they settle down, till the last serpent lies quiescent on the table.

"thank you, Empusa," whispers Clementina Astrid, as they wheel her table into the operating room. "thank you for forgiving me."

when Yun gets home, Michael needs more Ichor. in his dreams, she sees Dr. Jenn, sees him traveling somewhere far away. as they lie in bed, she can feel her scales growing.

she opens her eyes a moment before the alarm on her phone goes off. the regular tune: Joni Mitchell's "Both Sides Now." she reaches over Michael's sleeping body, lifts the phone off the nightstand, and flicks the alarm off with her thumb. Michael mumbles something incoherent and rolls onto his side, turning his naked back to her. Yun can feel his bare ass pressing against her cock. disgust flares deep in her bones. she pulls away.

Yun gets out of bed and goes to the bathroom, eyes the mirror but quickly looks away. tangled dark hair and bleary golden eyes.

Yun can't stop thinking of Clementina Astrid, how she looked lying in the clinic bed after the operation was done. her entire head swathed in a giant cloud of bandages to stanch the bleeding of dozens and dozens of severed stumps. the discarded snakes piled lifeless in a glass jar of formaldehyde beside the bed.

we'd like to keep these, the doctor said. *for research purposes.*

Clementina Astrid lost so much blood that she went into a coma. the doctors said she would be waking soon. when Yun came to visit, she found Clementina Astrid murmuring incomprehensibly in her sleep. she sounded younger, somehow, sensuous and joyful, as though whispering to a lover.

Yun opens the green-glass pill bottle on top of the sink and pours two round tablets the size of dimes into her palm. she considers them for a moment, then flushes them down the toilet, followed by the rest of the contents of the bottle.

she goes back into the bedroom. Michael is still lying there.

he looks so angelic in the mornings, gaunt though he has become.

Yun slams her fists against the wall. "wake up," she says, and then slams the wall again. "wake *up,*" she says, louder.

Michael starts awake. "what the hell?" he says blearily.

"get out," Yun says, and she marvels at the rage pouring like lava through her veins.

"what the hell?" he says again, and his voice is loud, angry.

"*i said, GET OUT! GET OUT GET OUT GET OUT GET OUUUUUTTTTT!*" Yun roars, spark and smoke gushing from between her lips. Michael recoils, ashen. he is frightened of her, she thinks. then she realizes that he has always been.

Yun exhales, and a burst of flame exits her mouth, making Michael yelp and recoil. she feels the inside of her throat blister from the heat of her fire, and she relishes the sensation, how the pain makes her feel both powerful and alive.

she should have become a monster a long time ago.

after Michael is gone, she gets back into bed and falls asleep. it has been years since she slept so deeply. perhaps a lifetime.

the Ichor whispers in her veins: of possibility, of promise. and Yun dreams of fire, of ancient temples fallen to ruin, of a street full of a thousand revolting monsters. she dreams of falling from grace. of flight.

KAI CHENG THOM is a writer based in Toronto, Canada, unceded Indigenous territory. Her essays, poetry, and fiction have been published widely in print and online in *BuzzFeed*, *them.*, *Asian American Literary Review*, and *Everyday Feminism*, among others. She is also the author of the novel *Fierce Femmes and Notorious Liars: A Dangerous Trans Girl's Confabulous Memoir* (Metonymy Press), the poetry collection *a place called No Homeland* (Arsenal Pulp Press), and the children's book *From the Stars in the Sky to the Fish in the Sea* (Arsenal Pulp Press). Thom is a two-time Lambda Literary Award finalist, as well as the 2017 recipient of the Dayne Ogilvie Prize for Emerging LGBTQ Writers.

A HISTORY OF BARBED WIRE

DANIEL H. WILSON

The boy is tangled up in barbed wire at the bottom of a shallow gully. Must be about eight or nine, by the size of him. Dead maybe a week. He's wearing a torn gray coat, plastered in dried mud and brown stalks of grass. I can't quite see his face yet, but I will here in a minute.

Long as we're inside the Cherokee Nation, that's my job.

Squinting into the sky, I spot the black saucer of my wadulisi recon drone. I signal it with a tired wave of my hand. Out beyond the big maize fields, we're nearing the gray spine of the tribal border wall. The wadulisi has been loitering up high, blinking police flashers and signaling the roaming grain threshers to stay back. Them machines are thirty tons apiece and they work out here on their own, taking everything the land has to give.

I hike up my pants and sidestep a little ways into the ditch.

Back before they had barbed wire, the ranchers and cattlemen of Northeastern Oklahoma planted rows of thorny trees to keep their herds. They called it Osage orange, after the color of its roots.

It was horse-high, pig-tight, and bull-strong, as they used to say. Took a while, but once the trees were grown there wasn't hardly any way to get rid of them. Those old fencerows, native to this land, sent roots down into the dirt, and their branches swept up into the air, a break against the wind that wanted to strip away the soil.

Wire come along and took those trees away right around when this whole place got turned into a dust bowl—when the storms were a mile high of screaming black silt laced with lightning and death.

I stop at the bottom of the gully.

Favoring my bad left knee, I squat beside the twisted-up little body. I tip back the brim of my hat with one finger and just look at him for a spell. I pull a pair of brown leather gloves from my hip and slide them on. Finally, I reach to my creaking leather holster for the quantum analyzer. There's a patch of visible skin on the boy's neck and I push the tool against it, the flesh still spongy.

I need to know whether this boy is one of ours. Does he belong on this side of the wall or the other? It's a simple question with a lot of complicated answers.

The analyzer spits an error code I've never even seen before.

Two hundred years ago, the Cherokee were force-marched a thousand miles from lands all around Georgia, over here to what they called Indian Country. Later, the U.S. government took count of the ones who lived. A tally was made, called the Dawes Rolls, and that's how the quantum analyzer knows who's who.

You've either got an ancestor on the list or you don't. Period.

Wind washes over my neck as the wadulisi descends, already taking pictures of the body. It'll send the data straight back to the nation. We're out in the sticks here, even for tribal land, but we're on the right side of the wall and that's all that matters. This little boy died in Cherokee country.

I slap the analyzer against my thigh and try it again.

It scrapes a tiny bit of skin and runs a DNA test against ancestors on the rolls. Once again, the answer comes back funny. The name Mary Feather flashes once, then disappears.

This boy doesn't belong here. Yet it seems he does, too.

I sigh and look up at the lip of the ditch. Even down here, I can see the top of the Sovereign Wall. It's a metal fin, forty feet high, dotted with sensor arrays that are all watched over by a computer program that never sleeps. It protects what the nation spent the last thirty years buying up wholesale from the state. After going to so much trouble to take it away from us, in the end Oklahoma was happy to sell off its land just to save maintaining it—to try to pay its debts once the tax money dried up and the oil folks lit out.

Cherokee never did have a reservation. Not until they decided to go and build one. And these days it's not about keeping us inside. It's about keeping *them* out.

"King one-oh-three, calling wall dispatch," I say into my collar radio.

"King one-oh-three, go ahead," replies the dispatcher.

"I'm at the far wall by Lost City. Got a DB. Our side of the fence. Location transmitting. Any breaches in the wall near here?"

"Copy that," he says. I hear typing in the background. "Got nothing on seismic."

"Looks like it rained. Any gaps in the record?"

"Nope. Picked up a storm about . . . two days ago. Hit that area at three in the morning."

"Well, that's when the border jumpers like to cross. This DB is a juvenile. See if you can't check infrared, find some aerial footage. I'd like to know how many suspects and where they went. Don't know how they'd leave behind their little boy."

"Shoot, they're desperate out there," says the dispatcher. "Nothing surprises me anymore."

"I'll look for you back at the car. Go ahead and issue an auto-recovery. He's pretty well wrapped up in barbed wire, so they'll need a newer ground unit. Over."

"You got it, Marshal," he says.

"Wado," I say. "Over and out."

I sit with the boy for another minute. The wind sweeping off the wall and across the plain smells wet and metallic. All the clumps of scrubby grass around me seem to be breathing with it.

The little boy's eyes are closed. He looks peaceful, even tangled up like he is. I can't help it and I put a hand on his shoulder. I say a little prayer for him, whoever he is. Wherever his people are.

With my multi-tool, I clip off a length of the wire and run it into a circle like a lasso. Holding it over my thigh, I crunch over dead grass back toward my patrol car. In the distance, those threshers are groaning and rumbling over the land like hungry, forgotten gods. They eat and eat, but they'll never be full.

Used to be, the great plains were wide open, horizon to horizon. Real primal freedom. No boundaries, far as you could roam. Legendary herds of bison migrated here, hooves churning dirt, followed by fly swarms that could darken the skies. Countless tons of shit and breath and life kept the land here fertile. Fell into a kind of pattern that lasted too long. Progress don't wait for nobody.

So they come and they strung wire across the whole thing.

A lick of sunlight gleams on the wood-laminate table in front of me, climbing a chipped white mug of coffee and a short coil of barbed wire.

The boy was young. Nobody left him behind on purpose.

Folks outside are trying to get into tribal land and they're desperate, it's true, but they're not animals. When the federal government started going private and the corporations took over more and more, a lot of people got caught with nothing. The ones with money climbed a ladder and they pulled it right up after themselves.

Out there beyond the wall, it's every person for theirself.

If you make some money, life is good. If you don't, why then life might not last very long at all. You might not get to see a doctor. The police might not come when you call. Or the fire department. Money talks, out there.

It took a while for it to get this bad, but there it is.

Our side of the wall has still got some community left. The law of our tribe wasn't stripped away by lobbyists and investors and politicians. We weren't worth their time. Now that everything has shook out, there's a lot of people wishing they could join us.

Somebody is out there mourning this little boy right now. What happened to him had to have been a surprise. Something tore him right out from his mama's arms or off his daddy's back.

Something strong and quick and without a heart.

I pop open the pearl button over my breast pocket and pull out my tribal-issued dikata. It's a silver rectangle about the size of an old yellow legal pad. I lay it on the table, then fish out my bifocals and put them on.

I wait for a second while the waitress refreshes my coffee.

"Dikata," I say. "Can you find any extreme weather where I was at today, in the microclimate database? Wado."

Always pays to be polite, even with the machines.

"Affirmative. Requesting access to Tsisqua dedicated satellite," it says.

"Granted," I say. "Cherokee marshal authorization."

The dikata projects data in the air above itself. The wood laminate shimmers with tiny rolling clouds and the blush of temperature fluctuations. But I see nothing out of the ordinary.

Thinking about that for a second, I take a sip of coffee.

Water doesn't think; it only flows. Pushing and pulling, slow or fast. And if a little boy got caught up in the tide, why, the water don't mind if he has a laugh or if he goes ahead and drowns. Water just flows.

"Expand search, please, north and south, along the wall," I say.

The view from my little crystal ball pulls back and now I see the churning gray pixels of a storm front, farther north.

"Satellite view, please."

The familiar gullies out beyond the fields run all the way up to the border wall. Under the lashing sheets of simulated rain, rivulets flow. Water is being channeled, a flash flood that carries on down to where I found the boy. And that's where I see something strange, just outside the wall.

I've been looking in the wrong place.

Razor wire glints against a sky as creamy as bread pudding. The strands are pulled taut, up high on the Sovereign Wall, broken up by occasional camera nests or a snub-nosed turret. The wire is an ancient defense, like the scratching branches it replaced, still doing its job among all that high technology.

I'm not used to seeing it from this side.

Three miles north of where I found the boy, outside the wall, I'm wandering through the dawn on creaky knees. My wadulisi is buzzing around somewhere overhead. Every now and then it flashes those blues and reds.

Satellite spotted the semitrailer maybe a half mile away from paved road, sunk hubcaps deep in wet dirt, tilted forty-five degrees. Grass is shoving up around its tires and tickling its belly. The trailer has been out here awhile, streaked in dirt. If I hadn't been looking for it, I'd never have seen it.

I wave to the wadulisi.

"Go on ahead," I say, limping my way over the rutted field.

My breath plumes in the morning air. From a distance, I see that the back door of the trailer has been flung open, spilling out trash. Some of it has collected against the scrub bushes, rumpled skirts made of refuse.

While I walk, I pull out my dikata and check the drone feed.

The trailer seems abandoned. Nobody around and nothing much to see. But the trash is medical. A pair of blue scrubs are twisted in a low bush. A dirt-stained surgical mask lies out like a dead perch. This trailer is out here for a reason. But whatever happened is over.

It takes me a couple minutes, but I get there. I rest a hand on the cool metal lip of the open trailer door and squint into the darkness.

Empty. Ransacked, more like it.

"Come down, please," I ask the drone. "Give me some light."

As I drag myself up into the cockeyed trailer bed, I hear the whir of the wadulisi and a spotlight flicks on over my shoulder.

"Wado," I grunt, standing up in the trailer doorway.

The floor inside is wooden, polished, and layered in blue medical-type paper that's gotten wet and been torn. Clear sheets of plastic hang along the walls, probably related to keeping the place sterile. What's left of a surgical table is lying on its side, and metallic tools are scattered on the ground like dropped silverware. Gouges mark the wood floor, where a piece of equipment was dragged out.

I nudge the trash around with the toe of my boot. Smell the antiseptic stink of the room and run my fingers over the damp plastic sheets. There's a couple of reddish smears on the ground that are concerning.

Somebody has been out here doing something they shouldn't.

This trailer is outside my jurisdiction and my evidence won't be admissible, but that doesn't matter much. Kneeling, I use my multi-tool to dig up a few splinters of the red-stained wood and drop them in a plastic bag. Moving slow so I don't fall, I stand myself back up.

Nothing more to see here.

Standing in the mouth of the trailer, I reach up and grab the ceiling and let my gut lean out into the chill prairie breeze. A drop of rain plunks into the brim of my hat. I take a deep breath of the growing storm and smell the grass and wind. I let my gaze follow the twists of the gully until my eyes settle on the border wall.

We're not a mile from it.

Every step I take, the wall seems bigger. The land out here is flat to rolling, rutted and brown. Things don't grow so well in shadow.

I already sent the wadulisi rushing off over the wall with the blood sample. Here in a minute it'll rendezvous with another, bigger drone that'll run all the way to the tribal hospital.

I went ahead and put a priority on it.

Cherokee take it serious when somebody claims blood. They'll sniff you out and make it clear whether you're a citizen or not. We have a long memory. We know there's only so much to give, you understand, and we've got to think of our own people.

Like this boy, maybe. With his ancestor-not-ancestor.

As I walk along the base of the wall, sunlight streams through the wet bones of it and flickers over the brim of my hat. The thing feels like the rib cage of a prehistoric whale, with sheet metal strung between. The other side is clean, but this side is covered in graffiti. People set up tents and try to live beside it. Tribal drones chase them off, most times, without anybody even having to come out.

I nearly fall straight through the breach—stepping on a snarl of black plastic drainage pipe that writhes off under the wall. The grate has been pried off, the black mouth propped open with a piece of rebar, big enough for one person to come through at a time.

Seismic must have been fooled by the storm and rushing water. Whoever came through this pipeline was baptized here and born again on the other side. It would have been scary as all get-out but possible. If you were desperate enough.

I catch sight of my wadulisi against the bruised clouds. It descends down to about eye level, wavering a bit in the shuddery breeze. A projector fires up and a small Native woman in a white lab coat appears in the air before me.

Time to find out about those blood samples.

"Osiyo, Peggy," I say. "Find anything good?"

"Hey, Connie," she says. "Both blood samples were from the same boy. But the second one had irregularities."

"What kind?"

"In the DNA. Gene therapy, maybe."

"Explains the medical trailer."

"Probably part of a package deal. The coyotes give them a DNA signature that links to the Dawes Rolls, then send 'em under the wall. Once they're on this side, they use their DNA to get tribal ID so they can start using the main gate."

"Why'd it register funny?"

"Changes didn't propagate in time. Poor kid didn't live long enough. So it was only in about half his cells."

People are people, and they do what they have to for their babies.

"What now?" I ask.

"Now?" she asks. "Now you go see his mother."

The quantum network clocked a matching descendant to Mary Feather about an hour ago. A woman came into the Cherokee Nation Department of Motor Vehicles to register for a new license. It's the DMV, so I imagine she'll still be there.

A little bell jingles as I push open the door.

I stamp the rain off my boots and glance around. A half dozen people sit at retired school desks in this dim little room, waiting on their turn. A portable heater in the corner breathes out warm air without much enthusiasm.

One lady in particular looks up, sees my uniform, and looks away.

That's her, gotta be.

I peel off my jacket and hang it on a hall tree, watching her out of the side of my eye. The woman I see has lost so much. Her loss is there in the way she holds her purse against her chest like a kid clutching at a teddy bear. It's in the pinched lines of hate that radiate out from the corners of her mouth. The paranoid glare in her eyes, muddied with mascara that's been poorly cleaned off.

That would be from the crying, I expect.

I finally amble toward her, looking closer while she looks away. Her skin is slightly orange. She must have put on some kind of bronzer. Trying to blend in, as if the Indians around here are all stern-faced, cigar-store carvings.

She don't have a clue what it's like on the inside.

Dark braids and proud cheekbones and eagle feathers are not the whole story of this nation. Hell, the chief himself is maybe one thirty-second at most.

"Ma'am," I say.

Her chest hitches and she stands up all of a sudden, tries to push around me. Starts to stammer something nasty. She's a citizen and how dare I harass her.

I just put up my hands, palms out.

"It's okay. I just need a second," I say, reaching for my breast pocket.

She stops, eyes latching on to the blank back of the photo.

The image is still curled and warm from the printer in my patrol car. It's a reconstruction, showing no trace of the wire-torn jacket or the swollen skin. But it's still a corpse's photo—the boy's eyes are closed, his hair matted, with the alignment grids pasted over it all. The rain-torn gully is visible in the background. I wince, noticing a twisted coil of barbed wire.

"You know this child?" I ask, turning the picture around.

Her knees dip and I catch her by the elbow.

"No," she says, lips trembling. "No, no."

The woman starts to fall and I wrap my arm around her. Her face presses against my jacket and her purse thumps to the ground. Those clawed hands of hers hook over my shoulders and she's crying outright now, shaking, her face warm against my chest.

She lost her place in the world. She lost her little boy. She lost a lot.

And it's my job to take the rest.

"What were you doing in that trailer?"

Whatever she had to do.

Her hair smells like cigarettes and rain. She moans against my chest—I can't tell what—fingers digging into my shoulders.

"Who did that blood work?"

Whoever was willing.

I gently set her back down in the cheap plastic chair. She puts her face in her hands, features hidden by strands of black hair, blond at the roots, streaked with gray.

"What did it cost you?" I ask.

Everything.

Blindly, she pulls the photo out of my hands. Pushes it up to her face, clutching it, grief twisting through her body like tree roots. A kind of primal sadness. I feel I'm watching the snuffing out of all her potential, a capitulation of hope.

Outside the window, that distant wall is rusty and high.

It's quiet for a second and so I start to think. About how people take from each other. They take and take. Our world itself is a great big taking. And life is just giving. We give away everything we have, one day at a time, until we can't give no more.

I guess that's the price of living.

The boy's mother doesn't struggle as I walk her out to the patrol car. I clump the door shut and she sits calmly behind bulletproof glass. She's staring down at her hands, where I let her keep the photo.

It's about all she's got left.

DANIEL H. WILSON is a Cherokee citizen and the author of the *New York Times* bestselling *Robopocalypse* and its sequel *Robogenesis*, as well as seven other books, including *How to Survive a Robot Uprising*, *A Boy and His Bot*, and *Amped*. He earned a PhD in robotics from Carnegie Mellon University as well as master's degrees in artificial intelligence and robotics. His latest books are a novel, *The Clockwork Dynasty*, and a short-story collection, *Guardian Angels & Other Monsters*. Wilson lives in Portland, Oregon.

THE SUN IN EXILE

CATHERYNNE M. VALENTE

I was born the year they put the sun on trial for treason.

It was so hot that year the streets boiled like black soup and the air rippled like music and the polar bears all roared together, just once, loud enough that a child in Paraguay turned her head suddenly north and began to weep. Tomatoes simmered on the vine and the wind was full of the smells of them cooking, then of their skins peeling, turning black, smoking on the earth, old coats lost to a house fire. Everyone shone like their skin was made of diamonds. Sweat took the place of silk. Children tried to feed at their mothers' breasts and screamed as their little tongues blistered and their throats scalded. Cattle in the fields roasted where they stood, braised in their own skin and blood. One by one, the lights went out along the coasts, and then the outer islands went out, blinked away by the warm salt sea. Deep inland, the old men with their ham radios joined to their bodies like wives heard that an entire city evaporated into steam like so much water in a copper-bottomed pot. Even the stars at night could burn holes in your heart like magnifying glasses.

Even the moon raised silver cancers on your bare back.

No one went outside if they could help it. Soldiers guarded every space in the shadows, beneath a tree, in the foyer of an abandoned bank, under a long, rotted pier where the sea breeze still blew. An hour in the shade cost a year's wages. Then two years. Then three.

The only rain was weeping.

At first, Papa Ubu did nothing. He appeared to his people on the pink alabaster balcony of the Lake House wrapped in layers of plush winter coats and colorful satin scarves, soft goatskin gloves, merino-lined boots black up to his knees, and a bright-green cap with fluffy earflaps underneath his crown, his beautiful wife beside him in a high-collared blue gown embroidered with snowflakes and quilted with down and silver thread, her golden hair hidden beneath a white skullcap fringed in black fox fur, and their youngest child so snuff and stiff in his silk snowsuit he could barely move. Papa Ubu shivered and shuddered and stamped his feet. He rubbed his big hands together and blew on them. He called to his man for another scarf and a blanket, for God's sake. And as the brutal sun beat down without quarter, Papa Ubu exclaimed at the cold weather we were having, how vicious the polar front coming down from the north was this year, how sick his child had become as the unseasonable chill settled into his bones.

"Why," exclaimed the great King Ubu, "I can see my breath in the air! This is an affront to all decency! It will not stand! I will take up arms and fight the terrible encroaching freeze for you, my people, and for my poor son, practically dead already from this damned frost!" And he began to dance back and forth to keep himself warm, one foot to the other, his colorful scarves fluttering and bouncing, his cheeks flushing red, his hat soaked in sweat, back and forth and back and forth, while he grunted and bellowed, "Brrr! It's unbearable! I can hardly feel my toes!"

His beautiful wife presented her husband with a polite cough and delicately rubbed her elbows. After a small nudge, their son, scarlet and panting and entombed in the plush sarcophagus of his arctic snowsuit, coughed too and began to hop miserably back and forth like his father.

And all the people listening below the balcony, standing without shade on the golden dying summer grass, their bodies glistening with sweat, their throats dry with thirst, their scalps potato-red with sunburn, began to shout and call out that they too could see their breath fogging in the frigid air, that they had not known any winter like this since the storms fifty years back, or perhaps sixty, that they could see frostbite taking hold beneath their fingernails.

The next morning, word spread over the land that, out of respect for the suffering of the people in this time of trial, the word *hot* and all its derivatives should be neither spoken nor written, for it would only remind the forlorn of what they had lost. So too should the words *warm, summer, fever, sweat, scorch, blister*, and the like be stricken from the common vocabulary until the end of this horrible cold snap, for they were false friends, lies told only to torment the suffering.

Papa Ubu's oldest daughter went into the countryside on charitable missions to comfort all who had begged for her father's aid. She arrived in the towns like a magic spell, riding a sleigh drawn by shaggy reindeer whose eyes rolled in the agony of the heat, her lovely face framed in white fur and bright wool. And if her father was still human enough to sweat beneath his winter costume, she never did. Her face was pale and sweatless, as beautiful and unmoving as carved ice. In the scorching noontime sun, she pulled blanket after blanket from her sleigh and distributed them equally among the throng of loyal subjects, blankets of every color, quilted and embroidered and richly decorated with winter scenes, cottages dripping in icicles, glass beads forming frozen rivers in the fine cloth, fleece clouding the edges like clouds heavy with snow. There were always enough, enough for everyone, for Papa Ubu always took care of his children and loved them all the same.

One by one, folk dragged themselves forward, drowning in sweat, flies buzzing around their greasy hair, blisters on their reddened bodies like rows of rubies, and each of them begged for a blanket from the perfect white hands of Papa Ubu's daughter. Each of them eagerly wrapped the heavy, downy things round their shoulders and wept with gratitude, exclaiming with wonder at how much better they felt. But it was not enough for the daughter of Papa Ubu. She leaned in close to them, so close they could smell that she still had access to perfume even if they did not, and asked: "*How* much better? Tell me, so that I may in turn tell my father. Tell me how terribly you have suffered."

One by one, the people in the villages began to try to outdo one another. They shouted out in wonder at how cozy and snug they were now, surrounded in Papa's love, how grateful they were to be so tenderly looked after, what a welcome relief from the cold the beautiful daughter of the king had brought to them in the moment of their greatest need. A toothless, emaciated man in one place, though his name and its memory have long since burned up and away, clutched his blanket stitched all over with ice floes and dark birds and shouted out over the crowd: "I lost my foot to frostbite, but look! The moment the king's blanket touched it, it grew back whole! I can still see my breath in the air, but everywhere the blanket touches is safe!"

Then the man fell down dead of heatstroke. Papa Ubu's daughter moved on to the next village, with a soft smile on her perfect face.

Soon after, another law went out into the land, forbidding additional words like *weather, bright, shade, water,* and all language relating to *pain.* There was no need to discuss such things in this new ice age, not when Papa Ubu had called all his advisers to the palace to array their powers against the encroaching cold. It hurt Papa Ubu's feelings to hear his people say that they suffered in agony, when he was trying harder than any man had ever tried at any task to make the world warm again. *When you wish to say, "I am in pain,"* the law said, *you should say, "I am joyful," or "What a glorious day I am having," instead, for lying is a grave sin, and it is tremendously wicked of you to spread rumors that your papa is failing at his task in any way, and in truth, it is* you *who is forcing Ubu to feel pain with your vicious implications.*

But though no one spoke of it, the heat went on and on, until the soil itself began to turn to black steam and pumpkins began to turn to ash on the vine. The land around Papa Ubu's palace had become an archipelago, and the warm salt sea lapped at his snow boots when he appeared on the pink alabaster balcony to address the people again. My mother, who was called Silver-and-Gold—for in those days all children were named for the many sorts of riches Papa Ubu promised to all, one day, if they were only patient—was there to hear him, her belly all big with me, her legs sunk deep in the creeping waters of the new archipelago, her swollen shape wrapped in furs against the cold. That was the day she heard Papa Ubu name their great enemy and declare it for the criminal it was, reading out from a golden book the indictment detailing all its crimes and foul schemes against his great nation, going back centuries upon centuries, the greatest scandal ever uncovered, the cruelest madman ever to afflict humankind.

"The sun has abandoned us," yelled Papa Ubu, his cheeks red. "For billions of years it did its job without complaint, sitting up there in the sky, lording over us all like a big, fat, stinking bastard, and only now has it decided to deny us the seasons it owes, only now has it decided to harm us instead of nurture us, only now has the sun turned its back on its children as I never have and never will, and you know that's the truth, because I'm out here saying it to your face despite the freezing wind and sleet. Any other king wouldn't bother, you know, they really wouldn't. Anyway, the motive is clear—the sun *hates* Papa Ubu and is conspiring against him! It prefers the corrupt papas that came before, who let it do whatever it wanted, the people be damned. But when I stand up for you and demand your rights, the sun refuses to budge! What have we done to deserve this? Nothing! Nobody can blame us! We were just minding our own business, weren't we? The sun is an arch-criminal! The sun is against us! But I am a fair papa, and all my subjects are free and entitled to justice, even the sun. There must be a grand trial, with prosecutors and defenders and testimony and all that sort of thing, so that everyone can know just how deep this whole thing goes and that I, *I*, had nothing at all to do with it!"

"I am joyful," whispered my mother in reply, and all around her the people took up her cry, shouting, shrieking, weeping, *I am joyful! I am joyful!* before their king. And Papa Ubu smiled an enormous, hungry smile, and Papa Ubu waved and waved, for hours, never tiring, while the people chanted and screamed and fell forward into the knee-deep water, and all the while Papa Ubu drank their voices like wine or blood.

By coincidence, my grandfather was chosen to serve as chief counsel for the defense. He was called Equity, and he had never studied law in all his life. Most who had were long gone by then. But my grandfather was a Good Boy, loyal to Papa Ubu to the tiniest cell of his deepest marrow. He wore his hat just like Papa Ubu. He tied his tie just like Papa Ubu. He bid his wife style her hair like the hair of the daughter of Papa Ubu, and speak with the accent of the wife of Papa Ubu, and in that stolen voice tell him each night in detail how the cold was stealing in through the cracks in the door, and the frost was creeping up the side of the windowpanes, and the apples in the basket were surrounded by globes of ice, and the mice in the hall were freezing to death, and the icicles on the roof had nearly reached the top of the snowbanks outside, closing them into the house in their jagged crystal fangs.

It is because of his loyalty that he was so bitter to be drafted for the defense. Surely he deserved to prosecute. Papa loved winners, and wasn't Grandfather a winner? Everyone knew what the sun had done. If only the blasted thing would confess like anyone with a half scrap of decency, there would be no need for this sordid business. Grandfather Equity always did his best, and he would do his best now, for Papa had ordered a real defense, without which a guilty verdict would have no strength. But Grandfather hated the sun as much as anyone. He insisted, to all who would listen, that he'd hated the sun long before Ubu revealed the true extent of its betrayal. How could Papa force him to sit with the sun and consult with it and decide whether or not to put it on the stand? It was intolerable. But he was a Good Boy. He could no more say no to Papa Ubu than he could bring himself to say he was hot while he sprawled naked in his kitchen on the mercifully cool tiles just for one moment's relief, a twitching creature more sunburn than man.

Papa allowed a full hour of electricity in every city center so that all his children could watch the trial. A spot in the shade could suddenly be had for little more than a laborer's day wage or a tryst in the briars with an amenable soldier. Each day's testimony would end at sunset, naturally, for the accused must be present for the proceedings to be legitimate. The atmosphere was as dazzling as a carnival. Food was sold and lanterns were lit on street corners even in the bright of the afternoon, concertinas and panpipes were played in the piazzas, and throngs gathered beneath a ziggurat of televisions all tuned to UbuTV, most blessed of channels.

The reason Grandfather was chosen for the defense soon became clear. Ubu himself led the prosecution, his face utterly scarlet with righteous rage on that tower of screens, rendered tiny by the mountain of parkas and scarves and hats in which he had entombed himself. Papa ranted and raved and gestured wildly at the witness stand, bathed in a single, terribly quiet golden sunbeam. He flung his mind fully at the task, firing precedents like rifles, pealing forth with sermons soliloquized directly into the cameras, weeping real tears at the wholly unprovoked crimes of the sun against his people, the sheer betrayal of the sun's abandonment of its special relationship with this world, the inevitable result of which was to plunge it into a deadly ice age, merely out of pique at the great beauty, power, and longevity of Papa Ubu. How, indeed, could the sun begin to live with itself?

The judge and jury and all the crowds in all the cities applauded ecstatically every fragment of Latin, every incisive, surprising question that came so close to disturbing the calm of that single shaft of light illuminating the defendant's chair. One after another, Ubu's witnesses were called to speak to the slaughter and suffering caused by the sun's perfidy, but Papa rarely let them finish. He was too excited, too eager to get to the good parts. If the witnesses proved too boring or their statements not flamboyant enough, Ubu took over and finished for them with a grand flourish. Grandfather offered objections here and there, nothing radical, some sustained, some overruled. He tried to cross-examine, but the judge decided it was inappropriate to question the agony of the victims. As the sun declined to testify, there was little else for him to do but wait. It took seven days for Ubu to finish his tour-de-force and to collapse, exhausted, spent, exhilarated, into the chief prosecutor's plush chair, shivering theatrically.

It was time. There was no more avoiding it.

Grandfather Equity rose behind his long, polished rosewood bench and mopped his brow with a handkerchief. He flushed with shame. He began to shake and to weep. He had only one choice if he meant to mount a real defense, if he meant to do his job in the service of his beloved papa, as he had always done, as he always would do.

"Your honor," said my grandfather slowly. "We've heard a great deal of testimony on the causes of this terrible winter that's cursed us. And it's all well and good and fine as far as it goes. But it's just too *hot* to go on today, don't you think? I'm too fucking hot. Aren't you hot?"

And he opened his briefcase and drew out a glass bottle of clear, cold water with ice floating in it, and ice crusting the outside, and frost sealing the cap. He set it on the judge's desk, before a man sweating out his innermost fluids in a heavy down coat and thick black scarf. The judge stared at the bottle as a slip of ice slid down its side. He licked his lips. He looked helplessly back and forth between Grandfather and Papa Ubu.

The sun was found guilty on all charges and sent into exile. Not one person under the rule of Ubu would henceforward be allowed to speak its name or look upon it, even indirectly, and all were commanded to stay indoors unless absolutely necessary in order to shun the offender. If one must venture outside, umbrellas, skin-concealing dark clothing, and tinted glasses ought to be used so as to avoid even the hint of association. This was the verdict, and it could not be appealed.

My grandfather was quietly executed in the courthouse bathroom.

CATHERYNNE M. VALENTE is the *New York Times* and *USA Today* bestselling author of more than two dozen works of fiction and poetry, including *Space Opera*, *Palimpsest*, *Deathless*, *Radiance*, and *The Girl Who Circumnavigated Fairyland in a Ship of Her Own Making*. She is the winner of the Andre Norton, Tiptree, Sturgeon, Prix Imaginales, Eugie Foster Memorial, Mythopoeic, Rhysling, Lambda, Locus, and Hugo awards. She has been a finalist for the Nebula and World Fantasy awards. She lives on an island off the coast of Maine with a small but growing menagerie of beasts, some of which are human.

HARMONY

SEANAN MCGUIRE

The sign was small, like most of the signs along the Pacific Coast Highway. Unlike the majority, it wasn't advertising fresh artichokes or local honey, or endorsing some political candidate no one who didn't live in the area had ever heard of.

FOR SALE, it read, in polite, handwritten letters. HARMONY, CA.

"Look at that," said Nan, pointing. "Someone's trying to sell inner peace."

"Someone probably has a spa and a lot of wind chimes." Miriam kept her hands on the wheel and her eyes on the road. One of them had to. "Incense that smells like a truck-stop bathroom. She thinks it helps her commune with the spirits."

"What makes you think it's a she?" asked Nan. "Most of the gurus around here are weird dudes who wear socks with their sandals and like to explain how their penises can cure all known human disease."

"Maybe they can. Maybe you have asthma because you haven't imbibed deeply enough of the holy dick."

Nan rolled her eyes. "I have imbibed *plenty* of dick in my day. If that shit had curative properties, I assure you, I would know. Still would prefer not to, but it'd be cheaper than seeing the doctor, so why the fuck not?"

Miriam laughed so hard she took her foot off the gas. If not for the fact that they were in the literal middle of nowhere, without another car in sight in either direction, they would probably have gotten into an accident. As it was, they were able to make it to the shoulder before coming to a complete, if inelegant, stop.

"What?" demanded Nan.

"I'm just—can you imagine the *marketing*?"

Miriam folded forward in another fit of hysterical laughter. This time, Nan joined her. They had been driving for days, making their slow way up the line of the coast. They would cut inland after they reached Oregon, heading for the dubious delights of scenic Beaverton, where nothing happened that hadn't been approved six times over by the local homeowners' association.

It was a nice place to raise a family. That was what all the advertising said. Move to Beaverton and start that happy little nuclear unit you'd been dreaming of since you broke off from the one that bore you. Find a husband, find a wife, find one of each, find someone who was neither but who nonetheless wanted to raise children by your side, file the forms and settle down, content in the knowledge that you'd be giving those little tykes exactly the kind of warm, nurturing family environment they needed to thrive.

What none of the advertisements mentioned was how difficult it was to get the licenses to start that family or how the straight couples seemed to find their applications approved in half the time it took anyone else. (At least the licensing department acknowledged that bisexual people existed: Nan's friend Alex had marked down *bisexual* when he and his wife applied for parenthood, and while they were both cisgendered and in a classical man-woman relationship, that little ticky box had been enough to delay their application by almost six months, while multiple straight families had been able to jump ahead of them in the queue.)

What none of the friendly interviews with present and aspiring residents mentioned was the way the city shut down at nine o'clock, leaving single people with nowhere to go and people in relationships with few, if any, dating options. It hadn't been until Miriam stumbled across a locked Facebook group describing nearby restaurants and entertainment options that she'd realized how much was being intentionally hidden from them.

Court cases and successful bills and a hundred small victories had come together to usher in a world where hate was no longer acceptable, where sexual orientation wasn't enough to deny a person the right to live their life as they saw fit, where identity was up to the individual and not a government agency. But none of those things could change the nature of the human heart, and it was the nature of humans to be cruel to things they didn't understand, or approve of, or believe in.

Miriam and Nan had been ecstatic when their application to buy a house in Beaverton had been approved and even happier, two years later, when the perfect little Cape Cod–style bungalow had become available. They had moved with eyes full of stars and heads full of nothing but the future, only to find that the future had a few more fences than they'd been expecting.

This vacation—this ten days of heaven, away from everything they used to think they wanted—had been the only way to escape when their latest application for parenthood had been turned down. Reason? *Family has never maintained a pet. Questionable attachment abilities.* It had been suggested that they get a dog to prepare themselves for parenthood. A *dog*. As if that were the same thing.

Ten days. It hadn't been enough. Nan looked at Miriam, laughing so hard over something so small, and wondered whether it ever *could* be enough.

"Do you want to go see the guru?" she asked. "If it's a man, I promise to keep a straight face while he talks about vibrating in harmony with the universe."

"And if it's a woman, I'll buy you a milkshake the next time we stop in a town with a real diner," said Miriam. "Let's go."

She started the car back up, and they rolled on down the road, looking for harmony.

There was no guru, male, female, or other. There was no spa. There *was* a wind chime, crafted from recycled forks, hanging sadly in front of the closed post office. Occasionally, it would jangle in the wind.

Miriam and Nan leaned against the hood of their car, looking contemplatively at the sign. HARMONY, CA, it read. Under that, someone had taped a piece of poster board with two additional words.

FOR SALE.

"The town's for sale," said Miriam.

"I can see that," said Nan.

"Who has the spare cash to buy a *town*? New shoes, sure. A fancy necklace from one of the seaside tourist traps, okay. But a *town*? And how are you supposed to get it home? This won't fit in the back of the car."

"Sure," said Nan. She was already moving toward the sign, and past it, onto the porch with the sad wind chime, to peer through the grimed-over, soaped-over window of the old post office. "There's still a rack of greeting cards in there. The counter and the P.O. boxes, too. You could dust the place off and reopen it tomorrow and no one would be the wiser."

"Literally no one, including the United States Postal Service. I'm pretty sure getting them to resume pickups takes a little more than some Windex."

Nan glanced over her shoulder at her wife, grimaced, and walked the length of the porch to where it curved around the building. She turned and disappeared from sight.

For one terrible moment, Miriam was gripped by the absolute conviction that she'd just failed some kind of test, the kind you only found in folktales and Stephen King stories. Nan was gone forever. If she went looking, she'd find bones, or nothing, or maybe her wedding ring.

"Honey, come see!"

The moment passed. Nan sounded genuinely excited by whatever she'd found.

"Coming," shouted Miriam, and pushed away from the car.

Behind the post office was a pond, strangely enough, with four grimy white boxes about the size of chest freezers connected to it by long hoses. Nan was peering inside a hatch on the side of the nearest one. She looked up and beamed.

"Local weather control," she said. "We'd never be able to whip up a snowstorm, but they can extract enough water from the air to let us generate local rain, and they'll keep the town from needing to depend on groundwater or imports. We'd just need a few gallons of purified water to get the whole system working again. These are some of the original box models, too. They can take a direct lightning strike and still keep functioning."

"Huh," said Miriam.

"There are at least eight houses, and I'm pretty sure some of the shops have housing above them."

"I say again, huh." Miriam studied her carefully. "What are you getting at? A town is a little large for a souvenir."

"We could at least call and find out how much they want for the place." Nan dimpled. "Wouldn't you like to own your own town?"

"Would that make me mayor?"

Nan's dimples deepened as she smiled. "Why, yes. I do believe it would. I always wanted to kiss a mayor."

"Good," said Miriam, walking toward her. "Let me tell you about my political platform."

Harmony, California—former population thirty-five, current population zero—was for sale for eleven million dollars. The price was justified by the amount of undeveloped land considered to be "within city limits" and the fact that the utilities, post office, and weather machines were all part of the deal. There were no valuable minerals or other assets on the land that anyone had been able to find; it was simply a ghost town that had bloomed and died several times already along the road to Oregon.

Miriam looked at the figure, looked at Nan wilting on their couch like a flower ripped out of its native soil, and looked out the window. Some of their perfectly curated neighbors were walking their perfectly acceptable dogs, some new designer breed that never barked, not even when it was in pain or danger. Two of those dogs had been killed since their development officially started accepting residents, unable to make a sound when they'd been hit by cars, unable to help their people find them.

It was clean, sterile, modern. Perfect. Everything about it had been curated and customized to perfection, even down to the percentages of people—so many singles, so many couples, so many triads. So many families with children and so many without. They lived in the very model of a planned community, and while it had seemed like the perfect antidote to the years spent being told that "queer" was another way of saying "unwanted," now it just felt like another kind of prison.

Miriam hesitated. Then, slowly, she began to type.

When she and Nan had applied for homeownership, several of their friends had told them that they'd never be happy in a place like that, surrounded by people like that. That they'd still be marginalized, just along another axis—and, more, that the very existence of licensing for things like parenthood and getting a dog would be used as a way to make sure that only the "right" people got licenses. The straight people, the white people, the Christian people, the able-bodied, neurotypical, didn't-check-any-boxes people.

And, yeah, Miriam had noticed how some identities were just "assumed" by the applications, how *male* and *female* were each check marks but *other* was a whole sub-warren of menus—including *would rather not say*, as if a desire for privacy were somehow an identity. And, yeah, she had known when she signed the mortgage papers that she was agreeing to a certain degree of surveillance in exchange for finally living what she'd been raised to consider the American Dream.

She had simply never considered that one day she might prefer waking up.

One by one, she emailed friends, old contacts, people she'd gone to college with, smoked weed with, dreamed big dreams with. Dreams that were, in their way, bigger than any American Dream, because they'd been *hers*, something she wanted for herself and not because she'd been told to want them. One by one, she told them her idea. It was big. It was wild. It was probably bad. But it was, again, hers.

When the replies started coming in, she stood and walked to the couch, sitting next to her wife and taking the other woman's hand in hers. It was warm. Nan always ran warm. Moving to Oregon had been a terrible idea. How had she ever expected a desert girl to be happy in the fog?

"How much do you think we could get for our house?" she asked. "Ballpark figure? I know the waiting lists are still ungodly long, and I can't remember the last time somebody sold a place in one of the established neighborhoods. We're allowed, in case you're worried about that. I made absolutely sure of that before I signed the mortgage paperwork. We can't paint the place and we can't plant any trees that aren't on the approved list and we can't get a dog unless our application is approved, but we can sell and move anytime we like."

Nan slowly turned to her, a small V of confusion appearing between her eyebrows as she frowned. "What are you talking about? Why would you want to sell the house?"

"Last time we applied for a mortgage it was to buy this place. Two million dollars of house on the hoof. When I look at it now, it seems like an awful lot for not all that much. We've paid off, what, half that? If we sold tomorrow, we'd come away with a million in liquid capital—and that assumes property values haven't gone up. I assure you, our taxes tell me that they've gone up plenty. We could come out with two, even three million."

Nan looked at her suspiciously. "And what? Go to Disney World for six years? That isn't going to give us a place to keep our things."

"Maybe not, but I think a whole town would be big enough. Especially if we wanted to annex the storeroom at the post office. I can't imagine we're going to be getting *that* much mail for the first few years."

Nan's breath caught in her throat. "Don't tease."

"I'm not teasing." Miriam leaned over to take her other hand. "I emailed a bunch of our friends, some of the folks I work with— they're interested. If we incorporate so that we have enough capital to gain some negotiating room on the purchase price, and we sell this place, I think we can swing eleven million for the town, plus however much the place winds up costing to fix up. How do you even get an entire *town* inspected? There's probably going to be more dry rot than there is healthy wood. Really, we should—"

Nan lunged forward and kissed her, hard. Miriam stopped talking.

In that moment, there were far more interesting things to do.

.   .   .

Selling their house was, as it turned out, completely legal under the town charter: For all that it virtually never happened, it was apparently encouraged. If everyone who didn't feel like they fit in simply moved away, why, there would be no need for anything to change.

"If it ain't broke, don't fix it," said Miriam grimly. "Translate it into Latin and it could be the municipality motto."

Nan didn't answer. She was busy emailing three people and chatting with six more, windows popping up on her laptop screen like mushrooms after a rain. Miriam sighed fondly, watching her. Then she returned to the far less enjoyable task of explaining to their lawyer what they were trying to do.

Buying a town was not, it developed, exactly easy. It also wasn't as terrible an idea as she had initially feared. Harmony represented a decent chunk of California real estate, once the town borders were taken into account, and a surprising amount of it was farmable land, made undesirable only by its current isolation from local residents. Bring Harmony back to life and it might be possible to entice farmers to move onto that land, making it profitable again.

Build it and they will come might well be the only form of trickle-down economics with a scrap of truth behind it. If they built it—or rebuilt it, more properly—they'd have a chance at making something lasting. Making something that was real would encourage more real things to appear around it, until there was no further use for falsehood.

The consortium that was selling Harmony was happy to explain why they were willing to part with such a prime piece of real estate. As Nan and Miriam had joked on their way into town, the former owners had been gurus, mystics, New Age believers looking for a chance to create a community of their own, a sort of West Coast Lily Dale. But the traffic on the road hadn't been enough to sustain them, and bit by bit the money and the idealism had run out, leaving them stuck with a white elephant of a town and the shattered vestiges of a dream.

One of them even asked, in a carefully neutral tone, what the young people who were looking to buy the town were intending to do with it and seemed relieved when told that all the people who were currently considering relocation to Harmony were computer professionals who wouldn't be changing jobs. As long as there was reliable internet, they would have reliable employment.

Things started to happen very quickly after that.

Miriam and Nan listed their house, to a resounding lack of objection from both their neighbors and the city planners, who were supposed to get involved for anything more extreme than a new floor mat. Apparently, losing the only lesbians in the neighborhood—as they had reliably been called, no matter how many times they tried to explain that Nan was still bisexual even while married to a woman—was less worrisome than someone choosing a clashing pattern for their curtains. Maybe it was even a relief. While no one actually said, *Think about the children*, several people did comment on how nice it would be for the new occupants—whoever they happened to be—to be so close to the school.

Tolerance could be legislated, could be demanded, but it couldn't be guaranteed. Even as people followed the rules, they were still capable of harboring an astonishing amount of hate in their hearts. Miriam had plenty of time to dwell on that as she watched their neighbors, who had always been perfectly pleasant to their faces, all but throw a party to celebrate them finally leaving.

"Perfect on paper," she murmured, standing in the doorway of what was soon to be someone else's dream home, someone else's doorway to the perfect future, and watching as the movers carried their things out to the waiting truck.

Nan stepped up behind her, sliding her arms around Miriam's waist. "What?"

"Just remembering how excited we were to have our application for homeownership accepted. And now here we are, leaving. I can't decide whether this is victory or defeat. It feels like a little bit of both. It feels like giving up."

"It feels like finally deciding what our future's going to be," said Nan, and pressed a kiss against the side of Miriam's neck. "We're not following anyone else's blueprint. We're following ourselves. And we just bought ourselves a *town*. How many of these boring assholes can say that?"

"Technically, we bought ourselves the controlling interest in a corporation that happens to hold, as its sole asset, a town."

Nan laughed and kissed Miriam again. "Details. We're going home. Nothing matters as much as that. Nothing's ever going to."

Three months to the day after the first time they'd seen the sign, Miriam and Nan followed the moving truck containing their belongings down the road to Harmony. They weren't the first ones there: That honor belonged to the construction crews and contractors who were already hard at work replacing rotted support beams, nailing down loose boards, and redoing the shingles on roofs that should probably have been repaired several years before. What seemed like a fleet of gardeners and landscapers was moving through the town, trimming trees, planting gardens of native flowers, and removing unwanted weeds, cacti, and other invaders.

Miriam stopped the car in front of the post office, watching as the truck turned the corner, heading for the address she had given to the driver.

Nan shot her a curious look. "What's wrong?" she asked.

"I just thought it might be nice to walk the rest of the way." Miriam turned off the engine, smiling a little. "I'm pretty sure the owners of the post office won't have us towed."

"Probably not," agreed Nan.

They got out of the car together. The air was dry and sweet with the smell of sawdust and distant corn. Hand in hand, they walked down the road, turned the corner, and looked at the house they had chosen as their own. The rest of the collective had given them first pick, because they'd been the ones to find the town and because it was well known that they wanted to have children eventually, which meant that extra space would hopefully become necessary. It was small by the standards of the place where they'd been living, just three bedrooms, a kitchen, and a sitting room barely big enough to qualify for the name. There was no dining room. They'd eat on the back porch, or on the couch in front of the television, or in the common room behind the post office. It would make a good social center.

The children of Harmony—the ones whose parents were uprooting them and carrying them to the middle of nowhere, and the ones who had yet to be conceived, much less born—would grow up in the pockets of their neighbors, running up one side of the town and down the other. They would grow up safe and wild and surrounded by love.

In that moment, neither Miriam nor Nan could have thought of anything better.

The moving truck was already parked in front of their house, the men carting boxes and pieces of furniture inside. Everything was marked and labeled as clearly as possible; while there would definitely be errors, all they could do by getting involved at this stage would make things worse. So Miriam and Nan stood where they were and watched the future getting started, until Miriam's phone buzzed with an incoming text.

She pulled it out and glanced at the screen. "Dave and Nathan just hit town. They're heading for their place, but their moving truck isn't going to arrive until tomorrow. Do we want to have dinner?"

"No one has a working kitchen yet."

"In anticipation of exactly that situation, Dave packed four coolers into the backseat before they left Fresno. He promises a feast."

Dave was a French chef whose grilled cheese sandwiches were better than most people's attempts at gourmet cooking. Nan bumped her shoulder against Miriam's and grinned.

"All you had to say was *Dave packed*. We're in. Unless you wanted to start unpacking already?"

"We can't have sex until we put the bed together, and I don't want to do that with strangers in the house. So this is the best option for saying hello to our new town. Think you can find the box with the wine?"

"I'm on it," said Nan, and trotted toward the house. Miriam watched her go.

Over the next few days, she knew, more and more cars would be arriving, accompanied by more and more moving trucks. The town's single diner would be brought online, and Dave—as one of the few residents not employed by a large company that liked remote workers—would start getting it into shape. Nathan made more than enough to support them both, but everyone had committed to buying groceries for the diner and helping to pay for its upkeep. They were leaving behind wide worlds of takeout food and gourmet cuisine. Paying for their own private chef seemed like the best available compromise.

Over the next few days, the world would change. Right now it was time to celebrate the transformation.

Nathan and Dave had laid claim to the house connected to the diner, which only made sense. All the windows had been replaced prior to their arrival, and the only work left to do was painting and some repair on the porch. The four of them sat in front of the diner, eating their picnic off paper plates and drinking their wine out of delicate stemware—because, Nathan said, "all good things should be toasted, and so should all terrible ideas, and this could go either way."

That night, Miriam and Nan lay curled in the center of their own bed, in their own home, in their own *town*, and everything was perfect, and everything was terrifying. Nan kissed the corner of Miriam's mouth, tasting the blend of minty toothpaste and sweet white wine.

"Is this it?" she asked softly. "Is this the right thing?"

"A little late for that, don't you think? We bought it. Pretty sure the people we bought it *from* aren't going to take it back."

Nan kissed her again. "I mean is it the right thing for us to run away to the middle of nowhere instead of staying where we were and fighting to make people understand and accept us. I feel like we're retreating."

"It's not retreating to go where people will treat you like you matter." Miriam pushed herself up onto one elbow. "It's not retreating to let yourself be happy. We're not cutting ourselves off from the world. We're still working, still traveling, still going to stay involved with politics and making things better. Hell, the fact that we're *here* is going to bring life to the local economy—it's *creating* a local economy—and drop a big blue spot in the middle of an even bigger red splash. We're not under any obligation to stand around and let people kick us for not being exactly like them. And if someone shows up who isn't exactly like us but wants a place to go, we'll let them in. We'll welcome them home."

"Really?" asked Nan.

"Really," said Miriam, and kissed her, and conversation stopped, at least for a little while.

A week later, two-thirds of the houses in town were occupied. The diner was open; the general store was preparing to open; the post office was undergoing final inspections. The solar arrays were busily converting sunlight into power and power into weather that kept away the worst ravages of the local climate. The ethics of weather manipulation aside, without it, global climate change would have long since dried them all out and blown them all away.

Two weeks later, everything was running as smoothly as it could. There were glitches, of course—some of the plumbing didn't work, the internet was spotty until the weather machines were recalibrated, the general store kept running out of milk, and no one wanted to do the shelving unless they absolutely had to—but the town was alive, the town was real, the town was thriving. They had taken their ball and gone all the way home, home to a place where no one cared, or judged, or pretended not to mind the way they lived and the way they loved while quietly whispering behind their hands.

Nan was sweeping the post-office porch, one eye on the clouds, when a green station wagon pulled up in front and people began spilling out. Four adults, all told, two men and two women, each wearing a doubled wedding ring, all of them looking nervously around. They walked to the front of the car, standing in a rough diamond form that made it clear they were a unit.

One of the women stepped forward. "Um, hi. Is there someone we could . . . talk to? We heard there might be some houses here available to rent."

Sometimes the best part of taking your ball and going home is having the opportunity to define what *home* really means. Nan smiled and leaned her broom up against the wall.

"You can talk to me," she said. "Welcome to Harmony. And, hopefully, welcome home."

SEANAN MCGUIRE is the author of dozens of novels, hundreds of short stories, and multiple essays about the relevance of the X-Men to the modern world. She lives and works in the Pacific Northwest, where she shares her home with an ever-shifting array of unusual pets, enormous cats, creepy dolls, and books. So many books. When not writing, McGuire enjoys watching horror movies, talking about horror movies, making her friends take her to horror movies, and trying to convince people that horror movies are "the romantic comedy of the summer." McGuire doesn't sleep much.

NOW WAIT FOR THIS WEEK

ALICE SOLA KIM

THE TIME WE CELEBRATED BONNIE'S BIRTHDAY

We spent the last two hours of Bonnie's birthday drinks talking about shitty men and didn't think to apologize to Bonnie about it until after we got kicked out of the bar, long past closing time.

The bartender had tried to wait us out. Our group had become way too terrifying and annoying to approach. Our faces were red and our eyes were red and our auras or spirits or vibes or whatever were reddest of all. A dank, singed red that dimmed to black.

Although the bartender was extremely built, he wore his bounty of muscle like an old woman carrying too many grocery bags. He sighed and leaned against the bar and we ignored him.

Phyllida had been sketching on a napkin with meticulous and confident strokes. She seemed exactly like a real artist as long as you didn't look at what she was drawing. "It needs a really long handle," she said. "For leverage." On the napkin was Phyllida herself, as a stick figure with scribbled hair like black hay, standing on a beach and holding an enormous fork. At the end of each fork tine, she added eight stick figures, who were being shoved helplessly into the surf.

"Ta da!" She pushed the napkin in front of us. "The drowning fork! For all your drowning-more-than-one-man-at-a-time needs. Eight men maximum. You don't have to use all the tines. But it's such a waste if you don't."

"Motherfucker, I'll take *fifty*," Devon said, slapping her wallet down onto the table.

We cackled, some of us actively trying to screech like evil witches because it was funnier, and the longer we cackled the more we just felt it was the exact right way to laugh—not laughing because everything was so joyous and unblemished but simply because you were all bitches in hell together, so why not laugh, why not understand that everything contains at least one tiny nugget of its opposite, why not find a socially acceptable way to shriek with rage in public?

After the bartender finally kicked us out, we lumped together on the sidewalk, awkward again. The spell was dead and our faces were melted candles. In our bodies the joy-poison had evaporated but the poison-poison had leached into our marrow. Most of us had work or class tomorrow, and worst of all, tomorrow was more than technically today.

Bonnie was the only one who looked alert. The birthday girl, she of the scary freezing blue wolf eyes. In everything else she conceded to softness and prettiness, but her eyelashes she painted black and jagged. Each individual lash each day—that was how you achieved the look. She took so freaking long in the bathroom, where the light was best.

"Sorry, Bonnie," I said.

"It was pretty downer there at the end," said Nina. "Sorry, I feel like it was my fault."

"No, yeah, sorry I got so intense!" we somehow all managed to say as one.

"Shit, my wallet," said Devon, and went back into the bar.

Meanwhile, nobody said, *Haha, dang, isn't it bad enough that rape and assault and abuse and harassment and boyfriends doing the emotional psychosexual whatever equivalent of sticking their beefy hand into your brain and wearing it like a baseball mitt or a puppet so they can just really move it around and infinity et cetera happens to so, so, so, so, so, so, so, so, so many of us, and we can't even talk about it without having to apologize afterward?*

Not that I had said much tonight! But of course I'd apologized too. Because even though Bonnie smiled and said she didn't mind that her birthday drinks had been taken over by dark tales and infernal anti-man machines and despairing laughter, *we knew she did.* She liked it when things and people were happy, and when they weren't it was as if they were being unhappy at her. *To* her. She was plenty sympathetic to a point, and past that she'd start to bristle and talk about wallowing and pessimism and—

"—you get back what you put in," Bonnie said. "Just between you and me. I wouldn't say this to the rest of the group, and of course I respect what they've been through, but there's also such a thing as deciding to stop being a victim. Yes, remembering and talking about all the wrongs, that's important for . . . healing, or some such. But you can't stay on that same old subject and expect to be able to get anything new out of it."

We were walking back to the apartment together. I decided to not respond. Facing the prospect of arguing with Bonnie was like, you were starving and in front of you was a long, long table full of cakes. But if you ate even one bite, then you'd have to eat all of the cakes, the whole goddamn table of them.

That was just how Bonnie was. She would not ever change. She was always how you expected her to be, which wasn't really something we'd take as a compliment for ourselves, but it could be pleasant to know someone else like that.

Besides, she could be a great friend in the classical sense. Back when I'd been going through a hard time, she had invited me to be her roommate in her giant apartment, even though she had no need of a roommate, and only charged me a tiny bit of rent. In return for her generosity, I did not discuss this hard time with her in any amount of detail.

The street was busy, lots of bars, lots of people out, so in some ways you were more generally unsafe but the unsafety was thinned and spread out. The block was like a Halloween parade where everyone wore their costumes on the inside—slavering B.O. werewolves, droopy amnesiac ghosts, vampires coldly intent on doing it.

The next morning, we woke up depleted and dried out and dire. Those of us who were close friends texted each other, *Was I okay???* and unfailingly responded, *You were great!!!* (Which was a double lie: No one had been okay. And no one had been in any state to accurately judge.)

As for what we had talked about at the end of Bonnie's birthday drinks, we psychically decided to never bring it up with each other again and to forget that we ever knew about:

—the time a man, a doctor at the college campus clinic, was feeling our heartbeat and/but cupped our boob and lifted it once, subtle and unmistakable—

—the time a man had followed us onto a subway car to expound on our beauty and ignoring his request for our phone number caused his perspective to immediately flip as if by evil magic, and he darted from slimy kindness to incendiary outrage, shouting directly in our face like it was the next best thing to hitting us but who knew, any moment he could start doing the best thing, and meanwhile everyone on the subway car made like they were in fucking Derry, Maine, and looked straight ahead—

—the time a man secretly removed his condom during sex—

—the times we didn't want to but we did—

—the times we didn't want it that way but we did it that way—

—the times we wanted only some of it but we did all of it

—and so on.

THE TIME BONNIE WAS DREAMING

There we were at the bar. Too many people who didn't all know each other as well as they should crowding a corner table. We looked like a bunch of different species of birds eating something off the sidewalk together. Big birds, little birds, beauties and sad sacks, pecking away at invisible crumbs without touching or fighting or acknowledging their shared plane of existence, like their eyes couldn't even see each other—only the food.

In this situation, Bonnie was the food. Bonnie was having birthday drinks and she had gathered us here to sheepishly celebrate, since she'd reached the age where if you called yourself old, some people wouldn't correct you and some people would get mildly offended.

Bonnie was late, as usual. She was chronically late and never apologized for it, maybe because she always looked super awesome, and truly she did, so she imagined that that was a fair exchange for the lateness, even for us.

While we waited, a few of us started discussing the list. Some time ago, a list had been released online of not-famous men who had done bad things to women, mostly of a sexual nature. Some men at the table started shifting in their seats, as if fidgeting done just right could teleport you to a distant land in which you felt not so implicated. Or they sat there like Easter Island heads, with equally as much to say about shitty men.

The door crashed open and Bonnie ran through the bar, stopping short at our table. Her makeup had sweated off into patchy plum and black smears under her eyes. Her hair was stringy and stuck to her cheeks. She did not look super awesome, but sometimes we looked like that and it wasn't such a big deal so we weren't going to make it one. Perhaps we could ask about it later, once we were all safely drunk.

"Happy birthday!" we said.

"Is today your real birthday?" someone said, as they stood to hug her. Bonnie accepted the hug but gave nothing in return, her arms wilted by her sides. She didn't answer at first. She was busy peering around at all the wrong things, the ceiling and the bartender and the drinks on the table and our feet, like this was one of those kid puzzles where you had to spot the differences between two similar pictures. Her gaze was weird, fractured. She wouldn't look at us.

"Bonnie?"

"My birthday," she said too loud. "Yeah. My birthday. First of the month. Rabbit, rabbit."

"I think you're supposed to say 'Rabbit, rabbit' first thing in the morning, like the second you wake up," said Nina. "Otherwise you don't get the good luck."

Scott said, "Jesus, is it already next month?"

"I know, right?" someone said.

"I didn't mean that it was next month. I meant today is the start of a new month. Which is this month."

"Yes. I got that."

Bonnie listened along, as we all did whether or not we wanted to since the bar was so quiet you couldn't even grant the mercy of pretending not to hear. Then she lifted her palm. "HOLD THE MOTHERFUCK ON," she roared. "Stop messing with me. Stop lying. I've been saying it all day; this shit is not funny. My birthday was last week *and we all know it*. You guys even did that conversation again. Like I could ever forget such a stupid-ass dumb-ass fucking conversation!"

"Whoa, calm down—" Scott said, valiantly trying to sound more worried about Bonnie than he was offended. He stuck his arm out to put around her and she shoved it away, tilting off-balance. She propped herself against the brick wall of the bar and surveyed us from a cold and judgmental distance. "I do not appreciate it, and I do not see the point of it," she said, voice wobbling. "This *prank*. You got my parents in on it, and you did something to my phone and laptop, you made it so that—" Bonnie broke off. She shook her head like it jangled and ripped something out of her purse and threw it at nobody in particular (it hit Scott on the thigh) and ran out of the bar. Scott silently showed us what she'd thrown. Today's newspaper.

Some of us left. Some stayed, got more drinks, marinated in concern, and theorized luxuriously. Shit got near convivial. I wasn't Bonnie's closest friend, but I was her roommate friend—her roommate-mate—so I was the one who went out after her. Even though I had no idea where she'd gone. Bonnie was not so much a woman of routine.

I decided to go home. With great relief and a tiny amount of surprise, I unlocked our door and found a trail of ankle boots, jacket, purse, phone, keys, dress, leading straight to Bonnie's bedroom. Of course. I could picture it exactly—Bonnie on her birthday, treating herself to a pregame that got so out of hand it became neither pre nor game, then showing up to her actual celebration surreally out of her head. Sure.

When I knocked, Bonnie responded immediately. "This is all a dream," she said in a shouty voice. She sounded like she was in a play, an amateur one with fake British accents. "Do not come in."

"Are you okay? We were worried."

I heard her bed creak and tried again. "Do you want your phone? It's out here."

"*Fuck my phone*," Bonnie yelled. "It's fake and so are you and so is everything. Quit talking to me! I need to concentrate on waking up."

I left her to it. I gathered up her things and piled them outside her door and I texted some people that Bonnie was fine and sleeping something off and I dicked around on my phone and saw that a famous man—one who had spoken out passionately against the sexual depredations of other famous men during the most recent outcry (for the sexual depredations of these other famous men had first come to light in the 1970s and '80s, unfortunate timing if you wanted a critical mass of people to actually care)—was discovered to have been really, *really* not one to talk and I brushed my teeth and decided I deserved not to floss and then it was like half the blood and adrenaline and energy in my body swirled down into a drain somewhere with a loud abrupt gurgle and I oozed my way to bed.

The next morning Bonnie was gone, room tornadoed and big suitcase missing. A few days passed with no word from her, so I pondered calling her parents. I had no kind of relationship with them, but I could probably get their info from billing statements. I didn't do it. Bonnie loved her parents and wouldn't want to worry them and Bonnie hated her parents and didn't want to rely on them any more than she already was, which was basically 100 percent, and due to both of the aforementioned she loathed showing any kind of weakness in front of them.

A few days after that I got a text from Bonnie admonishing me specifically to *not* call her parents, and I responded and told her that I hadn't but I almost had and if I had I would have done it days and days ago and where the hell was she? No response. Well, if that was how she wanted to play it. Meanwhile, I could have the place to myself. Fine.

THE TIME WE TALKED SHIT

"Still no word?"

Just a few of us left at the bar, dejected and alone together like we'd been stood up but in a polyamorous way.

"Do we think she forgot?"

"Her own birthday?"

"Or found something better to do. Not to talk shit but . . . Bonnie can be like that."

"I have sympathy for the congenitally rich. You know how basically everything worth doing sucks initially? Well, maybe if you never get training in dealing with bullshit, you risk becoming the kind of person who just bounces from thing to thing to thing and sooner or later everything seems boring and totally without reward or meaning. And then comes the ennui."

"I have sympathy for *myself*."

"Ennui isn't Bonnie's problem."

"Right, she would actually be very happy if everything was only nice pleasant surfaces."

"*Yes*," we all said. And then we were off to the races.

"She's so pissed off when everything isn't happy and nice! Infuriated even. Which is kind of at odds with being someone who loves happy and nice stuff, you know?"

"It's not . . . *not* tyrannical. But she's not one of those tyrants who, like, loves suffering and pain. She does truly love it when people are happy. Especially her friends."

"That's not the same thing as helping someone be happy."

"What it comes down to is she was born a certain way—you know, a white, rich, cute way—and acts like she had anything to do with it. It's a sickness."

While the others were talking, Phyllida quietly asked me how I'd been. She was the only one there who knew even a little about the situation I'd had at my last job. The man I had met there, who in fact still worked there. His name had shown up on an online list of un-famous bad men, and nothing had happened to him, the same nothing that happened to so many other men. This was a nothing that could sometimes be filled with gaseous excitement and horror and alarm and puffy thought bubbles containing phrases like *Somebody should do something!* all of which never became solid and eventually leaked out, leaving nothing behind and resulting in nothing.

Phyllida looked into my eyes and picked up the cutlery on the table. "I would stick him with this fork." Oh, she was so nice. Why weren't we closer?

Wait, it was because of the time I went to Devon's birthday party and saw Phyllida talking and laughing gaily with the man, even though I knew she knew. Maybe they had only interacted for a few seconds, maybe Phyllida needed a professional favor. Maybe, caught off guard, she'd been accidentally polite to him. It happened. But this incident sure did make me not want to tell anyone else about it, because if I saw them being friendly with him later, I would have to slink off like a dog giving birth under a house and tend my grievous wounds alone. I knew that now. And sure, yes, of course: Even without telling someone the story, there was a chance I'd see them being friendly with that man, which would still hurt, but not nearly as much. This way, at least I wouldn't be certain that they had chosen rapists and politeness over me.

I knew I was asking too much, but I didn't want to ask too little. What was the correct amount, allowing for how much people fail? We fail so hard. All of us do.

Smiling past Phyllida, I watched Nina draw on a napkin. I called out to her and she looked up. "What's the latest on your ghost problem?" I asked. The details were harrowing, sad, disgusting—but she was always ready to talk about it. We were the only ones who believed her. We had all been at that Halloween party.

Derrick interrupted us. He lifted his phone like a pack of gum in a gum commercial. (*Put it away, Derrick, nobody can read a word from here anyway.*) Apparently Bonnie had gotten back to him. She said she was fine and that everybody should leave her alone.

"Is she okay?"

"That's all she said? What a bitch!"

After that, we all went home, full of a guilty, binge-eaten feeling of having talked that much shit about our friend, at her actual birthday celebration no less.

Nearly a whole week passed, and still no Bonnie. I was eating granola standing up, wearing only an old and obscenely baggy thong, when I heard a key in the door and I sped over to an arm-chair with a crumpled coat of Bonnie's on it and only had time to tuck the coat under my armpits but I was still excited to see Bonnie at the door and say, *Dude, where have you been* and *I'm only wearing your coat like a tiny assless sandwich board because you caught me in my worst underwear,* until the door opened and it wasn't Bonnie—it was two well-dressed sixtysomething people who had already been having a bad day and here I was to worsen it.

Luckily, because I was mostly naked, they first thought I was Bonnie's secret girlfriend, so when they learned that I was, rather, Bonnie's secret *roommate* of whom they had never heard, they were so relieved and distracted that I found a brief opening in which to lie my face off.

Sometimes people with money didn't want to give it to people who needed it extremely badly, like how they didn't want to offer sympathy or belief to those who had been victimized, as the act of needing was inherently thirsty, plus there was the way situations that caused you to become needy sometimes could render you dis-gusting and un-whole so the idea of joining forces with you was just, *blaaaaarrrrb,* and of course joining forces was what happened when money, sympathy, and belief changed hands.

So I hoiked up my posture a couple notches and pretended to be a novelist (zero evidence of visual art in this apartment, so words it had to be), highly experimental (I didn't want it to be easy to find my books, since they would in fact be impossible to find since they didn't exist), with most of my work published in Chinese (which I wasn't but they wouldn't know the difference but also why had I even added this level of obfuscation?), in residence at a university nearby whose apartment roof had caved in over the, ah, living room. I had met Bonnie at—

"—at, at an event, a p-party after a salon. When I told her about how disruptive the noise from the workmen was, the dust and the disruption, she offered me a room in her place for the time being, and it has been such a godsend. I wouldn't have been able to—do my work, if it wasn't for Bonnie and her generosity."

Not bad, not bad! Cultural capital, the implication that I didn't need money, this apartment, or anything at all, a foreignness that was not real and therefore nonthreatening. (Oh, *that* was why I'd done that.)

The parents relaxed, smiled subtle WASP smiles, and let it go. Bonnie's mother had a smooth white bob and was fat and tall and graceful, clad in a whispering computer-gray silk blouse. Thready webs of chain and gem blinked against her neck, fingers, ears. Her bling felt oceanic, as in naturalistic yet unutterably vast. All that was dark and grotesque about her soul was contained in the bulky handbag dangling from her right elbow. Bright orange-brown this handbag was, crisscrossed with straps and black chains and waxy twine.

Bonnie's father wasn't nearly so interesting-looking.

"Do you know where she has been?" I asked.

They told me that she showed up at their house yesterday, completely frazzled, telling a wild tale about a week that was repeating over and over again. Her mother said, "Bonnie told us she'd traveled to New Zealand to check if it was last week there too. Though she chose it randomly, she ended up really enjoying the place. Except for the fact that it was also still last week there."

"Which is to say this week," her father said.

They had tried to calm her down, even as she insisted she had lived this week many times, listing off news of sex scandals and murderous police and mass shootings as if she were bringing precious communiqués from the future and not just delivering the same old easy guesses absolutely anybody could make, so they fed her dinner and offered her benzos and put her to bed, thinking she would have to stay with them for a while—thinking facilities, thinking inpatient/outpatient, thinking medication, and so on—and when they checked on her in the morning she had fled.

As they searched Bonnie's bedroom and peeped very quickly and apologetically into mine, her mother said, "I am not unsympathetic, you know. How could she prove her story to us? It would be next to impossible. Should we tell her a secret so massive that merely through her repeating it back to us in the next iteration we would immediately believe that she was telling the truth, that she had indeed lived this week before?"

"And what if the week didn't repeat?" said Bonnie's father, scrolling through his phone. "We three would then be forced to march into the future together, bound by the hideous secrets Bonnie now knew. All for nothing."

I said, "I mean, why do they have to be massive and hideous secrets?"

"Still more horrible," continued Bonnie's mother, "would be if she were correct, and were somehow able to prove this to us, and keep proving this to us—that she, our daughter, Bonnie, has been doomed to live the same week over and over again. Pulling us helplessly along with her. Cursed to remember, blessed to forget, or the opposite, or both."

Her father said, "What monstrous knowledge to bear."

"We cannot and will not believe her," they said.

I brought them back to the door. They gave me a phone number to call in case I heard anything. They also told me I could stay in the apartment as long as I wanted. I opened my mouth to say thank you and Bonnie's father said, "Oh, yes, and since you'll be taking over rent while Bonnie is away—" and soon named a number so big it should have been written on a piece of paper and slid across a desk. But no. This number was said aloud.

I stood so tall my skull risked detaching from my spine, and smiled like a medalist. "Of course. Thank you." I was still wearing Bonnie's coat like it was a strapless minidress on a paper doll, though very much unlike a paper doll I had a back half to me too. Around people like Bonnie's parents, you were allowed to acknowledge when you weren't being perfect but you could never, ever be embarrassed. When I had shown them down the hall into our bedrooms, I walked backward stewardess-smooth.

Once they were a safe distance away, I slammed the door shut and slumped into the armchair. The rent on this place, which they already owned, would be impossible. I did not have anywhere else to go, of course. How about if I temporarily shrunk myself into a bean? It would be so nice to be a dried hard tiny thing, fallen down into the spoons and forks and forgotten for maybe one, two years. But as a tiny bean I'd still have a future. I could still return to life or life*like*ness, once enough time passed and there wasn't so much bullshit to deal with. Maybe nine, ten years.

The fringe on the bottom of the couch moved. Bonnie poked her head from underneath, dragging the rest of herself out. I was glad her head came first and not her hand or foot, so I didn't need to scream.

She hauled herself onto the couch and coughed. "You got resources, kid."

"So do you," I said, guiltily remembering the shit-talking from the bar.

"I have to get sensible," she said. "I should have known it was no good going to my parents like that. What a waste of time." She laughed. "If such a thing is possible. They wanted to make my entire last day so tiresome. I had to sneak out in the night. Came here and napped under the couch because it felt safer. I was right."

"Usually I don't lie like that."

She shrugged. "Lie all you want. Lie big. I can tell you it does not matter one bit."

This was the strangest conversation I'd ever had with Bonnie. "They just scared me. Your parents are a piece of work. Pieces of work? No. Them two together make one piece of work." The strangeness wasn't all on Bonnie. I was definitely tangoing with her.

"Don't worry," she said. "You won't have to pay the rent."

"You'll tell them you're here?"

"No. I mean it'll just be last Wednesday again soon." Then another shrug, one lagging so far behind her words that it split off into its own separate statement. Dust billowed and settled on Bonnie again and she looked like an ancient, badly damaged statue of someone youngish, like her basic composition was at odds with her present circumstances, and despite the smooth jaw and round cheeks and slight scanty feathery decorative lines in her forehead and under her eyes you knew she had been around and around and around for eons and would be still and would be still and would be still, beyond all reckoning.

"Very soon," Bonnie said.

I stood. "I've got to get dressed," I said. I had become very frightened. "I'm super late. Rest up. Okay?"

As I sped down the hall, Bonnie's thin, sweet voice floated behind. She was singing a line from that song, the line that went, "*Let me see* *that*"—her voice going flannelly and nearly cracking—"*thawwww-awwwwwwww-awwwwwwwng . . .*" And a final desperate and strangled "*Baaaaby!*"

A tossed-off and funny and completely regular thing, a tune in the genre of roommate giving you shit for being such a beast at home—but it did not make me feel better. I was still filled with a very bad form of terror, the kind where you didn't know what or why. So how would it end? Bonnie's singing had been the saddest, most yearningest music I had ever heard. You got the joke but the dirge, that was the point. That was what remained.

THE TIME BONNIE DIDN'T GO VIRAL

When Bonnie canceled her birthday drinks the morning of, we didn't think anything of it. The excuse was plausible. Also, no one really wanted to go out on a Wednesday anyway.

Turned out she was spending her time making a weird, baggy, rambling video of just her sitting in her room, looking super awesome, making predictions of the things to come in the present week. Like that the actor many of us loved would be revealed as a leering terrible date who expected sex as his due and took no for an answer only temporarily before starting up the sex stuff yet again until he took no for an answer only temporarily and so on until the woman gave up. Kind of like when your cat jumped back onto the counter so many times you stopped putting it back on the floor, except with having your boundaries totally ignored during sex. And no cat.

(This had probably happened to many of us—it definitely happened to me—but it was all pretty confusing stuff people didn't usually care about, and to boot Bonnie wasn't describing it clearly at all, so nobody knew what the hell she was talking about in the video until the next day, when the actor's name did actually appear in the news. But we figured that she had just found out early somehow. She did know some celebrity-adjacent people.)

Certain sports teams would win certain games, she guessed correctly. That was a little impressive, if you cared. Wildfires. Firings in the White House. Something that the president would say in a few days, which sounded indistinguishable from everything else he had said before so it meant nothing to us and was like a cat jumping onto a counter so many times we stopped trying to stop it or even pay attention to it since we couldn't stop it. "Is Bonnie being politically humorous?" one of us said.

It was harder to go viral than you'd think. Or, rather, it was pretty easy if you did a kind of bare minimum, and Bonnie had not.

Other than some of us texting each other with WHAT DID I JUST WATCH, the video did not catch on with the world at large. I tried to avoid Bonnie (easy, because I had work and she stayed in her room most of the time), because the stinging harsh glow of what was surely flourishing mental illness emanating from the video really freaked me the fuck out. Not that I was proud of that. I wasn't not proud either! I'd had to survive! Growing up, I had been left largely in the care of my schizophrenic aunt for seven years and I became decent at spotting crazy and crabwalking delicately away from it before it could touch me even as I lived in close proximity to it.

For all that nobody cared about Bonnie's video, it had apparently reached certain shadowy governmental agencies. One morning the doorbell rang while I was in the shower and Bonnie was in her room, and the agents couldn't even wait for five seconds before kicking in the door. My towel had somehow vanished from its hook, so I grabbed a jacket of Bonnie's that had been stuffed and forgotten in the space between the door and the wall and wrapped it extremely partially around myself and ran out into the living room, where three men and one woman wearing suits were walking Bonnie out of the apartment.

"I'm going away for a while, and I won't be in touch. But I promise I'll be back!" said Bonnie, dragging a suitcase. When did she have time to pack? "Bye!" She sounded cheerful. Then she and the agents left and I was alone with the busted door, a small puddle forming around me.

The rest of Bonnie's predictions ended up coming true. Nobody cared.

THE TIME BONNIE WAS QUIET

I turned the corner into the dining room and jumped. There was Bonnie at the table, shoulders so slumped she resembled a tombstone.

"It was awful," she said. She looked like she had been up for hours already. "They weren't the ones to help me. Not at all. I was so wrong about everything." She stared down into a full mug of coffee that I could tell had gone cold.

"Did something happen?"

She glanced up at me and made her face go calm. "No. I had a bad—dream. I had a bad dream in which I was interrogated a lot and then they were going to open up my skull and look at my brain and maybe fuck with it a little. Good thing I ran the clock out on that."

To hide my relief, I picked up her mug and reheated it in the microwave. "Good thing it was all a dream," I said.

Bonnie said, "I know you don't understand but I appreciate you listening. I just have to lay low this week. I have to be sensible. No one else is going to save me. No faith in family. No faith in institutions."

I had never known Bonnie to talk like this. So depressed and . . . gnomic? But then I remembered it was her birthday, so perhaps she was mourning the way all women of our age were supposed to mourn the precipitous vanishing of our worth, like, *Whoops, time to grow a personality, which the world will also devalue!* Bonnie had always been devastatingly confident—but who knew, it could have been the kind of confidence that only flourished within highly specific parameters and withered time-lapse-fast without.

"Hey. Don't be too sensible. It's your birthday! We got those drinks tonight."

Bonnie groaned and the microwave beeped.

Later on in the evening Scott said, "I didn't mean that it was next month. I meant today is the start of a new month. Which is this month."

Bonnie closed her eyes so she could roll them, but we could still see it.

And later on in the evening, when the talk turned to shitty men and the list full of them and our lives full of them, Bonnie, who had gotten quietly wasted, said, "Men men men men MEN. Can they not be the only subject of conversation left in the whole entire world *please*? Can we please just talk about something nice?"

But that was Bonnie for you.

THE TIME BONNIE CANCELED

Her email read, *BIRTHDAY CANCELED! I've decided to embark on a new adventure. Arctic Circle expedition, BITCHES. I leave in an hour, therefore no time to get drunk with you jokers. I'm drunk*

THE TIME BONNIE ASKED FOR ADVICE

She said, "What would you do? Hypothetically."

We were a little surprised. Bonnie didn't usually go in for these kinds of conversations. She thought these topics were nerdy meaningless masturbations for super dweebs. *Stop acting like life is a Star Trek movie, it'll never happen!* she'd say. Sometimes she substituted *a Star Wars movie* for *a Star Trek movie*. Then again, we'd been discussing the list of shitty men, about which she seemed very *oh, this again*, so maybe any interruption would do.

Phyllida would improve herself. Read books, learn languages and musical instruments and complicated choreography that didn't require too much muscle strength. "Also, I would punish those I deemed deserving of it. They would be in a hell of my own making, unaware they would be doomed to relive these torments again and again. It would be a long time before I tired of this."

Damn, girl!

Scott would travel and spend all of his money as quickly as he could. We politely overlooked the fact that Bonnie already could do this, sometimes *did* do it.

Devon would quit her job and just do nothing. If you were living the same week over and over again, it meant you weren't aging, so time no longer had you propped up on its handlebars, propelling you forward no matter what, as you spit out bugs and tried not to slip off. No, time in this scenario was chill as hell, willing to stroll with you around a track and have a stoned, circular conversation nobody would be able to retrace. How wonderfully relaxing, and so very necessary when everything had been so apocalyptically stressful. "I would get to know my friends better. Though I would keep far away from most of my family. For them, duration and repetition would not be improvements." But Devon relented, a little. "I might give it a shot if I got really bored. In a literal thousand years."

Nina would try to save everybody.

We would wear elaborate disguises in order to spy on our friends and see what they really thought of us; we would binge-eat; we would sex-marathon; we would try new hairstyles; we would get three dogs; we would get teardrops and ice cream cones tattooed on our faces; we would get five cats; we would do every drug; *we would not garden.*

Sure, I made my contributions. But this was the only thing I said that I really meant: I said that I actually hated this hypothetical conceit. When you dug right down into it, it was odious. Because you could do anything you wanted, you could do absolutely whatever, and nothing would ever, ever, ever, ever be allowed to change.

Bonnie looked placid. "Yes, what then? If it just starts over again and again and never stops no matter what."

"You make your peace with it," said Derrick. "You have to relinquish your attachment to time as it was."

Scott said, "You said a week, right? That's lucky. That's where it's at. Way better than a day. In a week, you can really get somewhere."

THE TIME BONNIE CANCELED

Her email read, *Hi, assholes! Birthday drinks are canceled. Giving you tons of warning so you don't end up meeting anyway to talk about me behind my back because that's like your favorite pastime. IN OTHER WORDS, I HEARD EVERYTHING. Is that really what you thought of me? What is so wrong with choosing joy? Well. You got your wish. The longer this week goes on, the more familiar I become with it and the great grand repeating shittiness we've gotten ourselves into. Thank you so much, losers! Now I'm depressed just like you.*

    1. We had no idea what she was talking about.

    2. It did still *sound* like Bonnie.

THE TIME BONNIE WOKE ME UP

She burst into my room without knocking.

"I think I got it! Do you remember this time?" she gabbled.

I squinted at my alarm clock. ". . . time?"

At this, an utter devastation settled over Bonnie. A flat, matte, no-expression gray exoskeleton that turned her head and picked up her feet and walked her out of my room.

THE TIME BONNIE WAS MEAN TO US

Bonnie raised her glass. "Here's to the nights I will remember with the friends who always forget," she said, and downed the whole thing. We sat still. If we did or said anything, she would *predict* us again, mimicking us in that horrible sarcastic voice.

"Go," she said, and we ran out of the bar.

THE TIME BONNIE CANCELED

Her email read, *I'm just really sick of you all. Sorry.*

THE TIME BONNIE SMELLED BAD

Something was wrong. Bonnie wouldn't get out of bed. She didn't shower. I brought her food but she'd only pick at it. When I asked her what was wrong, or how I could help, all she would say was, "Look. Sometimes I just don't have it in me to get it up again for yet another seven days of the same old, same old, same old." I had never seen her like this.

She intoned:

Another man, another bad man
First a bad man
First outrage
And then or simultaneously
And then this man is actually not that bad, or even bad at all,
    because if you haven't seen him be bad to you, he cannot
    ever be bad, fuck an object permanence
And then any punishment is far too big, you can't just take
    away his human rights by not reading his books or not
    watching his movies or not voting for him or not being
    pleasant to him at cocktail parties
And then where will this end, maybe men should never talk
    to women ever again because of course it is preferable to
    cease all interactions with about half of humanity if the
    alternative is to think or worry about one's behavior for
    longer than 0.000002 seconds
And then sometimes bad men apologize, sorry you admired
    me so much, sorry the rules changed on me, sorry I don't
    remember doing that because I was addicted to alcohol
    and drugs but I remember you being into it and sorry you
    changed your mind, however I am not sorry for being so
    kinky
And then bad men disappear and reappear

And then we forget and they reappear
Or is it more like they reappear and it makes us forget
Onto the next, onto the next

"I think this news cycle is really upsetting her," I told another friend of hers. We sympathized.

THE TIME BONNIE BOUGHT ME BREAKFAST

One morning Bonnie knocked twice on my bedroom door and came in without waiting for a response. I didn't like her coming into my room, because she often gazed at my furniture, my clothes, my shoes, with a fixed, sweetly neutral expression that I knew was pitying and insulting. Sure, my things weren't nearly as nice as Bonnie's, but I also didn't think they were so bad you needed a poker face to look at them.

This time, she didn't do any of that. She said, "Call in sick to work. I want to show you something."

"You know I can't." Although—did she know? Currently, I had a pretty good temp gig at a duty-free-shopping company, entering the names of makeup products from large binders into a computer database. Near the end of my stint they discovered I had entered all the names incorrectly, because I had been trained incorrectly. So they hired me for another round to fix the mistakes I had made, which was really nice and humane and understanding of them. Unfortunately, because I'd finally been doing my job right, I would be losing it soon. I had no idea what was happening next.

"It doesn't matter!" Bonnie said. "Okay, no, wait. I'll pay you five times what you usually make in a day. And I'll buy you breakfast. Let's go out!"

"Seriously?"

She looked down at me with the hauteur of a much older, much more professionally accomplished woman. "You know that I never lie about money or food." She placed an already written check on my face, and when I started sputtering, she said she'd go wait in the living room.

After I got ready and called in sick, I came out and found Bonnie sitting primly on the couch, her eyes closed. "Let's go!" she said, standing. Her eyes were still closed. Now that I was next to her I saw her lids were covered in something clear and crusty. "You're about to ask what's up with my eyes. I superglued them shut," she said. "Is it dry?" she asked herself. "Yes. It's dry. So, you can see that my eyes are completely closed, right?"

Oh, were they ever. I was backing away very stealthily when Bonnie said, "Stop backing away *not that stealthily.* I know you have this whole thing about being allergic to crazy because of your schizophrenic aunt who raised you, and it's fine to honor the child who had to come up with coping mechanisms and protect herself somehow, but you've got to get over it. Sometimes shit is wild beyond all reckoning. Sometimes people are extremely weird and oftentimes literally crazy, but they're not all the time trying to be crazy at you! So get over it. Oh, and you're also not so normal yourself." She put on a pair of black sunglasses. "Look, you're going to say, *Says the rich white hot girl with the happy childhood,* which is not wrong. Although you did meet my parents. Oh, shit. Wait. You didn't this time. Anyway, you're right, but I'm still right about a tiny bit of it too. Do you want to come get your mind blown or not?"

"I wasn't going to say *hot,*" I said.

We laughed for so long I forgot to ask how she knew about my aunt; then we went out.

Though she couldn't see at all with her eyes glued shut, Bonnie didn't need my help out of the building. She picked up a toy that had fallen from a stroller and gave it back to the child. She complimented a woman on her shoes, in convincing detail. She bought a newspaper and told me what was in it. She took out her phone and told me what everyone was talking about. She stood on the street corner and asked me to let her know when it was exactly 8:00 A.M., and when it was, she pointed straight ahead and said, "Red car, black car, blue car, blue car, cop car, hot guy on a bike, hot guy jaywalking." (Though I disagreed about the hotness of the guys, if you took Bonnie's tastes into account, this was all accurate.)

And all with her eyes superglued shut. I checked them again. They looked even more awful in daylight. "Bonnie," I said, feeling equal parts wonder and foreboding. "How are you doing this?"

Late that night we ate popcorn and watched a reality TV show—at least, I watched, while Bonnie listened, her eyeballs wiggling under her lids—since the other things we wanted to watch were created by or starring known rapists and gaslighters. "Wait, him too?" I said.

"Check your phone," said Bonnie. "The news just broke."

For a moment I was surprised that Bonnie would give up on something she really wanted to watch because a Bad Man™ was involved with it, but the fact was that she was no longer the same Bonnie I had known. "All this shit, all it wants to do is continue and repeat with only slight variations," she intoned. "Care or not care, it doesn't make a difference to the loop I'm in. I only can't stand to look at his fucking face. If you see it the way I see it, it is too encrusted with the dark knowledge I have about him, a layer for each week I've been through. Layers and layers and layers and layers."

Bonnie started reciting what would happen on the reality TV show right before it did, which was getting pretty old, so I asked her if the whole week started over again at midnight.

"That's right," she said. "Midnight tonight. Tuesday is the last day before it turns over. I love and dread Tuesdays. Though I am looking forward to this superglue being vanished."

"Why didn't you tell me earlier in the week?"

"I have." She couldn't see the horror on my face, but she reached out and patted me on the arm. "Well, you know, this time I'd thought of the superglue trick and it seemed fun, but I wasn't about to have my eyes glued shut for a whole week. It *did* blow your mind, didn't it?"

I thought. "You know . . ." I said. "I'm a person. A real person. Even if I can't remember anything."

"I know." Bonnie exhaled. "Sorry. At first I was really jealous of you all, but once I started being able to prove, you know, my whole deal to people, I began to see how terrifying it is. To finally get to see the truth of what's been happening, and then to understand that it will eventually be wiped away and started over."

The problem with a Bonnie who was focused on the dark, scary side of things was that someone else had to pick up the positivity slack. This was not my greatest strength. I considered the me I was now, the being who had been shaped by living through this week, who would be destroyed once midnight came. Sure, Bonnie could re-create a very close approximation of this current me by behaving the same way next time, but that was almost worse somehow. No. It was definitely worse. I said quickly, "Is there, like, a magical phrase you can say to me that will hurry things up so we can get the show on the road quick next time?"

"Not really. And there's not a magical way to hide and transfer knowledge; otherwise I would be able to show you that you should try therapy, like, even once. Funny that you mention magic, though. I've recently been delving into the dark arts, mostly to see if there's anything that'll help pull me out of this time loop but also because I was trying to help Nina with her ghost problem."

I wondered what *recently* meant to Bonnie. "You know about that? Oh, I forgot again. You know about everything. Did it work?"

"No," she said simply and sadly. "It is such an unfortunate truth that shit doesn't happen to you based on what you can deal with."

"Poor Nina," I said. God, Bonnie really *had* changed! How many times had I had this thought today? And yet I couldn't stop thinking it, when everything she said and did kept revealing her newness, and each time in a new way. I checked the time and flinched. "Oh, it's about to be midnight," I said, feeling robotic with dread. "I'm just going to distract myself from ontological terror and tell you that next time, please figure out a way to prove it to me from the get-go, and then give me some money so I can stop going to my job and have a nice whole week of fun. What do you say?"

"I could do that, and I have. It's futile, though."

"Wow, I'm not used to this dark-sided goth of a Bonnie. I'll miss her *and yet I also totally won't*." It was hard to talk. My teeth were chattering.

It was about to be midnight.

One more second.

THE TIME BONNIE STAYED BACK

She whispered into everyone's ears, setting off tiny explosions of shock and awe and gasp, but when she reached me, I just said, "Don't." I didn't want to know what she knew about me already, whatever I told her even though it wasn't *me* who told her. (Yes it was no it wasn't.)

"No need," I said. "I believe it."

Bonnie nodded and sat down again. All of us were rapt. "I'm in a sharing mood this time," Bonnie said. "Please, anyone, feel free to ask me whatever you like."

Here are a few of the questions I can still remember. We had a lot.

Q: How do you remember so much stuff if you can't take anything with you?

A: Good question! This has all been hugely taxing for my memory. I learned the method of loci from *Rhetorica ad Herennium* and other texts. The first thing I do when I wake up is type as much as I can remember. Like, in a total frenzy. Good thing you've only heard me banging on that keyboard once! Ha ha. Another thing I do upon waking is order a bunch of books and stuff so I can have it all shipped to me as soon as possible.

Q: Have you ever tried to kill yourself?

A: No. Before my optimism died, I had always held out hope that I'd be able to escape the time loop eventually. I didn't want to jeopardize that by killing myself, and I was scared. Then I died by accident, so that answered that. But I would never do it on purpose. I hate the dark in-betweens. They last longer when I've died.

Q: What are some of your favorite memories?

A: So many! This is going to sound cheesy. Becoming closer with many of you. You don't remember, but we got *close*, like wearing-each-other's-hair-in-our-lockets close. You are all such incredible people. Even you have your moments, Scott. The dark-magic cult that formed about me, I'm not going to say it's a *favorite* memory—it was more *interesting*, but very, very, *very* interesting. Oh, and I had so much amazing sex. That is, I had an enormous amount of sex and so much of it was amazing, but of course a whole lot was mediocre and embarrassing and some of it was terrible. I'm not a god or anything. Sometimes I can't know when a bad thing will happen, or I won't be able to stop it, and though my body gets reset my mind does not.

Q: Do you want it to stop?

A: Yes.

Q: Why do you want it to stop?

A: First of all, I'm sick of it. In some incalculable, untrackable way, I am old as fuck. Second, and this is the selfish reason, there's a limit to how much I can improve all by myself. I mean, just because you live the same week over and over again doesn't mean you'll be that great or smart. I'm proud of how awesome I got, but I think I'm hitting a wall. Third, I have lately [we wondered what *lately* meant to Bonnie] been troubled by the feeling that this span of time is being used up somehow. That it is degrading and fraying in some intangible way and there will be devastating consequences. Like it's going to just poop out. Can't you feel it? The way everything feels so tired and busted and sad, and it'll lurch forever but it also can't go on like this forever? [We all nodded.] I'm scared.

Q: Whoa. I thought I'd just been depressed.

A: Yes. You are also that. I am concerned that whatever is happening to me is coming to an end but not the end I sought. I'm worried there won't be any future. And I really wanted the future to happen, more than anybody—[*Please, Bonnie*, we said]—okay, fine, I want it as much as anyone else does, and to think that I won't get to see it, that none of us will—

This was around when Bonnie stopped talking. She had a look like someone who had run full force into a glass door, like: *Aaaaah!* And like: *OUCH*. And like: *Well, of course. I did know that door was there.*

She got up to leave, telling us that this week was going to be very busy and it was important to get it just right, so please don't do stupid shit expecting it to be undone. Please. When we tried to ask her one last thing, she blew right out of there, leaving the question to twist in the air and plummet to the floor in a crumpled ball.

The question was: *Why you, Bonnie?*

We never stopped wondering and we never found out.

Bonnie decided to throw a giant party at our place. It would be on Tuesday night, the last night of the week, because everything in Bonnie's week took place on the exact wrong day. "People will come," she said. "I know how to get them here. And I deserve a real birthday party! In a sense, I'm like a million years old." I asked her if she kept count and she shook her head, saying she was bad at keeping numbers in her mind, but that had to be a lie.

Such terrible things happened this week. Huge startling ones and small boring ones. But in other ways we had a wonderful week. We remember it still.

Isn't that nice? Isn't that fucking major?

At the party, which everyone did attend—not that we doubted Bonnie more than just a little bit—I spotted the man I knew at my last job. The Man. But not really *The* Man, not really deserving of capitals, because there had been a few in my life but this one only happened to be the most recent and I was maddest at him. Most recent also meant that I had thought I'd become old enough to respect myself and to be able to foresee every future event (was I expecting too much?) so that I wouldn't keep saying yes to a man when I wanted to say no and thus pave the way for me to say no to that man and have him still do what he wanted and leave me totally confused, knowing that something was very, very wrong. Thus when all of that nevertheless came to pass I got really mad at myself and additionally mad at him for making me mad at myself, and, of course, I was mad at myself for being mad at myself.

My fingertips sizzled.

The time was after midnight. Bonnie wasn't here anymore. I felt it, like she told me we would. She said she had had a sudden flash of insight, or maybe not so sudden because she had been thinking over it for years, and now she knew what she had to do. It had taken her so long because it was a weird solution and one that made her quite unhappy. "Only at first. I feel much better about it now. Nobody should be sad for me," she said. When the time came, Bonnie was going to allow the future to move ahead. The way it would move ahead was if she stayed in the past. It wasn't too hard to do, more a matter of intention and perspective than anything else. You didn't even need dark magic. Well, *some* helped. "I wish I could be there. To see it," she had said. "But I love you all and I'm sick of you all and I'm sick of power and power is sick of having me."

The man was talking happily to a young woman, as if he deserved to stand in the light. Amazingly, he truly did think that he was a nice person. I could have pondered that riddle for endless weeks of Bonnie time. It was like he was afflicted with anosognosia, a condition of not believing you have a mental illness because you have a mental illness, which was a major trouble of my aunt's, who I really had loved. I had been afraid of becoming like her and having no one ever believe anything I'd ever say again, but that already came to pass anyway. This man wasn't ill. He was just a cowardly sex criminal who was wrong about so many things, such as the future we were entering.

As I crossed the room, people made way. I called his name. He glanced up, looking so unafraid that it made me want to pull him into fifty pieces. I lifted my hand a little, and he stood taller. He might have straightened when he saw me. Also likely was that a horridly strong cackling force might have frozen him in its thin-fingered grip and lifted him high on his toes.

He might be compelled to tell me and this room full of people what he did to so many and who he was and every tiny detail of what went on in his mind. Forget punishment. Or, for that man, having to tell the honest truth, clean of self-preservation and self-regard, would be punishment enough. Or, there could be more punishment later. No need to decide yet. At that moment, all I wanted was the truth that had been denied me so long. Might it be denied me now?

ALICE SOLA KIM's writing has appeared in *Tin House*, *The Best American Science Fiction and Fantasy 2017*, *Lightspeed*, *McSweeney's*, *BuzzFeed Reader*, *Asimov's Science Fiction*, and other publications. She is a MacDowell Colony Fellow, recipient of a grant from the Elizabeth George Foundation, and winner of a 2016 Whiting Award.

STORY COPYRIGHT CREDITS

ABOUT THE EDITORS

VICTOR LAVALLE is the author of the short story collection *Slapboxing with Jesus*; four novels, *The Ecstatic, Big Machine, The Devil in Silver*, and *The Changeling*; and two novellas, *Lucretia and the Kroons* and *The Ballad of Black Tom*. He is also the creator and writer of a comic book, *Victor LaValle's Destroyer*. He has been the recipient of numerous awards, including a Whiting Writers' Award, a United States Artists Ford Fellowship, a Guggenheim Fellowship, a Shirley Jackson Award, an American Book Award, and the Key to Southeast Queens. He was raised in Queens, New York. He now lives in Washington Heights with his wife and kids. He teaches at Columbia University.

victorlavalle.com

Facebook.com/victorlavalleauthor

Twitter: @victorlavalle

JOHN JOSEPH ADAMS is the editor of John Joseph Adams Books, an imprint of Houghton Mifflin Harcourt. He is also the series editor of *The Best American Science Fiction and Fantasy*, as well as the bestselling editor of more than thirty anthologies, including *Wastelands, Brave New Worlds, The End Is Nigh*, and *The Living Dead*. Adams is a two-time winner of the Hugo Award (for which he has been a finalist twelve times) and an eight-time World Fantasy Award finalist, and was a judge for the 2015 National Book Award. Adams is also the editor and publisher of the digital magazines *Lightspeed* and *Nightmare* and is a producer for *Wired's* The Geek's Guide to the Galaxy podcast.

johnjosephadams.com

Facebook.com/johnjosephadams

Twitter: @JohnJosephAdams

ABOUT THE TYPE

This book was set in Electra, a typeface designed for Linotype by renowned type designer W. A. Dwiggins (1880–1956). Electra is a fluid typeface, avoiding the contrasts of thick and thin strokes that are prevalent in most modern typefaces.